NEW YORK FANTASTIC

ALSO EDITED BY PAULA GURAN

Embraces
Best New Paranormal Romance
Best New Romantic Fantasy 2
The Year's Best Dark Fantasy & Horror: 2010
Zombies: The Recent Dead
Vampires: The Recent Undead
The Year's Best Dark Fantasy & Horror: 2011
Halloween
New Cthulhu: The Recent Weird
Brave New Love
Witches: Wicked, Wild & Wonderful
Obsession: Tales of Irresistible Desire
The Year's Best Dark Fantasy & Horror: 2012
Extreme Zombies
Ghosts: Recent Hauntings
Rock On: The Greatest Hits of Science Fiction & Fantasy
Season of Wonder
Future Games
Weird Detectives: Recent Investigations
The Mammoth Book of Angels & Demons
The Year's Best Dark Fantasy & Horror: 2013
Halloween: Magic, Mystery, and the Macabre
Once Upon a Time: New Fairy Tales
Magic City: Recent Spells
The Year's Best Dark Fantasy & Horror: 2014
Zombies: More Recent Dead
Time Travel: Recent Trips
New Cthulhu 2: More Recent Weird
Blood Sisters: Vampire Stories by Women
Mermaids and Other Mysteries of the Deep
The Year's Best Dark Fantasy & Horror: 2015
The Year's Best Science Fiction & Fantasy Novellas: 2015
Warrior Women
Street Magicks
The Mammoth Book of Cthulhu: New Lovecraftian Fiction
Beyond the Woods: Fairy Tales Retold
The Year's Best Dark Fantasy & Horror: 2016
The Year's Best Science Fiction & Fantasy Novellas: 2016
The Mammoth Book of the Mummy
Swords Against Darkness
Ex Libris: Stories of Librarians, Libraries, and Lore
The Year's Best Dark Fantasy & Horror: 2017

NEW YORK FANTASTIC

Fantasy Stories from the City That Never Sleeps

Edited by Paula Guran

Night Shade Books
New York

Night Shade books may be purchased in bulk at special discounts for sales promotion, corporate gifts, fund-raising, or educational purposes. Special editions can also be created to specifications. For details, contact the Special Sales Department, Night Shade Books, 307 West 36th Street, 11th Floor, New York, NY 10018 or info@skyhorsepublishing.com.

Night Shade Books® is a registered trademark of Skyhorse Publishing, Inc. ®, a Delaware corporation.

Visit our website at www.nightshadebooks.com.

10 9 8 7 6 5 4 3 2 1

Library of Congress Cataloging-in-Publication Data

Names: Guran, Paula editor.
Title: New York fantastic : fantasy stories from the city that never sleeps / edited by Paula Guran.
Description: New York : Night Shade Books , 2017.
Identifiers: LCCN 2017023269 | ISBN 9781597809313 (pbk. : alk. paper)
Subjects: LCSH: New York (N.Y.)--Fiction. | Short stories, American. | American fiction--20th century. | American fiction--21st century.
Classification: LCC PS648.N39 F36 2017 | DDC 813/.010897471--dc23
LC record available at https://lccn.loc.gov/2017023269

ISBN: 978-1-59780-931-3

Cover design by Jason Snair

Please see page 403 for an extension of this copyright page.

Printed in the United States of America

CONTENTS

INTRODUCTION: A PLACE APART

"As for New York City, it is a place apart. There is not its match in any other country in the world."

—Pearl S. Buck

New York City is a very real place, but no one can deny it is also somewhere magic occurs and all sorts of fantastical things happen. The metropolis is the epitome of urban action, romance, and excitement. It has no shortage of wonders: mysterious portals to other times and locations, magical hidden sites, and enchantments galore. Fascinating folks can be found just about anywhere and there are more exotic beasts than one might expect. Myths are born in its five boroughs. For countless people, New York has long been a city of dreams, the only destination that can truly fulfill all their hopes and desires.

The city that never sleeps—perhaps because of that famous wakefulness—has its dark side too, of course, and gives birth to nightmares as well as dreams. But there's no likelier place to find help, heroes, or the special power needed to overcome the nefarious than New York.

It has been called the Center of the Universe. Anything can happen in New York—and when it does, it is accepted as part of the everyday and sometimes never noticed at all!

If that is the reality, then is it any wonder that New York has inspired imaginative writers, from Washington Irving to any number of contemporary authors to combine fantasy with the tangible?

Welcome to a volume of twenty fantastic tales that may never have happened . . . but if they ever did, they could only happen in New York City!

Written on the eighty-sixth anniversary of the dedication of the Empire State Building.

Paula Guran

NEW YORK FANTASTIC

We'll start with a story set in the past, when many Irish immigrants came to New York to find a new life. But humans weren't the only creatures to leave Eire and cross the Atlantic.

HOW THE POOKA CAME TO NEW YORK CITY

DELIA SHERMAN

Early one morning in the spring of 1855, the passengers from the *Irish Maid* out of Dublin Bay trudged down the gangway of the steam lighter *Washington*. Each of them carried baggage: clothes and boots, tools and household needments, leprechauns and hobs, fleas, and the occasional ghost trailing behind like a soiled veil. Liam O'Casey, late of Ballynoe in County Down, brought a tin whistle and the collected poetry of J. J. Callanan, two shirts and three handkerchiefs rolled into a knapsack, a small leather purse containing his savings, and a great black hound he called Madra, which is nothing more remarkable than "dog" in Irish.

Liam O'Casey was a horse trainer by trade, a big, handsome man with a wealth of greasy black curls that clustered around his neat, small ears and his broad, fair temples. His eyes were blue, his shoulders wide, and he had a smile to charm a holy sister out of her cloister. He'd the look of a rogue, a scalawag, faster with a blow than a quip, with an eye to the ladies and an unquenchable thirst for strong drink.

Looks can be misleading. Liam had an artist's soul in his breast and a musician's skill in his fingers. One night in the hold of the *Irish Maid,* with the seas running high and everyone groaning and spewing out their guts, he pulled out his tin whistle to send "Molly's Lament" sighing sweetly through the fetid air. All through that long night he played, and if his music had no power to soothe the seas, it soothed the terror of those who heard it and quieted the sobbing of more than one small child.

After, the passengers of steerage were constantly at Liam to pull out his tin whistle for a slip jig or a reel. Liam was most willing to oblige, and might have been the best-loved man on board were it not for his great black dog.

Madra was a mystery. As a general rule, livestock and pets were not welcome on the tall ships that sailed between the old world and the new. They made more mouths to feed, more filth to clean up. Birds in cages were tolerated, but a tall hound black as the fabled Black Dog, with long sharp teeth and eyes yellow as piss? It was the wonder of the world he'd been let aboard. And once aboard, it was a wonder he survived the journey.

"A dog, seasick?" Liam's neighbor, a man from Cork, pulled his blanket up around his nose as Madra retched and whined. "Are you sure it's nothing catching?"

Liam stroked Madra's trembling flank. "He's a land-loving dog, I fear. I'd have left him behind if he'd have stood for being left. Perhaps he'll be easier in my hammock."

Which proved to be the case, much to the amusement of the man from Cork.

"The boy's soft, is what it is," he told his card-playing cronies.

"Leave him be," one of them said. "Fluters and fiddlers are not like you and me."

When the *Irish Maid* sailed into New York Harbor, New York Bay was wide as an inland sea to Liam's eyes, the early morning sun pouring its honey over forested hills and warehouses and riverside mansions and a myriad of ships. Islands slid past the *Washington* on both sides, some wild and bare, some bristling with buildings and docks and boats. The last of these, only a stone's throw from Manhattan itself, was occupied by a round and solid edifice, like a reservoir or a fort, that swarmed with laborers like ants on a stony hill.

The Cork man broke the awestruck silence. "Holy Mother of God," he said. "And what do you think of Dublin Bay after that?"

With all of America spread out before him like a meal on a platter and the sea birds welcoming him into port, Liam had no wish to think of Dublin Bay at all. He'd come to America to change his life, and he intended to do it thoroughly. Country bred, he was determined to live in a city, surrounded by people whose families he did not know. He'd live in a house with more than one floor, none of them dirt, and burn coal in a stove that vented through a pipe.

He'd eat meat once a week.

As the lighter slowed, the hound at his feet reared himself, with some effort, to plant his forepaws on the *Washington*'s rail and panted into the wind that blew from the shore. After a moment, he sneezed and shook his head irritably.

The Cork man laughed. "Seems your dog doesn't think much of the new world, Liam O'Casey. Better, perhaps, you should have left him in the old."

Madra bared his fangs at that, for all the world, the Cork man said, as though he spoke Gaelic like a Christian. Liam stroked the poor animal's ears while the lighter docked and the steerage passengers of the *Irish Maid* began to gather their bundles and their boxes, their ghosts and their memories and staggered down the gangway. On the pier, customs officials herded them to a shed where uniformed clerks checked their baggage and their names against the ship's manifest. These formalities concluded, the new immigrants were free to start their new lives where and when they pleased.

The lucky ones, the provident ones, embraced their families or greeted friends who had come to meet them, and moved off, chattering. A group of the less well prepared, including Liam and the man from Cork, lingered on the dock, uncertain where their next steps should take them.

With a sinking heart, Liam looked about at the piled boxes, the coils of rope, the wagons, the nets and baskets of fish, thinking he might as well have been on a wharf in Dublin. There was the same garbage and mud underfoot, the same air thick with the stink of rotting fish and salt and coal fires, the same dirty, raw-handed men loading and unloading wagons and boats and shouting to each other in a babel of strange tongues.

"That'll be you in a week or so," the Cork man said, slapping Liam on the shoulder hard enough to raise dust. "I'm for the Far West, where landlords are as rare as hen's teeth and the streams run with gold."

A new voice joined the conversation—in Irish, happily, since his audience had only a dozen English words between them. "You'll be needing a place to sleep the night, I'm thinking. Come along of me, and I'll have you suited in a fine, clean, economical boardinghouse before the cat can lick her ear."

The newcomer was better fed than the dockworkers, his frock coat only a little threadbare and his linen next door to clean. He had half a pound of pomade on his hair and a smile that would shame the sun. But when the boardinghouse runner saw Madra, his sun went behind a cloud and he kicked the dog square in the ribs.

"Hoy!" Liam roared, shocked out of his usual good humor. "What ails you to be kicking my dog?"

"Dogs are dirty creatures, as all the world knows, as thick with fleas as hairs."

"A good deal thicker," the man from Cork said, and everyone snickered, for Madra's coat after five weeks on shipboard was patchy and dull, with great sores on his flank and belly.

The boardinghouse runner grinned, flashing a golden tooth. "Just so. Mistress O'Leary'd not be thanking me for bringing such a litany of miseries and stinks into her good clean house. A doorway's good enough for the pair of you." And then he turned and herded his catch away inland.

Liam sat himself down on a crate, his knapsack and his mangy dog at his feet, and wondered where he might find a glass and a bite in this great city and how much they'd cost him.

"Yon was the villain of the world," Madra remarked. "Stinking of greed and goose fat. You're well shut of him."

"The goose fat I smelled for myself," Liam answered. "The greed I took for granted. Still, a bed for the night and a guide through the city might have been useful. Are you feeling any better, at all, now we've come to shore?"

Madra growled impatiently. "I'm well enough to have kept my ears to the wind and my nose to the ground for news of where we may find a welcome warmer than yon gold-toothed cony-catcher's."

"And where would that be, Madra? In Dublin, perhaps? Or back home in Ballynoe, where I wish to heaven I'd never left?"

The hound sighed. "Don't be wishing things you don't want, not in front of me. Had I my full strength, you'd be back in Ballynoe before you'd taken another breath, and sorry enough to be there after all the trouble you were put to leaving in the first place." He heaved himself wearily to his feet. "There's a public house north of here, run by the kind of folk who won't turn away a fellow countryman and his faithful hound."

"You're not my hound," Liam said, shouldering his pack. "I told you back in Ballynoe. I did only what I'd do for any living creature. You owe me nothing."

"I owe you my life." Madra lifted his nose to sniff the air. "That way." Moving as though his joints hurt him, Madra stalked away from the water with Liam strolling behind, gawking left and right at the great brick warehouses of the seaport of New York.

The Pooka was not happy. His eyes ran, his lungs burned, his skin galled him as if he'd been stung by a thousand bees, and the pads of his paws felt as though he'd walked across an unbanked fire. He was sick of his dog shape, sick of this mortal man he was tied to, sick of cramped quarters with no space to run and the stink of death that clung to mortals like a second skin. Most of all, he was sick, almost to dissolution, of the constant presence of cold iron.

He'd thought traveling with Liam O'Casey was bad, with the nails in his shoes and the knife in his pack, but Dublin had been worse. The weeks aboard the *Irish Maid* had been a protracted torture, which he'd survived only because Liam had given over his hammock to him. This new city was worst of all, as hostile to the Fair Folk as the most pious priest who'd ever sung a mass.

Yet in this same city, on this poisonous dock, the Pooka had just met a selkie in his man shape, hauling boxes that stank of iron as strongly as the air stank of dead fish.

The Pooka had smelled the selkie—sea air with an animal undertang of fur and musk—and followed his nose to a group of longshoremen loading crates onto a dray. As he sniffed curiously about their feet, one of them grabbed the Pooka by the slack of his neck and hauled him off behind a stack of barrels as though he'd been a puppy.

"What the devil kind of thing are you?" asked the selkie in the broadest of Scots.

"I'm a Pooka," he said, with dignity. "From County Down."

"Fresh off the boat and rotten with the iron-sickness, no doubt. Well, you're a lucky wee doggie to have found me, and that's a fact."

The Pooka's ears pricked. "You have a cure for iron-sickness?"

"Not I," the selkie said. "There's a Sidhe woman runs a lager saloon in Five Points. All the Gaelic folk who land here must go to her. It's that or die." The selkie pulled a little wooden box from his pocket and opened it. "Take a snort."

The Pooka filled his nose with a scent of thin beer, sawdust, and faerie magic. "One last question, of your kindness," he said. "Would a mortal be welcome at this Sidhe woman's saloon at all?"

The selkie replaced the box. "Maybe he will and maybe he won't. What's it to you?"

"We're by way of being companions," said the Pooka.

"Dinna tell me he knows you for what you are?" The selkie whistled. "That'd be a tale worth the hearing. Tell it me, and we'll call my help well paid."

The Pooka knew very well that his tale was a small enough price for such valuable information, but it was a price he was reluctant to pay. Stories in which he was the hero and the mortal his endlessly stupid dupe—those he told with pleasure to whoever would hear them. A story in which the stupidity had been his own was a different pair of shoes entirely. Still, a favor must be repaid.

"I will so," he said.

The selkie bared strong white teeth. "But no just now: I've work to do, and you, an Irish fay to see. Shall we say before midsummer? Ask for Iain. Everybody kens me here on the docks. Oh, and dinna fash yourself over yon mortal. The woman'll no harm him—if he keeps a civil tongue in his head."

"Oh, he's civil enough," the Pooka had answered, somewhat sourly. "He's the gentleman of the world, he is. The creature."

Which was why, as much as the Pooka resented Liam O'Casey, he could not dislike him, and why, after six months in Liam's company, he was far from home, iron-sick and mangy and too feeble to shift his shape, burdened with an unpaid blood debt and no prospect of paying it.

The Pooka had a nose as sharp as a kelpie's teeth, but lower New York was a maze of bewildering and distracting smells. The streets reeked of dung and garbage, of dogs marking their territory and the sweat of horses pulling heavy drays. The Pooka was startled out of what remained of his fur when a scrawny, half-wild sow squealed at him. Prudently, the Pooka whined and wagged his tail submissively. The sow snorted at him and trotted on.

Bowing to a pig! If the iron-sickness did not finish him, surely shame would do the job. The Pooka thought he'd like to kill Liam for bringing him here. But not until he'd saved his miserable life.

Liam had been hungry and thirsty when he got off the *Washington* at dawn. By noon, he was tired and footsore as well, and as bewildered as he'd ever been in his life. Listlessly, he watched Madra sniff the door of Maeve McDonough's Saloon, which looked no different to him than the fifty other such establishments he'd sniffed along the way, except for a sign in the window offering a free lunch. Liam read the fare on offer—cold meat, pickles, onions—and sent up a short and heartfelt prayer to the Virgin that their journey might end here. He sent a second prayer of thanks when Madra pricked his ears, raised his tail, and trotted down the filthy steps and into the dark room beyond.

Upon inquiry at the wooden counter, Liam learned that the free lunch came at the cost of two five-cent beers, which he was happy to pay, even though the beer was poor, sour stuff and the meat more gristle than fat. While he ate, a woman, well supplied with dark hair and bold eyes and an expanse of rosy-brown skin above the neck of her flowered gown, cuddled up, giving him an excellent view of her breasts and a noseful of her musky scent.

"Like what you see, boyo? I can arrange for a closer look."

Head swimming, he was on the point of agreeing when another woman's voice spoke, tuneful and sweet as a silver bell. The whore hissed, showing teeth a thought too long and pointed for beauty, and slid back into the crowd of drinkers.

Startled, Liam looked up into the face of the tall, redheaded woman on the other side of the bar. She'd a faded-green woolen shawl tied across her bosom and a look about her he was coming to recognize after six months in the Pooka's company: a luminous look, as though her skin were fairer, her hair more lustrous, her eyes more lambent, her whole person altogether more light-filled than an ordinary woman's. It was not a look he'd expected to see in the new world.

"Welcome to Five Points," said the woman. "There's a fine dog you have."

Liam looked down to see Madra sitting by his leg, panting cryptically. "Oh, he's not mine," he said. "Not in the way of ownership. Our paths lie together for a while, that's all it is."

The woman's smile broadened. Liam noted, with relief, that her teeth were remarkable only in being uncommonly white and even. "A good answer, young man. You may call me Maeve McDonough. I am the proprietress of this place. You are welcome to drink here. Should you be looking for a place to lay your head this night, I've beds above, twenty cents a night or four dollars a month, to be paid up front, if you please."

Liam laid the silver coins in Maeve's hand with a bow that made her laugh like a stream over rocks, then recklessly ordered another beer and carried it toward a knot of Irishmen who looked as though they'd been in New York a week or two longer than he.

The Pooka yawned nervously and licked at a sore on his flank. It seemed to him that it, like everything else in this forsaken place, tasted of iron. How many nails were in this building? How many iron bands around the barrels of beer? He could sense a stove, too, and most of the customers, unless he was much mistaken, were armed with steel knives. Some even carried pistols. It was almost unbearable.

It *was* unbearable, and the Pooka was beginning to realize that there was nowhere in this city where he might escape from the pain that gnawed at his bones. Hemmed in by mortals, surrounded by iron, with more mortals and iron outside on the street, the Pooka was ready to bite everyone around him and keep on biting until he died or the pain went away, whatever came first.

A cool hand touched his head. A fresh scent, as of spring fields after a rain, soothed his hot nose and cleared the red mists from his brain. The Pooka looked up into the amused green eyes of a Sidhe woman.

"I am called Maeve," she said. "Follow me."

The room Maeve led the Pooka to was, if anything, darker and hotter than the saloon itself. Stacked beer barrels lined the walls, and a complex apparatus of glass and tin on a table smelled strongly of raw spirits.

"A Pooka," Maeve said, setting down her lantern. "I've not seen your like before on this side of the wide ocean. A word for you, my heart. The city's no place for a creature of the bogs and wilds."

"Yet here I am," the Pooka said irritably. "On the point of paying with my life for the privilege, too."

"Well, perhaps it needn't be as costly as that." Maeve regarded him gravely. "What is your life worth, Pooka?"

"I haven't much to give you," the Pooka said. "Would you accept my everlasting gratitude?"

Maeve laughed. "What a joy it is to have a trickster to bargain with, even one half dead. I'd save you for the pure pleasure of your company, but that would be bad business. Come, give me a dozen hairs from your tail, that I may call upon you at my need."

"Good will is good business, lady. Three hairs will buy you my respect and affection as well as my service."

"Seven hairs I'll take, and no less. Unless you're willing to give the mortal over to my hands, to do with as I will."

The Pooka hesitated. "Much as it galls me to admit it, there's a small matter of a blood debt beween us." He sighed heavily. "Seven times I'll come to you, then. You drive a hard bargain, missus."

"Sure, and it's a hard city for the Fair Folk to live in." Then Maeve went to a shelf and brought back a charm, which she wove into the thick fur of the Pooka's ruff.

The charm bit like flies and nettles. The Pooka whined and scratched at his neck.

"It won't help you if you get rid of it," Maeve said mildly. "It's tear it off and die, or endure it and live. It becomes less irksome with time."

"I'll endure it," said the Pooka.

Out in the saloon, Liam was learning a number of facts.

Item: Work, although possible to come by, was not as plentiful in New York as poor men eager to do it.

Item: What work there was stretched from dawn to dusk, taxed a man's back more than his mind, and paid barely enough to keep body and soul together.

Item: Not all the poor men looking for work in New York were mortal.

Among Liam's new drinking companions were a midget in a bottle-green coat, sporting a pair of coppery sideburns to rival Prince Albert's, a boyo in threadbare moleskin with black curls hanging down around his ears, and a shortish man with curly golden hair and a clay pipe between his teeth.

Mindful of his purse, Liam refused a bet on a race between a horse and a pig and an opportunity to invest his savings in a sure money-making business. But when the golden-haired man pressed him for his name and county, Liam bethought him that his purse was not the only thing in danger here.

He made a dive for his knapsack and withdrew his tin whistle. "Anybody for a tune?"

The midget brightened. "D'ye know 'Whiskey Before Breakfast'?"

"Do I not?" said Liam, and began to play. If he hadn't been tipsy and perhaps a little more than tipsy, it's likely he'd have made a pig's ear of it, with his heart thundering in his breast and the spit dry in his mouth. As it was, "Whiskey Before Breakfast" came pouring out of his tin whistle as clear and clean as a May morning in Ballynoe, with all the birds singing.

The midget tapped his tiny, beautifully shod feet. The boyo hooked his elbows over the shelf nailed along the wall and sighed. The small man laid down his clay pipe and clapped time. "Whiskey Before Breakfast" rippled out over the room, until the whole saloon was listening to the bright notes skip through the rafters and ring against the stone bottles ranged behind the bar.

After playing the air three times through, Liam dropped the tin whistle from his lips and opened his eyes.

"Another," the midget said hoarsely.

Liam gave them "The Witch of the Glen" and "The Lady's Pantaloons" and "I Buried My Wife and Danced on Top of Her," which jig had them dancing as they roared out the words. And then he segued, without thinking about it, into an air he'd made before he'd decided to make his fortune in America.

When he was done, the boyo embraced him, dripping salt tears on the top of his head.

"All hail the fluter!" the midget shouted, and lifted his tankard.

"The fluter!" the others echoed.

A tankard appeared at his hand. When he'd drained it, another took its place. Liam wet his mouth and played again.

By and by, Liam felt a nudge at his knee and looked down to see Madra, looking, if possible, more miserable than he'd looked before, with a great mat of twigs and mud tangled in the fur at his neck and a wild look in his piss-yellow eyes.

Liam tucked the whistle away and knelt. "Is it well with you, Madra, my dear?"

"It is not so," said Madra, irritably. "How do you think it makes me feel, responsible for you as I am, to see you hobnobbing with leprechauns and cluricans and gancanagh and other such scrapings from the depths of the faerie barrel? And me no more fit to protect you than a day-old puppy?"

Liam laughed. "Is that what they are? Well, they seem to like my music well enough. They'll not harm me, I'm thinking, as long as I play for them."

"Very likely," said Madra dryly.

Liam felt a hand upon his shoulder and looked up to see Maeve McDonough herself smiling down at him.

"My thanks, sir, for the entertainment. You've put a thirst on my customers the like of which I've not seen since I came to these shores. I've sold enough drink this night to pay for your dinner—yes, and your dog's, too, if he's a stomach for a bit of meat. Come eat it in the back room, away from this moither, and then you'd best take yourself off to bed before they suck you dry entirely."

Left to himself, Liam might have taken the dinner and forgone the bed, so flown was he on beer and praise and his own dancing music. But he'd Madra to think of, and Madra looked to be on his last legs. So Liam followed Maeve into the back room, where he absorbed a bowl of quite reasonable stew, as well as Madra's portion, which the poor beast was far too ill to eat.

Indeed, the Pooka could not have been worse. The charm Maeve had given him to counteract the iron-sickness bit into his neck like a wolf. His muscles trembled, his vision blurred, and he'd a mighty thirst on him that water did nothing to assuage. In all the long years of his existence, he'd never suffered so—not even when he'd stumbled into a steel trap set for poachers, which he'd been saved from by a stale-drunk horse trainer named Liam O'Casey.

By the time Liam had eaten, the Pooka was too weak and sore even to stand. Clucking, Liam scooped him up in his arms and carried him bodily up the rickety stairs.

The state of Maeve's saloon had given Liam a tolerably accurate notion of the accommodations she had to offer.

It was a dismal enough apartment, low ceilinged and airless, with a door at each end. The side walls were lined with wooden shelves upon which Maeve's boarders were stacked four high and two deep. Liam found an unclaimed space on the lowest shelf, near the far door and right over the piss pot, and tucked Madra into it. He fit himself as best he could around the dog's burning, shivering body and fell asleep.

Thanks to the excitement of the day and the number of five-cent beers he'd downed, Liam slept heavily. He woke once when his fellow boarders retired, drunk and stumbling on the rickety ladders to the upper sleeping shelves. He woke once again when someone trod on his hand climbing down to use the piss pot. The third time he woke, it was to the piteous whines of a dog in agony.

Liam opened his eyes to see a dozen tiny, glowing creatures. Their gauzy wings whirred as they hovered about Madra, pulling at his ears and whiskers and the small hairs about his eyes. Liam shooed them away like bees, and like bees they turned upon him and pinched at his face with sharp little fingers. Owning himself defeated, Liam gathered Madra in his arms and bore him carefully down the stairs to the saloon. And there the pair of them spent the balance of the night, curled on a floor only a little fouler than the sleeping shelf above.

In the gray dawn, the Pooka woke to the toe of a boot in his ribs and Maeve's face looking down at him. "The top of the morning to you, trickster," she said. "And how are you finding yourself this lovely spring day?"

The Pooka levered himself to his feet. His body was sore but no longer wracked with pain, and the burning glede upon his neck had cooled a degree or perhaps more. He yawned hugely and shook himself from ears to tail. "I'm alive," he said. "Which comes as a pleasant surprise. As to the rest, I wish I were back in Erin, deep in a nice bog, and a rainy night descending."

"And so do I, trickster. So do I." For a moment, Maeve allowed her true face to show through the glamour, gaunt and fierce as a mewed hawk. "Now wake your mortal, trickster. I've the floor to sweep and the charms to make for any iron-sick Folk who chance to wash up at my door the day."

So the Pooka nudged Liam O'Casey with his nose and gave him to know it was time to be up and about.

Liam awoke with a foul mouth, a griping in his belly, and an aching head. Dunking his head in a barrel of stale water did something to resign him to a new day. A five-cent beer and a slice of soda bread hot from the oven did more. Thus fortified, Liam O'Casey set out into the April morning in search of employment.

Madra came with him.

Left to his own devices, Liam might have stopped to pass the time of day with someone, preferably a mortal like himself, who might give him advice a mortal could use. As it was, he could only follow Madra, trying not to get knocked down by a heavily laden cart or trip over a feral pig or run into a pushcart or one of the hundreds of gray-faced men on their way to work. He was hot and out of breath when Madra stopped in front of a big square clapboard warehouse.

Liam looked up at the sign: GREEN'S FINE FURNITURE. EST. 1840. EBENEZER GREEN, PROP.

"No doubt it's slipped your mind that I'm a horseman, Madra, not a carpenter."

Madra heaved a sigh. "There's a stable behind, you great idiot—I can smell it. Go on in now; it can't hurt to ask."

Liam brushed down his jacket, straightened his cap, and walked into the warehouse. The place was busy as an ant's nest, with an army of roughly dressed men running about with raw lumber and finished furniture, while a burly man in a loud silk waistcoat over his shirtsleeves and a porkpie hat shouted orders. Presuming this to be Ebenezer Green, Liam approached and greeted him in his best English.

Mr. Green turned a pig-eyed glare on him. "Speak American, Paddy, or git out. Better yet, do both. This is a Know-Nothing shop. We don't do business with Micks and such-like trash."

The man's voice was flat and loud, his accent unfamiliar. His tone and look, however, were as clear as the finest glass goblet.

"I'll be bidding you good day, then," Liam said. "Mr. Know-Nothing, sir." Then he turned on his heel and marched out.

"It seems a strange thing to be bragging of," he said as he and Madra left Green's Fine Furniture behind them.

"He certainly knows nothing about horses," Madra said. "Did you see his nags? Like harrows they were, draped in moth-eaten hides. You're well out of there."

The next stable Madra found was attached to a hauling company near the docks. It was run by Cornelius Vanderhoof, who, like all Dutchmen, didn't care which language a man spoke as long as he was willing to take a dollar in payment for ten hours of work.

"I've no need of a stableman," he told Liam kindly enough. "I have two horse boys, and that's all I need."

"All boys are good for is to feed and water and muck out," Liam said. "I'd care for them like children, I would."

Mr. Vanderhoof shook his head. "Come back in May. I might have work for you, if you can handle a team."

And so it went all the weary day. One livery stable proprietor had just hired someone. Another offered Liam fifty cents to shovel muck. Another shook his head before Liam even opened his mouth.

"It's April," he said. "Nobody will be hiring until summer. You're Irish, right? Why not carry bricks or dig foundations like the rest of your countrymen?"

"I'm a horse trainer," Liam said, hating the pleading note in his voice.

"I don't care if you're the king of County Down," the livery man said. "Ostlers are a dime a dozen in these parts. You want to work with horses, take a train west."

As they emerged from the livery stable, Madra broke the heavy silence. "It's getting on toward dusk. Shall we be heading home?"

Liam looked at the heavy carts piled high with crates and boxes lumbering over the rutted streets, at the ragged, gray-faced men plodding homeward in the fading light, at the street children, dirty and barefoot, lingering by pushcarts in hopes of a dropped apple or an unwatched cabbage. His ears rang with the rumble of wheels, the squeak of unoiled axles, the shouting and swearing and laughter.

"I have no home," he said. "Just now it seems to me I'll never have a home again."

He waited for Madra to call him a pitiful squinter or prescribe a pint or a song to clear his mind. But Madra just plodded down the street, head down and tail adroop, as tired and discouraged as Liam himself.

Being immortal, Folk do not commonly find time hanging heavy on their hands. A day is but an eyeblink in their lives; a month can pass in the drawing of a breath. The Pooka had never imagined being as aware of the arc of the sun across the sky or the length of time separating one meal from the next as he had been since his life had been linked to Liam's.

Today had been a weary length indeed.

At first, the Pooka had simply been glad to be alive and reasonably well. Maeve's charm itched, but it was a healing itch, and he felt some strength return to his limbs. He kept running up to railings and barrels and iron-shod wheels just to touch them and sniff them and prove once again that they had no power to hurt him.

The encounter with Ebenezer Green shook him. Had he been on his game, the Pooka would have nosed out what manner of man Green was before they'd even crossed the threshold.

But the Pooka was not on his game. A whole day on the town, and he hadn't tricked so much as the price of a drink out of a living soul. The fear grew on him that Maeve's charm had cured his iron-sickness at the expense of his magic. What he needed was something to knock him loose from the limited round of mortal concerns he'd been treading since Liam had freed him from the poacher's trap. He needed a bet or a challenge or a trick. Something tried and true, for preference not too dangerous, that would put him on his mettle and bring Liam a bit of silver.

"Liam," he said. "I have an idea. Tomorrow, as soon as it's light, we'll take ourselves up out of this sty to wherever it is the rich folk live. You shall sell me as a ratter for the best price you can get."

"Shall I so?" asked Liam wearily. "And what if no man needs a ratter or will not buy an Irish one?"

"There's always a man wants to buy a dog," the Pooka said confidently.

Liam shook his head. "I will not, and there's an end. What kind of man do you take me for, to sell a friend for silver money?"

"Oh, I'd not stay sold," the Pooka assured him. "I'd run away and meet you at Maeve's before the cat can lick her ear."

"And if you can't escape? What then? Will I steal you back again? It's stark mad you are, Madra. The city's gone to your head."

The Pooka was charmed with his plan and argued it with cunning and passion. Yet Liam would not be moved. It was illegal, he said, immoral, and dangerous, and that was an end on it. All of which confirmed the Pooka in his opinion that Liam was no more suited for city life than a wild deer. Were the Pooka not there to look after him, he'd surely have been stripped of his savings and left to starve in a ditch before he'd so much as fully exhaled the ship's air from his lungs.

West, the Pooka thought. *He'd like it out west. Tomorrow I'll think about getting him on a train.*

A furious squeal interrupted the Pooka's planning. Hackles rising, he turned to find himself nose to bristly snout with a big, ugly, foul-breathed sow.

A fight's as good as a trick for clearing the mind.

The Pooka bared his teeth and growled. The sow's amber eye glittered madly, and she wheeled and trotted back for the charge. The Pooka spared a glance at Liam, saw him surrounded by a handful of half-grown shoats, squealing and shoving at his legs. Liam was laying about him with his knapsack, cursing and trying to keep his feet in the mired street. If he were to fall, they'd trample him sure as taxes, and possibly eat him where he lay.

Fury rose in the Pooka's breast, then, pure and mighty. Ducking the sow's charge, he leaped into the melee around Liam, landing square on the largest of the shoats. The pig threw him off, but not before the Pooka had nipped a chunk out of its ear. Spitting that out, he fastened his teeth into the nearest ham. The shoat it belonged to squealed and bolted, leaving only four and their dam for the Pooka to fight.

He'd not endured a battle so furious since St. Patrick drove the snakes into the sea and the Fair Folk under hill. This fight he intended to win.

At home on his own turf, the Pooka would have made short work of the pigs. At home, even in his dog shape there, he was faster than a bee, mighty as a bull, and tireless as the tide. But weeks of iron-sickness and short commons, stuck in one shape like a chick in its shell, had sapped his strength.

The Pooka slipped in the slurry of mud and dung; a sharp trotter caught him a glancing blow. He felt the bright blood run burning down his flank, and a wave of pain and terror washed through and through him. Immortals cannot die, but they can be killed.

Instinct told the Pooka that he must shift to save himself. Fear whispered that he could not shift, that he'd lost the knack, that he'd been a dog so long, he'd forgotten what it felt like to have hooves or horns or two legs and a coat he could take off.

Seeing her enemy falter, the sow took heart and charged, squealing like a rusty hinge, her tusks aimed like twin spears straight at the Pooka's soft belly.

Instinct triumphed.

Tossing his streaming mane, the Pooka screamed and aimed his heavy, unshod hooves at the sow's spine. Quick as he was, she was quicker yet, scrambling out from under his feet at the last instant. The Pooka turned upon the shoats around Liam like an angry sea, striking with hoof and tooth.

The sow, seeing her shoats threatened, charged again, barreling toward the Pooka like a storm full of lightning. Wheeling, the Pooka reared again. This time, his hooves crushed the sow into the mud.

The Pooka stood over the bodies of his enemies and trumpeted his victory into the evening air.

An arm snaked across his withers and clung there. Liam's voice, shaky with relief, breathed in his ear. "Oh, my heart, my beauty, my champion of champions. That was a battle to be put in songs, and I shall do so. Just as soon as my legs will bear me and my heart climbs down from my throat."

The Pooka arched his neck proudly and pawed at the corpses piled at his feet. A shoat, recovering from its swoon, heaved up on its trotters and staggered away down the street, straight into the path of a bay gelding harnessed to a shiny black buggy driven by a man in a stovepipe hat.

Bruised and shaken as he was, Liam was no more able to leave a horse in difficulties than swim home to Eire. No sooner did he see the shoat run between the bay's feet and the bay shy and startle and kick its traces, than he ran to its head and grabbed its harness.

The bay tossed him to and fro like a terrier with a rat, but Liam hung on, murmuring soothing inanities in Irish and English, until the gelding's terror calmed and it stood silent and shivering.

Liam stroked the bay's nose and looked around him.

The street was a shambles, with the corpses of his late assailants bleeding into the mud. A crowd of day laborers stood all around, goggling with their mouths at half cock. Off to one side, Madra the hound was licking the blood from a gash on his flank.

The gelding's driver climbed down from the buggy, his cheeks as white as his snowy shirtfront.

"Thank you." His voice, though flatly American, was kind. "That was bravely done. I take it you know something about horses?"

Liam touched his forehead with his knuckle. "I do so, sir."

"Ostler?" the gentleman asked.

"Back in my own country, I was a trainer. Racehorses."

The gentleman looked startled. "A horse trainer? I'll be blowed! Do you mind if I ask your name?"

"It's Liam O'Casey, if it please your honor."

The gentleman laughed, showing strong teeth. "Honor me no honors, Mr. O'Casey. I'm plain William Graves, and I breed horses." Mr. Graves produced a pasteboard card. "Here's my card. I've a little farm up past the orphan asylum—Eighty-fifth Street, more or less. If you care to come there tomorrow, it may be that we'll find something to talk about."

Mr. Graves shook Liam's nerveless hand, climbed back up into his buggy, collected the reins, and drove off.

"Well, that was a piece of luck and no mistake."

It was Madra's voice, but when Liam turned, he saw no dog beside him but a tall man in a black-skirted coat as filthy as it was out of fashion. His skin was pale, his crow-black hair was tied with a strip of leather, and his narrow eyes were set on an upward tilt, with his black brows flying above them like wings.

"You can be shutting your jaw now, Liam O'Casey," the Pooka said. "I'm not such a sore sight as that, surely."

"Madra?"

"For shame, and me standing before you on my two legs as fine a figure of a man as you are yourself." The Pooka linked his arm through Liam's and propelled him down the street. "Come away to Maeve McDonough's and stand yourself a whiskey for a good day's work well done. You may stand me to one as well."

Looking back over his shoulder, Liam saw a pair of cart horses in thick collars pulling a piano in a wagon over the broken bodies of the swine. "My knapsack," he said sadly. "My tin whistle."

"The works of the late lamented J. J. Callanan were beyond saving," the Pooka said. "The tin whistle, on the other hand . . . " He held it out to Liam, dented, but whole. "I saved your purse, too."

"And my life." Liam stopped in the street and offered the Pooka his hand. "I'm forever in your debt."

The Pooka looked alarmed. "What are you after saying, Liam O'Casey? There's no question of debt between us. Favor for favor. Life for life. We're quits now."

"Will you be leaving me, then?" asked Liam, and the Pooka could not for the life of him tell whether it was with hope or dread he asked it.

"Not before I've had my drink," he said, and was ridiculously pleased to feel the arm in his relax its tension. "I'll see you safe up to Mr. Graves's farm first."

"Do you think he's prepared to employ me?"

"Of a certainty. And give you his daughter's hand in marriage, I shouldn't wonder."

Liam laughed aloud. "He's not much older than I, Madra. His daughter would be an infant, presuming he had one at all. This is the real world we're in, after all, not a fairy tale."

"Are we not?" They'd reached Maeve McDonough's by now and descended into the hot and noisy saloon. "And here am I, thinking there's room enough for both in a city the size of this. New York's got life in it, my friend. I'm minded to stay awhile. As long as you come down from the country from time to time and give us a tune. There's no joy in a city where you cannot hear 'Whiskey Before Breakfast.' "

Now, a quick journey to near-future Manhattan where a certain actor wakes up to find a griffin made of shining metal perched at the end of his bed.

. . . AND THE ANGEL WITH TELEVISION EYES

JOHN SHIRLEY

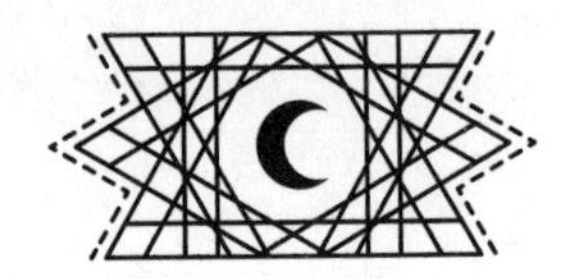

One gray April morning, Max Whitman woke in his midtown Manhattan apartment to find a living, breathing griffin perched on the righthand post at the foot of his antique four-poster bed. Max watched with sleep-fuzzed pleasure as the griffin—a griffin made of shining metal—began to preen its mirror-bright feathers with a hooked beak of polished cadmium. It creaked a little as it moved.

Max assumed at first that he was still dreaming; he'd had a series of oddly related Technicolor-vivid dreams recently. Apparently one of these dreams had spilled over onto his waking reality. He remembered the griffin from a dream of the night previous. It had been a dream bristling with sharp contrasts: of hard-edged shafts of white light—a light that never warms—breaking through clouds the color of suicidal melancholy. And weaving in and out of those shafts of light, the griffin came flying toward him ablaze with silvery glints. And then the clouds coming together, closing out the light, and letting go sheets of rain. Red rain. Thick, glutinous rain. A rain of blood. Blood running down the sheer wall of a high-towered, gargoyle-studded castle carved of transparent glass. Supported by nothing at all: a crystalline castle still and steady as Mount Everest, hanging in mid-air. And laying siege to the sky-castle was a flying army of wretched things led by a man with a barbed-wire head—

Just a bad dream.

Now, Max gazed at the griffin and shivered, hoping the rest of the dream wouldn't come along with the griffin. He hadn't liked the rain of blood at all.

Max blinked, expecting the griffin to vanish. It remained, gleaming. Fulsome. Something hungry . . .

The griffin noticed Max watching. It straightened, fluttered its two-meter wingspread, wingtips flashing in the morning light slanting through the broad picture window, and said, "Well, what do you want of me?" It had a strangely musical, male voice.

"Whuh?" said Max blearily. "Me? Want with you?" Was it a holograph? But it looked so solid . . . and he could hear its claws rasping the bedpost.

"I heard your call," the griffin went on. "It was too loud, and then it was too soft. You really haven't got the hang of mindsending yet. But I heard and I came. Who are you and why did you call me?"

"Look, I didn't—" He stopped, and smiled. "Sandra. Sandra Klein in special effects, right? This is her little cuteness." He yawned and sat up. "She outdid herself with you, I must admit. You're a marvel of engineering. Damn." The griffin was about a meter high. It gripped the bedpost with metallic eagle's claws; it sat on its haunches, and its lion's forepaws—from a lion of some polished argent alloy—rested on its pin-feathered knees. The pinfeathers looked like sweepings from a machine shop. The griffin had a lion's head, but an eagle's beak replaced a muzzle. Its feathered chest rose and fell.

"A machine that breathes . . ." Max murmured.

"Machine?" The griffin's opalescent eyes glittered warningly. Its wire-tufted lion's tail swished. "It's true my semblance is all alloys and plastics and circuitry. But I assure you I am not an example of what you people presume to call 'artificial intelligence'."

"Ah." Max felt cold, and pulled the bedclothes up to cover his goose-pimpled shoulders. "Sorry." *Don't make it mad.* "Sandra didn't send you?"

It snorted. "Sandra! Good Lord, no."

"I . . ." Max's throat was dry. "I saw you in a dream." He felt odd. Like he'd taken a drug that couldn't make up its mind if it were a tranquilizer or a psychedelic.

"You saw me in a dream?" The griffin cocked its head attentively. "Who else was in this dream?"

"Oh there were—*things*. A rain of blood. A castle that was there and wasn't there. A man—it looked like he was made of . . . of hot metal. And his head was all of wire. I had a series of dreams that were . . . Well, things like that."

"If you dreamed those things, then my coming here is ordained. You act as if you honestly don't know *why* I'm here." It blinked, tiny metal shutters closing with a faint *clink*. "But you're not much *surprised* by me. Most humans would have run shrieking from the room by now. You accept me.

Max shrugged. "Maybe. But you haven't told me why you're here. You said it was—ordained?"

"*Planned* might be a better word, I can tell you that I am Flare, and I am a Conservative Protectionist, a High Functionary in the Fiefdom of Lord Viridian. And you—if you're human—must be wild talent. At least. You transmitted the mindsend in your sleep, unknown to your conscious mind. I should have guessed from the confused signal. Well, well, well. Such things are outside the realm of my expertise. You might be one of the Concealed. We'll see, at the meeting. First, I've got to have something to eat. You people keep food in 'the kitchen,' I think. That would be through that hallway . . ."

The griffin of shining metal fluttered from the bedpost, alighted on the floor with a light clattering, and hopped into the kitchen, out of sight.

Max got out of bed, thinking: He's right. I should be at least disoriented. But I'm not. I *have* been expecting him.

Especially since the dreams started. And the dreams began a week after he'd taken on the role of Prince Red Mark. He'd named the character himself—there'd been last moment misgivings about the original name chosen by the scripters, and he'd blurted, "How about 'Prince Red Mark'?" And the producer went for it, one of the whims that shape show business. Four tapings for the first two episodes, and then the dreams commenced. Sometimes he'd dream he was Prince Red Mark; other times a flash of heat lightning; or a ripple of wind, a breeze that could think and feel, swishing through unseeable gardens of invisible blooms . . . And then the dreams became darker, fiercer, so that he awoke with his fists balled, his eyes wild, sweat cold on his chin. Dreams about griffins and rains of blood and sieges by wretched things. The things that flew, the things with claws.

He'd played Prince Red Mark for seven episodes now. He'd been picked for his athletic build, his thick black hair, and his air of what the PR people called "aristocratic detachment." Other people called it arrogance.

Max Whitman had found, to his surprise, he hadn't had to act the role. When he played Prince Red Mark, he *was* Prince Red Mark. Pure and simple . . . The set-hands would make fun of him, when they thought he couldn't hear, because he'd forget to step out of the character between shootings. He'd swagger about the set with his hand on the pommel of his sword, emanating Royal Authority.

This morning he didn't feel much like Prince Red Mark. He felt sleepy and confused and mildly threatened. He stretched, then turned toward the kitchen, worried by certain sinister noises: claws on glass. Splashings. Wet, slapping sounds. He burst out, "Damn, it got into my aquarium!" He hurried to the kitchen. "Hey—oh, hell. My fish." The griffin was perched beside the ten-gallon aquarium on the breakfast bar. Three palm-sized damsel fish were gasping, dying on the wet blue-tile floor. The griffin fluttered to the floor, snipped the fish neatly into sections with its beak, and gobbled them just as an eagle would have. The blue tile puddled with red. Max turned away, saddened but not really angry. "Was that necessary?"

"It's my nature. I was hungry. When we're bodied, we have to eat. I can't eat those dead things in your refrigerator. And after some consideration I decided it would be best if I didn't eat *you* . . . Now, let's go to the meeting. And don't say, 'What meeting?'"

"Okay. I won't."

"Just take a fast cab to 862 Haven, apartment 17. I'll meet you on their balcony . . . wait. Wait. I'm getting a send. They're telling me—it's a message for *you*." It cocked its head to one side as if listening. "They tell me I must apologize for eating your fish. Apparently you have some unusual level of respect in their circle." It bent its head. "I apologize. And they say you are to read a letter from 'Carstairs.' It's been in your computer's mail sorter for two weeks under *personal* and you keep neglecting to retrieve it. Read it. That's the send . . . Well, then . . ." The griffin, fluttering its wings, hopped into the living room. The French doors opened for it as if slid back by some ghostly hand. It went to the balcony, crouched, then sprang into the air and soared away. He thought he heard it shout something over its shoulder at him: something about Prince Red Mark.

It was a breezy morning, feeling like spring. The sun came and went.

Max stood under the rain shelter in the gridcab station on the roof of his apartment building. The grid was a webwork of metal slats and signal contacts, braced by girders and upheld by the buildings that jutted through the finely woven net like mountaintops through a cloud field. Thousands of wedge-shaped cabs and private gridcars hummed along the grid in as many different directions.

Impatiently, Max once more thumbed the green call button on the signal stanchion. An empty cab, cruising by on automatic pilot, was dispatched by the Uptown area's traffic computer; it detached from the feverishly interlacing main traffic swarm and arced neatly into the pick-up bay under the rain shelter. Max climbed inside and inserted his Unicard into the cab's creditor. The small terminal's screen acknowledged his bank account and asked, "Where to?" Max tapped his destination into the keyboard: the cab's computer, through the data-feed contacts threaded into the grid, gave the destination to the main computer, which maneuvered the cab from the bay and out onto the grid. *You are to read a letter from Carstairs*, the griffin had said.

He'd met Carstairs at a convention of fantasy fans. Carstairs had hinted he was doing "some rather esoteric research" for Duke University's parapsychology lab. Carstairs had made Max nervous—he could feel the man following him, watching him, wherever he went in the convention hotel. So he'd deliberately ignored the message. But he hadn't gotten around to deleting it.

As the cab flashed across the city, weaving in and out of the peaks of skyscrapers, over the narrow parks that had taken the place of the Avenue, Max punched a request to connect to his home computer. The cab charged his bank account again, tied him in, and he asked his system to print out a copy of the email from Carstairs. He scanned the message, focusing first on: ". . . when I saw you at the convention I knew the Hidden Race had chosen to favor you. They were there, standing at your elbow, invisible to you—invisible to me too, except in certain lights, and when I concentrate all my training on looking . . ." Max shivered, and thought: *A maniac. But—the griffin had been real.*

He skipped ahead, to: ". . . You'll remember, perhaps, back in the last century, people were talking about a 'plasma body' that existed within our own physiological bodies, an independently organized but interrelated skein of subatomic particles; this constituted, it was supposed, the so-called soul. It occurred to some of us that if this plasma body could exist in so cohesive a form within an organism, and could survive for transmigration after the death of that organism, then perhaps a race of creatures, creatures who seem to us to be 'bodiless,' could exist alongside the embodied creatures without humanity's knowing it. This race does exist, Max. It accounts for those well-documented cases of 'demonic' possession and poltergeists. And for much in mythology. My organization has been studying the Hidden Race—some call them plasmagnomes—for fifteen years. We kept our research secret for a good reason . . ."

Max was distracted by a peculiar noise. A scratching sound from the roof of the cab. He glanced out the window, saw nothing, and shrugged. Probably a news-sheet blown by the wind onto the car's roof. He looked again at the letter. ". . . for a good reason. Some of the plasmagnomes are hostile . . . The Hidden Race is very orderly. It consists of about ten thousand plasmagnomes, who live for the most part in the world's 'barren' places. Such places are not barren to them. The bulk of the plasmagnomes are a well-cared-for serf class, who labor in creating base plasma fields, packets of nonsentient energy to be consumed or used in etheric constructions. The upper classes govern, study the various universes, and most of all concern themselves with the designing and elaboration of their Ritual. But this monarchist hierarchy is factioned into two distinct opposition parties, the Protectionists and the Exploitationists: they gave us those terms as being the closest English equivalent. The Protectionists are sanctioned by the High Crown and the Tetrarchy of Lords. Lately the Exploitationists have increased their numbers, and they've become harder to police. They have gotten out of hand. For the first time since a Protectionist walked the Earth centuries ago as 'Merlin' and an Exploitationist as 'Mordred,' certain members of the Hidden Race have taken bodied form among us . . ."

Max glanced up again.

The scratching sound from the roof. Louder this time. He tried to ignore it; he wondered why his heart was pounding. He looked doggedly at the letter. ". . . The Exploitationists maintain that humanity is small-minded, destructive of the biosphere, too numerous, and in general suitable only for slavery and as sustenance. If they knew my organization studied them, they would kill me and my associates. Till recently, the Protectionists have prevented the opposition party from taking physical form. It's more difficult for them to affect us when they're unbodied, because our biologic magnetic fields keep them at a distance. . . . Centuries ago, they appeared to us as dragons, sorcerers, fairies, harpies, winged horses, griffins, angels, demons—"

Max leaned back in his seat and slowly shook his head. Griffins. He took a deep breath. This could still be a hoax. The griffin *could* have been a machine.

But he knew better. He'd known since he was a boy, really. Even then, certain Technicolor-vivid dreams—

He tensed: the phantom scrabbling had come again from overhead. He glimpsed a dark fluttering from the corner of one eye; he turned, thought he saw a leathery wingtip withdraw from the upper edge of the window frame.

"Oh God." He decided it might be a good idea to read the rest of the letter. Now. Quickly. Best he learn all he could about them. Because the scratching on the roof was becoming a grating, scraping sound. Louder and harsher.

He forced himself to read the last paragraph of the letter. ". . . in the old days they manifested as such creatures, because their appearance is affected by our expectation of them. They enter the visible plane only after filtering through our cultural psyche, the society's collective electromagnetic mental field. And their shapes apparently have something to do with their inner psychological make-up—each one has a different self-image. When they become bodied, they manipulate the atoms of the atomic-physical world with plasma-field telekinesis, and shape it into what at least seem to be actually functioning organisms, or machines. Lately they take the form of machines—collaged with more ancient imagery—because ours is a machine-minded society. They're myth robots, perhaps. They're not magical creatures. They're real, with their own subtle metabolism—and physical needs and ecological niche. They have a method of keeping records—in 'closed-system plasma fields'—and even constructing housing. Their castles are vast and complex and invisible to us, untouchable and all but undetectable. We can pass through them and not disturb them. The Hidden Race has a radically different relationship to matter, energy—and death. That special relationship is what makes them seem magical to us . . . Well, Mr. Whitman, we're getting in touch with you to ask you to attend a meeting of those directly involved in plans for defense against the Exploitationists' campaign to—"

He got no further in his reading. He was distracted. Naked terror is a distracting thing.

A squealing sound of ripped metal from just over his head made him cringe in his seat, look up to see claws of polished titanium, claws long as a man's fingers and wickedly curved, slashing the cab's thin roof. The claws peeled the metal back.

Frantically, Max punched a message into the cab's terminal: *Change direction for nearest police station. Emergency priority. I take responsibility for traffic disruption.*

The cab swerved, the traffic parting for it, and took an exit from the grid to spiral down the off-ramp. It pulled up in the concrete cab stop at street level, across from a cop just getting out of a patrol car at a police station. Wide-eyed, the cop drew his gun and ran toward the cab.

Claws snatched at Max's shoulders. He opened the cab door, and flung himself out of the car, bolting for shelter.

Something struck him between the shoulderblades. He staggered. There was an icy digging at his shoulders—he howled. Steel claws sank into his flesh and lifted him off his feet—he could feel the muscles of his shoulders straining, threatening to tear. The claws opened, released him, and he fell face down; he lay for a moment, gasping on his belly. He had a choppy impression of something blue-black flapping above and behind. He felt a tugging at his belt—and then he was lifted into the air, the clawed things carrying him by the belt as if it were a luggage handle.

He was two, three, five meters above the concrete, and spiraling upward. He heard a gunshot, thought he glimpsed the cop fallen, a winged darkness descending on him.

The city whirled into a gray blur. Max heard the regular beat of powerful wings just above. He thought: I'm too heavy. It's not aerodynamically possible.

But he was carried higher still, the flying things making creaking, whipping sounds with their pinions. Otherwise, they were unnervingly silent. Max stopped struggling to free himself. If he broke loose now, he'd fall ten stories to the street. He was slumped like a rabbit in a hawk's claws, hanging limply, humiliated.

He saw two of the flying things below, now, just climbing into his line of sight. They carried the policeman—a big bald man with a paunchy middle. They carried him between them; one had him by the ankles, the other by the throat. He looked lifeless. Judging by the loll of his head, his neck was broken.

Except for the rush of wind past his face, the pain at his hips where the belt was cutting into him, Max felt numb, once more in a dream. He was afraid, deeply afraid, but the fear had somehow become one with the world, a background noise that one grows used to, like the constant banging from a neighborhood construction site. But when he looked at the things carrying him, he had a chilling sense of déjà vu. He remembered them from the dreams. Two mornings before, he'd awakened, mumbling, "The things that flew, the things with claws . . ."

They were made of vinyl. Blue-black vinyl stretched over, he guessed, aluminum frames. They were bony, almost skeletal women, with little hard knobs for breasts, their arms merging into broad, scalloped imitation leather wings. They had the heads of women—with DayGlo wigs of green, stiff-plastic bristles—but instead of eyes there were the lenses of cameras, one in each socket; and when they opened their mouths he saw, instead of teeth, the blue-gray curves of razors following the line of the narrow jaws. Max thought: It's a harpy. A vinyl harpy.

One of the harpies, three meters away and a little below, turned its vinyl head, its camera lenses glittering, to look Max in the face; it opened its mouth and threw back its head like a dog about to howl and out came the sound of an air-raid warning: GO TO THE SHELTERS. GO IMMEDIATELY TO THE SHELTERS. DO NOT STOP TO GATHER POSSESSIONS. TAKE FAMILY TO THE SHELTERS. BRING NOTHING. FOOD AND WATER WILL BE PROVIDED. GO IMMEDIATELY—

And two others took it up. GO IMMEDIATELY—in a sexless, emotionless tone of authority. TAKE FAMILY TO THE SHELTERS—

And Max could tell that, for the harpies, the words had no meaning. It was their way of animal cawing, the territorial declaration of their kind.

They couldn't have been in the air more than ten minutes—flapping unevenly over rooftops, bits and pieces of the city churning by below—when they began to descend. They were going down beyond the automated zone. They entered Edgetown, what used to be the South Bronx. People still sometimes drove combustion cars here, on the pot-holed, cracked streets, when they could get contraband gasoline; here policemen were rarely seen; here the corner security cameras were always smashed, the sidewalks crusted with trash, and two-thirds of the buildings deserted.

Max was carried down toward an old-fashioned tar rooftop; it was the roof of a five-story building, wedged in between three taller ones. All four looked derelict and empty; the building across the street showed a few signs of occupation: laundry in the airshaft, one small child on the roof. The child, a little black girl, watched without any sign of surprise. Max felt a little better, seeing her.

Where the shadows of the three buildings intersected on the fourth, in the deepest pocket of darkness, there was a small outbuilding; it was the rooftop doorway into the building. The door hung brokenly to one side. A cherry-red light pulsed just inside the doorway, like hate in a nighted soul.

Max lost sight of the red glow as the vinyl harpies turned, circling for a landing. The rooftop rushed up at him. There was a sickening moment of freefall when they let go. He fell three meters to the rooftop, struck on the balls of his feet, plunged forward, shoulder-rolled to a stop. He gasped, trying to get his breath back. His ankles and the soles of his feet ached.

He took a deep breath and stood, swaying, blinking. He found he was staring into the open doorway. Within, framed by the dusty, dark entrance to the stairway, was a man made of red-hot steel. The heat-glow was concentrated in his torso and arms. He touched the wooden frame of the doorway—and it burst into flame. The harpies capered about the tar rooftop, leaping atop chimneys and down again, stretching their wings to flap, cawing, booming, GO IMMEDIATELY TO THE SHELTERS, GO IMMEDIATELY, GO GO GO . . .

The man made of hot metal stepped onto the roof. The harpies quieted, cowed. They huddled together, behind him, cocking their heads and scratching under their wings with pointed chins. To one side lay the lifeless body of the policeman, its back toward Max; the corpse's head had been twisted entirely around on its neck; one blue eye was open, staring lifelessly; the man's tongue was caught between clamped teeth, half severed.

For a moment all was quiet, but for the rustling of wings and crackling of the small fire on the outbuilding.

The man of hot chrome wore no clothes at all. He was immense, nearly two-and-a-half meters tall, and smooth as the outer hull of a factory-new fighter-jet. He was seamless—except for the square gate on his chest, with the little metal turn-handle on it. The gate was precisely like the door of an old-fashioned incinerator; in the center of the gate was a small, thick pane of smoke-darkened glass, through which blue-white fires could be seen burning restlessly. Except for their bright metal finish, his arms and legs and stylized genitals looked quite human. His head was formed of barbed wire—a densely woven wire sculpture of a man's head, cunningly formed to show grim, aristocratic features. There were simply holes for eyes, behind which red fires flickered in his hollow head; now and then flames darted from the eyeholes to play about his temples and then recede; his scalp was a crest of barbs; eyebrows and ears were shaped of barbs. Gray smoke gusted from his mouth when he spoke to the harpies: "Feed me." The wire lips moved like a man's; the wire jaw seemed to work smoothly. "Feed me, while I speak to this one." He stepped closer Max, who cringed back from the heat. "I am Lord Thanatos." A voice like metal rending.

Max knew him.

One of the harpies moved to the corpse of the policeman; it took hold of the arm, put one stunted foot on the cop's back, and began to wrench and twist. It tore the corpse's arm from its shoulder and dragged it to Thanatos, leaving a trail of red blood on black tar. The harpy reached out with its free hand and turned the handle on its lord's chest. The door swung open; an unbearable brightness flared in the opening; ducking its head, turning its eyes from the rapacious light, the vinyl harpy stuffed the cop's arm, replete with wrist-com and blue coat-sleeve, into the inferno, the bosom of Thanatos. Sizzlings and poppings and black smoke unfurling. And the smell of roasting flesh. Max's stomach recoiled; he took another step backward. He watched, feeling half paralyzed, as the harpies scuttled back and forth between the corpse and Thanatos, slowly dismembering and disemboweling the dead policeman, feeding the pieces into the furnace that was their lord.

And his fire burned more furiously; his glow increased.

"This is how it will be," said Thanatos. "You will serve me. You can look on me, Max Whitman, and upon my servants, and you do not go mad. You do not run howling away. Because you are one of those who has always known about us, in some way. We met on the dream-plane once, you and I, and I knew you for what you were then. You can serve me, and still live among men. You will be my emissary. You will be shielded from the cowards who would prevent my entry into your world. You will go to certain men, the few who control the many. The wealthy ones. You will tell them about a great source of power,

Lord Thanatos. I will send fiends and visitations to beset their enemies. Their power will grow, and they will feed me, and my power will grow. This is how it will be."

As he finished speaking, another harpy flapped down from the sky, dropping a fresh corpse into the shadows. It was a young Hispanic man in a smudged white suit. Thanatos opened the wiry mouth of his hollow head and sighed; blue smoke smelling of munitions factories dirtied the air. "They always kill them, somehow, as they bring them to me. I cannot break them of it. They always kill the humans. Men are more pleasurable to consume when there is life left in them. My curse is this: I'm served by half-minds."

Max thought: Why didn't the harpies kill me, then?

The vinyl harpies tore an arm from the sprawled dead man, and fed it into their master's fire. Their camera-lens eyes caught the shine of the fire. Thanatos looked at Max. "You have not yet spoken."

And Max thought: *Say anything. Anything to get the hell away.* "I'll do just what you ask. Let me go and I'll bring you lives. I'll be your, uh, your emissary."

Another long, smoky sigh. "You're lying. I was afraid you'd be loyal. Instinct of some sort, I suppose."

"Loyal to who?"

"I can read you. You see only the semblance I've chosen. But I see past your semblance. You cannot lie to one of us. I see the lie in you unfolding like the blossoming of a poisonous purple orchid. You cannot lie to a Lord."

He licked barbed wire lips with a tongue of flame.

So they will kill me, Max thought. They'll feed me into this monstrosity! Is that a strange death? An absurd death? No stranger than dying by nerve-gas on some foreign battlefield; no more absurd than my Uncle Danny's death: he drowned in a big vat of fluorescent pink paint.

"You're not going to die," said Thanatos. "We'll keep you in stasis, forever imprisoned, unpleasantly alive."

What happened next made Max think of a slogan stenciled on the snout of one of the old B-12 bombers from World War II: *Death From Above*. Because something silvery flashed down from above and struck the two harpies bending over the body of the man in the smudged white suit . . . both harpies were struck with a terrible impact, sent broken and lifeless over the edge of the roof.

The griffin pulled up from its dive, raking the tar roof, and soared over the burning outbuilding and up for another pass. The remaining harpies rose to meet it.

Other figures were converging on the roof, coming in a group from the north. One was a man who hovered without wings; he seemed to levitate. His body was angelic, his skin dazzling white; he wore a loincloth made of what looked like aluminum foil. His head was a man's, haloed with blond curls—but where his eyes and forehead should have been was a small television screen, projecting from the bone of his skull. On the screen was an image of human eyes, looking about; it was as if he saw from the TV screen. Two more griffins arrived, one electroplated gold, another of nickel, and just behind them came a woman who drifted like a bit of cotton blown on the breeze. She resembled Mother Mary, but nude: a plastic Madonna made of the stuff of which inflatable beach toys are made; glossy and striped in wide bands of primary colors. She seemed insubstantial as a soap bubble, but when she struck at a vinyl harpy it reeled back, turning end over end to fall senseless to the rooftop. Flanking her were two miniature helicopters—helicopters no bigger than horses. The lower section of each helicopter resembled a medieval dragon attired in armored metal, complete with clawed arms in place of landing runners. Each copter's cab was conventionally shaped—but no pilot sat behind the windows; and just below those sinister windows was a set of chrome teeth in a mouth opening to let loose great peals of electronically amplified laughter. The dragon copters dived to attack the remaining harpies, angling their whirring blades to shred the vinyl wings.

Thanatos grated a command, and from the burning doorway behind him came seven bats big as vultures, with camera-lens eyes and sawing electric knives for teeth and wings of paper-thin aluminum.

Max threw himself to the roof, coughing in the smoke of the growing fire; the bats whipped close over his head and climbed, keening, to attack Our Lady of the Plastics.

Two dog-sized spiders made of high-tension rubbery synthetics, their clashing mandibles forged of the best Solingen steel, raced on whirring copper legs across the roof to intercept the angel with television eyes. The angel alighted and turned to gesture urgently to Max. The spiders clutched at the angel's legs and dragged him down, slashed bloody hunks from his ivory arms.

Max saw Lord Thanatos catch a passing griffin by the tail and slam it onto the roof; he clamped the griffin in his white-hot hands. It shrieked and began to melt.

Two metal bats collided head-on with a copter dragon and all three disintegrated in a shower of blue sparks. Our Lady of the Plastics struck dents into the aluminum ribs of the vinyl harpies who darted at her, slashed, and boomed GO IMMEDIATELY, bellowing it in triumph as she burst open—but they recoiled in dismay, flapping clumsily out of reach, when she re-formed, gathering her fragments together, making herself anew in mid-air.

Max sensed that the real battle was fought in some other dimension of subatomic physicality, with a subtler weaponry; he was seeing only the distorted visual echoes of the actual struggle.

The spiders were wrapping the angel's legs with cords of optical fiber. He gave a mighty wrench and threw them off, levitating out of their reach, shouting at Max: "Take your life! You—"

"SILENCE HIM!" Thanatos bellowed, stabbing a hot finger at the angel. And instantly two of the harpies plummeted to sink their talons in the throat of the angel with television eyes. They tore at him, made a gouting, ragged wreckage of his white throat—and Max blinked, seeing a phosphorescent mist, the color of translucent turquoise, issuing from the angel's slack mouth as he fell to the ground.

I'm seeing his plasma body escape, Max thought. I'm realizing my talent.

He saw the blue phosphorescence, vaguely man-shaped, drift to hang in the air over the body of the dead Hispanic. It settled, enfolding the corpse. Possessing it.

Sans its right arm, half its face clawed away, the corpse stood. It swayed, shuddered, spoke with shredded lips. "Max, kill yourself and lib—"

Thanatos lunged at the wavering corpse, closed hot metal fingers around its throat, burned its voice box into char. The body slumped.

But Max stood. His dreams were coming back to him—or was someone sending them back? Someone mindsending. *You were of the Concealed.*

Thanatos turned from the battle, scowling, commanding: "Take him! Bind him, carry him to safety!" The spiders, gnawing on the corpse of the angel with television eyes, moved reluctantly away from their feeding and crept toward Max. A thrill of revulsion went through him. He forced himself forward. He knelt, within the spiders' reach. "Don't hurt him!" Thanatos bellowed. "Take care that he does not—"

But he did. He embraced a spider, clasping it to him as if it were something dear, and used its razor-sharp mandibles to slash his own throat. He fell, spasming, and knew inexpressible pain and numbness, and grayness. And a shattering white light.

He was dead. He was alive. He was standing over his own body, liberated. He reached out, and, with his plasma-field, extinguished the fire on the outbuilding. Instantly.

The battle noises softened, then muted—the combatants drew apart. They stood or crouched or hovered silently, watching him and waiting. They knew him for Prince Red Mark, a sleeping Lord of the Plasmagnomes, one of seven Concealed among humanity years before, awaiting the day of awakening, the hour when they must emerge to protect those the kin of Thanatos would slaughter for the eating.

He was arisen, the first of the Concealed. He would awaken the others, those hidden, sleeping in the hearts of the humble and the unknown. In old women and tired, middle-aged soldiers and—and there was one, hidden in a young sepia-skinned girl, not far away.

Thanatos shuddered and squared himself for the battle of wills.

Max, Lord Red Mark, scanned the other figures on the rooftop.

Now he could see past their semblances, recognize them as interlacing networks of rippling wavelength, motion that is thought, energy equal to will. He reached out, reached past the semblance of Lord Thanatos.

A small black girl, one Hazel Johnson, watched the battle from a rooftop across the street. She was the only one who saw it; she had the only suitable vantage.

Hazel Johnson was just eight years old, but she was old enough to know that the scene should have surprised her, should have sent her yelling for Momma. But she had seen it in a dream, and she'd always believed that dreams were real.

And now she saw that the man who'd thrown himself on the spider had died, and his body had given off a kind of blue glow; and the blue cloud had formed into something solid, a gigantic shape that towered over the nasty-looking wire-head of hot metal. All the flying things had stopped flying. They were watching the newcomer.

The newcomer looked, to Hazel, like one of the astronauts you saw on TV coming home from the space station; he wore one of those spacesuits they wore, and he even had the U.S. flag stitched on one of his sleeves. But he was a whole lot bigger than any astronaut, or any man she'd ever seen. He must have been four meters tall. And now she saw that he didn't have a helmet like a regular astronaut had. He had one of those helmets that the Knights of the Round Table wore, like she saw in the movie on TV. The knight in the spacesuit was reaching out to the man of hot metal . . .

Lord Red Mark was distantly aware that one of his own was watching from the rooftop across the street. Possibly Lady Day asleep in the body of a small human being; a small person who didn't know, yet, that she wasn't really human after all.

Now he reached out and closed one of his gloved hands around Lord Thanatos's barbed-wire neck (that's how it looked to the little girl watching from across the street) and held him fast, though the metal of that glove began to melt in the heat. Red Mark held him, and with the other hand opened the incinerator door, and reached his hand into the fire that burned in the bosom of his enemy—

And snuffed out the flame, like a man snuffing a candle with his thumb and forefinger.

The metal body remained standing, cooling, forever inert. The minions of Lord Thanatos fled squalling into the sky, pursued by the Protectionists, abandoning their visible physicality, becoming once more unseeable. And so the battle was carried into another realm of being.

Soon the rooftop was empty of all but the two corpses, and a few broken harpies, and the shell of Thanatos, and Lord Red Mark.

Red Mark turned to look directly at the little girl on the opposite roof. He levitated, rose evenly into the air, and drifted to her. He alighted beside her and took off his helm. Beneath was a light that smiled. He was beautiful. He said, "Let's go find the others."

She nodded, slowly, beginning to wake. But the little-girl part of her, the human shell, said, "Do I have to die too? Like you did?"

"No. That was for an emergency. There are other ways."

"I don't have to die now?"

"Not now and . . ." The light that was a smile grew brighter. "Not ever. You'll never die, my Lady Day."

The real estate market in Manhattan is always an adventure: everyone wants to live somewhere in the city and that includes elves, wizards, brownies, goblins, and other supernatural types.

PRICED TO SELL

NAOMI NOVIK

"I'm over getting offended," the vampire said despondently. "I just want to stop wasting my time. If the board isn't going to let me in, I don't care how much they smile and how polite they are. I'd rather they just tell me up front there's no chance."

"I know, it's terrible," Jennifer said. No co-op board was going to say anything like that, of course; it was asking for a Fair Housing lawsuit. "Have you thought about a townhouse?"

"Yeah, sure, because of course I've got a trust fund built on long-term compound interest," he said bitterly. "I'm only fifty-four."

He didn't look a day over twenty-five, with that stylish look vampires got if they didn't feed that often, pale and glamorous and hungry, staring into his Starbucks like it was nowhere near what he actually wanted. Jennifer wasn't too surprised he was getting turned down; right now she was feeling pretty excellent about the garlic salt she'd put on the quick slice of pizza that had been lunch.

"Well," Jennifer said, "maybe a property in Brooklyn?"

"Brooklyn?" the vampire said, like she'd suggested a beach vacation in Florida.

It took him five minutes wrapping up to leave the cafe: coat, gloves, hat, veil, scarf, and a cape over all that; Jennifer was so not envying him the rush-hour subway ride home on the Lexington Avenue line.

She walked the five blocks uptown and poked her head into Doug's office to report. The vampire had been bounced over to their team from a broker at Black Thomas Phillips, with blessings, after getting rejected by a second co-op board.

"Try him on some of the new condo developments, where the developer is still controlling the building," Doug said. "What's his budget?"

"A million two," Jennifer said.

"And he wants a three-bedroom?" Doug said. She winced and nodded. "Not a chance. Show him some convertible twos and see if the amenities make him happy."

"I was thinking maybe if we could shake something loose in the Victorian, on 76th?" she said. "I could send around postcards to the current owners."

"Keep it in your back pocket, but I wouldn't start there," Doug said. "The board there won't mind he's a vampire, but they'll mind that he's less than a hundred years old."

Tom knocked on the door and looked in. "Doug, sorry to interrupt, but you've got that 2:15 with the new client at their place on 32nd and 1st."

Doug didn't really know the building; it was a rental, and not a good one: near the Midtown Tunnel traffic, no views, and only an aggressive goblin minding the door, who scowled when Doug asked for 6B. "Six *B*?"

"Yes?" Doug said.

"You . . . friend?" the goblin asked, even more suspiciously.

"He's expecting me," Doug said, diplomatically—some tenants didn't want their landlord knowing they were apartment-hunting.

Unbelievably, the goblin went ahead and poked a foot at the watchcat sleeping under the front hall table. It raised its head and sniffed at Doug and said in a disgruntled voice, "What do you want from me, it's just a real estate broker."

"Broker?" the goblin said, brightening. "Broker, huh? He moving?"

"You'd have to ask him," Doug said, but that wasn't a good sign. Bad landlord references could sink a board application quicker than vampirism. He was starting to get doubts about the client anyway. Anyone who really had a $3 million budget, living here?

The IKEA furniture filling the apartment didn't give him a lot of added confidence, but the client said, "Oh, it's—it's in a trust fund," blinking at him myopically from behind small, thick-glassed round John Lennon specs. Henry Kell didn't seem like a candidate to piss off goblins: he was a skinny five-foot-six and talked softly enough that Doug had to lean forward to hear him. "I don't like to spend it, and—and I don't have very many needs, you know. Only—well—I think it would be best if, if we had our own property, and I think he's come around to the notion."

"Okay, so we're looking for a place for you and your—partner?" Doug said. "Should I meet him too?"

"Er," Mr. Kell said. He took his glasses off and wiped them with a cloth. "You very likely will, at some point, I would expect. But perhaps we could begin just the two of us?"

Kell didn't care about pre-war or post-war, didn't care about a view—"Although I would prefer," he said, "not to look directly into other apartments"—and only shrugged when Doug asked about neighborhoods.

"Okay," Doug said, giving up. He figured he was going to have to take Kell around a little to get some sense of the guy's taste. "I can show you some places tomorrow, if you have time?"

"That would be splendid," Kell said, and the next morning he set Doug's new personal best record by walking into the first place he was shown, looking around for a total of ten minutes, and coming back to say he'd take it for the asking price.

Not that Doug had a deep aversion to getting paid more for less work, but he felt like he wasn't doing his job. "Are you sure you don't want to see anything else?" he said. "Honestly—the ask here is a little high, the place has only been on the market a week."

"No, I," Kell said, "I think I would prefer, really, to tie everything up as quickly as possible. The apartment is quite excellent."

Not a lot of people would have called it that—it was an estate sale, the kitchen and the bathrooms were original, and the late owner had committed crimes against architecture with a pile of ugly built-ins. But nobody could deny it met Kell's criteria for privacy—three rooms facing into blank walls, another one into a courtyard, and the bedroom had a little slice of a view into Riverside Park. The neighborhood was quiet, the elves at Riverside kept it that way, and it was a condo.

"How soon can we sign a contract?" Kell asked.

"I'll get your lawyer in touch with the seller's lawyer," Doug said, and called Tom to cancel the rest of the viewings, shrugging a little helplessly to himself.

"Wow," Tom said, when Doug got back into the office.

"Yeah, that was really something," Doug said. "I think I get bragging rights for easiest commission ever made on this one. How did it go at Tudor City?"

Tom shook his head glumly. The Tudor City apartment was a beautiful place—view of the UN, formal dining room and two bedrooms, renovated kitchen, new subway tile bathrooms, and priced to move. Unfortunately, it had come on the market as part of a divorce settlement, and before moving out the owners had gotten into a knockdown, drag-out screaming fight that had ended in dueling curses in the living room.

People weren't even getting to the master suite. They came in, stuck their heads into the big entry closet, walked into the living room, saw the long wall swarming over with huge black bugs, and turned around and went right out. Sometimes they screamed, even though Doug always warned their brokers beforehand. But it was a tough market right now, and no one wanted to give up a chance for a sale.

The potential buyer this afternoon hadn't screamed: she was a herpetologist, and Tom had really thought that was going to be perfect—he'd pitched it to her as free food supply for her snakes. "But apparently they don't eat beetles," he said.

"Well, you win some, you lose some," Doug said. "Let's see if we can get the clients to put up the fee for another eradicator. It's breaking my heart to see that place list for half a million under market."

The real estate market in Manhattan was always an adventure: everyone wanted to live somewhere in the city. The elves fought tooth-and-nail with Wall Street wizards over Gramercy Park townhouses and Fifth Avenue co-ops, developers tried to pry brownies out of abandoned industrial buildings in Greenwich Village so they could build loft conversions for rock stars and advertising execs, college students squeezed in four-to-a-1BR with actors and alchemists trying for their big break.

Doug had slogged through the dark days of the early nineties, when there'd been seven years of inventory on the market and nothing selling. The immortals were the worst: unless you had a co-op with a limit on how long you could sublet, good luck getting a rakshasa or a vampire to lower their asking price no matter how bad the market was. It was always, "I'll hang in there another decade and see how things go."

Even then, he'd liked the challenge of finding the perfect match of buyer and seller that moved Manhattan real estate, and he liked it a lot more now that he had his own offices tucked into a corner of the Richard Merriman Inc. corporate headquarters, handling the clients with his own team and farming out the boring overhead to the firm.

Right now, though, it was getting a bit more challenging than he liked. Just last week, a $6M deal for one of his exclusives—down from an ask of $7.1M at peak, and happy to get it—had fallen through after an accepted offer. The buyer had lost a quarter of her net worth in the huge Ponzi scheme that had just gotten busted, as though there weren't enough bad news out there.

"Oh, it was brilliant," she'd said grimly, calling to tell him why the deal was off. "They put all these zombie investors on the books, paid them out of our money, then the zombies fell apart and their accounts went to the animators, who turn out to be working for a firm owned by the partners in the fund."

"Can you get any of the money back?" Doug asked.

"Ask me in five years after I finish paying the lawyers," she said.

It made every sale twice as important and ten times as fragile. He was a little surprised they'd gotten the vampire from Black Thomas Phillips, actually, even with the two co-op rejections.

Speaking of which, he sat down to make a few phone calls to people he knew with condo exclusives, but before he got the phone off the hook, it was ringing under his hand.

"What the hell kind of crazy buyer are you bringing me?" Rina Lazar said, without so much as a hello. She was the selling broker on the Riverside apartment.

"Oh, boy," Doug said. "What happened? Did Kell back out?" That would be great, two new records: quickest sale, quickest flameout.

"Ohhh, no," Rina said. "Backing out, backing out would have been fantastic. He got my sellers' number, don't ask me how, called them up and told them, quote, their bleeping apartment was a bleeping pile of bleep, the built-ins were a disgrace, and the place smelled like dead old lady—I am not kidding you here—and nobody in their right mind would pay more than one million for the wreck, take it or leave it, end quote. The daughter just called me up in tears!"

"Oh my God," Doug said.

"Plan on sending me a financial sheet on anyone you want to bring to any of my exclusives from now on," she said, and banged the phone down hard enough to make him wince.

"Oh, dear," Henry Kell said, when Doug called. "I gather that this means the deal is off . . . ?"

"Uh, *yeah*, the deal is off," Doug said. "Mr. Kell, maybe I need to explain this, since you're a first-time buyer. Once you make an offer, you can't just—"

"No, no, I perfectly understand," Kell said. "I assure you, I had no second thoughts myself. It must have been he must have had strong feelings on the subject, I can't think why—"

"Is this your partner we're talking about?" Doug said. "Mr. Kell, if you aren't the sole purchaser here—"

"Well, I am, legally speaking," Kell said. "Only, er, he can make his opinion felt in, in other ways, as you see."

Doug rubbed his forehead and looked at the balance sheet on the open laptop in front of him, although he really didn't need to; he could keep track of all the contracts he had out right now in his head. "Mr. Kell, I'm sure we can find a place that will make both of you completely happy," he said. "But I really am going to need to speak to your partner, too."

"Oh dear," Mr. Kell said.

"Wow, they're a super-interesting touch, very Kafkaesque," the art dealer said, considering the bug swarm on the wall.

"It's definitely a unique feature," Tom said, trying not to look at the wall too hard himself. The bugs made a low raspy sound climbing over each other, which he could hear even though he'd cracked the windows to let in some of the noise of the First Avenue traffic outside.

The buyer's broker—she was backed into the far corner of the living room—looked at him with raised eyebrows as her client went to poke around in the kitchen. Tom shrugged at her a little. What was he going to do?

"I do like the details," the art dealer said, coming back out. "There's something special in the contradiction between the formal style of the classic six, the stained glass windows and the wood paneling, and the raw brutality of the insect swarm."

"Oh?" Tom said. "That is—Yes, absolutely. The clients are very negotiable," he added, with a faint stirring of hope.

The art dealer stood looking around the apartment a little more, and then shook his head. "It's a really tough call, but I don't think so. The apartment is great, but, you know, Tudor City. It's so—stuffy. I just can't see it. It would be almost like living on the Upper East Side. But tell the sellers I love their style," he added.

"Why is the maintenance so high?" the vampire said suspiciously, reading the offering sheet for the Battery Park apartment.

"Well," the selling broker said, and then he admitted that it was a land-lease, meaning the co-op didn't actually own the ground underneath the building, and also the lease was running out in fifteen years and no one had any idea what the term renewal was going to be. "But we've got a brownie super, and there's a fantastic sundeck on the—" He stopped at the look Jennifer shot him.

Waiting in the lobby as the vampire dispiritedly bundled himself up again, Jennifer said, "I've got a few condos lined up that we could take a look at this weekend."

"I don't want to live in a condo," the vampire said, muffled, as he wrapped a scarf around his head. "Those places let anyone in."

Jennifer opened and shut her mouth. "Okay," she said, after a moment. "Okay, a co-op it is. You know what, could I maybe get you to send me your last board application?"

"I've got the money!" the vampire said, offended, his eyes glowing briefly red from behind the scarf.

"No, I'm sure you do!" Jennifer said, not-fumbling for the little crucifix she'd worn under her blouse. "I don't even really need the financials, I'm just thinking maybe there's something we could do to—polish it up a little extra for a board. It might be worth getting an early start on it."

"Oh," the vampire said, mollified. "All right, I'll have my last broker send it to you. I guess it couldn't hurt."

Oh, but it could. One of his three personal reference letters was from his mother.

"I thought it was sweet," the vampire protested. "Shows I haven't lost touch with my mortal life."

"She's ninety-six and lives in Arizona," Jennifer said. "When was the last time you saw her?"

The vampire looked guilty. "I call every day," he muttered.

The other two letters were from a pooka—just the kind of guest everyone wanted visiting their neighbor, especially in horse form and snorting flames—and a necromancer.

"The necromancer is in-house at Goldman Sachs, with the lost wealth research division," the vampire said.

"Okay, see, that's excellent," Jennifer said. "Let's maybe ask her to revise this letter to focus on that, and let's just skip mentioning the necromancer part. Now, about the pooka—"

"He's a biotech entrepreneur!" the vampire said.

"Let's see if there's someone else we can get, okay?" Jennifer said.

The goblin doorman let Doug up without any hassle this time, even doing a good goblin impression of beaming. It took some effort not to glare at him. No wonder he was so happy Kell and his partner were looking for a new place, if the other guy was some kind of nut.

Kell was in the apartment alone, looking even smaller and hunched in a large shapeless sweater, and he twisted his hands anxiously as he let Doug in. "I suppose," he said, "I suppose there's no way to reopen the deal? I'd be willing to pay more—"

"Not a chance," Doug said. "Mr. Kell, I don't think you get it. If you or your partner does something, uh, unusual, you look unreliable, and that scares sellers. Closing can take two or three months. Even if you pay more, it's not worth having a sale fall through at the last second."

"Oh," Kell said, dismally.

"Honestly, the solution here is to find a place that your partner will be happy with, too," Doug said. "Is he here? I really do need to meet him."

Kell sighed and said, "Just a moment." He went to a cabinet and opened it and took out a bottle of whiskey and a glass. He brought them over to the table and poured a glass.

Doug had seen a lot weirder things than a client needing a drink, but it did take him by surprise when Kell slid the glass over to him instead of downing it. "Thanks, but—"

"No," Kell said. "You'll want it in a moment."

Doug started to ask, except Kell wasn't talking anymore. He'd fallen back onto the couch, and he was doubled over with his face in his hands, and something weird was happening to him. He seemed to be—growing.

"Uh," Doug said, and then Kell lifted his face out of his hands, and it wasn't Kell anymore. The eyes were the same color, but bloodshot and wider-apart in a broader face, with a flattened nose and a jaw that looked like it had been carved out of rock. His neck was thickening even while Doug watched.

"Well, fucking finally," not-Kell said, straightening up even more. The couch creaked under him. "So you're the broker who took him to that shithole?"

Doug paused and said, "And you're—?"

Not-Kell was coughing a little bit, thumping himself on the chest as he finished growing. He would have made about two of Kell with some leftovers. He belched loudly and bared his teeth in what you could've called a grin, if by grin you meant a mouth full of more shining white teeth than anybody should've had. "Call me Hyde."

"Okay," Doug said, after a second. "So that would make him—"

Hyde snorted. "I know. He changed the name when he moved here. Fucking pathetic." He pointed to the drink. "Are you going to have that?"

Doug looked at the glass, then slid it back across the table. "So, Mr. Hyde," he said, "can you tell me what you're looking for in an apartment?"

The eradicator stepped back from the wall of bugs and shook his head slowly and lugubriously.

"Really? Nothing?" Tom said, heart sinking.

"Sorry," the eradicator said. "These people, they'd lived here like twenty years or something. They put down roots. This," he waved a hand at the bugs, "this goes way, way down. I could charge you ten grand and strip off the top layers of the curse, wipe the bugs out, but they'd be back in two months. Might be even worse—millipedes or something. I hate those things." The eradicator shuddered his shoulders up and down expressively. "Anyway, you're not getting this out for good until you rip down the whole building."

He stopped and thought about it, and after a moment added, "Or you could get the two sellers back in and get them to make up. That can clear stuff like this up sometimes."

Tom looked at him. "The sellers' divorce took two years to finish, and they're still in court on some issues."

The eradicator shrugged. "Do they want to sell their apartment or not?"

Tom sighed. Then he paused and said, "So—wait, if you tried to take off the whole curse, the bugs might get worse—"

"Right," the eradicator said.

"If you *didn't* try that," Tom said, "could you maybe—do something else with them?"

"What did you have in mind?" the eradicator asked.

The vampire's application was still pretty disheartening, especially when Jennifer compared it to the one she was putting the final touches on that afternoon. She didn't like to jinx things, but kitsune or not, it was pretty much guaranteed Mei Shinagawa would be a shoo-in at the no-dogs-allowed Berkeley. Six letters of reference, terrific financials, and she'd even tucked in tiny origami cranes to be included with the copies of the application, one for each of the board members. The vampire's tax return, on the other hand, had a suspicious reddish-brown stain on the front.

To make the day complete, after she'd gotten off the phone with the vampire, Jennifer's phone went off with another all-caps CALL ME!! text message from one of their former buyers, a lawyer who'd bought into the top-drawer Oryx co-op for the panoramic views from the twenty-fourth floor apartment. Now those were about to go away, thanks to a new development, and she was having fits.

"If the Landmarks Commission has approved the renovation, and there's nothing in the zoning to stop it . . ." Jennifer said, apologetically.

She felt bad, but what could you do? That was Manhattan: you put one building up, somebody else put a bigger one up next door.

"My view was supposed to be protected!" Angela said. "It faces onto a freaking landmarked church!"

"I'm sorry. They're going to preserve the exterior shell and put up a new building on the inside, mimicking the facade and carvings all the way up," Jennifer said. "We could look for a new place for you, if you want?"

"How can I afford a new place with this millstone around my neck? Who is going to pay two million for a one bedroom with a view of a brick wall accessorized by carvings of smiley angels or whatever these guys are putting on their monstrosity?" Angela said. "No one, that's who! Oh my god, why did I buy at peak? I knew better!"

Of course she hadn't known better; nobody knew better, that was why it was peak. Jennifer said some comforting things with half a mind while she collated pages of the kitsune's application, and got off the phone; then she stopped and picked the phone up again and called back. "Angela? Can you get a picture of the facade and email it to me?"

"Granite countertops!" Hyde said. "I want some granite fucking countertops. None of this cheap Formica shit."

"Okay," Doug said, adding that to the list under *high ceilings*, *Subzero fridge*, *central A/C*, and *hardwood floors*. The list was getting pretty long. "Any particular neighborhoods?"

"That's another thing, I want someplace where there's a little goddamn fucking *life*, you understand me?" Hyde said. "I mean, what the hell was he thinking, Riverside Park. Yeah, because I want to live next to a bunch of elves singing "Kum-ba-yah" to the sun every morning. Not unless I get to pick 'em off with a shotgun."

"That wouldn't be such a great idea," Doug said.

"Fun, though," Hyde said, sort of wistfully.

"So," Doug said, getting off that subject, "can you tell me anything about what your, er—what Mr. Kell wants? He hasn't been all that clear—"

"That asshole just wants to crawl under a rock and read books," Hyde said. "Look at this—" He pointed to the particleboard bookshelves, sagging with hardbacks. "All this IKEA crap everywhere, Jesus. And this is a dream compared to what he had in here before those. Purple fucking built-ins! I had to take a sledgehammer to the whole pile of shit."

He glared at the bookshelves, and then abruptly heaved himself up off the whimpering couch and headed for them with his fists clenching and unclenching, like he couldn't handle looking at them a second longer.

"So, you know," Doug said hastily, "I do have a place I'd like you to take a look at—"

Hyde paused before reaching the bookcases, distracted. "Yeah? What the hell, let's go now."

"I don't know if I can reach the broker—" Doug started.

"We can look at the outside," Hyde said.

The vampire called her up less than a minute after Jennifer forwarded the email. "What the hell was that!" he yelled. "I almost dropped my iPhone in the gutter!"

"Really?" Jennifer said. "So—that actually hurt?"

"It was a picture of five million crosses!"

"Fantastic," Jennifer said. "Can you meet me at 75th and 3rd in half an hour?"

Getting Hyde into a taxi involved waiting fifteen minutes for one of the minivan ones to come by empty, but Doug was just fine with that: he spent the time frantically texting back and forth with Tom to get the selling broker down to the apartment in time to meet them. He didn't completely trust Hyde not to just knock down the front door and go inside, otherwise.

He got a call back from the broker while they were heading downtown. "I just want to make sure you realize—" the guy said.

"Yes, I know," Doug said. "It's completely mint inside, though, right?"

"Oh, absolutely," the broker said. "Architect-designed gut renovation."

They got out in front of Marble Cemetery. One of the wispy sadeyed apparitions paused by the iron railing to watch as Hyde climbed out of the cab, which almost bounced as he finally stepped out. It looked up at him. Hyde glared down at it. "You want something, Casper?" he said. The apparition prudently whisked away.

"So Bowery is two blocks that way, and the Hell's Angels club is on the next street over," Doug said, leading the way to the townhouse next door.

"Looks small," Hyde said, and he did have to duck his head to get through the front door, but inside the ceilings were ten feet. He stamped his foot experimentally. "What is this stuff?"

"Brazilian hardwood," the selling broker said faintly, staring up at Hyde with rabbit-wide eyes.

"Maybe let's take a look at the kitchen," Doug said, encouragingly. "Do you have an offering sheet?"

"Uh, yeah," the broker said, still staring as he backed up slowly. "Right—this way—"

"All right, now this is fucking something," Hyde said approvingly, coming into the kitchen. There was a long magnetic strip mounted on the wall with five or so chef's knives stuck onto it. He picked off a cleaver and tossed it casually in his hand as the broker edged around him, pointing out the Miele appliances.

"And granite countertops, as requested," Doug added.

"Let's see the bathroom," Hyde said. He didn't leave the cleaver behind.

The master bath on the second floor had a big soaking tub and another small apparition hanging around outside the window, staring in with miserable empty eyes that spoke of endless despair and horrors beyond the grave. "Get lost," Hyde told it, and it disappeared.

"So, the uh, the third floor ceilings," the broker said, stumbling over his words as they came out back to the staircase, "—a little lower, I'm not sure—"

"Maybe we could have Mr. Kell take a look?" Doug suggested to Hyde. "Assuming that you like the place so far."

Hyde looked around and said, "Yeah, this is decent. But make sure that asshole doesn't try to negotiate." He gave his toothy grin to the selling broker, who shrank away. "I'll handle that part."

"Sure," Doug said, and Hyde's smile and shoulders curled in on themselves, and Kell was there, wobbling a little in his suddenly too-large clothing.

He looked around uncertainly and said, "I—I'm not sure. The front windows, on the street—anyone could see inside—"

"Why don't we go upstairs," Doug said, shepherding him onto the third floor.

Kell paused about halfway up as the built-in bookcases came into view before continuing up. "Well, those are nice," he said.

"And the windows look on the cemetery back here," Doug said. "Of course, I realize it's a little inconvenient," he added, and Kell looked at him. "Since Mr. Hyde won't be able to get up to this floor."

"Oh," Kell said. "*Oh.*"

Doug shook the selling broker's hand as they left the house. "Will you be around later?" he said.

"Um," the broker said, "could you—maybe not give my number to—"

"Don't worry about it," Doug said. "I'll handle going between." The other broker looked relieved. "The seller is totally negotiable," he added, throwing a look at the cemetery. A gardener was busy nearby, spraying a thin clutching revenant hand that was struggling out of an old grave.

"Who *is* the seller?" Doug asked, watching.

"Investment banker," the broker said.

Doug dropped Kell off and took the cab the rest of the way back to the office. Tom had just gotten back, beaming, with celebratory lattes. "What's this for?" Doug said.

"We need to order new photos for Tudor City," Tom said, and showed them the little video clip off his cameraphone. Doug squinted at it: the wall was still moving, but—

"Are those *butterflies*?" Jennifer said.

"Twenty-three varieties, some of them endangered," Tom said. "I used the catalog from the exhibit at the Museum of Natural History."

"Wow," Doug said. "Tom, this doesn't call for new photos, this calls for a relisting."

They clinked latte cups, then Jennifer shrugged into her coat. "I have to get to Hunter College, Community Board 8 is having a review meeting for a proposed new building next to the Oryx."

"Is Angela still yelling at you about that?" Doug said. "You want me to talk to her? We told her before she bought, there's pretty much no such thing as a protected view."

"No worries," Jennifer said, over her shoulder. "We're getting a Fair Housing protest in. There's a sponsor apartment on the thirteenth floor that would be facing the new development, they're selling it to the vampire. They'll have to keep the new building below that height."

She stopped short with her hand on the door, though, as a thundering knock hit, and then another. She glanced back at Doug and Tom, then shrugged and pulled it open.

A giant horse was standing outside in the hall gazing down at them, nostrils flaring, a thin trail of smoke rising from them. Glowing red flames shone in its eyes. There was a small pile of paint flakes and bits of wood in the hallway, where it had knocked with a front hoof. People were sticking their heads out of other offices down the hall to watch.

"Hi," the pooka said. "Marvin said you could help me."

"Marvin?" Tom said, under his breath.

"The vampire," Jennifer said.

The pooka nodded, mane flopping. "I'm looking for an apartment."

They all stood and considered. Jennifer suggested after a moment, "Maybe a ground-floor unit?"

Tom said, "Or a place with a good freight elevator? There's the Atlantica—"

Doug eyed the hooves. Parquet and hardwood were definitely out. Marble tile, maybe. He looked up at the pooka. "So, tell me, how do you feel about Trump buildings?"

There's an alley in one of the less-affluent neighborhoods of New York that is really a tiny kingdom with a very strange ruler.

THE HORRID GLORY OF ITS WINGS

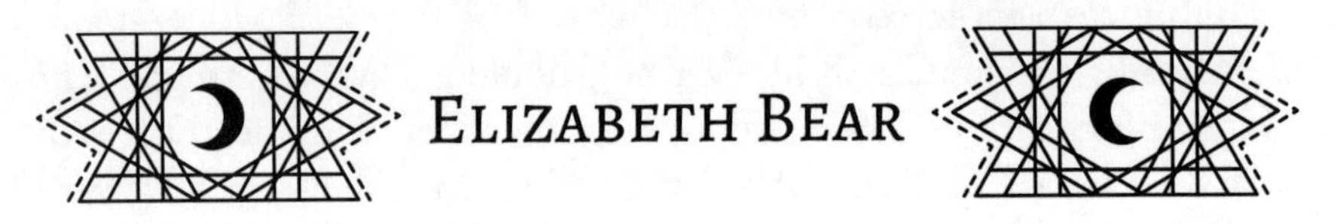

ELIZABETH BEAR

"Speaking of livers," the unicorn said, "Real magic can never be made by offering up someone else's liver. You must tear out your own, and not expect to get it back. The true witches know that."

—Peter S. Beagle, *The Last Unicorn*

My mother doesn't know about the harpy.

My mother, Alice, is not my *real* mom. She's my foster mother, and she doesn't look anything like me. Or maybe I don't look anything like her. Mama Alice is plump and soft and has skin like the skin of a plum, all shiny dark purple with the same kind of frosty brightness over it, like you could swipe it away with your thumb.

I'm sallow—Mama Alice says *olive*—and I have straight black hair and crooked teeth and no real chin, which is okay because I've already decided nobody's ever going to kiss me.

I've also got *lipodystrophy*, which is a fancy doctor way of saying I've grown a fatty buffalo hump on my neck and over each shoulderblade from the antiretrovirals, and my butt and legs and cheeks are wasted like an old lady's. My face looks like a dog's muzzle, even though I still have all my teeth.

For now. I'm going to have to get the wisdom teeth pulled this year, while I still get state assistance, because my birthday is in October and then I'll be eighteen. If I start having problems with them after then, well forget about it.

There's no way I'd be able to afford to get them fixed.

The harpy lives on the street, in the alley behind my building, where the dumpster and the winos live.

I come out in the morning before school, after I've eaten my breakfast and taken my pills (nevirapine, lamivudine, efavirenz). I'm used to the pills. I've been taking them all my life. I have a note in my file at school, and excuses for my classmates.

I don't bring home friends.

Lying is a sin. But Father Alvaro seems to think that when it comes to my sickness, it's a sin for which I'm already doing enough penance.

Father Alvaro is okay. But he's not like the harpy.

The harpy doesn't care if I'm not pretty. The harpy is beyond not pretty, way into ugly. Ugly as your mama's warty butt. Its teeth are snaggled and stained piss-yellow and char-black. Its claws are broken and dull and stink like rotten chicken. It has a long droopy blotchy face full of lines like Liv Tyler's dad, that rock star guy, and its hair hangs down in black-bronze rats over both feathery shoulders. The feathers look washed-out black and dull until sunlight somehow finds its way down into the grubby alley, bounces off dirty windows and hits them, and then they look like scratched bronze.

They are bronze.

If I touch them, I can feel warm metal.

I'd sneak the harpy food, but Mama Alice keeps pretty close track of it—it's not like we have a ton of money—and the harpy doesn't seem to mind eating garbage. The awfuller the better: coffee grounds, moldy cake, meat squirming with maggots, the stiff corpses of alley rats.

The harpy turns all that garbage into bronze.

If it reeks, the harpy eats it, stretching its hag face out on a droopy red neck to gulp the bits, just like any other bird. I've seen pigeons do the same thing with a crumb too big to peck up and swallow, but their necks aren't scaly naked, ringed at the bottom with fluffy down as white as a confirmation dress.

So every morning I pretend I'm leaving early for school—Mama Alice says "Kiss my cheek, Desiree"—and then once I'm out from under Mama Alice's window I sneak around the corner into the alley and stand by the dumpster where the harpy perches. I only get ten or fifteen minutes, however much time I can steal. The stink wrinkles up my nose. There's no place to sit. Even if there were, I couldn't sit down out here in my school clothes.

I think the harpy enjoys the company. Not that it *needs* it; I can't imagine the harpy needing anything. But maybe . . . just maybe it likes me.

The harpy says, I want you.

I don't know if I like the harpy. But I like being wanted.

The harpy tells me stories.

Mama Alice used to, when I was little, when she wasn't too tired from work and taking care of me and Luis and Rita, before Rita died. But the harpy's stories are better. It tells me about magic, and nymphs, and heroes. It tells me about adventures and the virgin goddesses like Artemis and Athena, and how they had adventure and did magic, and how Athena was cleverer than Poseidon and got a city named after her.

It tells me about Zephyrus, the West Wind, and his sons the magical talking horses. It tells me about Hades, god of the Underworld, and the feathers on its wings ring like bronze bells with excitement when it tells me about their mother Celaeno, who was a harpy also, but shining and fierce.

It tells me about her sisters, and how they were named for the mighty storm, and how when they all three flew, the sky was dark and lashed with rain and thunder. That's how it talks: *lashed with rain and thunder.*

The harpy says, We're all alone.

It's six thirty in the morning and I hug myself in my new winter coat from the fire department giveaway, my breath streaming out over the top of the scratchy orange scarf Mama Alice knitted. I squeeze my legs together, left knee in the hollow of the right knee like I have to pee, because even tights don't help too much when the edge of the skirt only comes to the middle of your kneecap. I'd slap my legs to warm them, but these are my last pair of tights and I don't want them to snag.

The scarf scrapes my upper lip when I nod. It's dark here behind the dumpster. The sun won't be up for another half hour. On the street out front, brightness pools under streetlights, but it doesn't show anything warm—just cracked black snow trampled and heaped over the curb.

"Nobody wants me," I say. "Mama Alice gets paid to take care of me." That's unfair. Mama Alice didn't *have* to take me or my foster brother Luis. But sometimes it feels good to be a little unfair. I sniff up a drip and push my chin forward so it bobs like the harpy swallowing garbage.

"Nobody would want to live with me. But I don't have any choice. I'm stuck living with myself."

The harpy says, There's always a choice. "Sure," I say. "Suicide is a sin."

The harpy says, Talking to harpies is probably a sin, too. "Are you a devil?"

The harpy shrugs. Its feathers smell like mildew. Something crawls along a rat of its hair, greasy-shiny in the street light. The harpy scrapes it off with a claw and eats it.

The harpy says, I'm a heathen monster. Like Celaeno and her sisters, Aello and Ocypete. The sisters of the storm. Your church would say so, that I am a demon. Yes.

"I don't think you give Father Alvaro enough credit."

The harpy says, I don't trust priests, and turns to preen its broken claws.

"You don't trust anybody."

That's not what I said, says the harpy—

You probably aren't supposed to interrupt harpies, but I'm kind of over that by now. "That's why I decided. I'm never going to trust anybody. My birth mother trusted somebody, and look where it got her. Knocked up and dead."

The harpy says, That's very inhuman of you. It sounds like a compliment.

I put a hand on the harpy's warm wing. I can't feel it through my glove. The gloves came from the fire department, too. "I have to go to school, Harpy."

The harpy says, You're alone there too.

I want to prove the harpy wrong.

The drugs are really good now. When I was born, a quarter of the babies whose moms had AIDS got sick too. Now it's more like one in a hundred. I could have a baby of my own, a healthy baby. And then I wouldn't be alone.

No matter what the harpy says.

It's a crazy stupid idea. Mama Alice doesn't have to take care of me after I turn eighteen, and what would I do with a baby? I'll have to get a job. I'll have to get state help for the drugs. The drugs are expensive.

If I got pregnant now, I could have the baby before I turn eighteen. I'd have somebody who was just mine. Somebody who loved me.

How easy is it to get pregnant, anyway? Other girls don't seem to have any problem doing it by accident.

Or by "accident."

Except whoever it was, I would have to tell him I was pos. That's why I decided I would sign the purity pledge and all that. Because then I have a reason not to tell.

And they gave me a ring. Fashion statement.

You know how many girls actually *keep* that pledge? I was going to. I meant to. But not just keep it until I got married. I meant to keep it forever, and then I'd never have to tell anybody.

No, I was right the first time. I'd rather be alone than have to explain. Besides, if you're having a baby, you should have the baby for the baby, not for you.

Isn't that right, Mom?

The harpy has a kingdom.

It's a tiny kingdom. The kingdom's just the alley behind my building, but it has a throne (the dumpster) and it has subjects (the winos) and it has me. I know the winos see the harpy. They talk to it sometimes. But it vanishes when the other building tenants come down, and it hides from the garbagemen.

I wonder if harpies can fly.

It opens its wings sometimes when it's raining as if it wants to wash off the filth, or sometimes if it's mad at something. It hisses when it's mad like that, the only sound I've ever heard it make outside my head.

I guess if it can fly depends on if it's magic. Miss Rivera, my bio teacher sophomore year, said that after a certain size things couldn't lift themselves with wings anymore. It has to do with muscle strength and wingspan and gravity. And some big things can only fly if they can fall into flight, or get a *headwind*.

I never thought about it before. I wonder if the harpy's *stuck* in that alley. I wonder if it's too proud to ask for help.

I wonder if I should ask if it wants some anyway.

The harpy's big. But condors are big, too, and condors can fly. I don't know if the harpy is bigger than a condor. It's hard to tell from pictures, and it's not like you can walk up to a harpy with a tape measure and ask it to stick out a wing.

Well, maybe you could. But I wouldn't.

Wouldn't it be awful to have wings that didn't work? Wouldn't it be worse to have wings that do work, and not be able to use them?

After I visit the harpy at night, I go up to the apartment. When I let myself in the door to the kitchen, Mama Alice is sitting at the table with some mail open in front of her. She looks up at me and frowns, so I lock the door behind me and shoot the chain. Luis should be home by now, and I can hear music from his bedroom. He's fifteen now. I think it's been three days since I saw him.

I come over and sit down in my work clothes on the metal chair with the cracked vinyl seat.

"Bad news?"

Mama Alice shakes her head, but her eyes are shiny. I reach out and grab her hand. The folded up paper in her fingers crinkles.

"What is it, then?"

She pushes the paper at me. "Desiree. You got the scholarship."

I don't hear her right the first time. I look at her, at our hands, and the rumply paper. She shoves the letter into my hand and I unfold it, open in, read it three times as if the words will change like crawly worms when I'm not looking at it.

The words are crawly worms, all watery, but I can see *hardship* and *merit* and *State*. I fold it up carefully, smoothing out the crinkles with my fingertips. It says I can be anything at all.

I'm going to college on a scholarship. Just state school.

I'm going to college because I worked hard. And because the state knows I'm full of poison, and they feel bad for me.

The harpy never lies to me, and neither does Mama Alice.

She comes into my room later that night and sits down on the edge of my bed, with is just a folded-out sofa with springs that poke me, but it's mine and better than nothing. I hide the letter under the pillow before she turns on the light, so she won't catch on that I was hugging it.

"Desiree," she says.

I nod and wait for the rest of it.

"You know," she says, "I might be able to get the state to pay for liposuction. Doctor Morales will say it's medically necessary."

"Liposuction?" I grope my ugly plastic glasses off the end table, because

I need to see her. I'm frowning so hard they pinch my nose.

"For the hump," she says, and touches her neck, like she had one too. "So you could stand up straight again. Like you did when you were little."

Now I wish I hadn't put the glasses on. I have to look down at my hands. The fingertips are all smudged from the toner on the letter. "Mama Alice," I say, and then something comes out I never meant to ask her. "How come you never adopted me?"

She jerks like I stuck her with a fork. "Because I thought . . . " She stops, and shakes her head, and spreads her hands.

I nod. I asked, but I know. Because the state pays for my medicine. Because Mama Alice thought I would be dead by now.

We were all supposed to be dead by now. All the HIV babies. Two years, maybe five. AIDS kills little kids really quick, because their immune systems haven't really happened yet. But the drugs got better as our lives got longer, and now we might live forever. Nearly forever.

Forty. *Fifty*.

I'm dying. Just not fast enough. If it were faster, I'd have nothing to worry about. As it is, I'm going to have to figure out what I'm going to do with my life.

I touch the squishy pad of fat on my neck with my fingers, push it in until it dimples. It feels like it should keep the mark of my fingers, like Moon Mud, but when I stop touching it, it springs back like nothing happened at all.

I don't want to get to go to college because somebody feels bad for me. I don't want anybody's pity.

The next day, I go down to talk to the harpy.

I get up early and wash quick, pull on my tights and skirt and blouse and sweater. I don't have to work after school today, so I leave my uniform on the hanger behind the door.

But when I get outside, the first thing I hear is barking. Loud barking, lots of it, from the alley. And that hiss, the harpy's hiss. Like the biggest maddest cat you ever heard.

There's junk all over the street, but nothing that looks like I could fight with it. I grab up some hunks of ice. My school shoes skip on the frozen sidewalk and I tear my tights when I fall down.

It's dark in the alley, but it's city dark, not real dark, and I can see the dogs okay. There's three of them, dancing around the dumpster on their hind legs. One's light-colored enough that even in the dark I can see she's all scarred up from fighting, and the other two are dark.

The harpy leans forward on the edge of the dumpster, wings fanned out like a cartoon eagle, head stuck out and jabbing at the dogs.

Silly thing doesn't know it doesn't have a beak, I think, and whip one of the ice rocks at the big light-colored dog. She yelps. Just then, the harpy sicks up over all three of the dogs.

Oh, God, the smell.

I guess it doesn't need a beak after all, because the dogs go from growling and snapping to yelping and running just like that. I slide my backpack off one shoulder and grab it by the strap in the hand that's not full of ice.

It's heavy and I could hit something, but I don't swing it in time to stop one of the dogs knocking into me as it bolts away. The puke splashes on my leg. It burns like scalding water through my tights.

I stop myself just before I slap at the burn. Because getting the puke on my glove and burning my hand too would just be smart like that. Instead, I scrub at it with the dirty ice in my other hand and run limping towards the harpy.

The harpy hears my steps and turns to hiss, eyes glaring like green torches, but when it sees who's there it pulls its head back. It settles its wings like a nun settling her skirts on a park bench, and gives me the same fishy glare.

Wash that leg with snow, the harpy says. Or with lots of water. It will help the burning.

"It's acid."

With what harpies eat, the harpy says, don't you think it would have to be?

I mean to say something clever back, but what gets out instead is, "Can you fly?"

As if in answer, the harpy spreads its vast bronze wings again. They stretch from one end of the dumpster to the other, and overlap its length a little.

The harpy says, Do these look like flightless wings to you?

Why does it always answer a question with a question? I know kids like that, and it drives me crazy when they do it, too.

"No," I say. "But I've never seen you. Fly. I've never seen you fly."

The harpy closes its wings, very carefully. A wind still stirs my hair where it sticks out under my hat.

The harpy says, There's no wind in my kingdom. But I'm light now, I'm empty. If there were wind, if I could get higher—

I drop my pack beside the dumpster. It has harpy puke on it now anyway. I'm not putting it on my back. "What if I carried you up?"

The harpy's wings flicker, as if it meant to spread them again. And then it settles back with narrowed eyes and shows me its snaggled teeth in a suspicious grin.

The harpy says, What's in it for you?

I say to the harpy, "You've been my friend."

The harpy stares at me, straight on like a person, not side to side like a bird. It stays quiet so long I think it wants me to leave, but a second before I step back it nods.

The harpy says, Carry me up the fire escape, then.

I have to clamber up on the dumpster and pick the harpy up over my head to put it on the fire escape. It's heavy, all right, especially when I'm holding it up over my head so it can hop onto the railing. Then I have to jump up and catch the ladder, then swing my feet up like on the uneven bars in gym class.

That's the end of these tights. I'll have to find something to tell Mama Alice. Something that isn't exactly a lie.

Then we're both up on the landing, and I duck down so the stinking, heavy harpy can step onto my shoulder with her broken, filthy claws. I don't want to think about the infection I'll get if she scratches me. Hospital stay. IV antibiotics. But she balances there like riding shoulders is all she does for a living, her big scaly toes sinking into my fat pads so she's not pushing down on my bones.

I have to use both hands to pull myself up the fire escape, even though I left my backpack at the bottom. The harpy weighs more, and it seems to get heavier with every step. It's not any easier because I'm trying to tiptoe and not wake up the whole building.

I stop to rest on the landings, but by the time I get to the top one my calves shake like the mufflers on a Harley. I imagine them booming like that too, which makes me laugh. Kind of, as much as I can. I double over with my hands on the railing and the harpy hops off.

"Is this high enough?"

The harpy doesn't look at me. It faces out over the empty dark street. It spreads its wings. The harpy is right: I'm alone, I've always been alone. Alone and lonely.

And now it's also leaving me.

"I'm dying," I yell, just as it starts the downstroke. I'd never told anybody. Mama Alice had to tell *me*, when I was five, but *I* never told anybody.

The harpy rocks forward, beats its wings hard, and settles back on the railing. It cranks its head around on its twisty neck to stare at me.

"I have HIV," I say. I press my glove against the scar under my coat where I used to have a G-tube. When I was little.

The harpy nods and turns away again. The harpy says, I know.

It should surprise me that the harpy knows, but it doesn't. Harpies know things. Now that I think about it, I wonder if the harpy only loves me because I'm garbage. If it only wants me because my blood is poison. My scarf's come undone, and a button's broken on my new old winter coat.

It feels weird to say what I just said out loud, so I say it again. Trying to get used to the way the words feel in my mouth. "Harpy, I'm dying. Maybe not today or tomorrow. But probably before I should."

The harpy says, That's because you're not immortal.

I spread my hands, cold in the gloves. Well *duh*. "Take me with you."

The harpy says, I don't think you're strong enough to be a harpy.

"I'm strong enough for this." I take off my new old winter coat from the fire department and drop it on the fire escape. "I don't want to be alone any more."

The harpy says, If you come with me, you have to stop dying. And you have to stop living. And it won't make you less alone. You are human, and if you stay human your loneliness will pass, one way or the other. If you come with me, it's yours. Forever.

It's not just empty lungs making my head spin. I say, "I got into college."

The harpy says, It's a career path.

I say, "You're lonely too. At least I decided to be alone, because it was better."

The harpy says, I am a harpy.

"Mama Alice would say that God never gives us any burdens we can't carry."

The harpy says, Does she look you in the eye when she says that? I say, "Take me with you."

The harpy smiles. A harpy's smile is an ugly thing, even seen edge-on. The harpy says, You do not have the power to make me not alone, Desiree.

It's the first time it's ever said my name. I didn't know it knew it. "You have sons and sisters and a lover, Celaeno. In the halls of the West Wind. How can you be lonely?"

The harpy turns over its shoulder and stares with green, green eyes. The harpy says, I never told you my name.

"Your name is Darkness. You told me it. You said you *wanted* me, Celaeno."

The cold hurts so much I can hardly talk. I step back and hug myself tight. Without the coat I'm cold, so cold my teeth buzz together like gears stripping, and hugging myself doesn't help.

I don't want to be like the harpy. The harpy is disgusting. It's *awful.*

The harpy says, And underneath the filth, I shine. I *salvage.* You choose to be alone? Here's your chance to prove yourself no liar.

I don't want to be like the harpy. But I don't want to be me any more, either. *I'm stuck living with myself.*

If I go with the harpy, I will be stuck living with myself *forever.*

The sky brightens. When the sunlight strikes the harpy, its filthy feathers will shine like metal. I can already see fingers of cloud rising across the horizon, black like cut paper against the paleness that will be dawn, not that you can ever see dawn behind the buildings. There's no rain or snow in the forecast, but the storm is coming.

I say, "You only want me because my blood is rotten. You only want me because I got thrown away."

I turn garbage into bronze, the harpy says. I turn rot into strength. If you came with me, you would have to be like me.

"Tell me it won't always be this hard."

I do not lie, child. What do you want?

I don't know my answer until I open my mouth and say it, but it's something I can't get from Mama Alice, and I can't get from a scholarship. "Magic."

The harpy rocks from foot to foot. I can't give you that, she says. You have to *make* it.

Downstairs, under my pillow, is a letter. Across town, behind brick walls, is a doctor who would write me another letter.

Just down the block in the church beside my school is a promise of maybe heaven, if I'm a good girl and I die.

Out there is the storm and the sunrise.

Mama Alice will worry, and I'm sorry. She doesn't deserve that. When I'm a harpy will I care? Will I care forever?

Under the humps and pads of fat across my shoulders, I imagine I can already feel the prickle of feathers.

I use my fingers to lift myself onto the railing and balance there in my school shoes on the rust and tricky ice, six stories up, looking down on the street lights. I stretch out my arms.

And so what if I fall?

A love story that could only happen in New York.

THE TALLEST DOLL IN NEW YORK CITY

MARIA DAHVANA HEADLEY

On a particular snowy Monday in February, at 5:02 p.m., I'm sixty-six flights above the corner of Lexington Avenue and Forty-second Street, looking down at streets swarming with hats and jackets. All the guys who work in midtown are spit into the frozen city, hunting sugar for the dolls they're trying to muddle from sour into sweet.

From up here I can see Lex fogged with cheap cologne, every citizen clutching his heart-shaped box wrapped in cellophane, red as the devil's drawers.

If you happen to be a waiter at the Cloud Club, you know five's the hour when a guy's nerves start to fray. This calendar square's worse than most. Every man on our member list is suffering the Saint Valentine's Cramp, and me and the crew up here are ready with a stocked bar. I'm in my Cloud Club uniform, the pocket embroidered with my name in the Chrysler's trademark typeface, swooping like a skid mark on a lonely road in Montana. Over my arm I've got a clean towel, and in my vest I have an assortment of aspirins and plasters in case a citizen shows up already bleeding or broken-nosed from an encounter with a lady lovenot.

Later tonight, it'll be the members' doll dinner, the one night a year we allow women into the private dining room. Valorous Victor, captain of the wait, pours us each a preparatory coupe. There are ice-cream sculptures shaped like Cupid in the walk-in. Each gal gets a corsage the moment she enters, the roses from Valorous Victor's brother's hothouse in Jersey. At least two dolls are in line for wife, and we've got their guy's rings here ready and waiting, to drop into champagne in one case and wedge into an oyster in another. Odds in the kitchen have the diamond in that particular ring consisting of a pretty piece of paste.

Down below, it's 1938, and things are not as prime as they are up here. Our members are the richest men left standing; their wives at home in Greenwich, their mistresses movie starlets with porcelain teeth. Me, I'm single. I've got a mother with rules strict as Sing Sing, and a sister with a face pretty as the Sistine's ceiling. My sister needs protecting from all the guys in the world, and so I live in Brooklyn, man of my mother's house, until I can find a wife or die waiting.

The members start coming in, and each guy gets led to his locker. Our members are the rulers of the world. They make automobiles and build skyscrapers, but none as tall as the one we're standing in right now. The Cloud Club's open since before the building got her spire, and the waitstaff in a Member's Own knows things even a man's miss doesn't. Back during Prohibition, we install each of the carved wood lockers at the Cloud Club with a hieroglyphic identification code straight out of ancient Egypt, so our members can keep their bottles safe and sound. Valorous Victor dazzles the police more than once with his rambling explanation of cryptographic complexities, and finally the blue boys just take a drink and call it done. No copper's going to Rosetta our rigmarole.

I'm at the bar mixing a Horse's Neck for Mr. Condé Nast, but I've got my eye on the mass of members staggering out of the elevators with fur coats, necklaces, and parcels of cling & linger, when, at 5:28 p.m. precisely, the Chrysler Building steps off her foundation and goes for a walk.

There is no warning.

She just shakes the snow and pigeons loose from her spire and takes off, sashaying southwest. This is something even we waiters haven't experienced before. The Chrysler is 1,046 feet tall, and, until now, she's seemed stationary. She's stood motionless on this corner for seven years so far, the gleamiest gal in a million miles.

None of the waitstaff lose their cool. When things go wrong, waiters, the good ones, adjust to the needs of both customers and clubs. In 1932, for example, Valorous himself commences to travel from midtown to Ellis Island in order to deliver a pistol to one of our members, a guy who happens to have a grievance against a brand new American in line for a name. Two slugs and a snick later, Victor's in surgery beneath the gaze of the Verdigris Virgin. Still, he returns to Manhattan in time for the evening napkin twist.

"The Chrysler's just taking a little stroll, sirs," Valorous announces from the stage. "No need to panic. This round is on me and the waiters of the Cloud Club."

Foreseeably, there is, in fact, some panic. To some of our members, this event appears to be more horrifying than Black Tuesday.

Mr. Nast sprints to the men's room with motion sickness, and The Soother, our man on staff for problems of the heart and guts, tails him with a tall glass of ginger ale. I decide to drink Nast's Horse's Neck myself. Nerves on the mend, I consider whether any our members on sixty-seven and sixty-eight might possibly need drinks, but I see Victor's already sending an expedition to the stairs.

I take myself to the windows. In the streets, people gawp and yawp and holler, and taxis honk their horns. Gals pick their way through icy puddles, and guys stand in paralysis, looking up.

We joke about working in the body of the best broad in New York City, but no one on the waitstaff ever thinks that the Chrysler might have a will of her own. She's beautiful, what with her multistory crown, her skin pale blue in daylight and rose-colored with city lights at night. Her gown's printed with arcs and swoops, and beaded with tiny drops of General Electric.

We know her inside out, or we think we do. We go up and down her stairs when her elevators are broken, looking out her triangular windows on the hottest day of summer. The ones at the top don't have panes, because the wind up there can kick up a field goal even when its breezeless down below, and the updrafts can grab a bird and fling it through the building like it's nothing. The Chrysler's officially seventy-seven floors, but she actually has eighty-four levels. They get smaller and smaller until, at eighty-three, there's only a platform the size of a picnic table, surrounded by windows; and, above that, a trapdoor and a ladder into the spire, where the lightning rod is. The top floors are tempting. Me and The Soother take ourselves up to the very top one sultry August night, knees and ropes, and she sways beneath us, but holds steady. Inside the spire, there's space for one guy to stand encased in metal, feeling the earth move.

The Chrysler is a devastating dame, and that's nothing new. I could assess her for years and never be done. At night we turn her on, and she glows for miles.

I'm saying, the waiters of the Cloud Club should know what kind of doll she is. We work inside her brain.

Our members retreat to the private dining room, the one with the etched glass working class figures on the walls. There, they cower beneath the table, but the waitstaff hangs onto the velvet curtains and watches as the Chrysler walks to Thirty-fourth Street, clicking and jingling all the way.

"We shoulda predicted this, boss," I say to Valorous.

"Ain't that the truth," he says, flicking a napkin over his forearm. "Dames! The Chrysler's in love."

For eleven months, from 1930 to 1931, the Chrysler's the tallest doll in New York City. Then the Empire is spired to surpass her, and winds up taller still. She has a view straight at him, but he ignores her.

At last, it seems, she's done with his silence. It's Valentine's Day.

I pass Victor a cigarette.

"He acts like a Potemkin village," I say. "Like he's got nothing inside him but empty floors. I get a chance at a doll like that, I give up everything, move to a two-bedroom. Or out of the city, even; just walk my way out. What've I got waiting for me at home? My mother and my sister. He's got royalty."

"No accounting for it," says Valorous, and refills my coupe. "But I hear he doesn't go in for company. He won't even look at her."

At Thirty-fourth and Fifth, the Chrysler stops, holds up the edge of her skirt, and taps her high heel. She waits for some time as sirens blare beneath her. Some of our fellow citizens, I am ashamed to report, don't notice anything out of place at all. They just go around her, cussing and hissing at the traffic.

The Empire State Building stands on his corner, shaking in his boots. We can all see his spire trembling. Some of the waitstaff and members sympathize with his wobble, but not me. The Chrysler's a class act, and he's a shack of shamble if he doesn't want to go out with her tonight.

At 6:03 p.m., pedestrians on Fifth Avenue shriek in terror as the Chrysler gives up and taps the Empire hard on the shoulder.

"He's gonna move," Valorous says. "He's got to! Move!"

"I don't think he is," says The Soother, back from comforting the members in the lounge. "I think he's scared. Look at her."

The Soother's an expert in both Chinese herbal medicine and psychoanalysis. He makes our life as waiters easier. He can tell what everyone at a table's waiting for with one quick look in their direction.

"She reflects everything. Poor guy sees all his flaws, done up shiny, for years now. He feels naked. It can't be healthy to see all that reflected."

The kitchen starts taking bets.

"She won't wait for him for long," I say. I have concerns for the big guy, in spite of myself. "She knows her worth, she heads uptown to the Metropolitan."

"Or to the Library," says The Soother. "I go there, if I'm her. The Chrysler's not a doll to trifle with."

"They're a little short," I venture, "those two. I think she's more interested in something with a spire. Radio City?"

The Empire's having a difficult time. His spire's supposedly built for zeppelin docking, but then the Hindenberg explodes, and now no zeppelin will ever moor there. His purpose is moot. He slumps slightly.

Our Chrysler taps him again, and holds out her steel glove. Beside me, Valorous pours another round of champagne. I hear money changing hands all over the club.

Slowly, slowly, the Empire edges off his corner.

The floor sixty-six waitstaff cheers for the other building, though I hear Mr. Nast commencing to groan again, this time for his lost bet.

Both buildings allow their elevators to resume operations, spilling torrents of shouters from the lobbies and into the street. By the time the Chrysler and the Empire start walking east, most of the members are gone, and I'm drinking a bottle of bourbon with Valorous and the Soother.

We've got no dolls on the premises, and the members still here declare formal dinner dead and done until the Chrysler decides to walk back to Lex. There is palpable relief. The citizens of the Cloud Club avoid their responsibilities for the evening.

As the Empire wades into the East River hand in hand with the Chrysler, other lovestruck structures begin to talk. We're watching from the windows as apartment towers lean in to gossip, stretching laundry lines finger to finger. Grand Central Station, as stout and elegant as a survivor of the Titanic, stands up, shakes her skirts, and pays a visit to Pennsylvania Station, that Beaux-Arts bangle. The Flatiron and Cleopatra's Needle shiver with sudden proximity, and within moments they're all over one another.

Between Fifty-Ninth Street and the Williamsburg Bridge, the Empire and the Chrysler trip shyly through the surf. We can see New Yorkers, tumbling out of their taxicabs and buses, staring up at the sunset reflecting in our doll's eyes.

The Empire has an awkward heart-shaped light appended to his skull, which Valorous and I do some snickering over. The Chrysler glitters in her dignified silver spangles. Her windows shimmy.

As the pedestrians of three boroughs watch, the two tallest buildings in New York City press against one another, window to window, and waltz in ankle-deep water.

I look over at the Empire's windows, where I can see a girl standing, quite close now, and looking back at me.

"Victor," I say.

"Yes?" he replies. He's eating vichyssoise beside a green-gilled tycoon, and the boxer Gene Tunney is opposite him smoking a cigar. I press a cool cloth to the tycoon's temples, and accept the fighter's offer of a Montecristo.

"Do you see that doll?" I ask them.

"I do, yes," Victor replies, and Tunney nods. "There's a definite dolly bird over there," he says.

The girl in the left eye of the Empire State, a good thirty feet above where we sit, is wearing red sequins, and a magnolia in her hair. She sidles up to the microphone. One of her backup boys has a horn, and I hear him start to play.

Our buildings sway, tight against each other, as the band in the Empire's eye plays "In the Still of the Night."

I watch her, that doll, that dazzling doll, as the Chrysler and the Empire kiss for the first time, at 9:16 p.m. I watch her for hours as the Chrysler blushes and the Empire whispers, as the Chrysler coos and the Empire laughs.

The riverboats circle in shock, as, at 11:34 p.m., the two at last walk south toward the harbor, stepping over bridges into deeper water, her eagle ornaments laced together with his girders. The Chrysler steps delicately over the Wonder Wheel at Coney Island, and he leans down and plucks it up for her. We watch it pass our windows as she inhales its electric fragrance.

"Only one way to get to her," Valorous tells me, passing me a rope made of tablecloths. All the waitstaff of the Cloud Club nod at me.

"You're a champ," I tell them. "You're all champs."

"I am too," says Tunney, drunk as a knockout punch. He's sitting in a heap of roses and negligees, eating bonbons.

The doll sings only to me as I climb up through the tiny ladders and trapdoors to the eighty-third, where the temperature drops below ice-cream Cupid. I inch out the window and onto the ledge, my rope gathered in my arms. As the Chrysler lays her gleaming cheek against the Empire's shoulder, as he runs his hand up her beaded knee, as the two tallest buildings in New York City begin to make love in the Atlantic, I fling my rope across the divide, and the doll in the Empire's eye ties it to her grand piano.

At 11:57 p.m., I walk out across the tightrope, and at 12:00 a.m., I hold her in my arms.

I'm still hearing the applause from the Cloud Club, all of them raising their coupes to the windows, their bourbons and their soup spoons, as, through the Chrysler's eye, I see the boxer plant his lips on Valorous Victor. Out the windows of the Empire State, the Cyclone wraps herself up in the Brooklyn Bridge. The Staten Island Ferry rises up and dances for Lady Liberty.

At 12:16 a.m., the Chrysler and the Empire call down the lightning into their spires, and all of us, dolls and guys, waiters and chanteuses, buildings and citizens, kiss like fools in the icy ocean off the amusement park, in the pale orange dark of New York City.

They went back a long ways, to the days when Warhol walked the earth, Manhattan was seamy and corroded, and an unending stream of young people came there to lose their identities and find newer, more exotic ones.

BLOOD YESTERDAY, BLOOD TOMORROW

RICHARD BOWES

1

"Ai Ling show Aunt Lilia and everyone else how you can play the Debussy 'Claire de Lune,'" Larry said as his partner Boyd beamed at his side. Lilia Gaines was at the dinner party as a friend of one of the hosts, Larry Stepelli.

She had, in fact, been his roommate in the bad old days. Twenty-five years before, she and Larry had entered Ichordone therapy as a couple and left it separate and apart.

The exquisitely dressed Asian girl sat, tiny but fully at ease, at the piano. At one time Lilia had wondered if only well-to-do gay couples should be allowed to raise kids.

Behind Ai Ling the windows of the West Street duplex looked over the Hudson and the lights of New Jersey on a late June evening. And amazingly, almost like a beautifully rendered piece of automata, the child played the piece with scarcely a flaw.

Amidst the applause of the dozen guests and her fathers, Ai Ling curtseyed and went off with her Nana. Lilia, not for the first time, considered Larry's upward mobility. This dinner party was for some of Boyd's clients, a few people whom Larry sought to impress and one or two like her whom he liked to taunt with his success.

A woman asked Boyd what preschool his daughter attended. One of his clients dropped the names of two senators and the president in a single sentence.

A young man who had been brought by an old and famous children's book illustrator talked about the novel he was writing, "It's YA and horror-light on what at the moment is a very timely theme," he said.

Larry smiled and said to Lilia, "I walked past Reliquary yesterday and you were closed."

"Major redecoration," she replied. Their connection had once been so close that at times each could still read the other. So they both knew that wasn't so.

He tilted his handsome head with only a subtle touch of grey and raised his left eyebrow a fraction of an inch.

Lilia knew he was going to ask her something about her shop and how long it could survive. She didn't want to discuss that just then.

Larry's question went unasked. At that moment the young author said, "It's a theme that sometimes gets overworked but never gets stale. The book I'm doing right now is titled, *Never Blood Today.* You know a variation on, 'Jam tomorrow and jam yesterday but never jam today' from *Alice in Wonderland.* In fact the book is Alice with Vampires! Set in a well-to-do private high school!"

The writer looked at Larry with fascination as he spoke. Boyd frowned. The illustrator who had a show of his art up in Larry's gallery rolled his eyes.

Larry smiled again, but just for a moment. For Lilia, the writer's conversation was an unplanned bonus.

A woman in an enviable silk dress with just a hint of shcath about it changed the subject to a reliably safe one: how nicely real estate prices had bottomed out.

Then Boyd suggested they all sit down to dinner. Boyd Lazlo was a corporate lawyer: solid, polite, nice looking, completely opaque. Lilia Gaines knew he didn't much trust her.

Lilia and Larry went back to the time when Warhol walked the earth, Manhattan was seamy and corroded and an unending stream of young people came there to loose their identities and find newer, more exotic ones. Back then, they two were roommates and Boyd was still a college kid preparing to go to Yale Law.

That summer Manhattan was gripped by nostalgia for the old sordid days and Lilia had something to show Larry that would evoke them.

But it was personal, private, and she hadn't found a moment alone with him.

At the end of the evening he stood at the door saying good-by to the illustrator. The young writer looked wide-eyed at Larry and even at Lilia. The mystique of old evil: she understood it well.

As Larry wished him farewell, Lilia caught the half wink her old companion gave the kid and was certain Larry was bored.

She remembered him in the Ichordone group therapy standing in tears and swearing that when he walked out of there—cured of his habit—he would establish a stable relationship and raise children.

Boyd was down the hall at the elevator kissing and shaking hands. Lilia and Larry were alone. Only then did he put his hands on her shoulders say, "You have a secret; give it up."

"Something I just found," she said, reached into her bag and handed him a folded linen napkin. You'd have had to know him as well as she did to catch the eyes widening by a millimeter. Stitched into the cloth was what, when Lilia first saw it years before, had looked like a small gold crown, a coronet. Curving below that in script were the words "Myrna's Place." The same words were above it upside down.

Before anything more could be said, Boyd came back, looking a bit concerned and as if he needed to speak to Larry alone. So Lilia thanked both of them for dinner and took her leave. She noticed Larry had made the napkin disappear.

Years ago—when New York was the wilder, darker place—Larry and Lilia had shared an apartment on a marginal street on the Lower East Side, pursued careers, and watched for their chance. He acted in underground films with Madonna before that meant anything, and took photos; she sold dresses she'd designed and made to East Village boutiques.

Patti Smith and Robert Mapplethorpe was the model for all the young couples like them: the poker-faced, serious girl with hair framing her face and the flashy bisexual guy. They were in the crowd at the Pyramid Club, Studio 54, and the Factory. Drugs and alcohol were their playthings. Love did enter into it, of course, and even sex when their stars crossed paths.

Since they needed money, they also had an informal business selling antiques and weird collectibles at the flea market on Sixth Avenue in the Twenties.

In those days that stretch of Manhattan was a place of rundown five-story buildings and wide parking lots—fallow land waiting for a developer. On weekends first one parking lot, then a second, then a third, then more blossomed with tables set up in the open air, tents pitched before dawn.

It became a destination where New Yorkers spent their weekend afternoons sifting through the trash and the gems. Warhol, the pale prince, bought much of his fabled cookie jar collection there.

During the week Larry and Lilia haunted the auction rooms on Fourth Avenue and Broadway south of Union Square, swooped down on forlorn vases and candy dishes, old toys, unwanted lots of parasols and packets of photos of doughboys and chorus girls, turn of the century nude swimming scenes, elephants wearing bonnets and top hats.

Since it kind of was their livelihood they both tried to be reasonably straight and sober at the moment that Sunday morning stopped being Saturday night. While it was still dark they'd go up to Sixth Avenue with their treasures in shopping carts, rent a few square feet of space and a couple of tables and set up their booth.

In the predawn, out-of-town antique dealers, edgy interior decorators, and compulsive collectors—all bearing flashlights—would circulate among the vans unloading furniture and the tables being carried to their places by the flea market porters.

Beams of light would scan the dark and suddenly, four, five, a dozen of them would circle around a booth where strange, interesting, perhaps even valuable stuff was being set up.

Lilia and Larry wanted that attention. Then came the very drowsy weekday auction when they found a lot consisting of several cartons of distressed goods: everything from matchbooks and champagne flutes to mirrors and tablecloths all with the words "Myrna's Place" in an oval and the gold design that looked like a small crown, a coronet.

The name meant nothing to them. They guessed that Myrna's was some kind of uptown operation—a speakeasy, a bordello, a bohemian salon—they didn't quite know.

Larry said, "Fleas—" old hard-bitten market dealers called themselves "fleas"—"call the trash they sell 'Stuff.' "

"And this looks like Stuff," Lilia replied.

"And plenty of it," they said at the same moment, something that happened with them back then. They bid fifty dollars, which was all the money they had, and got the lot.

That Sunday morning they rented their usual space and a couple of tables. Other recent finds included a tackily furnished tin dollhouse, a set of blue-and-white china bowls, a few slightly decayed leather jackets, several antique corsets, a box of men's assorted arm garters, and a golf bag and clubs bought at an apartment sale. They had dysfunctional old cameras and a cracked glass jar full of marbles. Prominently displayed was a selection of Myrna's Place stuff.

The couple in the booth across from theirs seemed to loot a different place each week. That Sunday it was an old hunting lodge. They had a moose head, skis, snowshoes, and blunt heavy ice skates; Adirondack chairs, and gun racks.

Larry and Lilia set up in the pre-dawn dark as flashlights darted about the lot. Then one beam fell on them. A flat-faced woman with rimless glasses, and eyes that showed nothing turned her light on the golf clubs.

She shrugged when she saw them up close. But as she turned to walk away, her flashlight caught a nicely draped tablecloth from Myrna's Place. "Thirty dollars for that lot," she said indicating all the Myrna items.

Larry and Lilia hesitated. Thirty dollars would pay the day's rent for the stall.

Then another light found the table. A middle-aged man with the thin, drawn look of a veteran of many Manhattan scenes was examining Myrna's wine glasses.

"Five dollars each," Lilia told him and he didn't back off.

To the woman who had offered thirty for the entire lot, Larry said, "Thirty for the tablecloth."

The woman ground them down to twenty. The thin, drawn man bought four wine glasses for fifteen dollars and continued examining the merchandise.

That morning, Lilia and Larry had the booth that attracted the flashlights. It was like being attacked by giant fireflies. It was all Myrna's Place. Nobody was interested in anything else. Old Fleas paused and looked their way.

As dawn began to slide in between the buildings, the thin, drawn man found a small ivory box.

"Myrna Lavaliere, who and where are you now?" he asked and opened the lid. It was full of business cards bearing the usual double Myrna's Place-and-coronet logo. Below that was an address on the Upper East Side, a Butterfield 8 telephone number and the motto, "Halfway between Park Avenue and Heaven."

"More like far from Heaven and down the street from Hell," the man said. "You kids have any idea what you have here?"

Larry and Lilia shrugged. Other customers wanted their attention.

"Wickedness always sells," the man told them. "And after the war in the late 1940s, rumor had it this place was wicked. Myrna's was a townhouse where you went in human and came out quite otherwise."

A tall woman with a black lace kerchief tied around her long neck and wearing sunglasses in the dawn light had stopped examining a pair of Myrna's Place candlesticks and paused to listen.

She gave a short, contemptuous laugh and said in an unplaceable accent, "Oh please, spare these not-terribly-innocent children all the sour grape stories spread by all the ones who couldn't get inside the front door of Myrna's. What happened there happened before and will happen again. If you know anything about these phenomena at all you know that."

She faced him and raised the glasses off her eyes for a moment. Neither Larry nor Lilia could see her face. But apparently her stare was enough to cause the man to first back away then scuttle off.

"Fifty gets you the candlesticks," Larry told her. They were getting bold.

"I just wanted to make sure these weren't as good as the pair I have. But I will let others know about you. I think the time is right."

That morning the wizened pack rats and sleek interior decorators were all at the booth hissing at each other as they pawed through the items. Lilia and Larry tried to spot people they thought might actually have gone to Myrna's.

As morning sunlight began to hit the Sixth Avenue Market, club kids coming from Danceteria in fifties drag found Larry and Lilia's stall. Dolled up boys in pompadours, girls in satin evening gowns who looked like inner tension was all that held them together, stopped on their way downtown. They seemed fascinated, whispered and giggled, but didn't buy much: a handkerchief, a cigarette holder.

But the stock of Myrna's Place items was almost cleaned out when a lone deathpunk girl, her eye shadow and black hair with green highlights looking sad in the growing light, appeared. She pawed through the remaining items, dug in her pockets and gave Larry three dollars and seventeen cents, all that she had with her, for a stained coaster.

Around then Lilia realized that if she held any of the items at a certain angle, the Myrna's Place design looked like an upper and lower lip and the coronet was a sharp, gold tooth. Once she saw that and pointed it out to Larry they couldn't see them any other way.

They weren't naive. In the demimonde they inhabited gossip lately concerned ones called the Nightwalkers. That morning they began wondering about Myrna's Place.

2.

Thirty years later, on the morning after the dinner party, Larry called Lilia on her cell phone several times.

But she was on an errand that took her uptown and onto the tram to Roosevelt Island. Though this situation hadn't occurred recently, Lilia remembered how to play Larry when she had something that he wanted.

Roosevelt Island lies in the East River between Manhattan and Queens. On that small spot in the midst of a great city is a little river town of apartment houses. Along the main street the buildings project out over the sidewalks providing a covered way.

In one period of Lilia's life the sun was unbearable and had to be avoided. Now walking under cover she was glad the habit had remained and helped her avoid skin cancer.

Lilia remembered the others who took the cure when she and Larry did: the old man with wild white hair and gleaming eyes who required three times as much Ichordone as anyone else in the program and wore a muzzle like a dog because he tried to bite, the mousy woman who had been turned into a vampire when she saw Bela Lugosi as Dracula on TV twenty years before.

Generations ago Roosevelt Island was called Welfare Island. It was where hospitals for contagious diseases were located. Their ruins still dot the place. Hospitals are still located there, most of them quite ordinary.

But in one there is a ward for patients with polymorphous light eruption (allergy to the sun) and hemophagia (strange reactions to blood) and several other exotic diseases. Behind that hospital are cottages.

In one of those sat the person Lilia had come to see. She was in a wheelchair, wrapped in blankets and looking out the window at the sunlight and water. The woman had seemed ancient to Lilia that morning years before at the Flea Market when she examined the candlesticks and told the man to spare her his sour grapes stories. Now Myrna Lavaliere was a mummy: nothing more than skin and bones and a voice.

"When one is old the smell of rot is omnipresent. Men are the worst but none are immune. Each time you come here you are awestruck by my age and corruption. I don't blame you. I am well over a hundred. My addiction, first to blood and then to Ichordone, prolonged my life, but look at the result.

"Up in the hospital they'd have me in restraints with my head immobilized because they are afraid I'd bite them." She laughed noiselessly and showed Lilia her toothless gums.

"All I want," she said, "is to die in this room with a bit of privacy, not up in that cadaver warehouse." She indicated the main hospital building. "Like everything else in this country, *that* requires money."

In earlier meetings she had told Lilia how much longer she had to live, how much that would cost, and how many treasures from Myrna's Place and other clubs she had stashed in storage lockers.

Lilia had told her of a plan she had. Today she told her what was required to implement it. "I need more bait for the market," she said.

Their eyes met and they understood one another. A nurse's aide was called and she brought Lilia a package of collectibles like the one she'd been given the week before.

3.

Lilia waited until she was back at her shop before answering one of Larry's calls.

Immediately he asked, "Where did you find it?" She heard voices echoing behind him in Stepelli, his large gallery space in West Chelsea.

She told him a tale of the Garage, that last sad remnant of the once sprawling Sixth Avenue Flea Markets, and the napkin she found the Sunday before when she ducked in there to get out of the rain.

"Was there anything else from Myrna's Place?" he asked.

"That's all that was left," she said. "But the dealer said there was quite a flurry when she opened. Young people apparently."

"Where did she get it? Does she have any more?"

"Yes," Lilia told him and gave no hint of her amusement. "She got it from a woman who got it from and a man who may have more. I have a lead on her source."

None of this was entirely true, but in his eagerness that escaped him.

It was Friday afternoon. They made plans to visit the Garage early Sunday morning.

Her shop, Reliquary: once so very trendy and notorious, later a charmingly creepy holdover, a bit of stylish nostalgia, now hung by a thread. The landlord, unable to find another tenant, had let Lilia slide on the rent from month to month. His patience was running out.

That afternoon as Lilia went on various errands, she remembered the Saturday night and Sunday morning after Larry and her first triumph.

That second week they brought all their good Myrna's Place stuff: the flasks, the scarves, the elephant foot umbrella stand. They were surrounded from the moment they set foot in the flea market. All the flashlights were around them. Customers from the previous week were back and others as well.

The dealers who looted a house each week had a daycare center's worth of children's chairs, toys. They paused to watch the commotion across the aisle.

Larry and Lilia discovered that the first deathpunk girl had been a harbinger. Out of the night, smelling of cigarettes and amyl nitrate, came club boys and girls in black from head to pointed-toe shoes. There were the retro and extreme retro kids, dressed as twenties flappers, Edwardian roués, and whores. One young man with a cravat and a face painted almost white carried a small, antique medical bag, and was called Doctor Jekyll.

They bought small souvenirs—a teacup or a doily. When asked what was so fascinating about Myrna's Place they shrugged and said this was Nightwalker stuff, the new thing.

Then, in the pre dawn, the club kids, awe-struck, watched as half a dozen figures flitted toward them like bats, like shadows. Lilia heard the flea across the way call out to someone, "Dracula and company just showed up!"

The newcomers all seemed tall, elongated. They wavered in the first light. Many of them actually wore capes. They were thin and their smiles were a brief flash of teeth.

As they moved through the kids around Larry and Lilia's tables, one of them reached over and, almost too fast to see, pulled down the collar of a girl's jacket, and first kissed then nipped her neck. The club girl shivered with ecstasy.

Lilia was uneasy, but Larry was star struck. Here was true glamour, the very heart of the most exclusive club back rooms. The sky was getting light. The newcomers surveyed the booth, nodded, put on sunglasses, exchanged glances and smiled. These people were impressed with him.

Raised cloaks hid what happened from the casual customers. In an eye-flash Larry's leather jacket and shirt were pulled off his shoulders. The smiles and fine sharp teeth looked like the ones on the Myrna's Place logo.

Larry's eyes went wide. A tiny trickle of blood ran down his chest. He stared after them as they left the market and didn't even notice Lilia pulling his clothes back in place.

Other customers appeared. Larry and Lilia were Flea celebrities and had a good day—even the dollhouse sold.

Larry was bedazzled. Lilia knew that he always gravitated to the key clique and always managed to get himself accepted. Now he'd found a group so special it was legend and they loved him.

That week Larry was distant and distracted. He got on her nerves. She got on his. The next Sunday morning they brought to market all the remaining Myrna's Place material and everything else they had for sale.

In the predawn the flashlights found them and so did the woman with the neck scarf and sunglasses. The club kids stared at her reverently. She glanced at Larry and almost smiled. She gave Lilia a slip of paper with some names.

"In one's old age, collections, however beloved become a burden. These are ones who are ready to give up theirs."

As she turned to go, the young Nightwalkers appeared. They bowed their heads and parted for her.

"Myrna," Lilia heard them murmur, "Myrna Lavaliere." The woman nodded and disappeared into the last of the night.

When the Nightwalkers exposed Larry's neck, Lilia told them not to because it had made him stupid. But he pointed at her and capes were raised, Lilia's arms were pinned, her blouse opened. Before she could even cry out, she felt teeth and a nick on the side of her neck.

Lilia turned to see who had done that but the effort made her head spin. Lilia knew a few things about drugs. None felt like this: it was like acid cut with heroin. She and Larry were in trances for the rest of that day and most of the next.

When they recovered, they took the list of names and telephone numbers the one the Nightwalkers called Myrna had given them. The people on the list were old and fragile, looking like they might break. But their eyes were sharp and sometimes their teeth. They all had memorabilia they were ready to get rid of. One or two liked to bite but they were mostly harmless.

4.

Late on a summer night thirty years later, Lilia met Larry in front of Reliquary on West Broadway at the trashy end of Soho. Tense, knowing things had to go just right; she noticed he wore the napkin with the Maud's Place logo displayed like a handkerchief in his jacket pocket. She did wonder where he had told Boyd he was going.

Cabs cruised and groups of young people searched for afterhours clubs. On weekends near the solstice, Saturday darkness comes later and Sunday morning is very early. There's almost no place left for the night.

Larry looked at the sign, the darkened windows, and shabby aura of the store. "Some amazing times here," he remarked and shook his head.

Once it had been different: *Cool Reliquary!* the ads in the *Village Voice* had said. *Not Your Mommy's Kind of Boutique—Not Your Daddy's Either* had been the title of the article in *New York Magazine* just after the shop opened in the early eighties.

Suitable designer styles were offered: capes in a variety of lengths, parasols to keep the sun out of the eyes, shirts and blouses that displayed best half open and exposing the throat and neck.

Then there was the tchotchkes, relics from what turned out to have been an endless succession of mysterious clubs and salons. Fra Diablo just off Union Square had attracted rumor and curiosity in the 1870s, the Bat Bar flourished just after the turn of the century. Club Indigo in Harlem in the late twenties had introduced white patrons to an impeccable African American staff and entertainment that could only be talked about in whispers.

"All those venues and every one of them produced artifacts," Larry said. "Certain individuals liked to have stuff like that around. Other people in the know would be aware of their interests without a word being spoken."

The two talked over old times as they walked toward Sixth Avenue while looking for a cab. They remembered the time that Nightwalkers first showed up at the Mudd Club, the way columnists in the *Village Voice* hinted at a craze that was not quite drugs or sex. *The New Yorker* had said, "Some call it a very old European tradition."

Everyone wanted artifacts, to take back to Westchester, to Chicago, to Paris, to Rome, a sign that they'd had at least a brush with the tingly and strange. Reliquary was where they got them.

"Daylight was something to be endured," Larry said. "We lived at night."

Lilia remembered those times like she'd seen them through the wrong end of binoculars. But she wasn't going to contradict him or mention the crash that followed the boom.

For her, it began when her dentist noticed the way her teeth had grown and ordered her out of his office. Then, on one of Lilia's rare visits to the Philadelphia suburbs, her mother mentioned the pallor. "Are those hickeys?" she had asked, catching sight of the bite marks on Lilia's neck.

She remembered the day the newspaper and magazine articles suddenly turned sour. *BLOOD CRAZED!* the tabloids screamed. *CONTAGIOUS DISEASE DISGUISED AS HIP CULT* the magazines cried.

Rich kids' families pulled them into elite and expensive therapy. Everyone else ended up in city hospitals and day clinics. Ichordone, horrible and soul deadening, was the methadone of vampirism. She wondered if Larry had managed to forget about that, guessed he had, and saw no reason to remind him.

At Sixth Avenue they found a cab and rode uptown through the Village and the old Ladies Mile. Groups hung about the corners, stood in front of the desecrated church that had been a nightclub. For a moment, on a side street, Lilia thought she saw a figure in a cape. She felt Larry tense and knew he'd seen it too.

"It's always been cycles, hasn't it?" he murmured. She said nothing. "Every twenty-five, thirty years: one is overdue," he said, and she nodded.

The cab turned on Twenty-Fifth Street and stopped at the Garage. This last stronghold of the Flea Market was set in the middle of the block and went right through to Twenty-Fourth. The official opening was eight a.m. but dealers were already getting read. Their vans rolled up and down the garage ramps and visitors were slipping in along with them.

A thin young woman and buff boy in black went down the ramp to the lower level. Lilia let Larry take the lead and follow them down. She wondered if all this was going to work.

The place had none of the mystery of the predawn flea market. It smelled of exhaust and bad coffee and was lighted so there was no need for flashlights. Older buyers watched dealers unpack their stock.

The couple in black drifted towards the back of the selling floor and a little knot of young people just out of the bars and clubs in a far corner.

Larry headed in that direction without looking to see if Lilia was with him. She was a step or two behind, following him back into a world they'd once known.

She knew what he was going to find: place cards with celebrity names: Cole Porter, Winston Guest, and Dorothy Parker from Club Indigo. Delicate fans decorated with cats baring their teeth from the Golden Palace, which had flourished down in Chinatown once upon a time. And, of course, salted into the mix were a few items from Myrna's Place. This was the contents of the parcel Lilia had been given on Roosevelt Island a couple of days before.

She watched the way Larry took in not only the items for sale but also the ones who had come to look at them. A few more kids stopped by. This was a gathering spot like their booth had been thirty years before.

They looked at Larry and his napkin with its crest of lips and teeth displayed. He asked the dealer where she had gotten the stuff and if she had any more.

The dealer was Eastern European and had trouble with English on certain occasions. She said a woman had sold them and hadn't left a name. No she didn't have any more. She was good at this and didn't once glance Lilia's way.

The onlookers stirred. Lilia turned and saw figures in sunglasses moving in the shadows cast by pillars and vans. Nightwalkers had arrived. A new, less formal generation in shorts and flip-flops, though Lilia noticed that several still wore capes.

Other dealers and their customers paused and shook their heads. Lilia's spine crawled. She wondered if all this was worth it. Then she saw something that again confirmed fate was with her.

The young writer of the Alice and the Vampires book was seemingly borne along as a kind of trophy by the Nightwalkers. His eyes were wide and he looked dazed. His shirt was open and several small puncture wounds ringed his neck and throat.

Larry's eyes widened and Lilia knew he'd once again found his exclusive clique. Clearly it was open to the young and pretty, but perhaps also to the well-to-do.

He reached for his wallet, asked the dealer how much she wanted for the lot of vampire tchotchkes. He didn't flinch at the gouger price Lilia had told her to charge. The crowd seemed disturbed by this interloper.

Lilia whispered, "I know the location of a treasure trove of similar stuff."

Larry nodded and distributed the items among the club kids and Nightwalkers alike. They became interested in this stranger. Then the young writer recognized Larry, got free of his handlers, hugged him and nipped his neck a little.

Lilia handed out faded cards for Reliquary while promising, "Memorabilia AND fashion. Come see us during the week."

As she did, she thought about T-shirts—hip, enigmatic ones. She knew distressed fashions that could be turned over for very little money, and she believed capes could be brought back one more time. Larry clearly was fascinated, so the money was there

The crowd broke up, headed to the exits. Larry and Lilia followed them, but when they reached the street all of them—club kids and Nightwalkers alike—had disappeared.

He seemed a little lost as they went toward a spot Lilia knew would be open at this hour. She wondered if he was remembering the Ichordone, the withdrawal, the dental clinics where teeth got filed down, the group therapy where a dozen other recovering vampires talked about their mothers.

"Don't worry, we'll get the audience back," Lilia said. There was a bit of blood on Larry's neck. When she pointed that out he dabbed it with the Myrna's Place napkin. And when she told Larry how much she'd need to get Reliquary up and going again, he nodded.

Lilia was certain she wasn't going to get hooked again. Larry probably would. For a moment she remembered his little adopted girl and hesitated.

Then she recalled the moment thirty years before in the flea market when she'd tried to keep the Nightwalkers away from him and he'd shut her up by siccing them on her.

So instead of little Ai Ling, Lilia thought of Boyd, who might dump Larry but would make sure his daughter was well taken care of. She took Larry's arm and led him to the spot where they could discuss the money.

The story Hat tells takes place far from New York, but you could never find Hat anywhere except New York.

PORK PIE HAT

PETER STRAUB

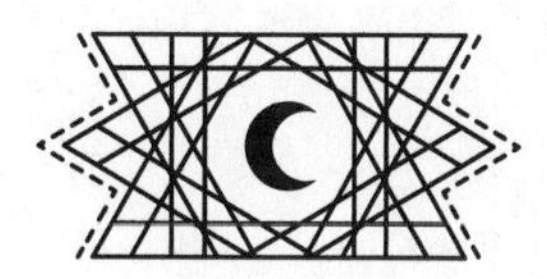

PART ONE

1

If you know jazz, you know about him, and the title of this memoir tells you who he is. If you don't know the music, his name doesn't matter. I'll call him Hat. What does matter is what he meant. I don't mean what he meant to people who were touched by what he said through his horn. (His horn was an old Selmer Balanced Action tenor saxophone, most of its lacquer worn off.) I'm talking about the whole long curve of his life, and the way that what appeared to be a long slide from joyous mastery to outright exhaustion can be seen in another way altogether.

Hat did slide into alcoholism and depression. The last ten years of his life amounted to suicide by malnutrition, and he was almost transparent by the time he died in the hotel room where I met him. Yet he was able to play until nearly the end. When he was working, he would wake up around seven in the evening, listen to Frank Sinatra or Billie Holiday records while he dressed, get to the club by nine, play three sets, come back to his room sometime after three, drink and listen to more records (he was on a lot of those records), and finally go back to bed around the time day people begin thinking about lunch. When he wasn't working, he got into bed about an hour earlier, woke up about five or six, and listened to records and drank through his long upside-down day.

It sounds like a miserable life, but it was just an unhappy one. The unhappiness came from a deep, irreversible sadness. Sadness is different from misery, at least Hat's was. His sadness seemed impersonal—it did not disfigure him, as misery can do. Hat's sadness seemed to be for the universe, or to be a larger than usual personal share of a sadness already existing in the universe. Inside it, Hat was unfailingly gentle, kind, even funny. His sadness seemed merely the opposite face of the equally impersonal happiness that shone through his earlier work.

In Hat's later years, his music thickened, and sorrow spoke through the phrases. In his last years, what he played often sounded like heartbreak itself. He was like someone who had passed through a great mystery, who was passing through a great mystery, and had to speak of what had seen, what he was seeing.

2

I brought two boxes of records with me when I first came to New York from Evanston, Illinois, where I'd earned a B.A. in English at Northwestern, and the first thing I set up in my shoebox at the top of John Jay Hall in Columbia University was my portable record player. I did everything to music in those days, and I supplied the rest of my unpacking with a soundtrack provided by Hat's disciples. The kind of music I most liked when I was twenty-one was called "cool" jazz, but my respect for Hat, the progenitor of this movement, was almost entirely abstract. I didn't know his earliest records, and all I'd heard of his later style was one track on a Verve sampler album. I thought he must almost certainly be dead, and I imagined that if by some miracle he was still alive, he would have been in his early seventies, like Louis Armstrong. In fact, the man who seemed a virtual ancient to me was a few months short of his fiftieth birthday.

In my first weeks at Columbia I almost never left the campus. I was taking five courses, also a seminar that was intended to lead me to a Master's thesis, and when I was not in lecture halls or my room, I was in the library. But by the end of September, feeling less overwhelmed, I began to go downtown to Greenwich Village. The IRT, the only subway line I actually understood, described a straight north-south axis which allowed you to get on at 116th Street and get off at Sheridan Square. From Sheridan Square radiated out an unimaginable wealth (unimaginable if you'd spent the previous four years in Evanston, Illinois) of cafes, bars, restaurants, record shops, bookstores, and jazz clubs. I'd come to New York to get a M.A. in English, but I'd also come for this.

I learned that Hat was still alive about seven o'clock in the evening on the first Saturday in October when I saw a poster bearing his name on the window of a storefront jazz club near St. Mark's Place. My conviction that Hat was dead was so strong that I first saw the poster as an advertisement of past glory. I stopped to gaze longer at this relic of a historical period. Hat had been playing with a quartet including a bassist and drummer of his own era, musicians long associated with him. But the piano player had been John Hawes, one of my musicians—John Hawes was on half a dozen of the records back in John Jay Hall. He must have been about twenty at the time, I thought, convinced that the poster had been preserved as memorabilia. Maybe Hawes' first job had been with Hat—anyhow, Hat's quartet must have been one of Hawes' first stops on the way to fame. John Hawes was a great figure to me, and the thought of him playing with a back number like Hat a disturbance in the texture of reality. I looked down at the date on the poster, and my snobbish and rule-bound version of reality shuddered under another assault of the unthinkable. Hat's engagement had begun on the Tuesday of this week—the first Tuesday in October, and its last night took place on the Sunday after next—the Sunday before Halloween. Hat was still alive, and John Hawes was playing with him. I couldn't have told you which half of this proposition was the more surprising.

To make sure, I went inside and asked the short, impassive man behind the bar if John Hawes were really playing there tonight. "He'd better be, if he wants to get paid," the man said.

"So Hat is still alive," I said.

"Put it this way," he said. "If it was you, you probably wouldn't be."

3

Two hours and twenty minutes later, Hat came through the front door, and I saw what he meant. Maybe a third of the tables between the door and the bandstand were filled with people listening to the piano trio. This was what I'd come for, and I thought that the evening was perfect. I hoped that Hat would stay away. All he could accomplish by showing up would be to steal soloing time from Hawes, who, apart from seeming a bit disengaged, was playing wonderfully. Maybe

Hawes always seemed a bit disengaged. That was fine with me. Hawes was *supposed* to be cool. Then the bass player looked toward the door and smiled, and the drummer grinned and knocked one stick against the side of his snare drum in a rhythmic figure that managed both to suit what the trio was playing and serve as a half-comic, half-respectful greeting. I turned away from the trio and looked back toward the door. The bent figure of a light-skinned black man in a long, drooping, dark coat was carrying a tenor saxophone case into the club. Layers of airline stickers covered the case, and a black porkpie hat concealed most of the man's face. As soon as he got past the door, he fell into a chair next to an empty table—really fell, as if he would need a wheelchair to get any farther.

Most of the people who had watched him enter turned back to John Hawes and the trio, who were beginning the last few choruses of "Love Walked In." The old man laboriously unbuttoned his coat and let it fall off his shoulders onto the back of the chair. Then, with the same painful slowness, he lifted the hat off his head and lowered it to the table beside him. A brimming shot glass had appeared between himself and the hat, though I hadn't noticed any of the waiters or waitresses put it there. Hat picked up the glass and poured its entire contents into his mouth. Before he swallowed, he let himself take in the room, moving his eyes without changing the position of his head. He was wearing a dark gray suit, a blue shirt with a tight tab collar, and a black knit tie. His face looked soft and worn with drink, and his eyes were of no real color at all, as if not merely washed out but washed clean. He bent over, unlocked the case, and began assembling his horn. As soon as "Love Walked In" ended, he was on his feet, clipping the horn to his strap and walking toward the bandstand. There was some quiet applause.

Hat stepped neatly up onto the bandstand, acknowledged us with a nod, and whispered something to John Hawes, who raised his hands to the keyboard. The drummer was still grinning, and the bassist had closed his eyes. Hat tilted his horn to one side, examined the mouthpiece, and slid it a tiny distance down the cork. He licked the reed, tapped his foot twice, and put his lips around the mouthpiece.

What happened next changed my life—changed me, anyhow. It was like discovering that some vital, even necessary substance had all along been missing from my life. Anyone who hears a great musician for the first time knows the feeling that the universe has just expanded. In fact, all that happened was that Hat had started playing "Too Marvelous For

Words," one of the twenty-odd songs that were his entire repertoire at the time. Actually, he was playing some oblique, one-time-only melody of his own that floated above "Too Marvelous For Words," and this spontaneous melody seemed to me to comment affectionately on the song while utterly transcending it—to turn a nice little song into something profound. I forgot to breathe for a little while, and goosebumps came up on my arms. Halfway through Hat's solo, I saw John Hawes watching him and realized that Hawes, whom I all but revered, revered *him*. But by that time, I did, too.

I stayed for all three sets, and after my seminar the next day, I went down to Sam Goody's and bought five of Hat's records, all I could afford. That night, I went back to the club and took a table right in front of the bandstand. For the next two weeks, I occupied the same table every night I could persuade myself that I did not have to study—eight or nine, out of the twelve nights Hat worked. Every night was like the first: the same things, in the same order, happened. Halfway through the first set, Hat turned up and collapsed into the nearest chair. Unobtrusively, a waiter put a drink beside him. Off went the pork pie and the long coat, and out from its case came the horn. The waiter carried the case, pork pie, and coat into a back room while Hat drifted toward the bandstand, often still fitting the pieces of his saxophone together. He stood straighter, seemed almost to grow taller, as he got on the stand. A nod to his audience, an inaudible word to John Hawes. And then that sense of passing over the border between very good, even excellent music and majestic, mysterious art. Between songs, Hat sipped from a glass placed beside his left foot. Three forty-five minute sets. Two half-hour breaks, during which Hat disappeared through a door behind the bandstand. The same twenty or so songs, recycled again and again. Ecstasy, as if I were hearing *Mozart* play Mozart.

One afternoon toward the end of the second week, I stood up from a library book I was trying to stuff whole into my brain—*Modern Approaches to Milton*—and walked out of my carrel to find whatever I could that had been written about Hat. I'd been hearing the sound of Hat's tenor in my head ever since I'd gotten out of bed. And in those days, I was a sort of apprentice scholar: I thought that real answers in the form of interpretations could be found in the pages of scholarly journals. If there were at least a thousand, maybe two thousand, articles concerning John Milton in Low Library, shouldn't there be at least a hundred about Hat? And out of the hundred shouldn't a dozen or so at least begin to explain what happened to me when I heard him play? I was looking for *close readings* of his solos, for analyses that would explain Hat's effects in terms of subdivided rhythms, alternate chords, and note choices, in the way that poetry critics parsed diction levels, inversions of meter, and permutations of imagery.

Of course I did not find a dozen articles that applied a musicological version of the New Criticism to Hat's recorded solos. I found six old concert write-ups in the *New York Times*, maybe as many record reviews in jazz magazines, and a couple of chapters in jazz histories. Hat had been born in Mississippi, played in his family band, left after a mysterious disagreement at the time they were becoming a successful "territory" band, then joined a famous jazz band in its infancy and quit, again mysteriously, just after its breakthrough into nationwide success. After that, he went out on his own. It seemed that if you wanted to know about him, you had to go straight to the music: there was virtually nowhere else to go.

I wandered back from the catalogues to my carrel, closed the door on the outer world, and went back to stuffing *Modern Approaches to Milton* into my brain. Around six o'clock, I opened the carrel door and realized that *I* could write about Hat. Given the paucity of criticism of his work—given the virtual absence of information about the man himself—I virtually had to write something. The only drawback to this inspiration was that I knew nothing about music. I could not write the sort of article I had wished to read. What I could do, however, would be to interview the man. Potentially, an interview would be more valuable than analysis. I could fill in the dark places, answer the unanswered questions—why had he left both bands just as they began to do well? I wondered if he'd had problems with his father, and then transferred these problems to his next bandleader. There had to be some kind of story. Any band within smelling distance of its first success would be more than reluctant to lose its star soloist—wouldn't they beg him, bribe him, to stay? I could think of other questions no one had ever asked: who had influenced him? What did he think of all those tenor players whom he had influenced? Was he friendly with any of his artistic children? Did they come to his house and talk about music?

Above all, I was curious about the texture of his life—I wondered what his life, the life of a genius, tasted like. If I could have put my half-formed fantasies into words, I would have described my naive, uninformed conceptions of Leonard Bernstein's surroundings. Mentally,

I equipped Hat with a big apartment, handsome furniture, advanced stereo equipment, a good but not flashy car, paintings . . . the surroundings of a famous American artist, at least by the standards of John Jay Hall and Evanston, Illinois. The difference between Bernstein and Hat was that the conductor probably lived on Fifth Avenue, and the tenor player in the Village.

I walked out of the library humming "Love Walked In."

4

The dictionary-sized Manhattan telephone directory chained to the shelf beneath the pay telephone on the ground floor of John Jay Hall failed to provide Hat's number. Moments later, I met similar failure back in the library after having consulted the equally impressive directories for Brooklyn, Queens, and the Bronx, as well as the much smaller volume for Staten Island. But of course Hat lived in New York: where else would he live? Like other celebrities, he avoided the unwelcome intrusions of strangers by going unlisted. I could not explain his absence from the city's five telephone books in any other way. Of course Hat lived in the Village—that was what the Village was *for*.

Yet even then, remembering the unhealthy-looking man who each night entered the club to drop into the nearest chair, I experienced a wobble of doubt. Maybe the great man's life was nothing like my imaginings. Hat wore decent clothes, but did not seem rich—he seemed to exist at the same oblique angle to worldly success that his nightly variations on "Too Marvelous For Words" bore to the original melody. For a moment, I pictured my genius in a slum apartment where roaches scuttled across a bare floor and water dripped from a rip in the ceiling. I had no idea of how jazz musicians actually lived. Hollywood, unafraid of cliche, surrounded them with squalor. On the rare moments when literature stooped to consider jazz people, it, too, served up an ambiance of broken bedsprings and peeling walls. And literature's bohemians—Rimbaud, Jack London, Kerouac, Hart Crane, William Burroughs—had often inhabited mean, unhappy rooms. It was possible that the great man was not listed in the city's directories because he could not afford a telephone.

This notion was unacceptable. There was another explanation—Hat could not live in a tenement room without a telephone. The man still possessed the elegance of his generation of jazz musicians, the generation that wore good suits and highly polished shoes, played in big bands, and lived on buses and in hotel rooms.

And there, I thought, was my answer. It was a comedown from the apartment in the Village with which I had supplied him, but a room in some "artistic" hotel like the Chelsea would suit him just as well, and probably cost a lot less in rent. Feeling inspired, I looked up the Chelsea's number on the spot, dialed, and asked for Hat's room. The clerk told me that he wasn't registered in the hotel. "But you know who he is," I said. "Sure," said the clerk. "Guitar, right? I know he was in one of those San Francisco bands, but I can't remember which one."

I hung up without replying, realizing that the only way I was going to discover Hat's telephone number, short of calling every hotel in New York, was by asking him for it.

5

This was on a Monday, and the jazz clubs were closed. On Tuesday, Professor Marcus told us to read all of *Vanity Fair* by Friday; on Wednesday, after I'd spent a nearly sleepless night with Thackeray, my seminar leader asked me to prepare a paper on James Joyce's "Two Gallants" for the Friday class. Wednesday and Thursday nights I spent in the library. On Friday I listened to Professor Marcus being brilliant about *Vanity Fair* and read my laborious and dimwitted Joyce paper, on each of the five pages of which the word "epiphany" appeared at least twice, to my fellow-scholars. The seminar leader smiled and nodded throughout my performance and when I sat down metaphorically picked up my little paper between thumb and forefinger and slit its throat. "Some of you students are so *certain* about things," he said. The rest of his remarks disappeared into a vast, horrifying sense of shame. I returned to my room, intending to lie down for an hour or two, and woke up ravenous ten hours later, when even the West End bar, even the local Chock Full O' Nuts, were shut for the night.

On Saturday night, I took my usual table in front of the bandstand and sat expectantly through the piano trio's usual three numbers. In the middle of "Love Walked In" I looked around with an insider's foreknowledge to enjoy Hat's dramatic entrance, but he did not appear, and the number ended without him. John Hawes and the other two musicians seemed untroubled by this break in the routine, and went on to play "Too Marvelous For Words" without their leader. During the next three songs, I kept turning around to look for Hat, but the set ended without him. Hawes announced a short break, and the musicians stood up and moved toward the bar. I fidgeted at my table, nursing my second beer of the night and anxiously checking the door. The minutes trudged by. I feared he would never show up. He had passed out in his room. He'd been hit by a cab, he'd had a stroke, he was already lying dead in a hospital room—just when I was going to write the article that would finally do him justice!

Half an hour later, still without their leader, John Hawes and other sidemen went back on the stand. No one but me seemed to have noticed that Hat was not present. The other customers talked and smoked—this was in the days when people still smoked—and gave the music the intermittent and sometimes ostentatious attention they allowed it even when Hat was on the stand. By now, Hat was an hour and a half late, and I could see the gangsterish man behind the bar, the owner of the club, scowling as he checked his wristwatch. Hawes played two originals I particularly liked, favorites of mine from his Contemporary records, but in my mingled anxiety and irritation I scarcely heard them.

Toward the end of the second of these songs, Hat entered the club and fell into his customary seat a little more heavily than usual. The owner motioned away the waiter, who had begun moving toward him with the customary shot glass. Hat dropped the porkpie on the table and struggled with his coat buttons. When he heard what Hawes was playing, he sat listening with his hands still on a coat button, and I listened, too—the music had a tighter, harder, more modern feel, like Hawes' records. Hat nodded to himself, got his coat off, and struggled with the snaps on his saxophone case. The audience gave Hawes unusually appreciative applause. It took Hat longer than usual to fit the horn together, and by the time he was up on his feet, Hawes and the other two musicians had turned around to watch his progress as if they feared he would not make it all the way to the bandstand. Hat wound through the tables with his head tilted back, smiling to himself. When he got close to the stand, I saw that he was walking on his toes like a small child. The owner crossed his arms over his chest and glared. Hat seemed almost to float onto the stand. He licked his reed. Then he lowered his horn and, with his mouth open, stared out at us for a moment. "Ladies, ladies," he said in a soft, high voice. These were the first words I had ever heard him speak. "Thank you for your appreciation of our pianist, Mr. Hawes. And now I must explain my absence during the first set. My son passed away this afternoon, and I have been . . . busy . . . with details. Thank you."

With that, he spoke a single word to Hawes, put his horn back in his mouth, and began to play a blues called "Hat Jumped Up," one of his twenty songs. The audience sat motionless with shock. Hawes, the bassist, and the drummer played on as if nothing unusual had happened—they must have known about his son, I thought. Or maybe they knew that he had no son, and had invented a grotesque excuse for turning up ninety minutes late. The club owner bit his lower lip and looked unusually introspective. Hat played one familiar, uncomplicated figure after another, his tone rough, almost coarse. At the end of his solo, he repeated one note for an entire chorus, fingering the key while staring out toward the back of the club, Maybe he was watching the customers leave—three couples and a couple of single people walked out while he was playing. But I don't think he saw anything at all. When the song was over, Hat leaned over to whisper to Hawes, and the piano player announced a short break. The second set was over.

Hat put his tenor on top of the piano and stepped down off the bandstand, pursing his mouth with concentration. The owner had come out from behind the bar and moved up in front of him as Hat tip-toed around the stand. The owner spoke a few quiet words. Hat answered. From behind, he looked slumped and tired, and his hair curled far over the back of his collar. Whatever he had said only partially satisfied the owner, who spoke again before leaving him. Hat stood in place for a moment, perhaps not noticing that the owner had gone, and resumed his tip-toe glide toward the door. Looking at his back, I think I took in for the first time how genuinely strange he was. Floating through the door in his gray flannel suit, hair dangling in ringlet-like strands past his collar, leaving in the air behind him the announcement about a dead son, he seemed absolutely separate from the rest of humankind, a species of one.

I turned as if for guidance to the musicians at the bar. Talking, smiling, greeting a few fans and friends, they behaved just as they did on every other night. Could Hat really have lost a son earlier today? Maybe this was the jazz way of facing grief—to come back to work, to carry on. Still it seemed the worst of all times to approach Hat with my offer. His playing was a drunken parody of itself. He would forget anything he said to me; I was wasting MY time.

On that thought, I stood up and walked past the bandstand and opened the door—if I was wasting my time, it didn't matter what I did.

He was leaning against a brick wall about ten feet up the alleyway from the club's back door. The door clicked shut behind me, but Hat did not open his eyes. His face tilted up, and a sweetness that might have been sleep lay over his features. He looked exhausted and insubstantial, too frail to move. I would have gone back inside the club if he had not produced a cigarette from a pack in his shirt pocket, lit it with a match, and then flicked the match away, all without opening his eyes. At least he was awake. I stepped toward him, and his eyes opened. He glanced at me and blew out white smoke. "Taste?" he said.

I had no idea what he meant. "Can I talk to you for a minute, sir?" I asked.

He put his hand into one of his jacket pockets and pulled out a half-pint bottle. "Have a taste." Hat broke the seal on the cap, tilted it into his mouth, and drank. Then he held the bottle out toward me.

I took it. "I've been coming here as often as I can."

"Me, too," he said. "Go on, do it."

I took a sip from the bottle—gin. "I'm sorry about your son."

"Son?" He looked upward, as if trying to work out my meaning. "I got a son—out on Long Island. With his momma." He drank again and checked the level of the bottle.

"He's not dead, then."

He spoke the next words slowly, almost wonderingly. "Nobody-told-me-if-he-is." He shook his head and drank another mouthful of gin. "Damn. Wouldn't that be something, boy dies and nobody tells me? I'd have to think about that, you know, have to really *think* about that one."

"I'm just talking about what you said on stage."

He cocked his head and seemed to examine an empty place in the dark air about three feet from his face. "Uh huh. That's right. I did say that. Son of mine passed."

It was like dealing with a sphinx. All I could do was plunge in. "Well, sir, actually there's a reason I came out here," I said. "I'd like to interview you. Do you think that might be possible? You're a great artist, and there's very little about you in print. Do you think we could set up a time when I could talk to you?"

He looked at me with his bleary, colorless eyes, and I wondered if he could see me at all. And then I felt that, despite his drunkenness, he saw everything—that he saw things about me that I couldn't see.

"You a jazz writer?" he asked.

"No, I'm a graduate student. I'd just like to do it. I think it would be important."

"Important." He took another swallow from the half pint and slid the bottle back into his pocket. "Be nice, doing an important interview."

He stood leaning against the wall, moving further into outer space with every word. Only because I had started, I pressed on: I was already losing faith in this project. The reason Hat had never been interviewed was that ordinary American English was a foreign language to him. "Could we do the interview after you finish up at this club? I could meet you anywhere you like." Even as I said these words, I despaired. Hat was in no shape to know what he had to do after this engagement finished. I was surprised he could make it back to Long Island every night.

Hat rubbed his face, sighed, and restored my faith in him. "It'll have to wait a little while. Night after I finish here, I go to Toronto for two nights. Then I got something in Hartford on the thirtieth. You come see me after that."

"On the thirty-first?" I asked.

"Around nine, ten, something like that. Be nice if you brought some refreshments."

"Fine, great," I said, wondering if I would be able to take a late train back from wherever he lived. "But where on Long Island should I go?"

His eyes widened in mock-horror. "Don't go nowhere on Long Island. You come see me. In the Albert Hotel, Forty-Ninth and Eighth. Room 821."

I smiled at him—I had guessed right about one thing, anyhow.

Hat did not live in the Village, but he did live in a Manhattan hotel. I asked him for his phone number, and wrote it down, along with the other information, on a napkin from the club. After I folded the napkin into my jacket pocket, I thanked him and turned toward the door.

"Important as a motherfucker," he said in his high, soft, slurry voice.

I turned around in alarm, but he had tilted his head toward the sky again, and his eyes were closed.

"Indiana," he said. His voice made the word seem sung. "Moonlight in Vermont. I Thought About You. Flamingo."

He was deciding what to play during his next set. I went back inside, where twenty or thirty new arrivals, more people than I had ever seen in the club, waited for the music to start. Hat soon reappeared through the door, the other musicians left the bar, and the third set began. Hat played all four of the songs he had named, interspersing them through his standard repertoire during the course of an unusually long set. He was playing as well as I'd ever heard him, maybe better than I'd heard on all the other nights I had come to the club. The Saturday night crowd applauded explosively after every solo. I didn't know if what I was seeing was genius or desperation.

An obituary in the Sunday *New York Times*, which I read over breakfast the next morning in the John Jay cafeteria, explained some of what had happened. Early Saturday morning, a thirty-eight year old tenor saxophone player named Grant Kilbert had been killed in an automobile accident. One of the most successful jazz musicians in the world, one of the few jazz musicians, known outside of the immediate circle of fans, Kilbert had probably been Hat's most prominent disciple. He had certainly been one of my favorite musicians. More importantly, from his first record, *Cool Breeze*, Kilbert had excited respect and admiration. I looked at the photograph of the handsome young man beaming out over the neck of his saxophone and realized that the first four songs on *Cool Breeze* were "Indiana," "Moonlight in Vermont," "I Thought About You," and "Flamingo." Sometime late Saturday afternoon, someone had called up Hat to tell him about Kilbert. What I had seen had not merely been alcoholic eccentricity, it had been grief for a lost son. And when I thought about it, I was sure that the lost son, not himself, had been the important motherfucker he'd apothesized. What I had taken for spaciness and disconnection had all along been irony.

PART TWO

1

On the 31st of October, after calling to make sure he remembered our appointment, I did go to the Albert Hotel, room 821, and interview Hat. That is, I asked him questions and listened to the long, rambling, often obscene responses he gave them. During the long night I spent in his room, he drank the fifth of Gordon's gin, the "refreshments" I brought with me—all of it, an entire bottle of gin, without tonic, ice, or other dilutants. He just poured it into a tumbler and drank, as if it were water. (I refused his single offer of a "taste.") I frequently checked to make sure that the tape recorder I'd borrowed from a business student down the hall from me was still working, I changed tapes until they ran out, I made detailed back-up notes with a ball-point pen in a stenographic notebook. A couple of times, he played me sections of records that he wanted me to hear, and now and then he sang a couple of bars to make sure that I understood what he was telling me. He sat me in his only chair, and during the entire night stationed himself, dressed in his pork pie hat, a dark blue chalk-stripe suit, and white button-down shirt with a black knit tie, on the edge of his bed. This was a formal occasion. When I arrived at nine o'clock, he addressed me as "Mr. Leonard Feather" (the name of a well-known jazz critic), and when he opened his door at six-thirty the next morning, he called me "Miss Rosemary". By then, I knew that this was an allusion to Rosemary Clooney, whose singing I had learned that he liked, and that the nickname meant he liked me, too. It was not at all certain, however, that he remembered my actual name.

I had three sixty-minute tapes and a notebook filled with handwriting that gradually degenerated from my usual scrawl into loops and wiggles that resembled Arabic more than English. Over the next month, I spent whatever spare time I had transcribing the tapes and trying to decipher my own handwriting. I wasn't sure that what I had was an interview. My carefully prepared questions had been met either with evasions or blank, silent refusals to answer—he had simply started talking about something else. After about an hour, I realized that this was his interview, not mine, and let him roll.

After my notes had been typed up and the tapes transcribed, I put everything in a drawer and went back to work on my M.A. What I had was even more puzzling than I'd thought, and straightening it out would have taken more time than I could afford. So the rest of that academic year was a long grind of studying for the comprehensive exam and getting a thesis ready. Until I picked up an old *Time* magazine in the John Jay lounge and saw his name in the "Milestones" columns, I didn't even know that Hat had died.

Two months after I'd interviewed him, he had begun to hemorrhage on a flight back from France; an ambulance had taken him directly from the airport to a hospital. Five days after his release from the hospital, he had died in his bed at the Albert.

After I earned my degree, I was determined to wrestle something useable from my long night with Hat—I owed it to him. During the first weeks of that summer, I wrote out a version of what Hat had said to me and sent it to the only publication I thought would be interested in it. *Downbeat* accepted the interview, and it appeared there about six months later. Eventually, it acquired some fame as the last of his rare public statements. I still see lines from the interview quoted in the sort of pieces about Hat never printed during his life. Sometimes they are lines he really did say to me; sometimes they are stitched together from remarks he made at different times; sometimes, they are quotations I invented in order to be able to use other things he did say.

But one section of that interview has never been quoted, because it was never printed. I never figured out what to make of it. Certainly I could not believe all he had said. He had been putting me on, silently laughing at my credulity, for he could not possibly believe that what he was telling me was literal truth. I was a white boy with a tape recorder, it was Halloween, and Hat was having fun with me. He was *jiving* me.

Now I feet different about his story and about him, too. He was a great man, and I was an unworldly kid. He was drunk, and I was priggishly sober, but in every important way, he was functioning far above my level. Hat had lived forty-nine years as a black man in America, and I'd spent all of my twenty-one years in white suburbs. He was an immensely talented musician, a man who virtually thought in music, and I can't even hum in tune. That I expected to understand anything at all about him staggers me now. Back then, I didn't know anything about grief, and Hat wore grief about him daily, like a cloak. Now that I am the age he was then, I see that most of what is called information is interpretation, and interpretation is always partial.

Probably Hat was putting me on, jiving me, though not maliciously. He certainly was not telling me the literal truth, though I have never been able to learn what the literal truth of this case was. It's possible that even Hat never knew what was the literal truth behind the story he told me—possible, I mean, that he was still trying to work out what the truth was, nearly forty years after the fact.

2

He started telling me the story after we heard what I thought were gunshots from the street. I jumped from the chair and rushed to the windows, which looked out onto Eighth Avenue. "Kids," Hat said. In the hard yellow light of the street lamps, four or five teenage boys trotted up the Avenue. Three of them carried paper bags. "Kids shooting?" I asked. My amazement tells you how long ago this was.

"Fireworks," Hat said. "Every Halloween in New York, fool kids run around with bags full of fireworks, trying to blow their hands off."

Here and in what follows, I am not going to try to represent the way Hat actually spoke. I cannot represent the way his voice glided over certain words and turned others into mushy growls, though he expressed more than half of his meaning by sound; and I don't want to reproduce his constant, reflexive obscenity. Hat couldn't utter four words in a row without throwing in a "motherfucker." Mostly, I have replaced his obscenities with other words, and the reader can imagine what was really said. Also, if I tried to imitate his grammar, I'd sound racist and he would sound stupid. Hat left school in the fourth grade, and his language, though precise, was casual. To add to these difficulties, Hat employed a private language of his own, a code to ensure that he would be understood only by the people he wished to understand him. I have replaced most of his code words with their equivalents.

It must have been around one in the morning, which means that I had been in his room about four hours. Until Hat explained the "gunshots," I had forgotten that it was Halloween night, and I told him this as I turned away from the window.

"I never forget about Halloween," Hat said. "If I can, I stay home on Halloween. Don't want to be out on the street, that night."

He had already given me proof that he was superstitious, and as he spoke he glanced almost nervously around the room, as if looking for sinister presences.

"You'd feel in danger?" I asked.

He rolled gin around in his mouth and looked at me as he had in the alley behind the club, taking note of qualities I myself did not yet perceive. This did not feel at all judgmental. The nervousness I thought I had seen had disappeared, and his manner seemed marginally more concentrated than earlier in the evening. He swallowed the gin and for a couple of seconds looked at me without speaking.

"No," he finally said. "Not exactly. But I wouldn't feel safe, either."

I sat with my pen half an inch from the page of my notebook, uncertain whether or not to write this down.

"I'm from Mississippi, you know."

I nodded.

"Funny things happen down there. Back when I was a little kid, it was a whole different world. Know what I mean?"

"I can guess," I said.

He nodded. "Sometimes people disappeared. They'd be *gone*. All kinds of stuff used to happen, stuff you wouldn't even believe in now. I met a witch-lady once who could put curses on you, make you go blind and crazy. Another time, I saw a mean, murdering son of a bitch named Eddie Grimes die and come back to life—he got shot to death at a dance we were playing, he was *dead*, and a woman went down and whispered to him, and Eddie Grimes stood right back up on his feet. The man who shot him took off double-quick and he must have kept on going, because we never saw him after that."

"Did you start playing again?" I asked, taking notes as fast as I could.

"We never stopped," Hat said. "You let the people deal with what's going on, but you gotta keep on playing."

"Did you live in the country?" I asked, thinking that all of this sounded like Dogpatch—witches and walking dead men.

He shook his head. "I was brought up in town, Woodland, Mississippi. On the river. Where we lived was called Darktown, you know, but most of Woodland was white, with nice houses and all. Lots of our people did the cooking and washing in the big houses on Miller's Hill, that kind of work. In fact, we lived in a pretty nice house, for Darktown—the band always did well, and my father had a couple of other jobs on top of that. He was a good piano player, mainly, but he could play any kind of instrument. And he was a big, strong guy, nice-looking, real light-complected, so he was called Red, which was what that meant in those days. People respected him."

Another long, rattling burst of explosions came from Eighth Avenue. I wanted to ask him again about leaving his father's band, but Hat once more gave his little room a quick inspection, swallowed another mouthful of gin, and went on talking.

"We even went out trick or treating on Halloween, you know, like the white kids. I guess our people didn't do that everywhere, but we did. Naturally, we stuck to our neighborhood, and probably we got a lot less than the kids from Miller's Hill, but they didn't have anything up there that tasted as good as the apples and candy we brought home in our bags. Around us, people made instead of bought, and that's the difference." He smiled at either the memory or the unexpected sentimentality he had just revealed—for a moment, he looked both lost in time and uneasy with himself for having said too much. "Or maybe I just remember it that way, you know? Anyhow, we used to raise some hell, too. You were *supposed* to raise hell, on Halloween."

"You went out with your brothers?" I asked.

"No, no, they were—" He flipped his hand in the air, dismissing whatever it was that his brothers had been. "I was always apart, you dig? Me, I was always into my own little things. I was that way right from the beginning. I play like that—never play like anyone else, don't even play like myself. You gotta find new places for yourself, or else nothing's happening, isn't that right? Don't want to be a repeater pencil." He saluted this declaration with another swallow of gin. "Back in those days, I used to go out with a boy named Rodney Sparks—we called him Dee, short for Demon, 'cause Dee Sparks would do anything that came into his head. That boy was the bravest little bastard I ever knew. He'd wrassle a mad dog. And the reason was, Dee was the preacher's boy. If you happen to be the preacher's boy, seems like you gotta prove every way you can that you're no Buster Brown, you know? So I hung with Dee, because I wasn't any Buster Brown, either. This is when we were eleven, around then—the time when you talk about girls, you know, but you still aren't too sure what that's about. You don't know what *anything's* about, to tell the truth. You along for the ride, you trying to pack in as much fun as possible. So Dee was my right hand, and when I went out on Halloween in Woodland, I went out with *him*."

He rolled his eyes toward the window and said, "Yeah." An expression I could not read at all took over his face. By the standards of ordinary people, Hat almost always looked detached, even impassive, tuned to some private wavelength, and this sense of detachment had intensified. I thought he was changing mental gears, dismissing his childhood, and opened my mouth to ask him about Grant Kilbert. But he raised his glass to his mouth again and rolled his eyes back to me, and the quality of his gaze told me to keep quiet.

"I didn't know it," he said, "but I was getting ready to stop being a little boy. To stop believing in little boy things and start seeing like a grown-up. I guess that's part of what I liked about Dee Sparks—he seemed like he was a lot more grown-up than I was, shows you what my head was like. The age we were, this would have been the last time we went out on Halloween to get apples and candy. From then on, we would have gone out mainly to raise hell. Scare the shit out of the little kids. But the way it turned out, it was the last time we ever went out on Halloween."

He finished off the gin in his glass and reached down to pick the bottle off the floor and pour another few inches into the tumbler. "Here I am, sitting in this room. There's my horn over there. Here's this bottle. You know what I'm saying?"

I didn't. I had no idea what he was saying. The hint of fatality clung to his earlier statement, and for a second I thought he was going to say that he was here but Dee Sparks was nowhere because Dee Sparks had died in Woodland, Mississippi, at the age of eleven on Halloween night. Hat was looking at me with a steady curiosity which compelled a response. "What happened?" I asked.

Now I know that he was saying *It has come down to just this, my room, my horn, my bottle.* My question was as good as any other response.

"If I was to tell you everything that happened, we'd have to stay in this room for a month." He smiled and straightened up on the bed. His ankles were crossed, and for the first time I noticed that his feet, shod in dark suede shoes with crepe soles, did not quite touch the floor. "And, you know, I never tell anybody everything, I always have to keep something back for myself. Things turned out all right. Only thing I mind is, I should have earned more money. Grant Kilbert, he earned a lot of money, and some of that was mine, you know."

"Were you friends?" I asked.

"I knew the man." He tilted his head and stared at the ceiling for so long that eventually I looked up at it, too. It was not a remarkable ceiling. A circular section near the center had been replastered not long before.

"No matter where you live, there are places you're not supposed to go," he said, still gazing up. "And sooner or later, you're gonna wind up there." He smiled at me again. "Where we lived, the place you weren't supposed to go was called The Backs. Out of town, stuck in the woods on one little path. In Darktown, we had all kinds from preachers on down. We had washerwomen and blacksmiths and carpenters, and we had some no-good thieving trash, too, like Eddie Grimes, that man who came back from being dead. In The Backs, they started with trash like Eddie Grimes, and went down from there. Sometimes, our people went out there to buy a jug, and sometimes they went there to get a woman, but they never talked about it. The Backs was *rough*. What they had was rough." He rolled his eyes at me and said, "That witch-lady I told you about, she lived in The Backs." He snickered. "Man, they were a mean bunch of people. They'd cut you, you looked at 'em bad. But one thing funny about the place, white and colored lived there just the same—it was *integrated*. Backs people were so evil, color didn't make no difference to them. They hated everybody anyhow, on principle." Hat pointed his glass at me, tilted his head, and narrowed his eyes. "At least, that was what everybody *said*. So this particular Halloween, Dee Sparks says to me after we finish with Darktown, we ought to head out to The Backs and see what the place is really like. Maybe we can have some fun.

"The idea of going out to The Backs kind of scared me, but being scared was part of the fun—Halloween, right? And if anyplace in Woodland was perfect for all that Halloween shit, you know, someplace where you might really see a ghost or a goblin, The Backs was better than the graveyard." Hat shook his head, holding the glass out at a right angle to his body. A silvery amusement momentarily transformed him, and it struck me that his native elegance, the product of his character and bearing much more than of the handsome suit and the suede shoes, had in effect been paid for by the surviving of a thousand unimaginable difficulties, each painful to a varying degree. Then I realized that what I meant by elegance was really dignity, that for the first time I had recognized actual dignity in another human being, and that dignity was nothing like the self-congratulatory superiority people usually mistook for it.

"We were just little babies, and we wanted some of those good old Halloween scares. Like those dumbbells out on the street, tossing firecrackers at each other." Hat wiped his free hand down over his face and made sure that I was prepared to write down everything he said. (The tapes had already been used up.) "When I'm done, tell me if we found it, okay?"

"Okay," I said.

3

"Dee showed up at my house just after dinner, dressed in an old sheet with two eyeholes cut in it and carrying a paper bag. His big old shoes stuck out underneath the sheet. I had the same costume, but it was the one my brother used the year before, and it dragged along the ground and my feet got caught in it. The eyeholes kept sliding away from my eyes. My mother gave me a bag and told me to behave myself and get home before eight. it didn't take but half an hour to cover all the likely houses in Darktown, but she knew I'd want to fool around with Dee for an hour or so afterwards.

"Then up and down the streets we go, knocking on the doors where they'd give us stuff and making a little mischief where we knew they wouldn't. Nothing real bad, just banging on the door and running like hell, throwing rocks on the roof, little stuff. A few places, we plain and simple stayed away from—the places where people like Eddie Grimes lived. I always thought that was funny. We knew enough to steer clear of those houses, but we were still crazy to get out to The Backs.

"Only way I can figure it is, The Backs was *forbidden*. Nobody had to tell us to stay away from Eddie Grimes' house at night. You wouldn't even go there in the daylight, 'cause Eddie Grimes would get you and that would be that.

"Anyhow, Dee kept us moving along real quick, and when folks asked us questions or said they wouldn't give us stuff unless we sang a song, he moaned like a ghost and shook his bag in their faces, so we could get away faster. He was so excited, I think he was almost shaking.

"Me, I was excited, too. Not like Dee—sort of sick-excited, the way people must feel the first time they use a parachute. Scared-excited.

"As soon as we got away from the last house, Dee crossed the street and started running down the side of the little general store we all used. I knew where he was going. Out behind the store was a field, and on the other side of the field was Meridian Road, which took you out into the woods and to the path up to The Backs. When he realized that I wasn't next to him, he turned around and yelled at me to hurry up. *No,* I said inside myself, *I ain't gonna jump outta of this here airplane, I'm not dumb enough to do that.* And then I pulled up my sheet and scrunched up my eye to look through the one hole close enough to see through, and I took off after him.

"It was beginning to get dark when Dee and I left my house, and now it was dark. The Backs was about a mile and a half away, or at least the path was. We didn't know how far along that path you had to go before you got there. Hell, we didn't even know what it was—I was still thinking the place was a collection of little houses, like a sort of shadow-Woodland. And then, while we were crossing the field, I stepped on my costume and fell down flat on my face. Enough of this stuff, I said, and yanked the damned thing off. Dee started cussing me out, I wasn't doing this stuff the right way, we had to keep our costumes on in case anybody saw us, did I forget that this is Halloween, on Halloween a costume *protected* you. So I told I him I'd put it back on when we got there. If I kept on falling down, it'd take us twice as long. That shut him up.

"As soon as I got that blasted sheet over my head, I discovered that I could see at least a little ways ahead of me. The moon was up, and a lot of stars were out. Under his sheet, Dee Sparks looked a little bit like a real ghost. It kind of glimmered. You couldn't really make out its edges, so the darn thing like *floated*. But I could see his legs and those big old shoes sticking out.

"We got out of the field and started up Meridian Road, and pretty soon the trees came up right to the ditches alongside the road, and I couldn't see too well any more. The road seemed like it went smack into the woods and disappeared. The trees looked taller and thicker than in the daytime, and now and then something right at the edge of the woods shone round and white, like an eye—reflecting the moonlight, I guess. Spooked me. I didn't think we'd ever be able to find the path up to The Backs, and that was fine with me. I thought we might go along the road another ten-fifteen minutes, and then turn around and go home. Dee was swooping around up in front of me, flapping his sheet and acting bughouse. *He* sure wasn't trying too hard to find that path.

"After we walked about a mile down Meridian Road, I saw headlights like yellow dots coming towards us fast—Dee didn't see anything at all, running around in circles the way he was. I shouted at him to get off the road, and he took off like a rabbit—disappeared into the woods before I did. I jumped the ditch and hunkered down behind a pine about ten feet off the road to see who was coming. There weren't many cars in Woodland in those days, and I knew every one of them. When the car came by, it was Dr. Garland's old red Cord—Dr. Garland was a white man, but he had two waiting rooms and took colored patients, so colored patients was mostly what he had. And the man was a heavy drinker, *heavy* drinker. He zipped by, goin' at least fifty, which was mighty fast for those days, probably as fast as that old Cord would go. For about a second, I saw Dr. Garland's face under his white hair, and his mouth was wide open, stretched like he was screaming. After he passed, I waited a long time before I came out of the woods. Turning around and going home would have been fine with me. Dr. Garland changed everything. Normally, he was kind of slow and quiet, you know, and I could still see that black screaming hole opened up in his face—he looked like he was being tortured, like he was in Hell. I sure as hell didn't want to see whatever *he* had seen.

"I could hear the Cord's engine after the tail lights disappeared. I turned around and saw that I was all alone on the road. Dee Sparks was nowhere in sight. A couple of times, real soft, I called out his name. Then I called his name a little louder. Away off in the woods, I heard Dee giggle. I said he could run around all night if he liked but I was going home, and then I saw that pale silver sheet moving through the trees, and I started back down Meridian Road. After about twenty paces, I looked back, and there he was, standing in the middle of the road in that silly sheet, watching me go. Come on, I said, let's get back. He paid me no mind. Wasn't that Dr. Garland? Where was he going, as fast as that? What was happening? When I said the doctor was probably out on some emergency, Dee said the man was going *home*—he lived in Woodland, didn't he?

"Then I thought maybe Dr. Garland had been up in The Backs. And Dee thought the same thing, which made him want to go there all the more. Now he was determined. Maybe we'd see some dead guy. We stood there until I understood that he was going to go by himself if I didn't go with him. That meant that I *had* to go. Wild as he was, Dee'd get himself into some kind of mess for sure if I wasn't there to hold him down. So I said okay, I was coming along, and Dee started swooping along like before, saying crazy stuff. There was no way we were going to be able to find some little old path that went up into the woods. It was so dark, you couldn't see the separate trees, only giant black walls on both sides of the road.

"We went so far along Meridian Road I was sure we must have passed it. Dee was running around in circles about ten feet ahead of me. I told him that we missed the path, and now it was time to get back home. He laughed at me and ran across to the right side of the road and disappeared into the darkness.

"I told him to get back, damn it, and he laughed some more and said I should come to *him*. Why? I said, and he said, Because this here is the path, dummy. I didn't believe him—came right up to where he disappeared. All I could see was a black wall that could have been trees or just plain night. Moron, Dee said, look down. And I did. Sure enough, one of those white things like an eye shone up from where the ditch should have been. I bent down and touched cold little stones, and the shining dot of white went off like a light—a pebble that caught the moonlight just right. Bending down like that, I could see the hump of grass growing up between the tire tracks that led out onto Meridian Road. He'd found the path, all right.

"At night, Dee Sparks could see one hell of a lot better than me. He spotted the break in the ditch from across the road. He was already walking up the path in those big old shoes, turning around every other step to look back at me, make sure I was coming along behind him. When I started following him, Dee told me to get my sheet back on, and I pulled the thing over my head even though I'd rather have sucked the water out of a hollow stump. But I knew he was right—on Halloween, especially in a place like where we were, you were safer in a costume.

"From then on in, we were in No Man's Land. Neither one of us had any idea how far we had to go to get to The Backs, or what it would look like once we got there. Once I set foot on that wagon-track I knew for sure The Backs wasn't anything like the way I thought. It was a lot more primitive than a bunch of houses in the woods. Maybe they didn't even have houses! Maybe they lived in caves!

"Naturally, after I got that blamed costume over my head, I couldn't see for a while. Dee kept hissing at me to hurry up, and I kept cussing him out. Finally I bunched up a couple handfuls of the sheet right under my chin and held it against my neck, and that way I could see pretty well and walk without tripping all over myself. All I had to do was follow Dee, and that was easy. He was only a couple of inches in front of me, and even through one eyehole, I could see that silvery sheet moving along.

"Things moved in the woods, and once in a while an owl hooted. To tell you the truth, I never did like being out in the woods at night. Even back then, give me a nice warm bar-room instead, and I'd be happy. Only animal I ever liked was a cat, because a cat is soft to the touch, and it'll fall asleep on your lap. But this was even worse than usual, because of Halloween, and even before we got to The Backs, I wasn't sure if what I heard moving around in the woods was just a possum or a fox or something a lot worse, something with funny eyes and long teeth that liked the taste of little boys. Maybe Eddie Grimes was out there, looking for whatever kind of treat Eddie Grimes liked on Halloween night. Once I thought of that, I got so close to Dee Sparks I could smell him right through his sheet.

"You know what Dee Sparks smelled like? Like sweat, and a little bit like the soap the preacher made him use on his hands and face before dinner, but really like a fire in a junction box. A sharp, kind of bitter smell. That's how excited he was.

"After a while we were going uphill, and then we got to the top of the rise, and a breeze pressed my sheet against my legs. We started going downhill, and over Dee's electrical fire, I could smell wood smoke. And something else I couldn't name. Dee stopped moving so sudden, I bumped into him. I asked him what he could see. Nothing but the woods, he said, but we're getting there. People are up ahead somewhere. And they got a still. We got to be real quiet from here on out, he told me, as if he had to, and to let him know I understood I pulled him off the path into the woods.

"Well, I thought, at least I know what Dr. Garland was after.

"Dee and I went snaking through the trees—me holding that blamed sheet under my chin so I could see out of one eye, at least, and walk without falling down. I was glad for that big fat pad of pine needles on the ground. An elephant could have walked over that stuff as quiet as a beetle. We went along a little further, and it got so I could smell all kinds of stuff—burned sugar, crushed juniper berries, tobacco juice, grease. And after Dee and I moved a little bit along, I heard voices, and that was enough for me. Those voices sounded angry.

"I yanked at Dee's sheet and squatted down—I wasn't going any farther without taking a good look. He slipped down beside me. I pushed the wad of material under my chin up over my face, grabbed another handful, and yanked that up, too, to look out under the bottom of the sheet. Once I could actually *see* where we were, I almost passed out. Twenty feet away through the trees, a kerosene lantern lit up the grease-paper window cut into the back of a little wooden shack, and a big raggedy guy carrying another kerosene lantern came stepping out of a door we couldn't see and stumbled toward a shed. On the other side of the building I could see the yellow square of a window in another shack, and past that, another one, a sliver of yellow shining out through the trees. Dee was crouched next to me, and when I turned to look at him, I could see another chink of yellow light from some way off in the woods over that way. Whether he knew it not, he'd just about walked us straight into the middle of The Backs.

"He whispered for me to cover my face. I shook my head. Both of us watched the big guy stagger toward the shed. Somewhere in front of us, a woman screeched, and I almost dumped a load in my pants. Dee stuck his hand out from under his sheet and held it out, as if I needed *him* to tell me to be quiet. The woman screeched again, and the big guy sort of swayed back and forth. The light from the lantern swung around in big circles. I saw that the woods were full of little paths that ran between the shacks. The light hit the shack, and it wasn't even wood, but tar paper. The woman laughed or maybe sobbed. Whoever was inside the shack shouted, and the raggedy guy wobbled toward the shed again. He was so drunk he couldn't even walk straight. When he got to the shed, he set down the lantern and bent to get in.

"Dee put his mouth up to my ear and whispered, *Cover up—you don't want these people to see who you are. Rip the eyeholes, if you can't see good enough.*

"I didn't want anyone in The Backs to see my face. I let the costume drop down over me again, and stuck my fingers in the nearest eyehole and pulled. Every living thing for about a mile around must have heard that cloth ripping. The big guy came out of the shed like someone pulled him out on a string, yanked the lantern up off the ground, and held it in our direction. Then we could see his face, and it was Eddie Grimes. You wouldn't want to run into Eddie Grimes anywhere, but The Backs was the last place you'd want to come across him. I was afraid he was going to start looking for us, but that woman started making stuck pig noises, and the man in the shack yelled something, and Grimes ducked back into the shed and came out with a jug. He lumbered back toward the shack and disappeared around the front of it. Dee and I could hear him arguing with the man inside.

"I jerked my thumb toward Meridian Road, but Dee shook his head. I whispered, *Didn't you already see Eddie Grimes, and isn't that enough for you?* He shook his head again. His eyes were gleaming behind that sheet. So what do you want, I asked, and he said, *I want to see that girl. We don't even know where she is,* I whispered, and Dee said, *All we got to do is follow her sound.*

"Dee and I sat and listened for a while. Every now and then, she let out a sort of whoop, and then she'd sort of cry, and after that she might say a word or two that sounded almost ordinary before she got going again on crying or laughing, the two all mixed up together. Sometimes we could hear other noises coming from the shacks, and none of them sounded happy. People were grumbling and arguing or just plain talking to themselves, but at least they sounded normal. That lady, she sounded like *Halloween*—like something that came up out of a grave.

"Probably you're thinking what I was hearing was sex—that I was too young to know how much noise ladies make when they're having fun. Well, maybe I was only eleven, but I grew up in Darktown, not

Miller's Hill, and our walls were none too thick. What was going on with this lady didn't have anything to do with fun. The strange thing is, Dee didn't know that—he thought just what you were thinking. He wanted to see this lady getting humped. Maybe he even thought he could sneak in and get some for himself, I don't know. The main thing is, he thought he was listening to some wild sex, and he wanted to get close enough to see it. Well, I thought, his daddy was a preacher, and maybe preachers didn't do it once they got kids. And Dee didn't have an older brother like mine, who sneaked girls into the house whenever he thought he wouldn't get caught.

"He started sliding sideways through the woods, and I had to follow him. I'd seen enough of The Backs to last me the rest of my life, but I couldn't run off and leave Dee behind. And at least he was going at it the right way, circling around the shacks sideways, instead of trying to sneak straight through them. I started off after him. At least I could see a little better ever since I ripped at my eyehole, but I still had to hold my blasted costume bunched up under my chin, and if I moved my head or my hand the wrong way, the hole moved away from my eye and I couldn't see anything at all.

"So naturally, the first thing that happened was that I lost sight of Dee Sparks. My foot came down in a hole and I stumbled ahead for a few steps, completely blind, and then I hit a tree. I just came to a halt, sure that Eddie Grimes and a few other murderers were about to jump on me. For a couple of seconds I stood as still as a wooden Indian, too scared to move. When I didn't hear anything, I hauled at my costume until I could see out of it. No murderers were coming toward me from the shack beside the still. Eddie Grimes was saying *You don't understand* over and over, like he was so drunk that one phrase got stuck in his head, and he couldn't say or hear anything else. That woman yipped, like an animal noise, not a human one—like a fox barking. I sidled up next to the tree I'd run into and looked around for Dee. All I could see was dark trees and that one yellow window I'd seen before. To hell with Dee Sparks, I said to myself, and pulled the costume off over my head. I could see better, but there wasn't any glimmer of white over that way. He'd gone so far ahead of me I couldn't even see him.

"So I had to catch up with him, didn't I? I knew where he was going—the woman's noises were coming from the shack way up there in the woods—and I knew he was going to sneak around the outside of the shacks. In a couple of seconds, after he noticed I wasn't there, he was going to stop and wait for me. Makes sense, doesn't it? All I had to do was keep going toward that shack off to the side until I ran into him. I shoved my costume inside my shirt, and then I did something else—set my bag of candy down next to the tree. I'd clean forgotten about it ever since I saw Eddie Grimes' face, and if I had to run, I'd go faster without holding onto a lot of apples and chunks of taffy.

"About a minute later, I came out into the open between two big old chinaberry trees. There was a patch of grass between me and the next stand of trees. The woman made a gargling sound that ended in one of those fox-yips, and I looked up in that direction and saw that the clearing extended in a straight line up and down, like a path. Stars shone out of the patch of darkness between the two parts of the woods. And when I started to walk across it, I felt a grassy hump between two beaten tracks. The path into The Backs off Meridian Road curved around somewhere up ahead and wound back down through the shacks before it came to a dead end. It had to come to a dead end, because it sure didn't join back up with Meridian Road.

"And this was how I'd managed to lose sight of Dee Sparks. Instead of avoiding the path and working his way north through the woods, he'd just taken the easiest way toward the woman's shack. Hell, I'd had to pull him off the path in the first place! By the time I got out of my sheet, he was probably way up there, out in the open for anyone to see and too excited to notice that he was all by himself. What I had to do was what I'd been trying to do all along, save his ass from anybody who might see him.

"As soon as I started going as soft as I could up the path, I saw that saving Dee Sparks' ass might be a tougher job than I thought—maybe I couldn't even save my own. When I first took off my costume, I'd seen lights from three or four shacks. I thought that's what The Backs was—three or four shacks. But after I started up the path, I saw a low square shape standing between two trees at the edge of the woods and realized that it was another shack. Whoever was inside had extinguished his kerosene lamp, or maybe wasn't home. About twenty-thirty feet on, there was another shack, all dark, and the only reason I noticed that one was, I heard voices coming from it, a man and a woman, both of them sounding drunk and slowed-down. Deeper in the woods past that one, another grease-paper window gleamed through the trees like a firefly. There were shacks all over the woods. As soon as I realized that Dee and I might not be the only people walking through The Backs on

Halloween night, I bent down low to the ground and damn near slowed to a standstill. The only thing Dee had going for him, I thought, was good night vision—at least he might spot someone before they spotted him.

"A noise came from one of those shacks, and I stopped cold, with my heart pounding away like a bass drum. Then a big voice yelled out, *Who's that?*, and I just lay down in the track and tried to disappear. *Who's there?* Here I was calling Dee a fool, and I was making more noise than he did. I heard that man walk outside his door, and my heart pretty near exploded. Then the woman moaned up ahead, and the man who'd heard me swore to himself and went back inside. I just lay there in the dirt for a while. The woman moaned again, and this time it sounded scarier than ever, because it had a kind of a chuckle in it. She was crazy. Or she was a witch, and if she was having sex, it was with the Devil. That was enough to make me start crawling along, and I kept on crawling until I was long past the shack where the man had heard me. Finally I got up on my feet again, thinking that if I didn't see Dee Sparks real soon, I was going to sneak back to Meridian Road by myself. If Dee Sparks wanted to see a witch in bed with the Devil, he could do it without me.

"And then I thought I was a fool not to ditch Dee, because hadn't he ditched me? After all this time, he must have noticed that I wasn't with him any more. Did he come back and look for me? The hell he did.

"And right then I would have gone back home, but for two things. The first was that I heard that woman make another sound—a sound that was hardly human, but wasn't made by any animal. It wasn't even loud. And it sure as hell wasn't any witch in bed with the Devil. It made me want to throw up. That woman was being *hurt*. She wasn't just getting beat up—I knew what that sounded like—she was being hurt bad enough to drive her crazy, bad enough to kill her. Because you couldn't live through being hurt bad enough to make that sound. I was in The Backs, sure enough, and the place was even worse than it was supposed to be. Someone was killing a woman, everybody could hear it, and all that happened was that Eddie Grimes fetched another jug back from the still. I froze. When I could move, I pulled my ghost costume out from inside my shirt, because Dee was right, and for certain I didn't want anybody seeing my face out there on *this* night. And then the second thing happened. While I was pulling the sheet over my head, I saw something pale lying in the grass a couple of feet back toward the woods I'd come out of, and when I looked at it, it turned into Dee Sparks' Halloween bag.

"I went up to the bag and touched it to make sure about what it was. I'd found Dee's bag, all right. And it was empty. Flat. He had stuffed the content into his pockets and left the bag behind. What that meant was, I couldn't turn around and leave him—because he hadn't left me after all. He waited for me until he couldn't stand it any more, and then he emptied his bag and left it behind as a sign. He was counting on me to see in the dark as well as he could. But I wouldn't have seen it at all if that woman hadn't stopped me cold.

"The top of the bag was pointing north, so Dee was still heading toward the woman's shack. I looked up that way, and all I could see was a solid wall of darkness underneath a lighter darkness filled with stars. For about a second, I realized, I had felt pure relief. Dee had ditched me, so I could ditch him and go home. Now I was stuck with Dee all over again.

"About twenty feet ahead, another surprise jumped up at me out of darkness. Something that looked like a little tiny shack began to take shape, and I got down on my hands and knees to crawl toward the path when I saw a long silver gleam along the top of the thing. That meant it had to be metal—tar paper might have a lot of uses, but it never yet reflected starlight. Once I realized that the thing in front of me was metal, I remembered its shape and realized it was a car. You wouldn't think you'd come across a car in a down-and-out rathole like The Backs, would you? People like that, they don't even own two shirts, so how do they come by cars? Then I remembered Dr. Garland driving away speeding down Meridian Road, and I thought *You don't have to live in The Backs to drive there.* Someone could turn up onto the path, drive around the loop, pull his car off onto the grass, and no one would ever see it or know that he was there.

"And this made me feel funny. The car probably belonged to someone I knew. Our band played dances and parties all over the county and everywhere in Woodland, and I'd probably seen every single person in town, and they'd seen me, too, and knew me by name. I walked closer to the car to see if I recognized it, but it was just an old black Model T. There must have been twenty cars just like it in Woodland. Whites and coloreds, the few coloreds that owned cars, both had them. And when I got right up beside the Model T, I saw what Dee had left for me on the hood—an apple.

"About twenty feet further along, there was an apple on top of a big old stone. He was putting those apples where I couldn't help but see them. The third one was on top of a post at the edge of the woods, and it was so pale it looked almost white. Next to the post one of those paths running all through The Backs led back into the woods. If it hadn't been for that apple, I would have gone right past it.

"At least I didn't have to worry so much about being making noise once I got back into the woods. Must have been six inches of pine needles and fallen leaves underfoot, and I walked so quiet I could have been floating—I've worn crepe soles ever since then, and for the same reason. You walk *soft*. But I was still plenty scared—back in the woods there was a lot less light, and I'd have to step on an apple to see it. All I wanted was to find Dee and persuade him to leave with me.

"For a while, all I did was keep moving between the trees and try to make sure I wasn't coming up on a shack. Every now and then, a faint, slurry voice came from somewhere off in the woods, but I didn't let it spook me. Then, way up ahead, I saw Dee Sparks. The path didn't go in a straight line, it kind of angled back and forth, so I didn't have a good clear look at him, but I got a flash of that silvery-looking sheet way off through the trees. If I sped up I could get to him before he did anything stupid. I pulled my costume up a little further toward my neck and started to jog.

"The path started dipping *downhill*. I couldn't figure it out. Dee was in a straight line ahead of me, and as soon as I followed the path downhill a little bit, I lost sight of him. After a couple more steps, I stopped. The path got a lot steeper. If I kept running, I'd go ass over teakettle. The woman made another terrible sound, and it seemed to come from everywhere at once. Like everything around me had been *hurt*. I damn near came unglued. Seemed like everything was *dying*. That Halloween stuff about horrible creatures wasn't any story, man, it was the way things really were—you couldn't know anything, you couldn't trust anything, and you were surrounded by *death*. I almost fell down and cried like a baby boy. I was lost. I didn't think I'd ever get back home.

"Then the worst thing of all happened.

"I heard her die. It was just a little noise, more like a sigh than anything, but that sigh came from everywhere and went straight into my ear. A soft sound can be loud, too, you know, be the loudest thing you ever heard. That sigh about lifted me up off the ground, about blew my head apart.

"I stumbled down the path, trying to wipe my eyes with my costume, and all of a sudden I heard men's voices from off to my left. Someone was saying a word I couldn't understand over and over, and someone else was telling him to shut up. Then, behind me, I heard running—heavy running, a man. I took off, and right away my feet got tangled up in the sheet and I was rolling downhill, hitting my head on rocks and bouncing off trees and smashing into stuff I didn't have any idea what it was. *Biff bop bang slam smash clang crash ding dong.* I hit something big and solid and wound up half-covered in water. Took me a long time to get upright, twisted up in that sheet the way I was. My ears buzzed and I saw stars—yellow and blue and red ones, not real ones. When I tried to sit up, the blasted sheet pulled me back down, so I got a faceful of cold water. I scrambled around like a fox in a trap, and when I finally got so I was sitting up, I saw a slash of real sky out the corner of one eye, and I got my hands free and ripped that hole in the sheet wide enough for my whole head to fit through it.

"I was sitting in a little stream next to a fallen tree. The tree was what had stopped me. My whole body hurt like the dickens. I had no idea where I was. Wasn't even sure I could stand up. Got my hands on top of the fallen tree and pushed myself up with my legs—blasted sheet ripped in half, and my knees almost bent back the wrong way, but I got up on my feet. And there was Dee Sparks, coming toward me through the woods on the other side of the stream.

"He looked like he didn't feel any better than I did, like he couldn't move in a straight line. His silvery sheet was smearing through the trees. *Dee got hurt, too,* I thought—he looked as if he was in some total panic. The next time I saw the white smear between the trees it was twisting about ten feet off the ground. *No,* I said to myself and closed my eyes. Whatever that thing was, it wasn't Dee. An unbearable feeling, an absolute despair, flowed out from it. I fought against this despair with every weapon I had. I didn't want to know that feeling—I was eleven years old. If that feeling reached me when I was eleven years old, my entire life would be changed, I'd be in a different universe altogether.

"But it did reach me, did it? I could say *no* all I liked, but I couldn't change what had happened. I opened my eyes and the white smear was gone.

That was almost worse—I wanted it to be Dee after all, doing something crazy and reckless, climbing trees, running around like a wild man, trying to give me a big whopping scare. But it wasn't Dee Sparks, and it meant the worst things I'd ever imagine were true. Everything was dying. You couldn't know anything. you couldn't trust anything, we were all lost in the midst of the death that surrounded us.

"Most people will tell you growing up means you stop believing in Halloween things—I'm telling you the reverse. You start to grow up when you understand that the stuff that scares you is part of the air you breathe.

"I stared at the spot where I'd seen that twist of whiteness, I guess trying to go back in time to before I saw Dr. Garland fleeing down Meridian Road. My face looked like his, I thought—because now I knew that you really *could* see a ghost. The heavy footsteps I'd heard before suddenly cut through the buzzing in my head, and after I turned around and saw who was coming at me down the hill, I thought it was probably my own ghost I'd seen.

"Eddie Grimes looked as big as an oak tree, and he had a long knife in one hand. His feet slipped out from under him, and he skidded the last few yards down to the creek, but I didn't even try to run away. Drunk as he was, I'd never get away from him. All I did was back up alongside the fallen tree and watch him slide downhill toward the water. I was so scared I couldn't even talk. Eddie Grimes' shirt was flapping open, and big long scars ran all across his chest and belly. He'd been raised from the dead at least a couple of times since I'd seen him get killed at the dance. He jumped back up on his feet and started coming for me. I opened my mouth, but nothing came out.

"Eddie Grimes took another step toward me, and then he stopped and looked straight at my face. He lowered the knife. A sour stink of sweat and alcohol came off him. All he could do was stare at me. Eddie Grimes knew my face all right, he knew my name, he knew my whole family—even at night, he couldn't mistake me for anyone else. I finally saw that Eddie was actually afraid, like he was the one who'd seen a ghost. The two of us just stood there in the shallow water for a couple more seconds, and then Eddie Grimes pointed his knife at the other side of the creek.

"That was all I needed, baby. My legs unfroze, and I forgot all my aches and pains. Eddie watched me roll over the fallen tree and lowered his knife. I splashed through the water and started moving up the hill, grabbing at weeds and branches to pull me along. My feet were frozen, and my clothes were soaked and muddy, and I was trembling all over.

About half way up the hill, I looked back over my shoulder, but Eddie Grimes was gone. It was like he'd never been there at all, like he was nothing but the product of a couple of good raps to the noggin.

"Finally, I pulled myself shaking up over the top of the rise, and what did I see about ten feet away through a lot of skinny birch trees but a kid in a sheet facing away from me into the woods, and hopping from foot to foot in a pair of big clumsy shoes? And what was in front of him but a path I could make out from even ten feet away? Obviously, this was where I was supposed to turn up, only in the dark and all I must have missed an apple stuck onto a branch or some blasted thing, and I took that little side trip downhill on my head and wound up throwing a spook into Eddie Grimes.

"As soon as I saw him, I realized I hated Dee Sparks. I wouldn't have tossed him a rope if he was drowning. Without even thinking about it, I bent down and picked up a stone and flung it at him. The stone bounced off a tree, so I bent down and got another one. Dee turned around to find out what made the noise, and the second stone hit him right in the chest, even though it was his head I was aiming at.

"He pulled his sheet up over his face like an Arab and stared at me with his mouth wide open. Then he looked back over his shoulder at the path, as if the real me might come along at any second. I felt like pegging another rock at his stupid face, but instead I marched up to him. He was shaking his head from side to side. *Jim Dawg*, he whispered, *what happened to you?* By way of answer, I hit him a good hard knock on the breastbone. *What's the matter?* he wanted to know. *After you left me, I say, I fell down a hill and ran into Eddie Grimes.*

"That gave him something to think about, all right. Was Grimes coming after me, he wanted to know? Did he see which way I went? Did Grimes see who I was? He was pulling me into the woods while he asked me these dumb-ass questions, and I shoved him away. His sheet flopped back down over his front, and he looked like a little boy. He couldn't figure out why I was mad at him. From his point of view, he'd been pretty clever, and if I got lost, it was my fault. But I wasn't mad at him because I got lost. I wasn't even mad at him because I'd run into Eddie Grimes. It was everything else. Maybe it wasn't even him I was mad at.

"I want to get home without getting killed, I whispered. *Eddie ain't gonna let me go twice.* Then I pretended he wasn't there any more and tried to figure out how to get back to Meridian Road. It seemed to me

that I was still going north when I took that tumble downhill, so when I climbed up the hill on the other side of the creek I was still going north. The wagon-track that Dee and I took into The Backs had to be off to my right. I turned away from Dee and started moving through the woods. I didn't care if he followed me or not. He had nothing to do with me any more, he was on his own. When I heard him coming along after me, I was sorry. I wanted to get away from Dee Sparks. I wanted to get away from everybody.

"I didn't want to be around anybody who was supposed to be my friend. I'd rather have had Eddie Grimes following me than Dee Sparks.

"Then I stopped moving, because through the trees I could see one of those grease-paper windows glowing up ahead of me. That yellow light looked evil as the Devil's eye—everything in The Backs was evil, poisoned, even the trees, even the air. The terrible expression on Dr. Garland's face and the white smudge in the air seemed like the same thing—they were what I didn't want to know.

"Dee shoved me from behind, and if I hadn't felt so sick inside I would have turned around and punched him. Instead, I looked over my shoulder and saw him nodding toward where the side of the shack would be. He wanted to get closer! For a second, he seemed as crazy as everything else out there, and then I got it: I was all turned around, and instead of heading back to the main path, I'd been taking us toward the woman's shack. That was why Dee was following me.

"I shook my head. No, I wasn't going to sneak up to that place. Whatever was inside there was something I didn't have to know about. It had too much power—it turned Eddie Grimes around, and that was enough for me. Dee knew I wasn't fooling. He went around me and started creeping toward the shack.

"And damndest thing, I watched him slipping through the trees for a second, and started following him. If he could go up there, so could I. If I didn't exactly look at whatever was in there myself, I could watch Dee look at it. That would tell me most of what I had to know. And anyways, probably Dee wouldn't see anything anyhow, unless the front door was hanging open, and that didn't seem too likely to me. He wouldn't see anything, and I wouldn't either, and we could both go home.

"The door of the shack opened up, and a man walked outside. Dee and I freeze, and I mean *freeze*. We're about twenty feet away, on the side of this shack, and if the man looked sideways, he'd see our sheets. There were a lot of trees between us and him, and I couldn't get a very good look at him, but one thing about him made the whole situation a lot more serious. This man was white, and he was wearing good clothes—I couldn't see his face, but I could see his rolled up sleeves, and his suit jacket slung over one arm, and some kind of wrapped-up bundle he was holding in his hands. All this took about a second. The white man started carrying his bundle straight through the woods, and in another two seconds he was out of sight.

"Dee was a little closer than I was, and I think his sight line was a little clearer than mine. On top of that, he saw better at night than I did. Dee didn't get around like me, but he might have recognized the man we'd seen, and that would be pure trouble. Some rich white man, killing a girl out in The Backs? And us two boys close enough to see him? Do you know what would have happened to us? There wouldn't be enough left of either one of us to make a decent smudge.

"Dee turned around to face me, and I could see his eyes behind his costume, but I couldn't tell what he was thinking. He just stood there, looking at me. In a little bit, just when I was about to explode, we heard a car starting up off to our left. I whispered at Dee if he saw who that was. *Nobody*, Dee said. Now, what the hell did that mean? Nobody? You could say Santa Claus, you could say J. Edgar *Hoover*, it'd be a better answer than Nobody. The Model T's headlights shone through the trees when the car swung around the top of the path and started going toward Meridian Road. *Nobody I ever saw before*, Dee said. When the headlights cut through the trees, both of us ducked out of sight. Actually, we were so far from the path, we had nothing to worry about. I could barely see the car when it went past, and I couldn't see the driver at all.

"We stood up. Over Dee's shoulder I could see the side of the shack where the white man had been. Lamplight flickered on the ground in front of the open door. The last thing in the world I wanted to do was to go inside that place—I didn't even want to walk around to the front and look in the door. Dee stepped back from me and jerked his head toward the shack. I knew it was going to be just like before. I'd say no, he'd say yes, and then I'd follow him wherever he thought he had to go. I felt the same way I did when I saw that white smear in the woods—hopeless, lost in the midst of death. *You go, if you have to*, I whispered to him, *it's what you wanted to do all along*. He didn't move, and I saw that he wasn't too sure about what he wanted any more.

"Everything was different now, because the white man made it different. Once a white man walked out that door, it was like raising the stakes in a poker game. But Dee had been working toward that one shack ever since we got into The Backs, and he was still curious as a cat about it. He turned away from me and started moving sideways in a straight line, so he'd be able to peek inside the door from a safe distance.

"After he got about half way to the front, he looked back and waved me on, like this was still some great adventure he wanted me to share. He was afraid to be on his own, that was all. When he realized I was going to stay put, he bent down and moved real slow past the side. He still couldn't see more than a sliver of the inside of the shack, and he moved ahead another little ways. By then, I figured, he should have been able to see about half of the inside of the shack. He hunkered down inside his sheet, staring in the direction of the open door. And there he stayed.

"I took it for about half a minute, and then I couldn't any more. I was sick enough to die and angry enough to explode, both at the same time. How long could Dee Sparks look at a dead whore? Wouldn't a couple of seconds be enough? Dee was acting like he was watching a goddamn Hopalong Cassidy movie. An owl screeched, and some man in another shack said *Now that's over*, and someone else shushed him. If Dee heard, he paid it no mind. I started along toward him, and I don't think he noticed me, either. He didn't look up until I was past the front of the shack, and had already seen the door hanging open, and the lamplight spilling over the plank floor and onto the grass outside.

"I took another step, and Dee's head snapped around. He tried to stop me by holding out his hand. All that did was make me mad. Who was Dee Sparks to tell me what I couldn't see? All he did was leave me alone in the woods with a trail of apples, and he didn't even do that right. When I kept on coming, Dee started waving both hands at me, looking back and forth between me and the inside of the shack. Like something was happening in there that I couldn't be allowed to see. I didn't stop, and Dee got up on his feet and skittered toward me.

"*We gotta get out of here*, he whispered. He was close enough so I could smell that electrical stink. I stepped to his side, and he grabbed my arm. I yanked my arm out of his grip and went forward a little ways and looked through the door of the shack.

"A bed was shoved up against the far wall, and a woman lay naked on the bed. There was blood all over her legs, and blood all over the sheets, and big puddles of blood on the floor. A woman in a raggedy robe, hair stuck out all over her head, squatted beside the bed, holding the other woman's hand. She was a colored woman—a Backs woman—but the other one, the one on the bed, was white. Probably she was pretty, when she was alive. All I could see was white skin and blood, and I near fainted.

"This wasn't some white-trash woman who lived out in The Backs—she was brought there, and the man who brought her had killed her. More trouble was coming down than I could imagine, trouble enough to kill lots of our people. And if Dee and I said a word about the white man we'd seen, the trouble would come right straight down on us.

"I must have made some kind of noise, because the woman next to the bed turned halfways around and looked at me. There wasn't any doubt about it—she saw me. All she saw of Dee was a dirty white sheet, but she saw my face, and she knew who I was. I knew her, too, and she wasn't any Backs woman. She lived down the street from us. Her name was Mary Randolph, and she was the one who came up to Eddie Grimes after he got shot to death and brought him back to life. Mary Randolph followed my dad's band, and when we played roadhouses or colored dance halls, she'd be likely to turn up. A couple of times she told me I played good drums—I was a drummer back then, you know, switched to saxophone when I turned twelve. Mary Randolph just looked at me, her hair stuck out straight all over her head like she was already inside a whirlwind of trouble. No expression on her face except that look you get when your mind is going a mile a minute and your body can't move at all. She didn't even look surprised. She almost looked like she *wasn't* surprised, like she was expecting to see me. As bad as I'd felt that night, this was the worst of all. I liked to have died. I'd have disappeared down an anthill, if I could. I didn't know what I had done—just be there, I guess—but I'd never be able to undo it.

"I pulled at Dee's sheet, and he tore off down the side of the shack like he'd been waiting for a signal. Mary Randolph stared into my eyes, and it felt like I had to pull myself away—I couldn't just turn my head, I had to *disconnect*. And when I did, I could still feel her staring at me. Somehow I made myself go down past the side of the shack, but I could still see Mary Randolph inside there, looking out at the place where I'd been.

"If Dee said anything at all when I caught up with him, I'd have knocked his teeth down his throat, but he just moved fast and quiet through the trees, seeing the best way to go, and I followed after. I felt like I'd been kicked by a horse. When we got on the path, we didn't bother trying to sneak down through the woods on the other side, we fit out and ran as hard as we could—like wild dogs were after us. And after we got onto Meridian Road, we ran toward town until we couldn't run any more.

"Dee clamped his hand over his side and staggered forward a little bit. Then he stopped and ripped off his costume and lay down by the side of the road, breathing hard. I was leaning forward with hands on my knees, as winded as he was. When I could breathe again, I started walking down the road. Dee picked himself up and got next to me and walked along, looking at my face and then looking away, and then looking back at my face again.

"*So?* I said.

"*I know that lady*, Dee said.

"Hell, that was no news. Of course he knew Mary Randolph—she was his neighbour, too. I didn't bother to answer, I just grunted at him. Then I reminded him that Mary hadn't seen his face, only mine.

"*Not* Mary, he said. *The other one.*

"He knew the dead white woman's name? That made everything worse. A lady like that shouldn't be in Dee Sparks' world, especially if she's going to wind up dead in The Backs. I wondered who was going to get lynched, and how many.

"Then Dee said that I knew her, too. I stopped walking and looked him straight in the face.

"*Miss Abbey Montgomery*, he said. *She brings clothes and food down to our church, Thanksgiving and Christmas.*

"He was right—I wasn't sure if I'd ever heard her name, but I'd seen her once or twice, bringing baskets of ham and chicken and boxes of clothes to Dee's father's church. She was about twenty years old, I guess, so pretty she made you smile just to look at. From a rich family in a big house right at the top of Miller's Hill. Some man didn't think a girl like that should have any associations with colored people, I guess, and decided to express his opinion about as strong as possible. Which meant that we were going to take the blame for what happened to her, and the next time we saw white sheets, they wouldn't be Halloween costumes.

"*He sure took a long time to kill her*, I said.

"And Dee said, *She ain't dead.*

"So I asked him, What the hell did he mean by that? I saw the girl. I saw the blood. Did he think she was going to get up and walk around?

Or maybe Mary Randolph was going to tell her that magic word and bring her back to life?

"*You can think that if you want to*, Dee said. *But Abbey Montgomery ain't dead.*

"I almost told him I'd seen her ghost, but he didn't deserve to hear about it. The fool couldn't even see what was right in front of his eyes. I couldn't expect him to understand what happened to me when I saw that miserable . . . that *thing*. He was rushing on ahead of me anyhow, like I'd suddenly embarrassed him or something. That was fine with me. I felt the exact same way. I said, *I guess you know neither one of us can ever talk about this*, and he said, *I guess you know it, too*, and that was the last thing we said to each other that night. All the way down Meridian Road Dee Sparks kept his eyes straight ahead and his mouth shut. When we got to the field, he turned toward me like he had something to say, and I waited for it, but he faced forward again and ran away. just ran. I watched him disappear past the general store, and then I walked home by myself.

"My mom gave me hell for getting my clothes all wet and dirty, and my brothers laughed at me and wanted to know who beat me up and stole my candy. As soon as I could, I went to bed, pulled the covers up over my head, and closed my eyes. A little while later, my mom came in and asked if I was all right. Did I get into a fight with that Dee Sparks? Dee Sparks was born to hang, that was what she thought, and I ought to have a better class of friends. *I'm tired of playing those drums, Momma*, I said, *I want to play the saxophone instead*. She looked at me surprised, but said she'd talk about with Daddy, and that it might work out.

"For the next couple days, I waited for the bomb to go off. On the Friday, I went to school, but couldn't concentrate for beans. Dee Sparks and I didn't even nod at each other in the hallways—just walked by like the other guy was invisible. On the weekend I said I felt sick and stayed in bed, wondering when that whirlwind of trouble would come down. I wondered if Eddie Grimes would talk about seeing me—once they found the body, they'd get around to Eddie Grimes real quick.

"But nothing happened that weekend, and nothing happened all the next week. I thought Mary Randolph must have hid the white girl in a grave out in The Backs. But how long could a girl from one of those rich families go missing without investigations and search parties? And, on top of that, what was Mary Randolph doing there in the first place? She liked to have a good time, but she wasn't one of those wild girls with a razor under her skirt—she went to church every Sunday, was good to people, nice to kids. Maybe she went out to comfort that poor girl, but how did she know she'd be there in the first place? Misses Abbey Montgomerys from the hill didn't share their plans with Mary Randolphs from Darktown. I couldn't forget the way she looked at me, but I couldn't understand it, either. The more I thought about that look, the more it was like Mary Randolph was saying something to me, but what? *Are you ready for this? Do you understand this? Do you know how careful you must be?*

"My father said I could start learning the C-melody sax, and when I was ready to play it in public, my little brother wanted to take over the drums. Seems he always wanted to play drums, and in fact, he's been a drummer ever since, a good one. So I worked out how to play my little sax, I went to school and came straight home after, and everything went on like normal, except Dee Sparks and I weren't friends any more. If the police were searching for a missing rich girl, I didn't hear anything about it.

"Then one Saturday I was walking down our street to go the general store, and Mary Randolph came through her front door just as I got to her house. When she saw me, she stopped moving real sudden, with one hand still on the side of the door. I was so surprised to see her that I was in a kind of slow-motion, and I must have stared at her. She gave me a look like an X-ray, a look that searched around down inside me. I don't know what she saw, but her face relaxed, and she took her hand off the door and let it close behind her, and she wasn't looking inside me any more. *Miss Randolph*, I said, and she told me she was looking forward to hearing our band play at a Beergarden dance in a couple of weeks. I told her I was going to be playing the saxophone at that dance, and she said something about that, and all the time it was like we were having two conversations, the top one about me and the band, and the one underneath about her and the murdered white girl in The Backs. It made me so nervous, my words got all mixed up. Finally she said *You make sure you say hello to your daddy from me, now*, and I got away.

"After I passed her house, Mary Randolph started walking down the street behind me. I could feel her watching me, and I started to sweat. Mary Randolph was a total mystery to me. She was a nice lady, but probably she buried that girl's body. I didn't know but that she was going to come and kill me, one day. And then I remembered her kneeling down beside Eddie Grimes at the roadhouse. She had been *dancing* with Eddie Grimes, who was in jail more often than he was out. I wondered if you could be a respectable lady and still know Eddie Grimes well enough to dance with him. And how did she bring him back to life? Or was that what happened at all? Hearing that lady walk along behind me made me so uptight, I crossed to the other side of the street.

"A couple days after that, when I was beginning to think that the trouble was never going to happen after all, it came down. We heard police cars coming down the street right when we were finishing dinner. I thought they were coming for me, and I almost lost my chicken and rice. The sirens went right past our house, and then more sirens came toward us from other directions—the old klaxons they had in those days. It sounded like every cop in the state was rushing into Darktown. This was bad, bad news. Someone was going to wind up dead, that was certain. No way all those police were going to come into our part of town, make all that commotion, and leave without killing at least one man. That's the truth. You just had to pray that the man they killed wasn't you or anyone in your family. My daddy turned off the lamps, and we went to the window to watch the cars go by. Two of them were state police. When it was safe, Daddy went outside to see where all the trouble was headed. After he came back in, he said it looked like the police were going toward Eddie Grimes' place. We wanted to go out and look, but they wouldn't let us, so we went to the back windows that faced toward Grimes' house. Couldn't see anything but a lot of cars and police standing all over the road back there. Sounded like they were knocking down Grimes' house with sledge hammers. Then a whole bunch of cops took off running, and all I could see was the cars spread out across the road. About ten minutes later, we heard lots of gunfire coming from a couple of streets further back. It like to have lasted forever. Like hearing the Battle of the Bulge. My momma started to cry, and so did my little brother. The shooting stopped. The police shouted to each other, and then they came back and got in their cars and went away.

"On the radio the next morning, they said that a known criminal, a Negro man named Edward Grimes, had been killed while trying to escape arrest for the murder of a white woman. The body of Eleanore Monday, missing for three days, had been found in a shallow grave by Woodland police searching near an illegal distillery in the region called The Backs. Miss Monday, the daughter of grocer Albert Monday, had been in poor mental and physical health, and Grimes had apparently taken advantage of her weakness to either abduct or lure her to The Backs, where she had been savagely murdered. That's what it said on the radio—I still remember the words. *In poor mental and physical health. Savagely murdered.*

"When the paper finally came, there on the front page was a picture of Eleanore Monday, a girl with dark hair and a big nose. She didn't look anything like the dead woman in the shack. She hadn't even disappeared on the right day. Eddie Grimes was never going to be able to explain things, because the police had finally cornered him in the old jute warehouse just off Meridian Road next to the general store. I don't suppose they even bothered trying to arrest him—they weren't interested in *arresting* him. He killed a white girl. They wanted revenge, and they got it.

"After I looked at the paper, I got out of the house and ran between the houses to get a took at the jute warehouse. Turned out a lot of folks had the same idea. A big crowd strung out in a long line in front of the warehouse, and cars were parked all along Meridian Road. Right up in front of the warehouse door was a police car, and a big cop stood in the middle of the big doorway, watching people file by. They were walking past the doorway one by one, acting like they were at some kind of exhibit. Nobody was talking. It was a sight I never saw before in that town, whites and colored all lined up together. On the other side of the warehouse, two groups of men stood alongside the road, one colored and one white, talking so quietly you couldn't hear a word.

"Now I was never one who liked standing in lines, so I figured I'd just dart up there, peek in, and save myself some time. I came around the end of the line and ambled toward the two bunches of men, like I'd already had my look and was just hanging around to enjoy the scene. After I got a little past the warehouse door, I sort of drifted up alongside it. I looked down the row of people, and there was Dee Sparks, just a few yards away from being able to see in. Dee was leaning forward, and when he saw me he almost jumped out of his skin. He looked away as fast as he could. His eyes turned as dead as stones. The cop at the door yelled at me to go to the end of the line. He never would have noticed me at all if Dee hadn't jumped like someone just shot off a firecracker behind him.

"About half way down the line, Mary Randolph was standing behind some of the ladies from the neighborhood. She looked terrible. Her hair stuck out in raggedy clumps, and her skin was ashy, like she hadn't slept in a long time. I sped up a little, hoping she wouldn't notice me, but after I took one more step, Mary Randolph looked down and her eyes hooked into mine. I swear, what was in her eyes almost knocked me down. I couldn't even tell what it was, unless it was pure hate. Hate and pain. With her eyes hooked into mine like that, I couldn't look away. It was like I was seeing that miserable, terrible white smear twisting up between the trees on that night in The Backs. Mary let me go, and I almost fell down all over again.

I got to the end of the line and started moving along regular and slow with everybody else. Mary Randolph stayed in my mind and blanked out everything else. When I got up to the door, I barely took in what was inside the warehouse—a wall full of bulletholes and bloodstains all over the place, big slick ones and little drizzly ones. All I could think of was the shack and Mary Randolph sitting next to the dead girl, and I was back there all over again.

"Mary Randolph didn't show up at the Beergarden dance, so she didn't hear me play saxophone in public for the first time. I didn't expect her, either, not after the way she looked out at the warehouse. There'd been a lot of news about Eddie Grimes, who they made out to be less civilized than a gorilla, a crazy man who'd murder anyone as long as he could kill all the white women first. The paper had a picture of what they called Grimes' 'lair,' with busted furniture all over the place and holes in the walls, but they never explained that it was the police tore it up and made it look that way.

"The other thing people got suddenly all hot about was The Backs. Seems the place was even worse than everybody thought. Seems white girls besides Eleanore Monday had been taken out there—according to some, there was even white girls living out there, along with a lot of bad coloreds. The place was a nest of vice, Sodom and Gomorrah. Two days before the town council was supposed to discuss the problem, a gang of white men went out there with guns and clubs and torches and burned every shack in The Backs clear down to the ground. While they were there, they didn't see a single soul, white, colored, male, female, damned or saved. Everybody who lived in The Backs had skedaddled. And the funny thing was, long as The Backs had existed right outside of Woodland, no one in Woodland could recollect the name of anyone who had ever lived there. They couldn't even recall the name of anyone who had ever gone there, except for Eddie Grimes. In fact, after the place got burned down, it appeared that it must have been a sin just to say its name, because no one ever mentioned it. You'd think men so fine and moral as to burn down The Backs would be willing to take the credit, but none ever did.

"You could think they must have wanted to get rid of some things out there. Or wanted real bad to forget about things out there. One thing I thought, Dr. Garland and the man I saw leaving that shack had been out there with torches.

"But maybe I didn't know anything at all. Two weeks later, a couple things happened that shook me good.

"The first one happened three nights before Thanksgiving. I was hurrying home, a little bit late. Nobody else on the street, everybody inside either sitting down to dinner or getting ready for it. When I got to Mary Randolph's house, some kind of noise coming from inside stopped me. What I thought was, it sounded exactly like somebody trying to scream while someone else was holding a hand over their mouth. Well, that was plain foolish, wasn't it? How did I know what that would sound like? I moved along a step or two, and then I heard it again. Could be anything, I told myself. Mary Randolph didn't like me too much, anyway. She wouldn't be partial to my knocking on her door. Best thing I could do was get out. Which was what I did. Just went home to supper and forgot about it.

"Until the next day, anyhow, when a friend of Mary's walked in her front door and found her lying dead with her throat cut and a knife in her hand. A cut of fatback, we heard, had boiled away to cinders on her stove. I didn't tell anybody about what I heard the night before. Too scared. I couldn't do anything but wait to see what the police did.

"To the police, it was all real clear. Mary killed herself, plain and simple.

"When our minister went across town to ask why a lady who intended to commit suicide had bothered to start cooking her supper, the chief told him that a female bent on killing herself probably didn't care *what* happened to the food on her stove. Then I suppose Mary Randolph nearly managed to cut her own head off, said the minister. A female in despair possesses a godawful strength, said the chief. And asked, wouldn't she have screamed if she'd been attacked? And added, couldn't it be that maybe this female here had secrets in her life connected to the late savage murderer named Eddie Grimes? We might all be better off if these secrets get buried with your Mary Randolph, said the chief. I'm sure you understand me, Reverend. And yes, the Reverend did understand, he surely did. So Mary Randolph got laid away in the cemetery, and nobody ever said her name again. She was put away out of mind, like The Backs.

"The second thing that shook me up and proved to me that I didn't know anything, that I was no better than a blind dog, happened on Thanksgiving day. My daddy played piano in church, and on special days, we played our instruments along with the gospel songs. I got to church early with the rest of my family, and we practiced with the choir. Afterwards, I went to fooling around outside until the people came, and saw a big car come up into the church parking lot. Must have been the biggest, fanciest car I'd ever seen. Miller's Hill was written all over that vehicle. I couldn't have told you why, but the sight of it made my heart stop. The front door opened, and out stepped a colored man in a fancy gray uniform with a smart cap. He didn't so much as dirty his eyes by looking at me, or at the church, or at anything around him. He stepped around the front of the car and opened the rear door on my side. A young woman was in the passenger seat, and when she got out of the car, the sun fell on her blond hair and the little fur jacket she was wearing. I couldn't see more than the top of her head, her shoulders under the jacket, and her legs. Then she straightened up, and her eyes lighted right on me. She smiled, but I couldn't smile back. I couldn't even begin to move.

"It was Abbey Montgomery, delivering baskets of food to our church, the way she did every Thanksgiving and Christmas. She looked older and thinner than the last time I'd seen her alive—older and thinner, but more than that, like there was no fun at all in her life anymore. She walked to the trunk of the car, and the driver opened it up, leaned in, and brought out a great big basket of food. He took into the church by the back way and came back for another one. Abbey Montgomery just stood still and watched him carry the baskets. She looked—she looked like she was just going through the motions, like going through the motions was all she was ever going to do from now on, and she knew it. Once she smiled at the driver, but the smile was so sad that the driver didn't even try to smile back. When he was done, he closed the trunk and let her into the passenger seat, got behind the wheel, and drove away.

"I was thinking, *Dee Sparks was right, she was alive all the time.* Then I thought, *No, Mary Randolph brought her back, too, like she did Eddie Grimes. But it didn't work right, and only part of her came back.*

"And that's the whole thing, except that Abbey Montgomery didn't deliver food to our church, that Christmas—she was traveling out of the country, with her aunt. And she didn't bring food the next Thanksgiving, either, just sent her driver with the baskets. By that time, we didn't expect her, because we'd already heard that, soon as she got back to town, Abbey Montgomery stopped leaving her house. That girl shut herself up and never came out. I heard from somebody who probably didn't know any more than I did that she eventually got so she wouldn't even leave her room. Five years later, she passed away. Twenty-six years old, and they said she looked to be at least fifty."

4

Hat fell silent, and I sat with my pen ready over the notebook, waiting, for more. When I realized that he had finished, I asked, "What did she die of?"

"Nobody ever told me."

"And nobody ever found who had killed Mary Randolph."

The limpid, colorless eyes momentarily rested on me. "Was she killed?"

"Did you ever become friends with Dee Sparks again? Did you at least talk about it with him?"

"Surely did not. Nothing to talk about."

This was a remarkable statement, considering that for an hour he had done nothing but talk about what had happened to the two of them, but I let it go. Hat was still looking at me with his unreadable eyes. His face had become particularly bland, almost immobile. It was not possible to imagine this man as an active eleven-year-old boy. "Now you heard me out, answer my question," he said.

I couldn't remember the question.

"Did we find what we were looking for?"

Scares—that was what they had been looking for. "I think you found a lot more than that," I said.

He nodded slowly. "That's right. It was more."

Then I asked him some question about his family's band, he lubricated himself with another swallow of gin, and the interview returned to more typical matters. But the experience of listening to him had changed. After I had heard the long, unresolved tale of his Halloween night, everything Hat said seemed to have two separate meanings, the daylight meaning created by sequences of ordinary English words, and another, nighttime meaning, far less determined and knowable. He was like a man discoursing with eerie rationality in the midst of a surreal dream—like a man carrying on an ordinary conversation with one foot placed on solid ground and the other suspended above a bottomless abyss. I focused on the rationality, on the foot placed in the context I understood; the rest was unsettling to the point of being frightening. By six-thirty, when he kindly called me "Miss Rosemary" and opened his door, I felt as if I'd spent several weeks, if not whole months, in his room.

PART THREE

1

Although I did get my M.A. at Columbia, I didn't have enough money to stay on for a Ph.D., so I never became a college professor. I never became a jazz critic, either, or anything else very interesting. For a couple of years after Columbia, I taught English in a high school, until I quit to take the job I have now, which involves a lot of traveling and pays a little bit better than teaching. Maybe even quite a bit better, but that's not saying much, especially when you consider my expenses. I own a nice little house in the Chicago suburbs, my marriage held up against everything life did to it, and my twenty-two year old son, a young man who never once in his life for the purpose of pleasure read a novel, looked at a painting, visited a museum, or listened to anything but the most readily available music, recently announced to his mother and myself that he has decided to become an artist, actual type of art to be determined later, but probably to include aspects of photography, video tape, and the creation of "installations." I take this as proof that he was raised in a manner that left his self-esteem intact.

I no longer provide my life with a perpetual sound track (though my son, who has moved back in with us, does), in part because my income does not permit the purchase of a great many compact discs. (A friend presented me with a CD player on my forty-fifth birthday.) And these days, I'm as interested in classical music as in jazz. Of course, I never go to jazz clubs when I am home. Are there still people, apart from New Yorkers, who patronize jazz nightclubs in their own hometowns? The concept seems faintly retrograde, even somehow illicit. But when I am out on the road, living in airplanes and hotel rooms, I often check the jazz listings in the local papers to see if I can find some way to fill my evenings. Many of the legends of my youth are still out there, in most cases playing at least as well as before. Some months ago, while I was San Francisco, I came across John Hawes' name in this fashion. He was working in a club so close to my hotel that I could walk to it.

His appearance in any club at all was surprising. Hawes had ceased performing jazz in public years before. He had earned a great deal of fame (and undoubtedly, a great deal of money) writing film scores, and in the past decade, he had begun to appear in swallow-tail coat and white tie as a conductor of the standard classical repertoire. I believe he had a permanent post in some city like Seattle, or perhaps Salt Lake City. If he was spending a week playing jazz with a trio in San Francisco, it must have been for the sheer pleasure of it.

I turned up just before the beginning of the first set, and got a table toward the back of the club. Most of the tables were filled—Hawes' celebrity had guaranteed him a good house. Only a few minutes after the announced time of the first set, Hawes emerged through a door at the front of the club and moved toward the piano, followed by his bassist and drummer. He looked like a more successful version of the younger man I had seen in New York, and the only indications of the extra years were his silvergrey hair, still abundant, and a little paunch. His playing, too, seemed essentially unchanged, but I could not hear it in the way I once had. He was still a good pianist—no doubt about that—but he seemed to be skating over the surface of the songs he played, using his wonderful technique and good time merely to decorate their melodies. It was the sort of playing that becomes less impressive the more attention you give it—if you were listening with half an ear, it probably sounded like Art Tatum. I wondered if John Hawes had always had this superficial streak in him, or if he had lost a certain necessary passion during his years away from jazz. Certainly he had not sounded superficial when I had heard him with Hat.

Hawes, too, might have been thinking about his old employer, because in the first set he played "Love Walked In," "Too Marvelous For Words," and "Up Jumped Hat." In the last of these, inner gears seemed to mesh, the rhythm simultaneously relaxed and intensified, and the music turned into real, not imitation, jazz. Hawes looked pleased with himself when he stood up from the piano bench, and half a dozen fans moved to greet him as he stepped off the bandstand. Most of them were carrying old records they wished him to sign.

A few minutes later, I saw Hawes standing by himself at the end of the bar, drinking what appeared to be club soda, in proximity to his musicians but not actually speaking with them. Wondering if his allusions to Hat had been deliberate, I left my table and walked toward the bar. Hawes watched me approach out of the side of his eye, neither encouraging nor discouraging me. When I introduced myself, he smiled nicely and shook my hand and waited for whatever I wanted to say to him.

At first, I made some inane comment about the difference between playing in clubs and conducting in concert halls, and he replied with the non-committal and equally banal agreement that yes, the two experiences were very different.

Then I told him that I had seen him play with Hat all those years ago in New York, and he turned to me with genuine pleasure in his face. "Did you? At that little club on St. Mark's Place? That sure was fun. I guess I must have been thinking about it, because I played some of those songs we used to do."

"That was why I came over," I said. "I guess that was one of the best musical experiences I ever had."

"You and me both." Hawes smiled to himself. "Sometimes, I just couldn't believe what he was doing."

"It showed," I said.

"Well." His eyes slid away from mine. "Great character. Completely otherworldly."

"I saw some of that," I said. "I did that interview with him that turns up now and then, the one in *Downbeat*."

"Oh!" Hawes gave me his first genuinely interested look so far. "Well, that was him, all right."

"Most of it was, anyhow."

"You cheated?" Now he was looking even more interested.

"I had to make it understandable."

"Oh, sure. You couldn't put in all those ding-dings and bells and Bob Crosbys." These had been elements of Hat's private code. Hawes laughed at the memory. "When he wanted to play a blues in G, he'd lean over and say, 'Gs, please.' "

"Did you get to know him at all well, personally?" I asked, thinking that the answer must be that he had not—I didn't think that anyone had ever really known Hat very well.

"Pretty well," Hawes said. "A couple of times, around '54 and '55, he invited me home with him, to his parents' house, I mean. We got to be friends on a Jazz at the Phil tour, and twice when we were in the South, he asked me if I wanted to eat some good home cooking."

"You went to his hometown?"

He nodded. "His parents put me up. They were interesting people. Hat's father, Red, was about the lightest black man I ever saw, and he could have passed for white anywhere, but I don't suppose the thought ever occurred to him."

"Was the family band still going?"

"No, to tell you the truth, I don't think they were getting much work up toward the end of the forties. At the end, they were using a tenor player and a drummer from the high school band. And the church work got more and more demanding for Hat's father."

"His father was a deacon, or something like that?"

He raised his eyebrows. "No, Red was the Baptist minister. The Reverend. He ran that church. I think he even started it."

"Hat told me his father played piano in church, but . . ."

"The Reverend would have made a hell of a blues piano player, if he'd ever left his day job."

"There must have been another Baptist church in the neighborhood," I said, thinking this the only explanation for the presence of two Baptist ministers. But why had Hat not mentioned that his own father, like Dee Sparks's, had been a clergyman?

"Are you kidding? There was barely enough money in that place to keep one of them going." He looked at his watch, nodded at me, and began to move closer to his sidemen.

"Could I ask you one more question?"

"I suppose so," he said, almost impatiently.

"Did Hat strike you as superstitious?"

Hawes grinned. "Oh, he was superstitious, all right. He told me he never worked on Halloween—he didn't even want to go out of his room on Halloween. That's why he left the big band, you know. They were starting a tour on Halloween, and Hat refused to do it. He just quit." He leaned toward me. "I'll tell you another funny thing. I always had the feeling that Hat was terrified of his father—I thought he invited me to Hatchville with him so I could be some kind of buffer between him and his father. Never made any sense to me. Red was a big strong old guy, and I'm pretty sure a long time ago he used to mess around with the ladies, Reverend or not, but I couldn't ever figure out why Hat should be afraid of him. But whenever Red came into the room, Hat shut up. Funny, isn't it?"

I must have looked very perplexed. "Hatchville?"

"Where they lived. Hatchville, Mississippi—not too far from Biloxi."

"But he told me—"

"Hat never gave too many straight answers," Hawes said. "And he didn't let the facts get in the way of a good story. When you come to think of it, why should he? He was Hat."

After the next set, I walked back uphill to my hotel, wondering again about the long story Hat had told me. Had there been any truth in it at all?

2

Three weeks later I found myself released from a meeting at our Midwestern headquarters in downtown Chicago earlier than I had expected, and instead of going to a bar with the other wandering corporate ghosts like myself, made up a story about having to get home for dinner with visiting relatives. I didn't want to admit to my fellow employees, committed like all male business people to aggressive endeavors such as racquetball, drinking, and the pursuit of women, that I intended to visit the library. Short of a trip to Mississippi, a good periodical room offered the most likely means of finding out once and for all how much truth had been in what Hat had told me.

I hadn't forgotten everything I had learned at Columbia—I still knew how to look things up.

In the main library, a boy set me up with a monitor and spools of microfilm representing the complete contents of the daily newspapers from Biloxi and Hatchville, Mississippi, for Hat's tenth and eleventh years. That made three papers, two for Biloxi and one for Hatchville, but all I had to examine were the issues dating from the end of October through the middle of November—I was looking for references to Eddie Grimes, Eleanore Monday, Mary Randolph, Abbey Montgomery, Hat's family, The Backs, and anyone named Sparks.

The Hatchville *Blade*, a gossipy daily printed on peach-colored paper, offered plenty of references to each of these names and places, and the papers from Biloxi contained nearly as many—Biloxi could not conceal the delight, disguised as horror, aroused in its collective soul by the unimaginable events taking place in the smaller, supposedly respectable town ten miles west. Biloxi was riveted, Biloxi was superior, Biloxi was virtually intoxicated with dread and outrage. In Hatchville, the press maintained a persistent optimistic dignity: when wickedness had appeared, justice official and unofficial had dealt with it. Hatchville was shocked but proud (or at least pretended to be proud), and Biloxi all but preened. The *Blade* printed detailed news stories, but the Biloxi papers suggested implications not allowed by Hatchville's version of events. I needed Hatchville to confirm or question Hat's story, but Biloxi gave me at least the beginning of a way to understand it.

A black ex-convict named Edward Grimes had in some fashion persuaded or coerced Eleanore Monday, a retarded young white woman, to accompany him to an area variously described as "a longstanding local disgrace" (the *Blade*) and "a haunt of deepest vice" (Biloxi) and after "the perpetration of the most offensive and brutal deeds upon her person" (the *Blade*) or "acts which the judicious commentator must decline to imagine, much less describe" (Biloxi) murdered her, presumably to ensure her silence, and then buried the body near the "squalid dwelling" where he made and sold illegal liquor. State and local police departments acting in concert had located the body, identified Grimes as the fiend, and, after a search of his house, had tracked him to a warehouse where the murderer was killed in a gun battle. The *Blade* covered half its front page with a photograph of a gaping double door and a bloodstained wall. All Mississippi, both Hatchville and Biloxi declared, now could breathe more easily.

The *Blade* gave the death of Mary Randolph a single paragraph on its back page, the Biloxi papers nothing.

In Hatchville, the raid on The Backs was described as an heroic assault on a dangerous criminal encampment which had somehow come to flourish in a little-noticed section of the countryside. At great risk to themselves, anonymous citizens of Hatchville had descended like the army of the righteous and driven forth the hidden sinners from their dens. Troublemakers, beware! The Biloxi papers, while seeming to endorse the action in Hatchville, actually took another tone altogether. Can it be, they asked, that the Hatchville police had never before noticed the existence of a Sodom and Gomorrah so close to the town line? Did it take the savage murder of a helpless woman to bring it to their attention? Of course Biloxi celebrated the destruction of The Backs—such vileness must be eradicated—but it wondered what else had been destroyed along with the stills and the mean buildings where loose women had plied their trade. Men ever are men, and those who have succumbed to temptation may wish to remove from the face of the earth any evidence of their lapses. Had not the police of Hatchville ever heard the rumor, vague and doubtless baseless, that operations of an illegal nature had been performed in the selfsame Backs? That in an atmosphere of drugs, intoxication, and gambling, the races had mingled there, and that "fast" young women had risked life and honor in search of illicit thrills? Hatchville may have rid itself of a few buildings, but Biloxi was willing to suggest that the problems of its smaller neighbor might not have disappeared with them.

As this campaign of innuendo went on in Biloxi, the *Blade* blandly reported the ongoing events of any smaller American city. Miss Abigail Montgomery sailed with her aunt, Miss Lucinda Bright, from New Orleans to France for an eight-week tour of the continent. The Reverend Jasper Sparks of the Miller's Hill Presbyterian Church delivered a sermon on the subject "Christian Forgiveness." (Just after Thanksgiving, the Reverend Sparks's son, Rodney, was sent off with the blessings and congratulations of all Hatchville to a private academy in Charleston, South Carolina.) There were bake sales, church socials, and costume parties. A saxophone virtuoso named Albert Woodland demonstrated his astonishing wizardry at a well-attended recital presented in Temperance Hall.

Well, I knew the name of at least one person who had attended the recital. If Hat had chosen to disguise the name of his hometown, he had done so by substituting for it a name that represented another sort of home.

But, although I had more ideas about this than before, I still did not know exactly what Hat had seen or done on Halloween night in The Backs. It seemed possible that he had gone there with a white boy of his age, a preacher's son like himself, and had the wits scared out of him by whatever had happened to Abbey Montgomery—and after that night, Abbey herself had been sent out of town, as had Dee Sparks. I couldn't think that a man had murdered the young woman, leaving Mary Randolph to bring her back to life. Surely whatever had happened to Abbey Montgomery had brought Dr. Garland out to The Backs, and what he had witnessed or done there had sent him away screaming. And this event—what had befallen a rich young white woman in the shadiest, most criminal section of a Mississippi county—had led to the slaying of Eddie Grimes and the murder of Mary Randolph. Because they knew what had happened, they had to die.

I understood all this, and Hat had understood it, too. Yet he had introduced needless puzzles, as if embedded in the midst of this unresolved story were something he either wished to conceal or not to know. And concealed it would remain; if Hat did not know it, I never would. He had deliberately obscured even basic but meaningless facts: first Mary Randolph was a witch-woman from The Backs, then she was a respectable church-goer who lived down the street from his family. Whatever had really happened in The Backs on Halloween night was lost for good.

On the *Blade*'s entertainment page for a Saturday in the middle of November I had come across a photograph of Hat's family's band, and when I had reached this hopeless point in my thinking, I spooled back across the pages to look at it again. Hat, his two brothers, his sister, and his parents stood in a straight line, tallest to smallest, in front of what must have been the family car. Hat held a C-melody saxophone, his brothers a trumpet and drumsticks, his sister a clarinet. As the piano player, the Reverend carried nothing at all—nothing except for what came through even a grainy, sixty-year old photograph as a powerful sense of self. Hat's father had been a tall, impressive man, and in the photograph he looked as white as I did. But what was impressive was not the lightness of his skin, or even his striking handsomeness: what impressed was the sense of authority implicit in his posture, his straightforward gaze, even the dictatorial set of his chin. In retrospect, I was not surprised by what John Hawes had told me, for this man could easily be frightening. You would not wish to oppose him, you would not elect to get in his way. Beside him, Hat's mother seemed vague and distracted, as if her husband had robbed her of all certainty. Then I noticed the car, and for the first time realized why it had been included in the photograph. It was a sign of their prosperity, the respectable status they had achieved—the car was as much an advertisement as the photograph. It was, I thought, an old Model T Ford, but I didn't waste any time speculating that it might have been the Model T Hat had seen in The Backs.

And that would be that—the hint of an absurd supposition—except for something I read a few days ago in a book called *Cool Breeze: The Life of Grant Kilbert*.

There are few biographies of any jazz musicians apart from Louis Armstrong and Duke Ellington (though one does now exist of Hat, the title of which was drawn from my interview with him), and I was surprised to see *Cool Breeze* at the B. Dalton in our local mall. Biographies have not yet been written of Art Blakey, Clifford Brown, Ben Webster, Art Tatum, and many others of more musical and historical importance than Kilbert. Yet I should not have been surprised. Kilbert was one of those musicians who attract and maintain a large personal following, and twenty years after his death, almost all of his records have been released on CD, many of them in multi-disc boxed sets. He had been a great, great player, the closest to Hat of all his disciples. Because Kilbert had been one of my early heroes, I bought the book (for thirty-five dollars!) and brought it home.

Like the lives of many jazz musicians, I suppose of artists in general, Kilbert's had been an odd mixture of public fame and private misery. He had committed burglaries, even armed robberies, to feed his persistent heroin addiction; he had spent years in jail; his two marriages had ended in outright hatred; he had managed to betray most of his friends. That this weak, narcissistic louse had found it in himself to create music of real tenderness and beauty was one of art's enigmas, but not actually a surprise. I'd heard and read enough stories about Grant Kilbert to know what kind of man he'd been.

But what I had not known was that Kilbert, to all appearances an American of conventional northern European, perhaps Scandinavian or Anglo-Saxon, stock, had occasionally claimed to be black. (This claim had always been dismissed, apparently, as another indication of Kilbert's mental aberrancy.) At other times, being Kilbert, he had denied ever making this claim.

Neither had I known that the received versions of his birth and upbringing were in question. Unlike Hat, Kilbert had been interviewed dozens of times both in *Downbeat* and in mass market weekly news magazines, invariably to offer the same story of having been born in Hattiesburg, Mississippi, to an unmusical, working-class family (a plumber's family), of knowing virtually from infancy that he was born to make music, of begging for and finally being given a saxophone, of early mastery and the dazzled admiration of his teachers, then of dropping out of school at sixteen and joining the Woody Herman band. After that, almost immediate fame.

Most of this, the Grant Kilbert myth, was undisputed. He had been raised in Hattiesburg by a plumber named Kilbert, he had been a prodigy and high-school dropout, he'd become famous with Woody Herman before he was twenty. Yet he told a few friends, not necessarily those to whom he said he was black, that he'd been adopted by the Kilberts, and that once or twice, in great anger, either the plumber or his wife had told him that he had been born into poverty and disgrace and that he'd better by God be grateful for the opportunities he'd been given. The source of this story was John Hawes, who'd met Kilbert on another long JATP tour, the last he made before leaving the road for film scoring.

"Grant didn't have a lot of friends on that tour," Hawes told the biographer. "Even though he was such a great player, you never knew what he was going to say, and if he was in a bad mood, he was liable to put down some of the older players. He was always respectful around Hat, his whole style was based on Hat's, but Hat could go days without saying anything, and by those days he certainly wasn't making any new friends. Still, he'd let Grant sit next to him on the bus, and nod his head while Grant talked to him, so he must have felt some affection for him. Anyhow, eventually I was about the only guy on the tour that was willing to have a conversation with Grant, and we'd sit up in the bar late at night after the concerts. The way he played, I could forgive him a lot of failings. One of those nights, he said that he'd been adopted, and that not knowing who his real parents were was driving him crazy. He didn't even have a birth certificate. From a hint his mother once gave him, he thought one of his birth parents was black, but when he asked them directly, they always denied it. These were white Mississippians, after all, and if they had wanted a baby so bad that they taken in a child who looked completely white but maybe had a drop or two of black blood in his veins, they weren't going to admit it, even to themselves."

In the midst of so much supposition, here is a fact. Grant Kilbert was exactly eleven years younger than Hat. The jazz encyclopedias give his birth date as November first, which instead of his actual birthday may have been the day he was delivered to the couple in Hattiesburg.

I wonder if Hat saw more than he admitted to me of the man leaving the shack where Abbey Montgomery lay on bloody sheets; I wonder if he had reason to fear his father. I don't know if what I am thinking is correct—I'll never know that—but now, finally, I think I know why Hat never wanted to go out of his room on Halloween nights. The story he told me never left him, but it must have been most fully present on those nights. I think he heard the screams, saw the bleeding girl, and saw Mary Randolph staring at him with displaced pain and rage. I think that in some small closed corner deep within himself, he knew who had been the real object of these feelings, and therefore had to lock himself inside his hotel room and gulp gin until he obliterated the horror of his own thoughts.

Central Park is magic. This isn't a matter of opinion, it's the truth.

GRAND CENTRAL PARK

Delia Sherman

When I was little, I used to wonder why the sidewalk trees had iron fences around them. Even a city kid could see they were pretty weedy looking trees. I wondered what they'd done to be caged up like that, and whether it might be dangerous to get too close to them.

So I was pretty little, okay? Second grade, maybe. It was one of the things my best friend and I used to talk about, like why it's so hard to find a particular city on a map when you don't already know where it is, and why the fourth graders thought Mrs. Lustenburger's name was so hysterically funny.

My best friend's name was (is) Galadriel, which isn't even remotely her fault, and only her mother calls her that anyway. Everyone else calls her Elf.

Anyway. Trees. New York. Have I said I live in New York? I do. In Manhattan, on the West Side, a couple blocks from Central Park.

I've always loved Central Park. I mean, it's the closest to nature I'm likely to get, growing up in Manhattan. It's the closest to nature I want to get, if you must know. There's wild things in it—squirrels and pigeons and like that, and trees and rocks and plants. But they're city wild things, used to living around people. I don't mean they're tame. I mean they're streetwise. Look. How many squished squirrels do you see on the park transverses? How many do you see on any suburban road? I rest my case.

Central Park is magic. This isn't a matter of opinion, it's the truth. When I was just old enough for Mom to let me out of her sight, I had this place I used to play, down by the boat pond, in a little inlet at the foot of a huge cliff. When I was in there, all I could see was the water all shiny and sparkly like a silk dress with sequins and the great gray hulk of the rock behind me and the willow tree bending down over me to trail its green-gold hair in the water. I could hear people splashing and laughing and talking, but I couldn't see them, and there was this fairy who used to come and play with me.

Mom said my fairy friend came from me being an only child and reading too many books, but all I can say is that if I'd made her up, she would have been less bratty. She had long Saran-Wrap wings like a dragonfly, she was teensy, and she couldn't keep still for a second. She'd play princesses or Peter Pan for about two minutes, and then she'd get bored and pull my hair or start teasing me about being a big, galumphy, deaf, blind human being or talking to the willow or the rocks. She couldn't even finish a conversation with a butterfly.

Anyway, I stopped believing in her when I was about eight, or stopped seeing her, anyway. By that time I didn't care because I'd gotten friendly with Elf, who didn't tease me quite as much. She wasn't into fairies, although she did like to read. As we got older, mostly I was grateful she was willing to be my friend. Like, I wasn't exactly Ms. Popularity at school. I sucked at gym and liked English and like that, so the cool kids decided I was a super-geek. Also, I wear glasses and I'm no Kate Moss, if you know what I mean. I could stand to lose a few pounds—none of your business how many. It wasn't safe to be seen having lunch with me, so Elf didn't. As long as she hung with me after school, I didn't really care all that much.

The inlet was our safe place, where we could talk about whether the French teacher hated me personally or was just incredibly mean in general and whether Patty Gregg was really cool, or just thought she was. In the summer, we'd take our shoes off and swing our feet in the water that sighed around the roots of the golden willow.

So one day we were down there, gabbing as usual. This was last year, the fall of eleventh grade, and we were talking about boyfriends. Or at least Elf was talking about her boyfriend and I was nodding sympathetically. I guess my attention wandered, and for some reason I started wondering about my fairy friend. What was her name again? Bubble? Burble? Something like that.

Something tugged really hard on about two hairs at the top of my head, where it *really* hurts, and I yelped and scrubbed at the sore place. "Mosquito," I explained. "So what did he say?"

Oddly enough, Elf had lost interest in what her boyfriend had said. She had this look of intense concentration on her face, like she was listening for her little brother's breathing on the other side of the bedroom door. "Did you hear that?" she whispered.

"What? Hear what?"

"Ssh."

I sshed and listened. Water lapping; the distant creak of oarlocks and New Yorkers laughing and talking and splashing. The wind in the willow leaves whispering, *ssh, ssh*. "I don't hear anything," I said.

"Shut up," Elf snapped. "You missed it. A snapping sound. Over there." Her blue eyes were very big and round.

"You're trying to scare me," I accused her. "You read about that woman getting mugged in the park, and now you're trying to jerk my chain. Thanks, friend."

Elf looked indignant. "As if!" She froze like a dog sighting a pigeon. "There."

I strained my ears. It seemed awfully quiet all of a sudden.

There wasn't even a breeze to stir the willow. Elf breathed, "Omigod. Don't look now, but I think there's a guy over there, watching us."

My face got all prickly and cold, like my body believed her even though my brain didn't. "I swear to God, Elf, if you're lying, I'll totally kill you." I turned around to follow her gaze. "Where? I don't see anything."

"I said, don't *look*," Elf hissed. "He'll know."

"He already *knows*, unless he's a moron. If he's even there. Omigod!"

Suddenly I saw, or thought I saw, a guy with a stocking cap on and a dirty, unshaven face peering around a big rock.

It was strange. One second, it looked like a guy, the next, it was more like someone's windbreaker draped over a bush. But my heart started to beat really fast anyway. There weren't that many ways to get out of that particular little cove if you didn't have a boat.

"See him?" she hissed triumphantly.

"I guess."

"What are we going to do?"

Thinking about it later, I couldn't quite decide whether Elf was really afraid, or whether she was pretending because it was exciting to be afraid, but she sure convinced me. If the guy was on the path, the only way out was up the cliff. I'm not in the best shape *and* I'm scared of heights, but I was even more scared of the man, so up we went.

I remember that climb, but I don't want to talk about it. I thought I was going to die, okay? And I was really, really mad at Elf for putting me though this, like if she hadn't noticed the guy, he wouldn't have been there. I was sweating, and my glasses kept slipping down my nose and . . .

No. I won't talk about it. All you need to know is that Elf got to the top first and squirmed around on her belly to reach down and help me up.

"Hurry up," she panted. "He's behind you. No, don't look"—as if I could even bear to look all that way down—"just hurry."

I was totally winded by the time I got to the top and scrambled to my feet, but Elf didn't give me time to catch my breath. She grabbed my wrist and pulled me to the path, both of us stumbling as much as we were running.

It was about this time I realized that something really weird was going on. Like, the path was empty, and it was two o'clock in the afternoon of a beautiful fall Saturday, when Central Park is so full of people it's like Times Square with trees. And I couldn't run just like you can't run in dreams.

Suddenly, Elf tripped and let go of me. The path shook itself, and she was gone. Poof. Nowhere in sight.

By this time, I'm freaked totally out of my mind. I look around, and there's this guy, hauling himself over the edge of the cliff, stocking cap jammed down over his head, face gray-skinned with dirt, half his teeth missing. I don't know why I didn't scream—usually, it's pitiful how easy it is to make me scream—I just turned around and ran.

Now, remember that there's about fifty million people in the park that day. You'd think I would run into one or two, which would mean safety because muggers don't like witnesses. But no.

So I'm running and he's running, and I can hear him *breathing* but I can't hear his footsteps, and we've been running, like, *forever*, and I don't know where the hell I am, which means I must be in the Ramble, which isn't that near the Boat Pond, but hey, I'm running for my life. And I think he's getting closer and I really want to look, just stop and let him catch me and get it all over with, but I keep running anyway, and suddenly I remember what my fairy's name was (is) and I shriek out, "Bugle! Help me!"

I bet you thought something would happen.

So did I, and when it didn't, I started to cry. Gulping for breath, my glasses all runny with tears, I staggered up a little rise, and I'm in a clear spot with a bench in it and trees all around and a low stone wall in front of another granite cliff, this one going straight down, like, a mile or two.

The guy laughs, low and deep in his throat, and I don't know why because I don't really *want* to, but I turn around and face him.

So this is when it gets *really* weird. Because he's got a snout and really sharp teeth hanging out, and his stocking cap's fallen off, and he has *ears*—gray, leathery ones—and his skin isn't dirty, it's gray, like concrete, and he's impossible, but he's real—a real, like, rat-guy. I give this little *urk* and he opens his jaws, and things get sparkly around the edges.

"Gnaw-bone!" someone says. "Chill!"

I jump and look around everywhere, and there's this amazing girl standing right beside the rat-guy, who has folded up like a Slinky and is making pitiful noises over her boots. The boots are green, and so is her velvet mini and her Lycra top and her fitted leather jacket—all different shades of green, mostly olive and evergreen and moss and like that: dark greens. Browny, earthy greens. So's her hair—browny-green, in long, wild dreads around her shoulders and down her back. And her skin, but that's more brown than green.

She's beautiful, but not like a celebrity or a model or anything. She's way more gorgeous than that. Next to her, Taylor Swift is a complete dog.

"What's up?" she asks the rat-guy. Her voice is incredible, too. I mean, she talks like some wise-ass street kid, but there's leaves under it somehow. Sounds dumb, but that's what it was like.

"Games is up," he says, sounding just as ratty as he looks. "Fun-fun. She saw me. She's mine."

"I hear you," the green girl says thoughtfully. "The thing is, she knows Bugle's name."

I manage to make a noise. It's not like I haven't wanted to contribute to the conversation. But I'm kind of out of breath from all that running, not to mention being totally hysterical.

I'm not sure what old Gnaw-bone's idea of fun and games is, but I'm dead sure I don't want to play. If knowing Bugle's name can get me out of this, I better make the most of it. So, "Yeah," I croak. "Bugle and me go way back."

The green girl turns to look at me, and I kind of wish I'd kept quiet. She's way scary. It's not the green hair or the punk clothes or the fact that I've just noticed there's this humongous squirrel sitting on her shoulder and an English sparrow perched in her dreads. It's the way she looks at me, like I'm a St. Bernard that just recited the Pledge of Allegiance or something.

"I think we better hear Bugle's take on this beautiful friendship," she says. "Bugle says you're buds, fine. She doesn't, Gnaw-bone gets his fun and games. Fair?"

No, it's not fair, but I don't say so. There's a long silence, in which I can hear the noise of traffic, very faint and far away, and the panicked beating of my heart, right in my throat.

Gnaw-bone licks his lips, what there is of them, and the squirrel slithers down the green girl's shoulder and gets comfortable in her arms. If it's even a squirrel. I've seen smaller dogs.

Have I mentioned I'm really scared? I've never been this scared before in my entire life. And it's not even that I'm afraid of what Gnaw-bone might do to me, although I am.

I'm afraid of the green girl. It's one thing to think fairies are wicked cool, to own all of Brian Froud's *Faerie* books and see *Fairy Tale* three times and secretly wish you hadn't outgrown your fairy friend. But this girl doesn't look like any fairy I ever imagined. Green leather and dreads—get real! And I'm not really prepared for eyes like living moss and the squirrel curled like a cat in her arms and the sparrow in her hair like a bizzarroid hair clip. It's way too weird. I want to run away. I want to cry. But neither of these things seems like the right I thing to do, so I stand there with my legs all rubbery and wait for Bugle to show up.

After a while, I feel something tugging at my hair. I start to slap it away, and then I realize. Duh. It's Bugle, saying hi. I scratch my ear instead. There's a little tootling sound, like a trumpet: Bugle, laughing. I laugh too, kind of hysterically.

"See?" I tell the green girl and the humongous squirrel and Gnaw-bone. "She knows me."

The green girl holds out her hand—the squirrel scrambles up to her shoulder again—and Bugle flies over and stands on her palm. It seems to me that Bugle used to look more like a little girl and less like a teenager. But then, so did I.

The green girl ignores me. "Do you know this mortal?" she asks Bugle. Her voice is different, somehow: less street kid, more like Mom asking whether I've done my math homework. Bugle gives a little hop. "Yep. Sure do. When she was little, anyways. Now, she doesn't want to know me."

I've been starting to feel better, but now the green girl is glaring at me, and my stomach knots up tight. I give this sick kind of grin. It's true. I hadn't wanted to know her, not with Peggy and those guys on my case. Even Elf, who puts up with a lot, doesn't want to hear about how I saw fairies when I was little. I say, "Yeah, well. I'm sorry. I really did know you were real, but I was embarrassed."

The green girl smiles. I can't help noticing she has a beautiful smile, like sun on the boat pond. "Fatso is just saying that," she points out, "because she's afraid I'll throw her to Gnaw-bone."

I freeze solid. Bugle, who's been getting fidgety, takes off and flies around the clearing a couple of times. Then she buzzes me and pulls my hair again, lands on my shoulder and says, "She's not so bad. I like teasing her."

"Not fair!" Gnaw-bone squeaks.

The green girl shrugs. "You know the rules," she tells him. "Bugle speaks for her. She's off-limits. Them's the breaks. Now, scram. You bother me."

Exit Gnaw-bone, muttering and glaring at me over his shoulder, and am I ever glad to see him go. He's like every nightmare Mom has ever had about letting me go places by myself and having me turn up murdered. Mine, too.

Anyway, I'm so relieved I start to babble. "Thanks, Bugle.

Thanks a billion. I owe you big time."

"Yeah," says Bugle. "I know."

"You owe me, too," the green girl puts in.

Now, I can't quite see where she's coming from on this, seeing as how she was all gung-ho to let Gnaw-bone have his fun and games before Bugle showed up. Not to mention calling me names. On the other hand, she's obviously Very Important, and if there's one thing I've learned from reading all those fairy tales, it's that it's a very bad idea to be rude to people who wear live birds and squirrels like jewelry. So I shrug. Politely.

"Seven months' service should cover it," she says. "Can you sing? I'm mostly into salsa these days, but reggae or jazz is cool too."

My mouth drops open. Seven months? She's gotta be out of her mind. My parents will kill me if I don't come home for seven months.

"No?" Her voice is even more beautiful than it was before, like a fountain or wind in the trees. Her eyes sparkle like sun through leaves. She so absolutely gorgeous so not like anyone I can imagine having a conversation with, it's hard to follow what she's saying.

"I don't sing," I tell her.

"Dance, then?" I shake my head. "So, what can you do?"

Well, I know the answer to that one. "Nothing," I say. "I'm totally useless. Just ask my French teacher. Or my mom."

The beautiful face goes all blank and hard, like granite. "I said Gnawbone couldn't have you. That leaves all his brothers and sisters. You don't need much talent to entertain them."

You know how your brain goes totally spla when you're really scared? Well, my brain did that. And then I heard myself saying, "You said I was under Bugle's protection. Just because you're Queen of the Fairies doesn't mean you can do anything you want."

I was sure she'd be mad, but—get this—she starts to laugh. She laughs and laughs and laughs. And I get madder and madder, the way you do when you don't know what you've said that's so funny. Then I notice that she's getting broader and darker and shorter, and there's this scarf over her head, and she's wearing this dorky green housedress and her stockings are drooping around her ankles and she's got a cigarette in one hand. Finally she wheezes out, "The Queen of the Fairies! Geddouddaheah! You're killin' me!" She sounds totally different, too, like somebody's Aunt Ida from the Bronx.

"The Queen of the . . . Listen, kid. We ain't in the Old Country no more. We're in New York"—*Noo Yawk* is what she said—"New York, U. S. of A. We ain't got Queens, except across the bridge."

So now I'm really torqued, I mean, who knows what she's going to do next, right? She could turn me into a pigeon, for all I know. This is no time to lose it. I've got to focus. After all, I've been reading about fairies for years, right? New Age stuff, folklore, fantasy novels—everything I could get my hands on. I've done my homework. There's a chance I can b.s. my way out of this if I keep my cool.

"Oh, ha ha," I say. "Not. Like that rat-guy didn't say 'how high' when you said 'jump.' You can call yourself the Mayor of Central Park if you want, but you're still the Queen of the goddam Fairies."

She morphs back to dreads and leather on fast forward.

"So, Fatso. You think you're hot stuff." I shrug. "Listen. We're in this thing where I think you owe me, and you think you don't. I could *make* you pay up, but I won't." She plops down on the bench and gets comfortable. The squirrel jumps off her shoulder and disappears into a tree.

"Siddown, take a load off—have a drink. Here." Swear to God, she hands me a can of Diet Coke. I don't know where it came from, but the pop-top is popped, and I can hear the Coke fizzing and I realize I'm wicked thirsty. My hand goes, like all by itself, to take it, and then my brain kicks in. "No," I say. "Thank you."

She looks hurt. "Really? It's cold and everything." She shoves it towards me. My mouth is as dry as the Sahara Desert, but if there's one thing I'm sure I know about fairies, it's don't eat or drink anything a fairy gives you if you ever want to go home.

"Really," I say. "Thanks."

"Well, dag," she says, disgusted "You read fairy tales. Aren't you special. I suppose now you're going to ask for three wishes and a pot of gold. Go ahead. Three wishes. Have a ball."

This is more like it. I'm all prepared, too. In sixth grade, I worked out what my wishes would be, if I ever met a wish-granting fairy. And they were still perfectly good wishes, based on extensive research. Never, ever wish for more wishes. Never ask for money—it'll turn into dog doo in the morning. The safest thing to do was to ask for something that would make you a better citizen, and then you could ask for two things for yourself. I settled on a good heart, a really ace memory, and 20/20 vision. I didn't know about laser surgery in sixth grade.

So I'm all ready (except maybe asking to be a size 6 instead of the vision thing), and then it occurs to me that this is all way too easy, and Queenie is looking way too cheerful for someone who's been outsmarted by an overweight bookworm. Face it, I haven't done anything to earn those wishes.

All I've done is turn down a lousy Diet Coke. "Thanks all the same, but I'll pass," I say. "Can I go home now?"

Then she loses her temper. She's not foaming at the mouth or anything, but there are sparks coming out of her eyes like a Fourth of July sparkler, and her dreads are lifting and twining around her head like snakes. The sparrow gives a startled chirp and takes off for the nearest bush.

"Well, isn't this just my lucky day," Greenie snarls. "You're not as dumb as you look. On the bright side, though,"—her dreads settle slowly—"winning's boring when it's too easy, you know?"

I wouldn't know—I don't usually win. But then, I don't usually care that much. This is different. This time, there's a lot more at stake than my nonexistent self-esteem. I'm glad she thinks I'm a moron. It evens things up a little. "I tell you what," I tell her. "I'll play you for my freedom."

"You're on," she says. "Dealer's choice. That's me. What shall we play?" She leans back on the bench and looks up at the sky. "Riddles are trad, but everybody knows all the good ones. What's black and white and red all over? A blushing nun? A newspaper? Penguin roadkill? Puleeze. Anyway, riddles are boring. What do you say to Truth or Dare?"

"I hate it." I do, too. The only time I played it, I ended up feeling icky and raw, like I'd been sunbathing topless.

"Really? It's my favorite game. We'll play Truth or Dare. These are the rules. We ask each other personal questions, and the first one who won't answer loses everything. Deal?"

It doesn't sound like much of a deal to me. How can I know what question a Queen of Fairies would be too embarrassed to answer? On the other hand, what can a being who hangs out with squirrels and fairies and rat-guys know about human beings? And what choice do I have?

I shrug. "I guess."

"Okay. I go first."

Well, sure she does. She's the Queen of Central Park. And I see the question coming—she doesn't even pause to think about it. "So, how much do you weigh, anyway?"

Now you have to understand that nobody knows how much I weigh. Not Elf, not even my mom. Only the school nurse and the doctor and me. I've always said I'd rather die than tell anyone else. But the choice between telling and living in Central Park for seven months is a no-brainer. So I tell her. I even add a pound for the hotdog and the Mr. Softee I ate the boathouse.

"Geddouddaheah!" she says. "You really pork it down, huh?"

I don't like her comment, but it's not like I haven't heard it before. It makes me mad, but not so mad I can't think, which is obviously what she's trying for. Questions go through my mind, but I don't have a lot to go on, you know what I'm saying? And she's tapping her green boot and looking impatient. I have to say something, and what I end up asking is, "Why are you in Central Park, anyway? I mean, there's lots of other places that are more fairy-friendly. Why aren't you in White Plains or something?"

It sounds like a question to me, but she doesn't seem to think so. "I win. That's not personal," she says.

"It is too personal. Where a person lives is personal. Come on. Why do you live here, or let me go home."

"Can't blame a girl for trying," she says. "Okay, here goes. This is the heart of the city. You guys pass through all the time—like Grand Central Station, right? Only here, you stop or a while. You rest, you play, you kiss in the grass, you whisper your secrets, you weep, you fight. This ground, these rocks, are soaked through with love, hate, joy, sorrow, passion. And I love that stuff, you understand? It keeps me interested."

Wow. I stare at her, and all my ideas about fairies start to get rearranged. But they don't get very far because she's still talking.

"You think I don't know anything about you," she says. "Boy, are you wrong. I know everything I want to know. I know what's on your bio quiz next week. I know Patty Gregg's worst secret. I know who your real mother is, the one who gave you away when you were born." She gives me this look, like Elf's brother the time he stole a dirty magazine. "Wanna know?"

It's not what I'm expecting, but it's a question, all right, and it's personal. And it's really easy. Sure, I want to know all those things, a whole lot—especially about my biological mother.

Like more than anything else in the world. My parents are okay—I mean, they say they love me and everything. But they really don't understand me big time. I've always felt adopted, if you know what I mean—a changeling in a family of ordinary humans. I'd give anything to know who my real mother is, what she looks like and why she couldn't keep me. So I should say yes, right? I mean, it's the true answer to the green girl's question, and that's what the game is about, isn't it? There's a movement on my shoulder, a sharp little pinch right behind my ear. I've totally forgotten Bugle—I mean, she's been sitting there for ages, perfectly still, which is not her usual.

Maybe I've missed something. It's that too easy thing again. Sure, I want to know who my birth mom is. But it's more complicated than that. Because now that I think about it, I realize I don't want Greenie to be the one to tell me. I mean, it feels wrong, to learn something like that from someone who is obviously trying to hurt you.

"Answer the question," says the green girl. "Or give in. I'm getting bored."

I take a deep breath. "Keep your socks on. I was thinking how to put it. Okay, my answer is both yes and no. I do want to find out about my birth mom, but I don't want you to tell me. Even if you know, it's none of your business. I want to find out for myself. Does that answer your question?"

She nods briskly. "It does. Your turn."

She's not going to give me much time to come up with one, I can tell that. She wants to win. She wants to get me all torqued so I can't think, so I won't ask her the one question she won't answer, so I won't even see it staring me right in the face, the one thing she really, really can't answer, if the books I've read aren't all totally bogus.

"What's your name?" I ask.

I mean, it's obvious, isn't it? Like, how dumb does she think I am? Pretty dumb, I guess, from the look on her face.

"Guess," she says, making a quick recovery.

"Wrong fairy tale," I say, pushing it. "Come on. Tell me, or you lose."

"Do you know what you're asking?"

"Yes."

There's a long silence—a *long* silence, like no bird is ever going sing again, or squirrel chatter or wind blow. The green girl puts her fingers in her mouth and starts to bite her nails. I'm feeling pretty good. I know and she knows that I've won no matter what she says. If she tells me her name, I have total power over her, and if she doesn't, she loses the game. I know what I'd choose if I was in her place, but I guess she must really, really hate losing.

Watching her sweat, I think of several things to say, most of them kind of mean. She'd say them, if she was me. I don't.

It's not like I'm Mother Teresa or anything—I've been mean plenty of times, and sometimes I wasn't even sorry later. But she might lose her temper and turn me into a pigeon after all.

Besides, she looks so human all of a sudden, chewing her nails and all stressed out like she's the one facing seven months of picking up fairy laundry. Before, when she was winning, she looked maybe twenty, right? Gorgeous, tough, scary, in total control. Now she looks a lot younger and not tough at all.

So maybe if she loses, she's threatened with seven months of doing what I tell her. Maybe I don't realize what I'm asking. Maybe there's more at stake here than I know. A tiny whimpering behind my right ear tells me that Bugle is pretty upset. Suddenly, I don't feel so great. I don't care any more about beating the Queen of the Fairies at some stupid game.

I just want this to be over.

"Listen," I say, and the green girl looks up at me. Her wide, mossy eyes are all blurred with tears. I take a deep breath.

"Let's stop playing," I say.

"We can't stop," she says miserably. "It has begun, it must be finished. Those are the rules."

"Okay. We'll finish it. It's a draw. You don't have to answer my question. Nobody wins. Nobody loses. We just go back to the beginning."

"What beginning? When Gnaw-bone was chasing you? If I help you, you have to pay."

I think about this for a little while. She lets me. "Okay," I say. "How about this. You're in a tough spot, right? I take back question, you're off the hook, like you got me off the hook with Gnaw-bone. We're even."

She takes her fingers out of her mouth. She gnaws on her lip. She looks up into the sky, and around at the trees. She tugs on her dreads. She smiles. She starts to laugh. It's not teasing laugh or a mean laugh, but pure happiness, like a little kid in the snow.

"Wow," she says, and her voice is warm and soft as fleece. "You're right. Awesome."

"Cool," I say. Can I go home now?"

"In a minute." She puts her head to one side, and grins at me. I'm grinning back—I can't help it. Suddenly, I feel all mellow and safe and comfortable, like I'm lying on a rock in the sun and telling stories to Elf.

"Yeah," she says, like she's reading my mind. "I've heard you. You tell good stories. You should write them down. Now, about those wishes. They're human stuff—not really my business. As you pointed out. Besides, you've already got all those things. You remember what you need to know; you see clearly; you're majorly kind-hearted. But you deserve a present." She tapped her browny-green cheek with one slender finger. "I know. Ready?"

"Okay," I say. "Um. What is it?"

"It's a surprise," she says. "But you'll like it. You'll see."

She stands up and I stand up. Bugle takes off from my shoulder and goes and sits in the greeny-brown dreads like a butterfly clip. Then the Queen of the New York Fairies leans forward and kisses me on the forehead. It doesn't feel like a kiss—more like a very light breeze has just hit me between the eyes. Then she lays her finger across my lips, and then she's gone.

"So there you are!" It was Elf, red in the face, out of breath, with her hair coming out of the clip, and a tear in her jacket. "I've been looking all over. I was scared out of my mind! It was like you just disappeared into thin air!"

"I got lost," I said. "Anyway, it's okay now. Sit down. You look like hell."

"Thanks, friend." She sat on the bench. "So, what happened?"

I wanted to tell her, I really did. I mean, she's my best friend and everything, and I always tell her everything. But the Queen of the Fairies. I ask you. And I could feel the kiss nestling below my bangs like a little, warm sun and the Queen's finger cool across my lips. So all I did was look at my hands. They were all dirty and scratched from climbing up the cliff. I'd broken a fingernail.

"Are you okay?" Elf asked anxiously. "That guy didn't catch you or anything, did he? Jeez, I wish we'd never gone down there."

She was getting really upset. I said, "I'm fine, Elf. He didn't catch me, and everything's okay."

"You sure?"

I looked right at her, you know how you do when you want to be sure someone hears you? And I said, "I'm sure." And I was.

"Okay," she said slowly. "Good. I was worried." She looked at her watch. "It's not like it was that long, but it seemed like forever."

"Yeah," I agreed, with feeling. "I'm really thirsty."

So that's about it, really. We went to a coffee shop on Columbus Ave. and had blueberry pie and coffee and talked. For the first time, I told her about being adopted, and wanting to look for my birth mother, and she was really great about it after being mad because I hadn't told her before. I said she was a good friend and she got teary. And then I went home.

So what's the moral of this story? My life didn't get better overnight, if that's what you're wondering. I still need to lose a few pounds, I still need glasses, and the cool kids still hate me. But Elf sits with me at lunch now, and a couple other kids turned out to be into fantasy and like that, so I'm not a total outcast any more. And I'm writing down my stories. Elf thinks they're good, but she's my best friend. Maybe some day I'll get up the nerve to show them to my English teacher. Oh, and I've talked to my mom about finding my birth mother, and she says maybe I should wait until I'm out of high school. Which is okay with me, because, to tell you the truth, I don't need to find her right now—I just want to know I can.

And the Green Queen's gift? It's really weird. Suddenly, I see fairies everywhere.

There was this girl the other day—blonde, skinny, wearing a white leotard and her jeans unzipped and folded back, so she looked kind of like a flower in a calyx of blue leaves.

Freak, right? Nope. Fairy. So was an old black guy all dressed in royal blue, with butterflies sewn on his blue beret and painted on his blue suede shoes. And this Asian guy with black hair down to his butt and a big fur coat. And this Upper East Side lady with big blond hair and green bug-eyes. She had a fuzzy little dog on a rhinestone leash, and you won't believe this, but the dog was a fairy, too.

And remember the trees—the sidewalk ones? I know all about them now. No, I won't tell you, stupid. It's a secret. If you really want to know, you'll have to go find the Queen of Grand Central Park and make her an offer. Or play a game with her.

Don't forget to say hi to Gnaw-bone for me.

But if you want to meet fairies, Central Park is not the only place to find them in New York.

THE LAND OF HEART'S DESIRE

HOLLY BLACK

If you want to meet real-life members of the Sidhe—real faeries—go to the café Moon in a Cup, in Manhattan. Faeries congregate there in large numbers. You can tell them by the slight point of their ears—a feature they're too arrogant to conceal by glamour—and by their inhuman grace. You will also find that the café caters to their odd palate by offering nettle and foxglove teas, ragwort pastries. Please note too that foxglove is poisonous to mortals and shouldn't be tasted by you.

—posted in messageboard www.realfairies.com/forums by stoneneil

Lords of fairie sometimes walk among us. Even in places stinking of cold iron, up broken concrete steps, in tiny apartments where girls sleep three to a bedroom. Faeries, after all, delight in corruption, in borders, in crossing over and then crossing back again.

When Rath Roiben Rye, Lord of the Unseelie Court and Several Other Places, comes to see Kaye, she drags her mattress into the middle of the living room so that they can talk until dawn without waking anyone. Kaye isn't human either, but she was raised human. Sometimes, to Roiben, she seems more human than the city around her.

In the mornings, her roommates Ruth and Val (if she's not staying with her boyfriend) and Corny (who sleeps in their walk-in closet, although he calls it "the second bedroom") step over them. Val grinds coffee and brews it in a French press with lots of cinnamon. She shaved her head a year ago and her rust-colored hair is finally long enough that it's starting to curl.

Kaye laughs and drinks out of chipped mugs and lets her long green pixie fingers trace patterns on Roiben's skin. In those moments, with the smell of her in his throat, stronger than all the iron of the world, he feels as raw and trembling as something newly born.

One day in midsummer, Roiben took on a mortal guise and went to Moon in a Cup in the hope that Kaye's shift might soon be over. He thought they would walk through Riverside Park and look at the reflection of lights on the water. Or eat nuts rimed with salt. Or whatsoever else she wanted. He needed those memories of her to sustain him when he returned to his own kingdoms.

But walking in just after sunset, black coat flapping around his ankles like crow wings, he could see she wasn't there. The coffee shop was full of mortals, more full than usual. Behind the counter, Corny ran back and forth, banging mugs in a cloud of espresso steam.

The coffee shop had been furnished with things Kaye and her human friends had found by the side of the road or at cheap tag sales. Lots of ratty paint-stained little wooden tables that she'd decoupaged with post cards, sheets of music, and pages from old encyclopedias. Lots of chairs painted gold. The walls were hung with amateur paintings, framed in scrap metal.

Even the cups were mismatched. Delicate bone china cups sitting on saucers beside mugs with slogans for businesses long closed.

As Roiben walked to the back of the shop, several of the patrons gave him appraising glances. In the reflection of the shining copper coffee urn, he looked as he always did. His white hair was pulled back. His eyes were the color of the silver spoons.

He wondered if he should alter his guise.

"Where is she?" Roiben asked.

"Imperious, aren't we?" Corny shouted over the roar of the machine. "Well, whatever magical booty call the king of the faeries is after will have to wait. I have no idea where Kaye's at. All I know is that she should be here."

Roiben tried to control the sharp flush of annoyance that made his hand twitch for a blade.

"I'm sorry," Corny said, rubbing his hand over his face. "That was uncool. Val said she'd come help but she's not here and Luis, who's *supposed* to be my boyfriend, is off with some study partner for hours and hours and my scheme to get some more business has backfired in a big way. And then you come in here and you're so—you're always so—"

"May I get myself some nettle tea to bide with?" Roiben interrupted, frowning. "I know where you keep it. I will attend to myself."

"You can't," Corny said, waving him around the back of the bar. "I mean, you could have, but they drank it all, and I don't know how to make more."

Behind the bar was a mess. Roiben bent to pick up the cracked remains of a cup and frowned. "What's going on here? Since when have mortals formed a taste for—"

"Excuse me," said a girl with long wine-colored hair. "Are you human?"

He froze, suddenly conscious of the jagged edges of what he held. "I'm supposing I misheard you." He set the porcelain fragment down discreetly on the counter.

"You're one of them, aren't you? I knew it!" A huge smile split her face and she looked back eagerly toward a table of grinning humans. "Can you grant wishes?"

Roiben looked at Corny, busy frothing milk. "Cornelius," he said softly. "Um."

Corny glanced over. "If, for once, you just act like my best friend's boyfriend and take her order, I promise to be nicer to you. Nice to you, even."

Roiben touched a key on the register. "I'll do it if you promise to be more afraid of me."

"I envy what I fear and hate what I envy," Corny said, slamming an iced latte on the counter. "More afraid equals more of a jerk."

"What is it you'd like?" Roiben asked the girl. "Other than wishes."

"Soy mocha," said the girl. "But please, there's so much I want to know."

Roiben squinted at the scrawled menu on the chalkboard. "Payment, if you please."

She counted out some bills and he took them, looking helplessly at the register. He hit a few buttons and, to his relief, the drawer opened. He gave her careful change.

"Please tell me that you didn't pay her in leaves and acorns," Corny said. "Kaye keeps doing that and it's really not helping business."

"I knew it!" said the girl.

"I conjured nothing," Roiben said. "And you are not helping."

Corny squirted out Hershey's syrup into the bottom of a mug. "Yeah, remember what I said about my idea to get Moon in a Cup more business?"

Roiben crossed his arms over his chest. "I do."

"I might have posted online that this place has a high incidence of supernatural visitation."

Roiben narrowed his eyes and tilted his head. "You claimed Kaye's coffee shop is haunted?"

The girl picked up her mocha from the counter. "He said that faeries came here. Real faeries. The kind that dance in mushroom circles and—"

"Oh, did he?" Roiben asked, a snarl in his voice. "That's what he said?"

Corny didn't want to be jealous of the rest of them.

He didn't want to spend his time wondering how long it would be before Luis got tired of him. Luis, who was going places while Corny helped Kaye open Moon in a Cup because he had literally nothing else to do.

Kaye ran the place like a pixie. It had odd hours—sometimes opening at four in the afternoon, sometimes opening at dawn.

The service was equally strange when Kaye was behind the counter. A cappuccino would be ordered and chai tea would be delivered. People's change often turned to leaves and ash.

Slowly—for survival—things evolved so that Moon in a Cup belonged to all of them. Val and Ruth worked when they weren't at school. Corny set up the wireless.

And Luis, who lived in the dorms of NYU and was busy with a double major and flirting with a future in medicine, would come and type out his long papers at one of the tables to make the place look more full.

But it wouldn't survive like that for long, Corny knew.

Everything was too precarious. Everyone else had too much going on. So he made the decision to run the ad. And for a week straight, the coffee shop had been full of people. They could barely make the drinks in time. So none of the others could be mad at him. They had no right to be mad at him.

He had to stay busy. It was the only way to keep the horrible gnawing dread at bay.

Roiben listened to Corny stammer through an explanation of what he had done and why without really hearing it.

Then he made himself tea and sat at one of the salvaged tables that decorated the coffeehouse. Its surface was ringed with marks from the tens of dozens of watery cups that had rested there and any weight made the whole thing rock alarmingly. He took a sip of the foxglove tea—brewed by his own hand to be strong and bitter.

Val had come in during Corny's explanation, blanched, and started sweeping the floor. Now she and Corny whispered together behind the counter, Val shaking her head.

Faeries had, for many years, relied on discretion. Roiben knew the only thing keeping Corny from torment at the hands of the faeries who must have seen his markedly indiscreet advertisement was the implied protection of the King of the Unseelie Court. Roiben knew it and resented it.

It would be an easy thing to withdraw his protection. Easy and perhaps just.

As he considered that, a woman's voice behind him rose, infuriating him further. "Well, you see, my family has always been close to the faeries. My great great great great grandmother was even stolen away to live with them."

Roiben wondered why mortals so wanted to be associated with suffering that they told foolish tales. Why not tell a story where one's grandmother died fat, old, and beloved by her dozen children?

"Really?" the woman's friend was saying. "Like Robert Kirk on the faerie hill?"

"Exactly," said the woman. "Except that Great Grandma Clarabelle wasn't sleeping outdoors and she was right here in New York State. She got taken out of her own bed! Clarabelle had just given birth to a stillborn baby and the priest came too late to baptize her. No iron over the doors."

It happened like that sometimes, he had to concede.

"Oh," her friend said, shaking her head. "Yes, we've forgotten about iron and salt and all the other protections."

Clara. For a moment, thoughts of Corny and his betrayal went out of Roiben's head completely. He knew that name. And dozens upon dozens of Claras who have come into the world, in that moment, he knew the women were telling a true story. A story he knew. It shamed him that he had dismissed them so easily for being foolish.

Even fools tell the truth. Historically, the truth belongs especially to fools.

"Excuse me," Roiben said, turning in his chair. "I couldn't help overhearing"

"Do you believe in faeries?" she asked him, seeming pleased.

"I'm afraid I must," he said, finally. "May I ask you something about Clara?"

"My great great aunt" the woman said, smiling. "I'm named after her. I'm Clarabella. Well, it's really my middle name, but I still—"

"A pleasure to make your acquaintance" he said, extending his hand to shake hers. "Do you happen to know when your Clara went missing?"

"Some time in the eighteenth century, I guess," she said. Her voice slowed as she got to the end of the sentence, as though she'd become wary. Her smile dimmed. "Is something the matter?"

"And did she have two children?" he asked recklessly. "A boy named Robert and a girl named Mary?"

"How could you have known that?" Clarabella said, her voice rising.

"I didn't know it," Roiben said. "That is the reason I asked."

"But you—you shouldn't have been able to—" Everyone in the coffee shop was staring at them now. Roiben perceived a goblin by the door, snickering as he licked chocolate icing from his fingers.

Her friend put a hand on Clarabella's arm. "He's one of the fair folk," she said, hushed. "Be careful. He might want to steal you, too."

Roiben laughed, suddenly, but his throat felt full of thorns.

It is eternal summer in the Seelie Court, as changeless as faeries themselves. Trees hang eternally heavy with golden fruit and flowering vines climb walls to flood bark-shingled roofs with an endless rain of petals.

Roiben recalled being a child there, growing up in indolent pleasure and carelessness. He and his sister Ethine lived far from the faeries who'd sired them and thought no more of them than they thought of the sunless sky or of the patterns that the pale fishes in the stream made with their mad darting.

They had games to amuse themselves with. They dissected grasshoppers, they pulled the wings from moths and sewed them to the backs of toads to see if they could make the toads fly. And when they tired of those games they had a nurse called Clara with which to play.

She had mud brown hair and eyes as green as wet pools. In her more lucid moments, she hated her faerie charges. She must have known that she had been stolen away from home, from her own family and children, to care for beings she considered little better than soulless devils. When Ethine and Roiben would clamour for her lap, she thrust them away. When they teased her for her evening prayers, she described how their skin would crackle and smoke, as they roasted in hell after the final judgment day.

She could be kind, too. She taught them songs and chased them through meadows until they shrieked with laughter. They played fox and geese with acorns and holes dug by their fingers in the dirt. They played charades and forfeits. They played graces with hoops and sticks woven from willow trees. And after, Clara washed their dirty cheeks with her handkerchief, dipped in the water of the stream, and made up beds for them in the moss.

And when she kissed their clean faces and bid them goodnight, she would call them Robert and Mary. Her lost children. The children that she had been enchanted to think they were.

Roiben did not remember pitying Clara then, although thinking back on it, he found her pitiable. He and Ethine were young and their love for her was too selfish to want anything more than to be loved best. They hated being called by another's name and pinched her in punishment or hid from her until she wept.

One day, Ethine said that she'd come up with a plan to make Clara forget all about Robert and Mary. Roiben gathered up the mushrooms, just as his sister told him.

He didn't know that what was wholesome to him might poison Clara.

They killed her, by accident, as easily as they had pulled the wings from the moth or stabbed the grasshopper. Eventually, their faerie mother came and laughed at their foolishness and staged a beautiful funeral. Ethine had woven garlands to hang around the neck of Clara's corpse and no one washed their cheeks, even when they got smeared with mud.

And although the funeral was amusing and their faerie mother an entertaining novelty, Roiben could not stop thinking of the way Clara had looked at him as she died. As if, perhaps, she had loved her monstrous faerie children after all, and in that moment, regretted it. It was a familiar look, one that he had long thought was love but now recognized as hatred.

Corny watched Val foam milk and wondered if he should go home. The crowd was starting to die down and they could probably close in an hour or two. He was almost exhausted enough to be able to crawl into bed and let his body's need for sleep overtake his mind's need to race around in helpless circles.

Then Corny looked up and saw Roiben on his feet, staring at some poor woman like he was going to rip off her head. Corny had no idea what the lady had said, but if the girl at the counter was any indication, it could have been pretty crazy. He left a customer trying to decide whether or not she really wanted an extra shot of elderflower syrup to rush across the coffee shop.

"Everything okay over here?" Corny asked. Roiben flinched, like he hadn't noticed Corny getting so close and had to restrain some violent impulse.

"This woman was telling a story about her ancestor," Roiben said tightly, voice full of false pleasure. "A story that perhaps she read somewhere or which has been passed down through her family. About how a woman named Clarabelle was taken away by the faeries. I simply want to hear the whole thing."

Corny turned to the woman. "Okay, you two. Get out of here. Now." He pushed her and her friend toward the door.

They went, pulling on their coats and looking back nervously, like they wanted to complain but didn't dare.

"As for you," Corny said to Roiben, trying to keep from seeming as nervous as he now felt. His hands were sweating.

"People are idiots. So she made up some ridiculous story? It doesn't matter. You don't need to do . . . whatever it is you're thinking of doing to her."

"No," Roiben said and Corny cringed automatically.

"Please just let—" Corny started, but Roiben cut him off.

His voice was steely and his eyes looked like chips of ice.

"Mortal, you are trying my patience. This is all your doing. Were I to merely turn my back, they would come for you, they would drag you through the skies and torment you until madness finally, mercifully robbed you of your senses."

"You're a real charmer," Corny said, but his voice shook.

The door opened, bell ringing, and they both half-turned toward it. *He's looking for Kaye*, Corny thought. If she came through the door, she could charm Roiben into forgetting to be angry.

But it wasn't Kaye. Luis walked through the door with three college guys, backpacks and messenger bags slung over their shoulders. Luis took a quick look in Corny's direction, then walked to the table with them, dumped his bag.

"Come with me," Roiben said quietly.

"Where are we going?" Corny asked.

"There are always consequences. It's time for you to face yours."

Corny nodded, helpless to do anything else. He took a deep breath and let himself be guided to the door.

"Leave him alone," Luis said. Corny turned to find that Luis was holding Roiben's wrist. The welts in Luis's brown skin where the Night Court had ripped out his iron piercings, loop by loop, had healed to scars, but Luis's single cloudy eye, put out by a faerie because Luis had the Sight, would never get better.

Roiben raised one pale brow. He looked more amused than worried. Maybe he was angry enough to hope for an excuse to hurt someone.

"Don't worry about me," Corny told Luis stiffly. "I'll be right back. Go back to your friends."

Luis frowned and Corny silently willed him to go away. There was no point in both of them getting in trouble.

"You're not getting him without a fight," Luis said quietly.

"I mislike your tone," said Roiben, pulling his wrist free with a sudden twist of his arm. "Cornelius and I have some things to discuss. It's naught to do with you."

Luis turned to Corny. "You told him about the ad? Are you an idiot?"

"He figured it out for himself," Corny said.

"Is that all, Luis? Have we your permission to go outside?" Roiben asked.

"I'm going with you," Luis said.

"No you're not." Corny shoved at Luis' shoulder, harder than he'd intended. "You're never around for anything else, why be around for this? Go back to your friends. Why don't you go study with them or whatever you do? Go back and admit you're sick of me already. I bet you never even told them you had a boyfriend."

Luis blanched,

"That's what I thought," Corny said. "Just break up with me already."

"What's wrong with you?" asked Luis. "Are you really going to be pissed off at people who you've never met—just because I go to school with them? You hate them, that's why I don't tell them about you."

"I hate them because they're what you want me to be," Corny said. "Nagging me to register for classes. Wanting me to stay clear of faeries even though my best friend is one. Wanting me to be someone I'm never going to be."

Luis looked shocked, like each word was a slap. "All I want is for you not to get yourself killed."

"I don't need your pity," Corny said and pushed through the door, leaving Roiben to follow him. It felt good, the adrenaline rushing through his veins. It felt like setting the whole world on fire.

"Wait," Luis called from behind him. "Don't go."

But it was too late to turn back. Corny walked out of the warm coffee shop, onto the sidewalk and then turned into the mouth of the dark, stinking alley that ran next to Moon in a Cup. He heard Roiben's relentless footsteps approaching.

Corny leaned his forehead against the cold brick wall and closed his eyes. "I really screwed that up, didn't I?"

"You said that you envied what you feared and hated what you envied." Roiben rested his long fingers on Corny's shoulder.

"But it is as easy to hate what you love as to hate what you fear."

Roiben leaned against the wall of the alley, unsure of what else to say. His own rage at himself and his memories had dulled in the face of Corny's obvious misery. He had already come up with a vague idea for a fitting punishment, but it seemed cruel to do it now. Of course, perhaps cruelty should be the point.

"I don't know what's wrong with me," Corny said, head bent so that Roiben could see the nape of his neck, already covered in gooseflesh. Corny had left Moon in a Cup without his jacket and his thin T-shirt was no protection against the wind.

"You were only trying to keep him safe," Roiben said. "I think even he knows it."

Corny shook his head. "No, I wanted to hurt him. I wanted to hurt him before he got a chance to hurt me. I'm ruining our relationship and I just don't know how to stop myself."

"I'm hardly the person to advise you," Roiben said stiffly. "Recall Silarial. I have more than once mistaken hate for love. I have no wisdom here."

"Oh, come on," Corny said. "You're my best friend's boyfriend. You must talk to her sometimes—you must talk to her like this."

"Not like this," Roiben said, not without irony. But in truth the way that Corny was speaking felt dangerous, as though one's feelings might only continue to work if they remained undisturbed.

"Look, you seem grim and miserable most of the time, but I know you love her."

"Of course I love her," Roiben snapped.

"How can you?" Corny asked. He took a deep breath and spoke again, so quickly that the words tumbled over one another.

"How can you trust someone that much? I mean, she's just going to hurt you, right? What if someday she just stops liking you? What if she finds someone else—" Corny stopped abruptly, and Roiben realized he was frowning ominously. His fingers had dug into the pads of his own palms.

"Go on," Roiben said, deliberately relaxing his body.

Corny ran a hand through his dyed black hair. "She's going to eventually get tired of putting up with you never being around when the important stuff is going on, never changing while she's figuring out her own life. Eventually, you'll just be a shadow." Roiben found that he'd been clenching his jaw so tightly that his teeth ached. It was everything he was afraid of, laid before him like a feast of ashes.

"That's what I feel like I'm like. Going nowhere while Luis has gone from living on the street to some fancy university. He's going to be a doctor someday—a real one—and what am I going to be?"

Roiben nodded slowly. He'd forgotten they were talking about Corny and Luis.

"So how do you do it?" Corny demanded. "How do you love someone when you don't know if it's forever or not? When he might just leave you?"

"Kaye is the only thing that saves me from myself," Roiben said.

Corny turned at that and narrowed his eyes. "What do you mean?"

Roiben shook his head, unsure of how to express any of his tangled thoughts. "I hadn't recalled her in a long time—Clara. When I was a child, I had a human nurse enchanted to serve me. She couldn't love me," Roiben hesitated. "She couldn't love me, because she had no choices. She wasn't free to love me. She never had a chance. I too have been enchanted to serve. I understand her better now."

He felt a familiar revulsion thinking of his past, thinking of captivity with Nicnevin, but he pushed past it to speak. "After all the humiliations I have suffered, all the things I have done for my mistresses at their commands, here I am in a dirty human restaurant, serving coffee to fools. For Kaye. Because I am free to. Because I think it would please her. Because I think it would make her laugh."

"It's definitely going to make her laugh," Corny said.

"Thus I am saved from my own grim self," Roiben said, shrugging his shoulders, a small smile lifting his mouth.

Corny laughed. "So you're saying the world is cold and bleak, but infinitesimally less bleak with Kaye around? Could you be any more depressing?"

Roiben tilted his head. "And yet, here you are, more miserable than I."

"Funny." Corny made a face.

"Look, you can make someone appear to love you," Roiben said as carefully as he had put the jagged piece of broken china on the counter. "By enchantment or more subtle cruelties. You could cripple him such that he would forget that he had other choices."

"That's not what I want," Corny said.

Roiben smiled. "Are you sure?"

"Are *you*? Yes, I'm sure," Corny said hotly. "I just don't want to keep anticipating the worst. If it's going to be over tomorrow, then let it be over right now so I can get on with the pain and disappointment."

"If there is nothing but this," Roiben said. "If we are to be shadows, changeless and forgotten, we will have to dine on these memories for the rest of our days. Don't you want a few more moments to chew over?"

Corny shivered. "That's horrible. You're supposed to say that I'm wrong."

"I'm only repeating your words." Roiben brushed silver hair back from his face.

"But you believe them," said Corny. "You actually think that's what's going to happen with you and Kaye."

Roiben smiled gently. "And you're not the fatalist you pretend. What was it you said? *More afraid equals more of a jerk*. You're afraid, nothing more."

Corny snorted a little when Roiben said *jerk*.

"Yeah, I guess," he said, looking down at the asphalt and the strewn garbage. "But I can't *stop* being afraid."

"Perhaps, then, you could address the jerk part," Roiben said. "Or perhaps you could tell Luis, so he could at least try to reassure you."

Corny tilted his head, as if he was seeing Roiben for the first time. "You're afraid, too."

"Am I?" Roiben asked, but there was something in Cornelius's face that he found unnerving. He wondered what Corny thought he was looking at.

"I bet you're afraid you'll start hoping, despite your best intentions," Corny said. "You're okay with doom and gloom, but I bet it's really scary to think things might work out. I bet it's fucking terrifying to think she might love you the way you love her."

"Mayhaps." Roiben tried not to let anything show on his face. "Either way, before we go back inside I have a geas to place on you. Something to remind you of why you ought keep secrets secret."

"Oh come on," said Corny with a groan. "What about our meaningful talk? Aren't we friends now? Don't we get to do each other's nails and overlook each other's small, amusing betrayals?"

Roiben reached out one cold hand. "Afraid not."

Kaye was sitting on the counter of Moon in a Cup, looking annoyed, when Corny and Roiben walked back through the doors. Catching sight of them, her expression went slack with astonishment.

Luis, beside her, choked on a mouthful of hot chocolate and needed to be slapped several times on the back by Val before he recovered himself.

Cornelius's punishment was simple. Roiben had glamoured him to have small bone-pale horns jutting from his temples and had given his skin a light blue sheen. His ears tapered to delicate points. The glamour would last a single month from one fat, full moon to the next. And when he made coffee, he would have to face all those hopeful faerie seekers.

"I guess I deserve this," Corny said to no one in particular.

"Why did I even try to save you?" Luis said. Though his friends had gone, he was still there, still patiently waiting. Roiben hoped that Corny noticed that before all else.

Kaye walked toward Roiben. "I bet I know what you've been thinking," she said, shaking her head. "Bad things."

"Never when you're here," he told her, but he wasn't sure she heard as her arm wrapped around his waist so she could smother her helpless giggling against his chest. He drank in the warmth of her and tried, for once, to believe this could all last.

Don't sleep on the city that never sleeps, son, and don't fucking bring your squamous eldritch bullshit here, either!

THE CITY BORN GREAT

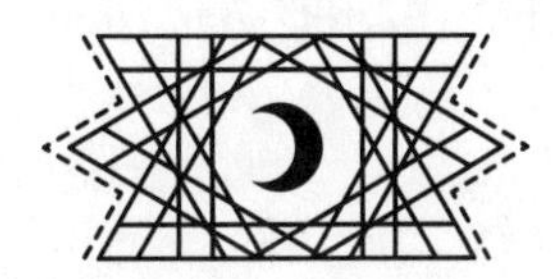

N. K. JEMISIN

I sing the city.

Fucking city. I stand on the rooftop of a building I don't live in and spread my arms and tighten my middle and yell nonsense ululations at the construction site that blocks my view. I'm really singing to the cityscape beyond. The city'll figure it out.

It's dawn. The damp of it makes my jeans feel slimy, or maybe that's 'cause they haven't been washed in weeks. Got change for a wash-and-dry, just not another pair of pants to wear till they're done. Maybe I'll spend it on more pants at the Goodwill down the street instead . . . but not yet. Not till I've finished going *AAAAaaaaAAAAaaaa* (breath) *aaaaAAAAaaaaaaa* and listening to the syllable echo back at me from every nearby building face. In my head, there's an orchestra playing "Ode to Joy" with a Busta Rhymes backbeat. My voice is just tying it all together.

Shut your fucking mouth! someone yells, so I take a bow and exit the stage.

But with my hand on the knob of the rooftop door, I stop and turn back and frown and listen, 'cause for a moment I hear something both distant and intimate singing back at me, basso-deep. Sort of coy.

And from even farther, I hear something else: a dissonant, gathering growl. Or maybe those are the rumblers of police sirens? Nothing I like the sound of, either way. I leave.

"There's a way these things are supposed to work," says Paulo. He's smoking again, nasty bastard. I've never seen him eat. All he uses his mouth for is smoking, drinking coffee, and talking. Shame; it's a nice mouth otherwise.

We're sitting in a cafe. I'm sitting with him because he bought me breakfast. The people in the cafe are eyeballing him because he's something not-white by their standards, but they can't tell what. They're eyeballing me because I'm definitively black, and because the holes in my clothes aren't the fashionable kind. I don't stink, but these people can smell anybody without a trust fund from a mile away.

"Right," I say, biting into the egg sandwich and damn near wetting myself. Actual egg! Swiss cheese! It's so much better than that McDonald's shit.

Guy likes hearing himself talk. I like his accent; it's sort of nasal and sibilant, nothing like a Spanish-speaker's. His eyes are huge, and I think, *I could get away with so much shit if I had permanent puppy eyes like that*. But he seems older than he looks—way, way older. There's only a tinge of gray at his temples, nice and distinguished, but he feels, like, a hundred.

He's also eyeballing me, and not in the way I'm used to. "Are you listening?" he asks. "This is important."

"Yeah," I say, and take another bite of my sandwich.

He sits forward. "I didn't believe it either, at first. Hong had to drag me to one of the sewers, down into the reeking dark, and show me the growing roots, the budding teeth. I'd been hearing breathing all my life. I thought everyone could." He pauses. "Have you heard it yet?"

"Heard what?" I ask, which is the wrong answer. It isn't that I'm not listening. I just don't give a shit.

He sighs. "Listen."

"I *am* listening!"

"No. I mean, listen, but not to me." He gets up, tosses a twenty onto the table—which isn't necessary, because he paid for the sandwich and the coffee at the counter, and this cafe doesn't do table service. "Meet me back here on Thursday."

I pick up the twenty, finger it, pocket it. Would've done him for the sandwich, or because I like his eyes, but whatever. "You got a place?"

He blinks, then actually looks annoyed. "*Listen*," he commands again, and leaves.

I sit there for as long as I can, making the sandwich last, sipping his leftover coffee, savoring the fantasy of being normal. I people-watch, judge other patrons' appearances; on the fly I make up a poem about being a rich white girl who notices a poor black boy in her coffee shop and has an existential crisis. I imagine Paulo being impressed by my sophistication and admiring me, instead of thinking I'm just some dumb street kid who doesn't listen. I visualize myself going back to a nice apartment with a soft bed, and a fridge stuffed full of food.

Then a cop comes in, fat florid guy buying hipster joe for himself and his partner in the car, and his flat eyes skim the shop. I imagine mirrors around my head, a rotating cylinder of them that causes his gaze to bounce away. There's no real power in this—it's just something I do to try to make myself less afraid when the monsters are near. For the first time, though, it sort of works: The cop looks around, but doesn't ping on the lone black face. Lucky. I escape.

I paint the city. Back when I was in school, there was an artist who came in on Fridays to give us free lessons in perspective and lighting and other shit that white people go to art school to learn. Except this guy had done that, and he was black. I'd never seen a black artist before. For a minute I thought I could maybe be one, too.

I can be, sometimes. Deep in the night, on a rooftop in Chinatown, with a spray can for each hand and a bucket of drywall paint that somebody left outside after doing up their living room in lilac, I move in scuttling, crablike swirls. The drywall stuff I can't use too much of; it'll start flaking off after a couple of rains. Spray paint's better for everything, but I like the contrast of the two textures—liquid black on rough lilac, red edging the black. I'm painting a hole. It's like a throat that doesn't start with a mouth or end in lungs; a thing that breathes and swallows endlessly, never filling. No one will see it except people in planes angling toward LaGuardia from the southwest, a few tourists who take helicopter tours, and NYPD aerial surveillance. I don't care what they see. It's not for them.

It's real late. I didn't have anywhere to sleep for the night, so this is what I'm doing to stay awake. If it wasn't the end of the month, I'd get on the subway, but the cops who haven't met their quota would fuck with me. Gotta be careful here; there's a lot of dumb-fuck Chinese kids west of Chrystie Street who wanna pretend to be a gang, protecting their territory, so I keep low. I'm skinny, dark; that helps, too. All I want to do is paint, man, because it's in me and I need to get it out. I need to open up this throat. I need to, I need to . . . yeah. Yeah.

There's a soft, strange sound as I lay down the last streak of black. I pause and look around, confused for a moment—and then the throat sighs behind me. A big, heavy gust of moist air tickles the hairs on my skin. I'm not scared. This is why I did it, though I didn't realize that when I started. Not sure how I know now. But when I turn back, it's still just paint on a rooftop.

Paulo wasn't shitting me. Huh. Or maybe my mama was right, and I ain't never been right in the head.

I jump into the air and whoop for joy, and I don't even know why.

I spend the next two days going all over the city, drawing breathing-holes everywhere, till my paint runs out.

I'm so tired on the day I meet Paulo again that I stumble and nearly fall through the cafe's plate-glass window. He catches my elbow and drags me over to a bench meant for customers. "You're hearing it," he says. He sounds pleased.

"I'm hearing coffee," I suggest, not bothering to stifle a yawn. A cop car rolls by. I'm not too tired to imagine myself as nothing, beneath notice, not even worth beating for pleasure. It works again; they roll on.

Paulo ignores my suggestion. He sits down beside me and his gaze goes strange and unfocused for a moment. "Yes. The city is breathing easier," he says. "You're doing a good job, even without training."

"I try."

He looks amused. "I can't tell if you don't believe me, or if you just don't care."

I shrug. "I believe you." I also don't care, not much, because I'm hungry. My stomach growls. I've still got that twenty he gave me, but I'll take it to that church-plate sale I heard about over on Prospect, get chicken and rice and greens and cornbread for less than the cost of a free-trade small-batch-roasted latte.

He glances down at my stomach when it growls. Huh. I pretend to stretch and scratch above my abs, making sure to pull up my shirt a little. The artist guy brought a model for us to draw once, and pointed to this little ridge of muscle above the hips called Apollo's Belt. Paulo's gaze goes right to it. *Come on, come on, fishy fishy. I need somewhere to sleep.*

Then his eyes narrow and focus on mine again. "I had forgotten," he says, in a faint wondering tone. "I almost . . . It's been so long. Once, though, I was a boy of the *favelas*."

"Not a lot of Mexican food in New York," I reply.

He blinks and looks amused again. Then he sobers. "This city will die," he says. He doesn't raise his voice, but he doesn't have to. I'm paying attention, now. Food, living: These things have meaning to me. "If you do not learn the things I have to teach you. If you do not help. The time will come and you will fail, and this city will join Pompeii and Atlantis and a dozen others whose names no one remembers, even though hundreds of thousands of people died with them. Or perhaps there will be a stillbirth—the shell of the city surviving to possibly grow again in the future but its vital spark snuffed for now, like New Orleans—but that will still kill *you*, either way. You are the catalyst, whether of strength or destruction."

He's been talking like this since he showed up—places that never were, things that can't be, omens and portents. I figure it's bullshit because he's telling it to *me*, a kid whose own mama kicked him out and prays for him to die every day and probably hates me. *God* hates me. And I fucking hate God back, so why would he choose me for anything? But that's really why I start paying attention: because of God. I don't have to believe in something for it to fuck up my life.

"Tell me what to do," I say.

Paulo nods, looking smug. Thinks he's got my number. "Ah. You don't want to die."

I stand up, stretch, feel the streets around me grow longer and more pliable in the rising heat of day. (Is that really happening, or am I imagining it, or is it happening *and* I'm imagining that it's connected to me somehow?) "Fuck you. That ain't it."

"Then you don't even care about that." He makes it a question with the tone of his voice.

"Ain't about being alive." I'll starve to death someday, or freeze some winter night, or catch something that rots me away until the hospitals have to take me, even without money or an address. But I'll sing and paint and dance and fuck and cry the city before I'm done, because it's mine. It's fucking *mine*. That's why.

"It's about *living*," I finish. And then I turn to glare at him. He can kiss my ass if he doesn't understand. "Tell me what to do."

Something changes in Paulo's face. He's listening, now. To me. So he gets to his feet and leads me away for my first real lesson.

This is the lesson: Great cities are like any other living things, being born and maturing and wearying and dying in their turn.

Duh, right? Everyone who's visited a real city feels that, one way or another. All those rural people who hate cities are afraid of something legit; cities really are *different*. They make a weight on the world, a tear in the fabric of reality, like . . . like black holes, maybe. Yeah. (I go to museums sometimes. They're cool inside, and Neil deGrasse Tyson is hot.) As more and more people come in and deposit their strangeness and leave and get replaced by others, the tear widens. Eventually it gets so deep that it forms a pocket, connected only by the thinnest thread of . . . something to . . . something. Whatever cities are made of.

But the separation starts a process, and in that pocket the many parts of the city begin to multiply and differentiate. Its sewers extend into places where there is no need for water. Its slums grow teeth; its art centers, claws. Ordinary things within it, traffic and construction and stuff like that, start to have a rhythm like a heartbeat, if you record their sounds and play them back fast. The city . . . quickens.

Not all cities make it this far. There used to be a couple of great cities on this continent, but that was before Columbus fucked the Indians' shit up, so we had to start over. New Orleans failed, like Paulo said, but it survived, and that's something. It can try again. Mexico City's well on its way. But New York is the first American city to reach this point.

The gestation can take twenty years or two hundred or two thousand, but eventually the time will come. The cord is cut and the city becomes a thing of its own, able to stand on wobbly legs and do . . . well, whatever the fuck a living, thinking entity shaped like a big-ass city wants to do.

And just as in any other part of nature, there are things lying in wait for this moment, hoping to chase down the sweet new life and swallow its guts while it screams.

That's why Paulo's here to teach me. That's why I can clear the city's breathing and stretch and massage its asphalt limbs. I'm the midwife, see.

I run the city. I run it every fucking day.

Paulo takes me home. It's just somebody's summer sublet in the Lower East Side, but it feels like a home. I use his shower and eat some of the food in his fridge without asking, just to see what he'll do. He doesn't do shit except smoke a cigarette, I think to piss me off. I can hear sirens on the streets of the neighborhood—frequent, close. I wonder, for some reason, if they're looking for me. I don't say it aloud, but

Paulo sees me twitching. He says, "The harbingers of the enemy will hide among the city's parasites. Beware of them."

He's always saying cryptic shit like this. Some of it makes sense, like when he speculates that maybe there's a *purpose* to all of it, some reason for the great cities and the process that makes them. What the enemy has been doing—attacking at the moment of vulnerability, crimes of opportunity—might just be the warm-up for something bigger. But Paulo's full of shit, too, like when he says I should consider meditation to better attune myself to the city's needs. Like I'mma get through this on white-girl yoga.

"White-girl yoga," Paulo says, nodding. "Indian man yoga. Stockbroker racquetball and schoolboy handball, ballet and merengue, union halls and SoHo galleries. You will embody a city of millions. You need not *be* them, but know that they are part of you."

I laugh. "Racquetball? That shit ain't no part of me, chico."

"The city chose you, out of all," Paulo says. "Their lives depend on you."

Maybe. But I'm still hungry and tired all the time, scared all the time, never safe. What good does it do to be valuable, if nobody values you?

He can tell I don't wanna talk anymore, so he gets up and goes to bed. I flop on the couch and I'm dead to the world. Dead.

Dreaming, dead dreaming, of a dark place beneath heavy cold waves where something stirs with a slithery sound and uncoils and turns toward the mouth of the Hudson, where it empties into the sea. Toward *me*. And I am too weak, too helpless, too immobilized by fear, to do anything but twitch beneath its predatory gaze.

Something comes from far to the south, somehow. (None of this is quite real. Everything rides along the thin tether that connects the city's reality to that of the world. The *effect* happens in the world, Paulo has said. The *cause* centers around me.) It moves between me, wherever I am, and the uncurling thing, wherever it is. An immensity protects me, just this once, just in this place—though from a great distance I feel others hemming and grumbling and raising themselves to readiness. Warning the enemy that it must adhere to the rules of engagement that have always governed this ancient battle. It's not allowed to come at me too soon.

My protector, in this unreal space of dream, is a sprawling jewel with filth-crusted facets, a thing that stinks of dark coffee and the bruised grass of a *futebol* pitch and traffic noise and familiar cigarette smoke.

Its threat display of saber-shaped girders lasts for only a moment, but that is enough. The uncurling thing flinches back into its cold cave, resentfully. But it will be back. That, too, is tradition.

I wake with sunlight warming half my face. Just a dream? I stumble into the room where Paulo is sleeping. "*São* Paulo," I whisper, but he does not wake. I wiggle under his covers. When he wakes he doesn't reach for me, but he doesn't push me away either. I let him know I'm grateful and give him a reason to let me back in, later. The rest'll have to wait till I get condoms and he brushes his ashy-ass mouth. After that, I use his shower again, put on the clothes I washed in his sink, and head out while he's still snoring.

Libraries are safe places. They're warm, in the winter. Nobody cares if you stay all day as long as you're not eyeballing the kids' corner or trying to hit up porn on the computers. The one at Forty-Second—the one with the lions—isn't that kind of library. It doesn't lend out books. Still, it has a library's safety, so I sit in a corner and read everything within reach: municipal tax law, *Birds of the Hudson Valley*, *What to Expect When You're Expecting a City Baby: NYC Edition*. See, Paulo? I told you I was listening.

It gets to be late afternoon and I head outside. People cover the steps, laughing, chatting, mugging with selfie sticks. There're cops in body armor over by the subway entrance, showing off their guns to the tourists so they'll feel safe from New York. I get a Polish sausage and eat it at the feet of one of the lions. Fortitude, not Patience. I know my strengths.

I'm full of meat and relaxed and thinking about stuff that ain't actually important—like how long Paulo will let me stay and whether I can use his address to apply for stuff—so I'm not watching the street. Until cold prickles skitter over my side. I know what it is before I react, but I'm careless again because I *turn to look* . . . Stupid, stupid, I fucking know better; cops down in Baltimore broke a man's spine for making eye contact. But as I spot these two on the corner opposite the library steps—short pale man and tall dark woman both in blue like black—I notice something that actually breaks my fear because it's so strange.

It's a bright, clear day, not a cloud in the sky. People walking past the cops leave short, stark afternoon shadows, barely there at all. But around these two, the shadows pool and curl as if they stand beneath their own private, roiling thundercloud. And as I watch, the shorter one begins to . . . *stretch*, sort of, his shape warping ever so slightly, until one eye is twice the circumference of the other. His right shoulder slowly develops a bulge that suggests a dislocated joint. His companion doesn't seem to notice.

Yooooo, nope. I get up and start picking my way through the crowd on the steps. I'm doing that thing I do, trying to shunt off their gaze—but it feels different this time. Sticky, sort of, threads of cheap-shit gum fucking up my mirrors. I *feel* them start following me, something immense and wrong shifting in my direction.

Even then I'm not sure—a lot of real cops drip and pulse sadism in the same way—but I ain't taking chances. My city is helpless, unborn as yet, and Paulo ain't here to protect me. I gotta look out for self, same as always.

I play casual till I reach the corner and book it, or try. Fucking tourists! They idle along the wrong side of the sidewalk, stopping to look at maps and take pictures of shit nobody else gives a fuck about. I'm so busy cussing them out in my head that I forget they can also be dangerous: Somebody yells and grabs my arm as I Heisman past, and I hear a man yell out, "He tried to take her purse!" as I wrench away. *Bitch, I ain't took shit*, I think, but it's too late. I see another tourist reaching for her phone to call 911. Every cop in the area will be gunning for every black male aged whatever now.

I gotta get out of the area.

Grand Central's right there, sweet subway promise, but I see three cops hanging out in the entrance, so I swerve right to take Forty-First. The crowds thin out past Lex, but where can I go? I sprint across Third despite the traffic; there are enough gaps. But I'm getting tired, 'cause I'm a scrawny dude who doesn't get enough to eat, not a track star.

I keep going, though, even through the burn in my side. I can feel *those* cops, the *harbingers of the enemy*, not far behind me. The ground shakes with their lumpen footfalls.

I hear a siren about a block away, closing. Shit, the UN's coming up; I don't need the Secret Service or whatever on me, too. I jag left through an alley and trip over a wooden pallet. Lucky again—a cop car rolls by the alley entrance just as I go down, and they don't see me. I stay down and try to catch my breath till I hear the car's engine fading into the distance. Then, when I think it's safe, I push up. Look back, because the city is squirming around me, the concrete is jittering and heaving, everything from the bedrock to the rooftop bars is trying its damnedest to tell me to go. Go. *Go*.

Crowding the alley behind me is . . . is . . . the shit? I don't have words for it. Too many arms, too many legs, too many eyes, and all of them fixed on me. Somewhere in the mass I glimpse curls of dark hair and a scalp of pale blond, and I understand suddenly that these are—this is—my two cops. One real monstrosity. The walls of the alley crack as it oozes its way into the narrow space.

"Oh. Fuck. No," I gasp.

I claw my way to my feet and haul ass. A patrol car comes around the corner from Second Avenue and I don't see it in time to duck out of sight. The car's loudspeaker blares something unintelligible, probably *I'm gonna kill you*, and I'm actually amazed. Do they not see the thing behind me? Or do they just not give a shit because they can't shake it down for city revenue? Let them fucking shoot me. Better than whatever that thing will do.

I hook left onto Second Avenue. The cop car can't come after me against the traffic, but it's not like that'll stop some doubled-cop monster. Forty-Fifth. Forty-Seventh and my legs are molten granite. Fiftieth and I think I'm going to die. Heart attack far too young; poor kid, should've eaten more organic; should've taken it easy and not been so angry; the world can't hurt you if you just ignore everything that's wrong with it; well, not until it kills you anyway.

I cross the street and risk a look back and see something roll onto the sidewalk on at least eight legs, using three or four arms to push itself off a building as it careens a little . . . before coming straight after me again. It's the Mega Cop, and it's gaining. *Oh shit oh shit oh shit please no.*

Only one choice.

Swing right. Fifty-Third, against the traffic. An old folks' home, a park, a promenade . . . fuck those. Pedestrian bridge? Fuck that. I head straight for the six lanes of utter batshittery and potholes that is FDR Drive, do not pass Go, do not try to cross on foot unless you want to be smeared halfway to Brooklyn. Beyond it? The East River, if I survive. I'm even freaked out enough to try swimming in that fucking sewage. But I'm probably gonna collapse in the third lane and get run over fifty times before anybody thinks to put on brakes.

Behind me, the Mega Cop utters a wet, tumid *hough*, like it's clearing its throat for swallowing. I go over the barrier and through the grass into fucking hell I go one lane silver car two lanes horns horns horns three lanes SEMI WHAT'S A FUCKING SEMI DOING ON THE FDR IT'S TOO TALL YOU STUPID UPSTATE HICK screaming four lanes GREEN TAXI screaming Smart Car hahaha cute five lanes moving truck six lanes and the blue Lexus actually brushes up against my clothes as it blares past screaming screaming screaming

screaming

screaming metal and tires as reality stretches, and nothing stops for the Mega Cop; it does not belong here and the FDR is an artery, vital with the movement of nutrients and strength and attitude and adrenaline, the cars are white blood cells and the thing is an irritant, an infection, an invader to whom the city gives no consideration and no quarter screaming, as the Mega Cop is torn to pieces by the semi and the taxi and the Lexus and even that adorable Smart Car, which actually swerves a little to run over an extra-wiggly piece. I collapse onto a square of grass, breathless, shaking, wheezing, and can only stare as a dozen limbs are crushed, two dozen eyes squashed flat, a mouth that is mostly gums riven from jaw to palate. The pieces flicker like a monitor with an AV cable short, translucent to solid and back again—but FDR don't stop for shit except a presidential motorcade or a Knicks game, and this thing sure as hell ain't Carmelo Anthony. Pretty soon there's nothing left of it but half-real smears on the asphalt.

I'm alive. Oh, God.

I cry for a little while. Mama's boyfriend ain't here to slap me and say I'm not a man for it. Daddy would've said it was okay—tears mean you're alive—but Daddy's dead. And I'm alive.

With limbs burning and weak, I drag myself up, then fall again. Everything hurts. Is this that heart attack? I feel sick. Everything is shaking, blurring. Maybe it's a stroke. You don't have to be old for that to happen, do you? I stumble over to a garbage can and think about throwing up into it. There's an old guy lying on the bench—me in twenty years, if I make it that far. He opens one eye as I stand there gagging and purses his lips in a judgy way, like he could do better dry-heaves in his sleep.

He says, "It's time," and rolls over to put his back to me.

Time. Suddenly I have to move. Sick or not, exhausted or not, something is . . . pulling me. West, toward the city's center. I push away from the can and hug myself as I shiver and stumble toward the pedestrian bridge. As I walk over the lanes I previously ran across, I look down onto flickering fragments of the dead Mega Cop, now ground into the asphalt by a hundred car wheels. Some globules of it are still twitching, and I don't like that. Infection, intrusion. I want it gone.

We want it gone. Yes. It's time.

I blink and suddenly I'm in Central Park. How the fuck did I get here? Disoriented, I realize only as I see their black shoes that I'm passing another pair of cops, but these two don't bother me. They should—skinny kid shivering like he's cold on a June day; even if all they do is drag me off somewhere to shove a plunger up my ass, they should *react* to me. Instead, it's like I'm not there. Miracles exist, Ralph Ellison was right, any NYPD you can walk away from, hallelujah.

The Lake. Bow Bridge: a place of transition. I stop here, stand here, and I know . . . everything.

Everything Paulo's told me: It's true. Somewhere beyond the city, the Enemy is awakening. It sent forth its harbingers and they have failed, but its taint is in the city now, spreading with every car that passes over every now-microscopic iota of the Mega Cop's substance, and this creates a foothold. The Enemy uses this anchor to drag itself up from the dark toward the world, toward the warmth and light, toward the defiance that is *me*, toward the burgeoning wholeness that is *my city*. This attack is not all of it, of course. What comes is only the smallest fraction of the Enemy's old, old evil—but that should be more than enough to slaughter one lowly, worn-out kid who doesn't even have a real city to protect him.

Not yet. It's time. *In* time? We'll see.

On Second, Sixth, and Eighth avenues, my water breaks. Mains, I mean. Water mains. Terrible mess, gonna fuck up the evening commute. I shut my eyes and I am seeing what no one else sees. I am feeling the flex and rhythm of reality, the contractions of possibility. I reach out and grip the railing of the bridge before me and feel the steady, strong pulse that runs through it. *You're doing good, baby. Doing great.*

Something begins to shift. I grow bigger, encompassing. I feel myself upon the firmament, heavy as the foundations of a city. There are others here with me, looming, watching—my ancestors' bones under Wall Street, my predecessors' blood ground into the benches of Christopher Park. No, *new* others, of my new people, heavy imprints upon the fabric of time and space. São Paulo squats nearest, its roots stretching all the way to the bones of dead Machu Picchu, watching sagely and twitching a little with the memory of its own relatively recent traumatic birth. Paris observes with distant disinterest, mildly offended that any city of our tasteless upstart land has managed this transition; Lagos exults to see a new fellow who knows the hustle, the hype, the fight. And more, many more, all of them watching, waiting to see if their numbers increase. Or not. If nothing else, they will bear witness that I, we, were great for one shining moment.

"We'll make it," I say, squeezing the railing and feeling the city contract. All over the city, people's ears pop, and they look around in confusion. "Just a little more. Come on." I'm scared, but there's no rushing this. *Lo que pasa, pasa*—damn, now that song is in my head, *in me* like the rest of New York. It's all here, just like Paulo said. There's no gap between me and the city anymore.

And as the firmament ripples, slides, tears, the Enemy writhes up from the deeps with a reality-bridging roar—

But it is too late. The tether is cut and we are here. We become! We stand, whole and hale and independent, and our legs don't even wobble. We got this. Don't sleep on the city that never sleeps, son, and don't fucking bring your squamous eldritch bullshit here.

I raise my arms and avenues leap. (It's real but it's not. The ground jolts and people think, *Huh, subway's really shaky today.*) I brace my feet and they are girders, anchors, bedrock. The beast of the deeps shrieks and I laugh, giddy with postpartum endorphins. *Bring it.* And when it comes at me I hip-check it with the BQE, backhand it with Inwood Park, drop the South Bronx on it like an elbow. (On the evening news that night, ten construction sites will report wrecking-ball collapses. City safety regulations are so lax; terrible, terrible.) The Enemy tries some kind of fucked-up wiggly shit—it's all tentacles—and I snarl and bite into it 'cause New Yorkers eat damn near as much sushi as Tokyo, mercury and all.

Oh, now you're crying! Now you wanna run? Nah, son. You came to the wrong town. I curb stomp it with the full might of Queens and something inside the beast breaks and bleeds iridescence all over creation. This is a shock, for it has not been truly hurt in centuries. It lashes back in a fury, faster than I can block, and from a place that most of the city cannot see, a skyscraper-long tentacle curls out of nowhere to smash into New York Harbor. I scream and fall, I can *hear* my ribs crack, and—no!—a major earthquake shakes Brooklyn for the first time in decades. The Williamsburg Bridge twists and snaps apart like kindling; the Manhattan groans and splinters, though thankfully it does not give way. I feel every death as if it is my own.

Fucking kill you for that, bitch, I'm not-thinking. The fury and grief have driven me into a vengeful fugue. The pain is nothing; this ain't my first rodeo. Through the groan of my ribs I drag myself upright and brace my legs in a pissing-off-the-platform stance. Then I shower the Enemy with a one-two punch of Long Island radiation and Gowanus toxic waste, which burn it like acid. It screams again in pain and disgust, but *Fuck you, you don't belong here, this city is mine, get out!* To drive this lesson home I cut the bitch with LIRR traffic, long vicious honking lines; and to stretch out its pain I salt these wounds with the memory of a bus ride to LaGuardia and back.

And just to add insult to injury? I backhand its ass with Hoboken, raining the drunk rage of ten thousand dudebros down on it like the hammer of God. Port Authority makes it honorary New York, motherfucker; you just got Jerseyed.

The Enemy is as quintessential to nature as any city. We cannot be stopped from becoming, and the Enemy cannot be made to end. I hurt only a small part of it—but I know damn well I sent that part back broken. Good. Time ever comes for that final confrontation, it'll think twice about taking me on again.

Me. *Us*. Yes.

When I relax my hands and open my eyes to see Paulo striding along the bridge toward me with another goddamned cigarette between his lips, I fleetingly see him for what he is again: the sprawling thing from my dream, all sparkling spires and reeking slums and stolen rhythms made over with genteel cruelty. I know that he glimpses what I am, too, all the bright light and bluster of me. Maybe he's always seen it, but there is *admiration* in his gaze now, and I like it. He comes to help support me with his shoulder, and he says, "Congratulations," and I grin.

I live the city. It thrives and it is mine. I am its worthy avatar, and together? We will never be afraid again.

Fifty years later.

I sit in a car, watching the sunset from Mulholland Drive. The car is mine; I'm rich now. The city is not mine, but that's all right. The person is coming who will make it live and stand and thrive in the ancient way . . . or not. I know my duty, respect the traditions. Each city must emerge on its own or die trying. We elders merely guide, encourage. Stand witness.

There: a dip in the firmament near the Sunset Strip. I can feel the upwelling of loneliness in the soul I seek. Poor, empty baby. Won't be long now, though. Soon—if she survives—she'll never be alone again.

I reach for my city, so far away, so inseverable from myself. *Ready?* I ask New York.

Fuck yeah, it answers, filthy and fierce.

We go forth to find this city's singer, and hopefully to hear the greatness of its birthing song.

Anything forbidden becomes mysterious. And mysterious things always become attractive, sooner or later. Usually sooner. Especially in New York.

LA PEAU VERTE

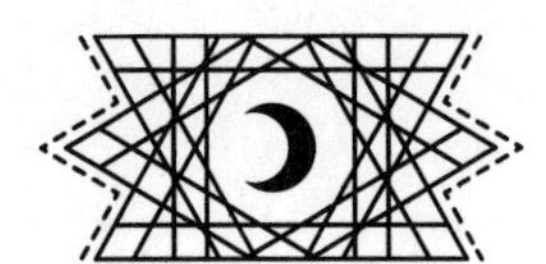

Caitlín R. Kiernan

1

In a dusty, antique-littered back room of the loft on St. Mark's Place, room with walls the color of ripe cranberries, Hannah stands naked in front of the towering mahogany-framed mirror and stares at herself. No—not *her* self any longer, but the new thing that the man and woman have made of her. Three long hours busy with their airbrushes and latex prosthetics, grease paints and powders and spirit gum, their four hands moving as one, roaming excitedly and certainly across her body, hands sure of their purpose. She doesn't remember their names, if, in fact, they ever told their names to her. Maybe they did, but the two glasses of brandy she's had have set the names somewhere just beyond recall. Him tall and thin, her thin but not so very tall, and now they've both gone, leaving Hannah alone. Perhaps their part in this finished; perhaps the man and woman are being paid, and she'll never see either of them again, and she feels a sudden, unexpected pang at the thought, never one for casual intimacies, and they have been both casual and intimate with her body.

The door opens, and the music from the party grows suddenly louder. Nothing she would ever recognize, probably nothing that has a name, even; wild impromptu of drumming hands and flutes, violins and cellos, an incongruent music that is both primitive and drawing-room practiced. The old woman with the mask of peacock feathers and gown of iridescent satin stands in the doorway, watching Hannah. After a moment, she smiles and nods her head slowly, appreciatively.

"Very pretty," she says. "How does it feel?"

"A little strange," Hannah replies and looks at the mirror again. "I've never done anything like this before."

"Haven't you?" the old woman asks her, and Hannah remembers her name, then—Jackie, Jackie something that sounds like Shady or Sadie, but isn't either. A sculptor from England, someone said. When she was very young, she knew Picasso, and someone said that, too.

"No," Hannah replies. "I haven't. Are they ready for me now?"

"Fifteen more minutes, give or take. I'll be back to bring you in. Relax. Would you like another brandy?"

Would I? Hannah thinks and glances down at the crystal snifter sitting atop an old secretary next to the mirror. It's almost empty now, maybe one last warm amber sip standing between it and empty. She wants another drink, something to burn away the last, lingering dregs of her inhibition and self-doubt, but "No," she tells the woman. "I'm fine."

"Then chill, and I'll see you in fifteen," Jackie Whomever says, smiles again, her disarming, inviting smile of perfect white teeth, and she closes the door, leaving Hannah alone with the green thing watching her from the mirror.

The old Tiffany lamps scattered around the room shed candy puddles of stained-glass light, light as warm as the brandy, warm as the dark-chocolate tones of the intricately carved frame holding the tall mirror. She takes one tentative step nearer the glass, and the green thing takes an equally tentative step nearer her. *I'm in there somewhere,* she thinks. *Aren't I?*

Her skin painted too many competing, complementary shades of green to possibly count, one shade bleeding into the next, an infinity of greens that seem to roil and flow around her bare legs, her flat, hard stomach, her breasts. No patch of skin left uncovered, her flesh become a rain-forest canopy, autumn waves in rough, shallow coves, the shells of beetles and leaves from a thousand gardens, moss and emeralds, jade statues and the brilliant scales of poisonous tropical serpents. Her nails polished a green so deep it might almost be black, instead. The uncomfortable scleral contacts to turn her eyes into the blaze of twin chartreuse stars, and Hannah leans a little closer to the mirror, blinking at those eyes, *with* those eyes, the windows to a soul she doesn't have. A soul of everything vegetable and living, everything growing or not, soul of sage and pond scum, malachite and verdigris. The fragile translucent wings sprouting from her shoulder blades—at least another thousand greens to consider in those wings alone—and all the many places where they've been painstakingly attached to her skin are hidden so expertly she's no longer sure where the wings end and she begins.

The one, and the other.

"I definitely should have asked for another brandy," Hannah says out loud, spilling the words nervously from her ocher, olive, turquoise lips.

Her hair—not *her* hair, but the wig *hiding* her hair—like something parasitic, something growing from the bark of a rotting tree, epiphyte curls across her painted shoulders, spilling down her back between and around the base of the wings. The long tips the man and woman added to her ears so dark that they almost match her nails, and her nipples airbrushed the same lightless, bottomless green, as well. She smiles, and even her teeth have been tinted a matte pea green.

There is a single teardrop of green glass glued firmly between her lichen eyebrows.

I could get lost in here, she thinks, and immediately wishes she'd thought something else instead.

Perhaps I am already.

And then Hannah forces herself to look away from the mirror, reaches for the brandy snifter and the last swallow of her drink. Too much of the night still lies ahead of her to get freaked out over a costume, too much left to do and way too much money for her to risk getting cold feet now. She finishes the brandy, and the new warmth spreading through her belly is reassuring.

Hannah sets the empty glass back down on the secretary and then looks at herself again. And this time it is her self, after all, the familiar lines of her face still visible just beneath the make-up. But it's a damn good illusion. *Whoever the hell's paying for this is certainly getting his money's worth,* she thinks.

Beyond the back room, the music seems to be rising, swelling quickly towards crescendo, the strings racing the flutes, the drums hammering along underneath. The old woman named Jackie will be back for her soon. Hannah takes a deep breath, filling her lungs with air that smells and tastes like dust and old furniture, like the paint on her skin, more faintly of the summer rain falling on the roof of the building. She exhales slowly and stares longingly at the empty snifter.

"Better to keep a clear head," she reminds herself.

Is that what I have here? And she laughs, but something about the room or her reflection in the tall mirror turns the sound into little more than a cheerless cough.

And then Hannah stares at the beautiful, impossible green woman staring back at her, and waits.

2

"Anything forbidden becomes mysterious," Peter says and picks up his remaining bishop, then sets it back down on the board without making a move. "And mysterious things always become attractive to us, sooner or later. Usually sooner."

"What is that? Some sort of unwritten social law?" Hannah asks him, distracted by the Beethoven that he always insists on whenever they play chess. *Die Geschöpfe des Prometheus* at the moment, and she's pretty sure he only does it to break her concentration.

"No, dear. Just a statement of the fucking obvious."

Peter picks up the black bishop again, and this time he almost uses it to capture one of her rooks, then thinks better of it. More than thirty years her senior and the first friend she made after coming to Manhattan, his salt-and-pepper beard and mustache that's mostly salt, his eyes as grey as a winter sky.

"Oh," she says, wishing he'd just take the damn rook and be done with it. Two moves from checkmate, barring an act of divine intervention. But that's another of his games, Delaying the Inevitable. She thinks he probably has a couple of trophies for it stashed away somewhere in his cluttered apartment, chintzy *faux* golden loving cups for his Skill and Excellence in Procrastination.

"Taboo breeds desire. Gluttony breeds disinterest."

"Jesus, I ought to write these things down," she says, and he smirks at her, dangling the bishop teasingly only an inch or so above the chessboard.

"Yes, you really should. My agent could probably sell them to someone or another. *Peter Mulligan's Big Book of Tiresome Truths.* I'm sure it would be more popular than my last novel. It certainly couldn't be *less*—"

"Will you stop it and *move* already? Take the damned rook, and get it over with."

"But it *might* be a mistake," he says and leans back in his chair, mock suspicion on his face, one eyebrow cocked, and he points towards her queen. "It could be a trap. You might be one of those predators that fakes out its quarry by playing dead."

"You have no idea what you're talking about."

"Yes, I do. You know what I mean. Those animals, the ones that only *pretend* to be dead. You might be one of those."

"I *might* just get tired of this and go the hell home," she sighs, because he knows that she won't, so she can say whatever she wants.

"Anyway," he says, "it's work, if you want it. It's just a party. Sounds like an easy gig to me."

"I have that thing on Tuesday morning though, and I don't want to be up all night."

"Another shoot with Kellerman?" asks Peter and frowns at her, taking his eyes off the board, tapping at his chin with the bishop's mitre.

"Is there something wrong with that?"

"You hear things, that's all. Well, *I* hear things. I don't think you ever hear anything at all."

"I need the work, Pete. The last time I sold a piece, I think Lincoln was still President. I'll never make as much money painting as I do posing for *other* people's art."

"Poor Hannah," Peter says. He sets the bishop back down beside his king and lights a cigarette. She almost asks him for one, but he thinks she quit three months ago, and it's nice having at least that one thing to lord over him; sometimes it's even useful. "At least you *have* a fallback," he mutters and exhales; the smoke lingers above the board like fog on a battlefield.

"Do you even know who these people are?" she asks and looks impatiently at the clock above his kitchen sink.

"Not firsthand, no. But then they're not exactly my sort. Entirely too, well . . . " and Peter pauses, searching for a word that never comes, so he continues without it. "But the Frenchman who owns the place on St. Mark's, Mr. Ordinaire—excuse me, *Monsieur* Ordinaire—I heard he used to be some sort of anthropologist. I think he might have written a book once."

"Maybe Kellerman would reschedule for the afternoon," Hannah says, talking half to herself.

"You've actually never tasted it?" he asks, picking up the bishop again and waving it ominously towards her side of the board.

"No," she replies, too busy now wondering if the photographer will rearrange his Tuesday schedule on her behalf to be annoyed at Peter's cat and mouse with her rook.

"Dreadful stuff," he says and makes a face like a kid tasting Brussels sprouts or Pepto-Bismol for the first time. "Might as well have a big glass of black jelly beans and cheap vodka, if you ask me. *La Fée Verte* my fat ass."

"Your ass isn't fat, you skinny old queen," Hannah scowls playfully, reaching quickly across the table and snatching the bishop from Peter's hand. He doesn't resist. This isn't the first time she's grown too tired of waiting for him to move to wait any longer. She removes her white rook off the board and sets the black bishop in its place.

"That's suicide, dear," Peter says, shaking his head and frowning. "You're aware of that, yes?"

"You know those animals that *bore* their prey into submission?"

"No, I don't believe I've ever heard of them before."

"Then maybe you should get out more often."

"Maybe I should," he replies, setting the captured rook down with all the other prisoners he's taken. "So, are you going to do the party? It's a quick grand, you ask me."

"That's easy for you say. You're not the one who'll be getting naked for a bunch of drunken strangers."

"A fact for which we should *all* be forevermore and eternally grateful."

"You have his number?" she asks, giving in, because that's almost a whole month's rent in one night and, after her last gallery show, beggars can't be choosers.

"There's a smart girl," Peter says and takes another drag off his cigarette. "The number's on my desk somewhere. Remind me again before you leave. Your move."

3

"How old were you when that happened, when your sister died?" the psychologist asks, Dr. Edith Valloton and her smartly cut hair so black it always makes Hannah think of fresh tar, or old tar gone deadly soft again beneath a summer sun to lay a trap for unwary, crawling things. Someone she sees when the nightmares get bad, which is whenever the painting isn't going well or the modeling jobs aren't coming in or both. Someone she can tell her secrets to who has to *keep* them secret, someone who listens as long as she pays by the hour, a place to turn when faith runs out and priests are just another bad memory to be confessed.

"Almost twelve," Hannah tells her and watches while Edith Valloton scribbles a note on her yellow legal pad.

"Do you remember if you'd begun menstruating yet?"

"Yeah. My periods started right after my eleventh birthday."

"And these dreams, and the stones. This is something you've never told anyone?"

"I tried to tell my mother once."

"She didn't believe you?"

Hannah coughs into her hand and tries not to smile, that bitter, wry smile to give away things she didn't come here to show.

"She didn't even *hear* me," she says.

"Did you try more than once to tell her about the fairies?"

"I don't think so. Mom was always pretty good at letting us know whenever she didn't want to hear what was being said. You learned not to waste your breath."

"Your sister's death, you've said before that it's something she was never able to come to terms with."

"She never tried. Whenever my father tried, or I tried, she treated us like traitors. Like we were the ones who put Judith in her grave. Or like we were the ones *keeping* her there."

"If she couldn't face it, Hannah, then I'm sure it did seem that way to her."

"So, no," Hannah says, annoyed that she's actually paying someone to sympathize with her mother. "No. I guess never really told anyone about it."

"But you think you want to tell me now?" the psychologist asks and sips her bottled water, never taking her eyes off Hannah.

"You said to talk about all the nightmares, all the things I think are nightmares. It's the only one that I'm not sure about."

"Not sure if it's a nightmare, or not sure if it's even a dream?"

"Well, I always thought I was awake. For years, it never once occurred to me I might have only been dreaming."

Edith Valloton watches her silently for a moment, her cat-calm, cat-smirk face, unreadable, too well trained to let whatever's behind those dark eyes slip and show. Too detached to be smug, too concerned to be indifferent. Sometimes, Hannah thinks she might be a dyke, but maybe that's only because the friend who recommended her is a lesbian.

"Do you still have the stones?" the psychologist asks, finally, and Hannah shrugs out of habit.

"Somewhere, probably. I never throw anything away. They might be up at Dad's place, for all I know. A bunch of my shit's still up there, stuff from when I was a kid."

"But you haven't tried to find them?"

"I'm not sure I *want* to."

"When is the last time you saw them, the last time you can remember having seen them?"

And Hannah has to stop and think, chews intently at a stubby thumbnail and watches the clock on the psychologist's desk, the second hand traveling round and round and round. Seconds gone for pennies, nickels, dimes.

Hannah, this is the sort of thing you really ought to try to get straight ahead of time, she thinks in a voice that sounds more like Dr. Valloton's than her own thought-voice. *A waste of money, a waste of time . . .*

"You can't remember?" the psychologist asks and leans a little closer to Hannah.

"I kept them all in an old cigar box. I think my grandfather gave me the box. No, wait. He didn't. He gave it to Judith, and then I took it after the accident. I didn't think she'd mind."

"I'd like to see them someday, if you ever come across them again. Wouldn't that help you to know whether it was a dream or not, if the stones are real?"

"Maybe," Hannah mumbles around her thumb. "And maybe not."

"Why do you say that?"

"A thing like that, words scratched onto a handful of stones, it'd be easy for a kid to fake. I might have made them all myself. Or someone else might have made them, someone playing a trick on me. Anyone could have left them there."

"Did people do that often? Play tricks on you?"

"Not that I can recall. No more than usual."

Edith Valloton writes something else on her yellow pad and then checks the clock.

"You said that there were always stones after the dreams. Never before?"

"No, never before. Always after. They were always there the next day, always in the same place."

"At the old well," the psychologist says, like Hannah might have forgotten and needs reminding.

"Yeah, at the old well. Dad was always talking about doing something about it, before the accident, you know. Something besides a couple of sheets of corrugated tin to hide the hole. Afterwards, of course, the county ordered him to have the damned thing filled in."

"Did your mother blame him for the accident, because he never did anything about the well?"

"My mother blamed *everyone*. She blamed him. She blamed me. She blamed whoever had dug that hole in the first goddamn place. She blamed God for putting water underground so people would dig wells to get at it. Believe me, Mom had blame down to an art."

And again, the long pause, the psychologist's measured consideration, quiet moments she plants like seeds to grow ever deeper revelations.

"Hannah, I want you to try to remember the word that was on the first stone you found. Can you do that?"

"That's easy. It was *follow*."

"And do you also know what was written on the last one, the very last one that you found?"

And this time she has to think, but only for a moment.

"*Fall*," she says. "The last one said *fall*."

4

Half a bottle of Mari Mayans borrowed from an unlikely friend of Peter's, a goth chick who DJs at a club that Hannah's never been to because Hannah doesn't go to clubs. Doesn't dance and has always been more or less indifferent to both music and fashion. The goth chick works days at Trash and Vaudeville on St. Mark's, selling Doc Martens and blue hair dye only a couple of blocks from the address on the card that Peter gave her. The place where the party is being held. *La Fête de la Fée Verte,* according to the small white card, the card with the phone number. She's already made the call, has already agreed to be there, seven o'clock sharp, seven on the dot, and everything that's expected of her has been explained in detail, twice.

Hannah's sitting on the floor beside her bed, a couple of vanilla-scented candles burning because she feels obligated to make at least half a half-hearted effort at atmosphere. Obligatory show of respect for mystique that doesn't interest her, but she's gone to the trouble to borrow the bottle of liqueur; the bottle passed to her in a brown paper bag at the boutique, anything but inconspicuous, and the girl glared out at her, cautious from beneath lids so heavy with shades of black and purple that Hannah was amazed the girl could open her eyes.

"So, you're supposed to be a friend of Peter's?" the girl asked suspiciously.

"Yeah, supposedly" Hannah replied, accepting the package, feeling vaguely, almost pleasurably illicit. "We're chess buddies."

"A painter," the girl said.

"Most of the time."

"Peter's a cool old guy. He made bail for my boyfriend once, couple of years back."

"Really? Yeah, he's wonderful," and Hannah glanced nervously at the customers browsing the racks of leather handbags and corsets, then at the door and the bright daylight outside.

"You don't have to be so jumpy. It's not illegal to have absinthe. It's not even illegal to drink it. It's only illegal to import it, which you didn't do. So don't sweat it."

Hannah nodded, wondering if the girl was telling the truth, if she knew what she was talking about. "What do I owe you?" she asked.

"Oh, nothing," the girl replied. "You're a friend of Peter's, and, besides, I get it cheap from someone over in Jersey. Just bring back whatever you don't drink."

And now Hannah twists the cap off the bottle, and the smell of odor is so strong, so immediate, she can smell it before she even raises the bottle to her nose. *Black jelly beans,* she thinks, just like Peter said, and that's something else she never cared for. As a little girl, she'd set the black ones aside—and the pink ones too—saving them for her sister. Her sister had liked the black ones.

She has a wine glass, one from an incomplete set she bought last Christmas, secondhand, and she has a box of sugar cubes, a decanter filled with filtered tap water, a spoon from her mother's mismatched antique silverware. She pours the absinthe, letting it drip slowly from the bottle until the fluorescent yellow-green liquid has filled the bottom of the glass. Then Hannah balances the spoon over the mouth of the goblet and places one of the sugar cubes in the tarnished bowl of the spoon. She remembers watching Gary Oldman and Winona Ryder doing this in *Dracula,* remembers seeing the movie with a boyfriend who eventually left her for another man, and the memory and all its associations are enough to make her stop and sit staring at the glass for a moment.

"This is so fucking silly," she says, but part of her, the part that feels guilty for taking jobs that pay the bills, but have nothing to do with painting, the part that's always busy rationalizing and justifying the way she spends her time, assures her it's a sort of research. A new experience, horizon-broadening something to expand her mind's eye, and, for all she knows, it might lead her art somewhere it needs to go.

"Bullshit," she whispers, frowning down at the entirely uninviting glass of Spanish absinthe. She's been reading *Absinthe: History in a Bottle* and *Artists and Absinthe,* accounts of Van Gogh and Rimbaud, Oscar Wilde and Paul Marie Verlaine and their various relationships with this foul-smelling liqueur. She's never had much respect for artists who use this or that drug as a crutch and then call it their muse; heroin, cocaine, pot, booze, what-the-hell-ever, all the same shit as far as she's concerned. An excuse, an inability in the artist to hold himself accountable for his *own* art, a lazy cop-out, as useless as the idea of the muse itself. And *this* drug, this drug in particular, so tied up with art and inspiration there's even a Renoir painting decorating the Mari Mayans label, or at least it's something that's supposed to *look* like a Renoir.

But you've gone to all this trouble. Hell, you may as well taste it, at least. Just a taste, *to satisfy curiosity, to see what all the fuss is about.*

Hannah sets the bottle down and picks up the decanter, pouring water over the spoon, over the sugar cube. The absinthe louches quickly to an opalescent, milky white-green. Then she puts the decanter back on the floor and stirs the half-dissolved sugar into the glass, sets the spoon aside on a china saucer.

"Enjoy the ride," the goth girl said as Hannah walked out of the shop. "She's a blast."

Hannah raises the glass to her lips, sniffs at it, wrinkling her nose, and the first, hesitant sip is even sweeter and more piquant than she expected, sugar-soft fire when she swallows, a seventy-proof flower blooming hot in her belly. But the taste not nearly as disagreeable as she'd thought it would be, the sudden licorice and alcohol sting, a faint bitterness underneath that she guesses might be the wormwood. The second sip is less of a shock, especially since her tongue seems to have gone slightly numb.

She opens *Absinthe: History in a Bottle* again, opening the book at random, and there's a full-page reproduction of Albert Maignan's *The Green Muse.* A blonde woman with marble skin, golden hair, wrapped in diaphanous folds of olive, her feet hovering weightless above bare floorboards, her hands caressing the forehead of an intoxicated poet. The man is gaunt and seems lost in some ecstasy or revelry or simple delirium, his right hand clawing at his face, the other hand open in what might have been meant as a feeble attempt to ward off the attentions of his unearthly companion. *Or,* Hannah thinks, *perhaps he's reaching for something.* There's a shattered green bottle on the floor at his feet, a full glass of absinthe on his writing desk.

Hannah takes another sip and turns the page.

A photograph, Verlaine drinking absinthe in the Café Procope.

Another, bolder swallow, and the taste is becoming familiar now, almost, *almost* pleasant.

Another page. Jean Béraud's *Le Boulevard, La Nuit.*

When the glass is empty, and the buzz in her head, behind her eyes is so gentle, buzz like a stinging insect wrapped in spider silk and honey, Hannah takes another sugar cube from the box and pours another glass.

5

"Fairies.

'Fairy crosses.'

Harper's Weekly, 50-715:

That, near the point where the Blue Ridge and the Allegheny Mountains unite, north of Patrick County, Virginia, many little stone crosses have been found.

A race of tiny beings.

They crucified cockroaches.

Exquisite beings—but the cruelty of the exquisite. In their diminutive way they were human beings. They crucified.

The 'fairy crosses,' we are told in *Harper's Weekly,* range in weight from one-quarter of an ounce to an ounce: but it is said, in the *Scientific American,* 79-395, that some of them are no larger than the head of a pin.

They have been found in two other states, but all in Virginia are strictly localized on and along Bull Mountain . . .

. . . I suppose they fell there."

Charles Fort, *The Book of the Damned* (1919)

6

In the dream, which is never the same thing twice, not precisely, Hannah is twelve years old and standing at her bedroom window watching the backyard. It's almost dark, the last rays of twilight, and there are chartreuse fireflies dappling the shadows, already a few stars twinkling in the high indigo sky, the call of a whippoorwill from the woods nearby.

Another whippoorwill answers.

And the grass is moving. The grass grown so tall because her father never bothers to mow it anymore. It could be wind, only there is no wind; the leaves in the trees are all perfectly, silently still, and no limb swaying, no twig, no leaves rustling in even the stingiest breeze. Only the grass.

It's probably just a cat, she thinks. *A cat, or a skunk, or a raccoon.*

The bedroom has grown very dark, and she wants to turn on a lamp, afraid of the restless grass even though she knows it's only some small animal, awake for the night and hunting, taking a short cut across their backyard. She looks over her shoulder, meaning to ask Judith to please turn on a lamp, but there's only the dark room, Judith's empty bunk, and she remembers it all again. It's always like the very first time she heard, the surprise and disbelief and pain always that fresh, the numbness that follows that absolute.

"Have you seen your sister?" her mother asks from the open bedroom door. There's so much night pooled there that she can't make out anything but her mother's softly glowing eyes the soothing color of amber beads, two cat-slit pupils swollen wide against the gloom.

"No, Mom," Hannah tells her, and there's a smell in the room then like burning leaves.

"She shouldn't be out so late on a school night."

"No, Mom, she shouldn't," and the eleven-year-old Hannah is amazed at the thirty-five-year-old's voice coming from her mouth. The thirty-five-year-old Hannah remembers how clear, how unburdened by time and sorrow, the eleven-year-old Hannah's voice could be.

"You should look for her," her mother says.

"I always do. That comes later."

"Hannah, have you seen your sister?"

Outside, the grass has begun to swirl, rippling round and round upon itself, and there's the faintest green glow dancing a few inches above the ground.

The fireflies, she thinks, though she knows it's not the fireflies, the way she knows it's not a cat, or a skunk, or a raccoon making the grass move.

"Your father should have seen to that damned well," her mother mutters, and the burning leaves smell grows a little stronger. "He should have done something about that years ago."

"Yes, Mom, he should have. You should have made him."

"No," her mother replies angrily. "This is not my fault. None of it's my fault."

"No, of course it's not."

"When we bought this place, I told him to see to that well. I *told* him it was dangerous."

"You were right," Hannah says, watching the grass, the softly pulsing cloud of green light hanging above it. The light is still only about as big as a basketball. Later, it'll get a lot bigger. She can hear the music now, pipes and drums and fiddles, like a song from one of her father's albums of folk music.

"Hannah, have you seen your sister?"

Hannah turns and stares defiantly back at her mother's glowing, accusing eyes.

"That makes three, Mom. Now you have to leave. Sorry, but them's the rules," and her mother does leave, that obedient phantom fading slowly away with a sigh, a flicker, a half second when the darkness seems to bend back upon itself, and she takes the burning leaves smell with her.

The light floating above the backyard grows brighter, reflecting dully off the windowpane, off Hannah's skin and the room's white walls. The music rises to meet the light's challenge.

Peter's standing beside her now, and she wants to hold his hand, but doesn't, because she's never quite sure if he's supposed to be in this dream.

"I am the Green Fairy," he says, sounding tired and older than he is, sounding sad. "My robe is the color of despair."

"No," she says. "You're only Peter Mulligan. You write books about places you've never been and people who will never be born."

"You shouldn't keep coming here," he whispers, the light from the backyard shining in his grey eyes, tinting them to moss and ivy.

"Nobody else does. Nobody else ever could."

"That doesn't mean—"

But he stops and stares speechlessly at the backyard.

"I should try to find Judith," Hannah says. "She shouldn't be out so late on a school night."

"That painting you did last winter," Peter mumbles, mumbling like he's drunk or only half awake. "The pigeons on your windowsill, looking in."

"That wasn't me. You're thinking of someone else."

"I hated that damned painting. I was glad when you sold it."

"So was I," Hannah says. "I should try to find her now, Peter. My sister. It's almost time for dinner."

"I am ruin and sorrow," he whispers.

And now the green light is spinning very fast, throwing off gleaming flecks of itself to take up the dance, to swirl about their mother star, little worlds newborn, whole universes, and she could hold them all in the palm of her right hand.

"What I need," Peter says, "is blood, red and hot, the palpitating flesh of my victims."

"Jesus, Peter, that's purple even for you," and Hannah reaches out and lets her fingers brush the glass. It's warm, like the spring evening, like her mother's glowing eyes.

"I didn't write it," he says.

"And I never painted pigeons."

She presses her fingers against the glass and isn't surprised when it shatters, explodes, and the sparkling diamond blast is blown inward, tearing her apart, shredding the dream until it's only unconscious, fitful sleep.

7

"I wasn't in the mood for this," Hannah says and sets the paper saucer with three greasy, uneaten cubes of orange cheese and a couple of Ritz crackers down on one corner of a convenient table. The table is crowded with fliers about other shows, other openings at other galleries. She glances at Peter and then at the long white room and the canvases on the walls.

"I thought it would do you good to get out. You never go anywhere anymore."

"I come to see you."

"My point exactly, dear."

Hannah sips at her plastic cup of warm merlot, wishing she had a beer instead.

"And you said that you liked Perrault's work."

"Yeah," she says. "I'm just not sure I'm up for it tonight. I've been feeling pretty morbid lately, all on my own."

"That's generally what happens to people who swear off sex."

"Peter, I didn't *swear off* anything."

And she follows him on their first slow circuit around the room, small talk with people that she hardly knows or doesn't want to know at all, people who know Peter better than they know her, people whose opinions matter and people whom she wishes she'd never met. She smiles and nods her head, sips her wine, and tries not to look too long at any of the huge, dark canvases spaced out like oil and acrylic windows on a train.

"He's trying to bring us down, down to the very core of those old stories," a woman named Rose tells Peter. She owns a gallery somewhere uptown, the sort of place where Hannah's paintings will never hang. "'Little Red Riding Hood,' 'Snow White,' 'Hansel and Gretel,' all those old fairy tales," Rose says. "It's a very post-Freudian approach."

"Indeed," Peter says. *As if he agrees,* Hannah thinks, *as if he even cares,* when she knows damn well he doesn't.

"How's the new novel coming along?" Rose asks him.

"Like a mouthful of salted thumbtacks," he replies, and she laughs.

Hannah turns and looks at the nearest painting, because it's easier than listening to the woman and Peter pretend to enjoy one another's company. A somber storm of blacks and reds and greys, dappled chaos struggling to resolve itself into images, images stalled at the very edge of perception. She thinks she remembers having seen a photo of this canvas in *Artforum*.

A small beige card on the wall to the right of the painting identifies it as *Night in the Forest*. There isn't a price, because none of Perrault's paintings are ever for sale. She's heard rumors that he's turned down millions, tens of millions, but suspects that's all exaggeration and PR. Urban legends for modern artists, and from the other things that she's heard he doesn't need the money, anyway.

Rose says something about the exploration of possibility and fairy tales and children using them to avoid any *real* danger, something that Hannah's pretty sure she's lifted directly from Bruno Bettelheim.

"Me, I was always rooting for the wolf," Peter says, "or the wicked witch or the three bears or whatever. I never much saw the point in rooting for silly girls too thick not to go wandering about alone in the woods."

Hannah laughs softly, laughing to herself, and takes a step back from the painting, squinting at it. A moonless sky pressing cruelly down upon a tangled, writhing forest, a path and something waiting in the shadows, stooped shoulders, ribsy, a calculated smudge of scarlet that could be its eyes. There's no one on the path, but the implication is clear—there will be, soon enough, and the thing crouched beneath the trees is patient.

"Have you seen the stones yet?" Rose asks and no, Peter replies, no we haven't.

"They're a new direction for him," she says. "This is only the second time they've been exhibited."

If I could paint like that, Hannah thinks, *I could tell Dr. Valloton to kiss my ass. If I could paint like that, it would be an exorcism.*

And then Rose leads them both to a poorly-lit corner of the gallery, to a series of rusted wire cages, and inside each one is a single stone. Large pebbles or small cobbles, stream-worn slate and granite, and each stone has been crudely engraved with a single word.

The first one reads "follow."

"Peter, I need to go now," Hannah says, unable to look away from the yellow-brown stone, the word tattooed on it, and she doesn't dare let her eyes wander ahead to the next one.

"Are you sick?"

"I need to go, that's all. I need to go *now*."

"If you're not feeling well," the woman named Rose says, trying too hard to be helpful, "there's a restroom in the back."

"No, I'm fine. Really. I just need some air."

And Peter puts an arm protectively around her, reciting his hurried, polite goodbyes to Rose. But Hannah still can't look away from the stone, sitting there behind the wire like a small and vicious animal at the zoo.

"Good luck with the book," Rose says and smiles, and Hannah's beginning to think she is going to be sick, that she will have to make a dash for the toilet, after all. there's a taste like foil in her mouth, and her heart like a mallet on dead and frozen beef, adrenaline, the first eager tug of vertigo.

"It was good to meet you, Hannah," the woman says. Hannah manages to smile, manages to nod her head.

And then Peter leads her quickly back through the crowded gallery, out onto the sidewalk and the warm night spread out along Mercer Street.

8

"Would you like to talk about that day at the well?" Dr. Valloton asks, and Hannah bites at her chapped lower lip.

"No. Not now," she says. "Not again."

"Are you sure?"

"I've already told you everything I can remember."

"If they'd found her body," the psychologist says, "perhaps you and your mother and father would have been able to move on. There could have at least been some sort of closure. There wouldn't have been that lingering hope that maybe someone would find her, that maybe she was alive."

Hannah sighs loudly, looking at the clock for release, but there's still almost half an hour to go.

"Judith fell down the well and drowned," she says.

"But they never found the body."

"No, but they found enough, enough to be sure. She fell down the well. She drowned. It was very deep."

"You said you heard her calling you."

"I'm not sure," Hannah says, interrupting the psychologist before she can say the things she was going to say next, before she can use Hannah's own words against her. "I've never been absolutely sure. I told you that."

"I'm sorry if it seems like I'm pushing," Dr. Valloton says.

"I just don't see any reason to talk about it again."

"Then let's talk about the dreams, Hannah. Let's talk about the day you saw the fairies."

9

The dreams, or the day from which the dreams would arise and, half-forgotten, seek always to return. The dreams or the day itself, the one or the other, it makes very little difference. The mind exists only in a moment, always, a single flickering moment, remembered or actual, dreaming or awake or something liminal between the two, the precious, treacherous illusion of Present floundering in the crack between Past and Future.

The dream of the day—or the day itself—and the sun is high and small and white, a dazzling July sun coming down in shafts through the tall trees in the woods behind Hannah's house. She's running to catch up with Judith, her sister two years older and her legs grown longer, always leaving Hannah behind. *You can't catch me, slowpoke. You can't even keep up.* Hannah almost trips in a tangle of creeper vines and has to stop long enough to free her left foot.

"Wait up!" she shouts, and Judith doesn't answer. "I want to see. Wait for me!"

The vines try to pull one of Hannah's tennis shoes off and leave bright beads of blood on her ankle. But she's loose again in only a moment, running down the narrow path to catch up, running through the summer sun and the oak-leaf shadows.

"I found something," Judith said to her that morning after breakfast. The two of them sitting on the back porch steps. "Down in the clearing by the old well," she said.

"What? What did you find?"

"Oh, I don't think I should tell you. No, I *definitely* shouldn't tell you. You might go and tell Mom and Dad. You might spoil everything."

"No, I wouldn't. I wouldn't tell them anything. I wouldn't tell anyone."

"Yes, you would, big mouth."

And, finally, she gave Judith half her allowance to tell, half to be shown whatever there was to see. Her sister dug deep down into the pockets of her jeans, and her hand came back up with a shiny black pebble.

"I just gave you a whole dollar to show me a *rock*?"

"No, stupid. *Look* at it," and Judith held out her hand.

The letters scratched deep into the stone—JVDTH—five crooked letters that almost spelled her sister's name, and Hannah didn't have to pretend not to be impressed.

"Wait for me!" she shouts again, angry now, her voice echoing around the trunks of the old trees and dead leaves crunching beneath her shoes. Starting to guess that the whole thing is a trick after all, just one of Judith's stunts, and her sister's probably watching her from a hiding place right this very second, snickering quietly to herself. Hannah stops running and stands in the center of the path, listening to the murmuring forest sounds around her.

And something faint and lilting that might be music.

"That's not all," Judith said. "But you have to *swear* you won't tell Mom and Dad."

"I swear."

"If you do tell, well, I *promise* I'll make you wish you hadn't."

"I won't tell anyone *anything*."

"Give it back," Judith said, and Hannah immediately handed the black stone back to her. "If you *do* tell—"

"I already said I won't. How many times do I have to say I won't tell?"

"Well then," Judith said and led her around to the back of the little tool shed where their father kept his hedge clippers and bags of fertilizer and the old lawnmowers he liked to take apart and try to put back together again.

"This better be *worth* a dollar," Hannah said.

She stands very, very still and listens to the music, growing louder. She thinks it's coming from the clearing up ahead.

"I'm going back home, Judith!" she shouts, not a bluff because suddenly she doesn't care whether or not the thing in the jar was real, and the sun doesn't seem as warm as it did only a moment ago.

And the music keeps getting louder.

And louder.

And Judith took an empty mayonnaise jar out of the empty rabbit hutch behind the tool shed. She held it up to the sun, smiling at whatever was inside.

"Let me see," Hannah said.

"Maybe I should make you give me another dollar first," her sister replied, smirking, not looking away from the jar.

"No way," Hannah said indignantly. "Not a snowball's chance in Hell," and she grabbed for the jar, then, but Judith was faster, and her hand closed around nothing at all.

In the woods, Hannah turns and looks back towards home, then turns back towards the clearing again, waiting for her just beyond the trees.

"Judith! This isn't funny! I'm going home right this second!"

Her heart is almost as loud as the music now. Almost. Not quite, but close enough. Pipes and fiddles, drums and a jingle like tambourines.

Hannah takes another step towards the clearing, because it's nothing at all but her sister trying to scare her. Which is stupid, because it's broad daylight, and Hannah knows these woods like the back of her hand.

Judith unscrewed the lid of the mayonnaise jar and held it out so Hannah could see the small, dry thing curled in a lump at the bottom. Tiny mummy husk of a thing, grey and crumbling in the morning light.

"It's just a damn dead mouse," Hannah said disgustedly. "I gave you a whole dollar to see a rock and a dead mouse in a jar?"

"It's *not* a mouse, stupid. Look closer."

And so she did, bending close enough that she could see the perfect dragonfly wings on its back, transparent, iridescent wings that glimmer faintly in the sun. Hannah squinted and realized that she could see its face, realized that it *had* a face.

"Oh," she said, looking quickly up at her sister, who was grinning triumphantly. "Oh, Judith. Oh my god. What is it?"

"Don't you know?" Judith asked her. "Do I have to tell you everything?"

Hannah picks her way over the deadfall just before the clearing, the place where the path through the woods disappears beneath a jumble of fallen, rotting logs. There was a house back here, her father said, a long, long time ago. Nothing left but a big pile of rocks where the chimney once stood, and also the well covered over with sheets of rusted corrugated tin. There was a fire, her father said, and everyone in the house died.

On the other side of the deadfall, Hannah takes a deep breath and steps out into the daylight, leaving the tree shadows behind, forfeiting her last chance not to see.

"Isn't it cool," Judith said. "Isn't it the coolest thing you ever seen?"

Someone's pushed aside the sheets of tin, and the well is so dark that even the sun won't go there. And then Hannah sees the wide ring of mushrooms, the perfect circle of toadstools and red caps and spongy brown morels growing round the well. The heat shimmers off the tin, dancing mirage shimmer as though the air here is turning to water, and the music is very loud now.

"I found it," Judith whispered, screwing the top back onto the jar as tightly as she could. "I found it, and I'm going to keep it. And you'll keep your mouth shut about it, or I'll never, *ever* show you anything else again."

Hannah looks up from the mushrooms, from the open well, and there are a thousand eyes watching her from the edges of the clearing. Eyes like indigo berries and rubies and drops of honey, like gold and silver coins, eyes like fire and ice, eyes like seething dabs of midnight.

Eyes filled with hunger beyond imagining, neither good nor evil, neither real nor impossible.

Something the size of a bear, squatting in the shade of a poplar tree, raises its shaggy charcoal head and smiles.

That's another pretty one," it growls.

And Hannah turns and runs.

10

"But you *know,* in your soul, what you must have really seen that day," Dr. Valloton says and taps the eraser end of her pencil lightly against her front teeth. There's something almost obscenely earnest in her expression, Hannah thinks, in the steady *tap, tap, tap* of the pencil against her perfectly spaced, perfectly white incisors. "You saw your sister fall into the well, or you realized that she just had. You may have heard her calling out for help."

"Maybe I *pushed* her in," Hannah whispers.

"Is that what you *think* happened?"

"No," Hannah says and rubs at her temples, trying to massage away the first dim throb of an approaching headache. "But, most of the time, I'd rather *believe* that's what happened."

"Because you *think* it would be easier than what you remember."

"Isn't it? Isn't easier to believe she pissed me off that day, and so I shoved her in? That I made up these crazy stories so I'd never have to feel guilty for what I'd done? Maybe that's what the nightmares are, my conscience trying to fucking force me to come clean."

"And what are the stones, then?"

"Maybe I put them all there myself. Maybe I scratched those words on them myself and hid them there for me to find, because I knew that would make it easier for me to believe. If there was something that real, that tangible, something solid to remind me of the story, that the story is supposed to be the truth."

A long moment that's almost silence, just the clock on the desk ticking and the pencil tapping against the psychologist's teeth. Hannah rubs harder at her temples, the real pain almost within sight now, waiting for her just a little ways past this moment or the next, vast and absolute, deep purple shot through with veins of red and black. Finally, Dr. Valloton lays her pencil down and takes a deep breath.

"Is this a confession, Hannah?" she asks, and the obscene earnestness is dissolving into something that may be eager anticipation, or simple clinical curiosity, or only dread. "Did you kill your sister?"

And Hannah shakes her head and shuts her eyes tight.

"Judith fell into the well," she says calmly. "She moved the tin, and got too close to the edge. The sheriff showed my parents where a little bit of the ground had collapsed under her weight. She fell into the well, and she drowned."

"Who are you trying so hard to convince? Me or yourself?"

"Do you really think it matters?" Hannah replies, matching a question with a question, tit for tat.

"Yes," Dr. Valloton says. "Yes, I do. You need to know the truth."

"Which one?" Hannah asks, smiling against the pain swelling behind her eyes, and this time the psychologist doesn't bother answering, lets her sit silently with her eyes shut until the clock decides her hour's up.

11

Peter Mulligan picks up a black pawn and moves it ahead two squares; Hannah removes it from the board with a white knight. He isn't even trying today, and that always annoys her. Peter pretends to bc surprised that's he's lost another piece, then pretends to frown and think about his next move while he talks.

"In Russian," he says, "*chernobyl* is the word for wormwood. Did Kellerman give you a hard time?"

"No," Hannah says. "No, he didn't. In fact, he said he'd actually rather do the shoot in the afternoon. So everything's jake, I guess."

"Small miracles," Peter sighs, picking up a rook and setting it back down again. "So you're doing the anthropologist's party?"

"Yeah," she replies. "I'm doing the anthropologist's party."

"*Monsieur* Ordinaire. You think he was born with that name?"

"I think I couldn't give a damn, as long as his check doesn't bounce. A thousand dollars to play dress-up for a few hours. I'd be a fool not to do the damned party."

Peter picks the rook up again and dangles it in the air above the board, teasing her. "Oh, his book," he says. "I remembered the title the other day. But then I forgot it all over again. Anyway, it was something on shamanism and shapeshifters, werewolves and masks, that sort of thing. It sold a lot of copies in '68, then vanished from the face of the earth. You could probably find out something about it online." Peter sets the rook down and starts to take his hand away.

"Don't," she says. "That'll be check mate."

"You could at least let me *lose* on my own, dear," he scowls, pretending to be insulted.

"Yeah, well, I'm not ready to go home yet." Hannah replies, and Peter Mulligan goes back to dithering over the chessboard and talking about Monsieur Ordinaire's forgotten book. In a little while, she gets up to refill both their coffee cups, and there's a single black and grey pigeon perched on the kitchen windowsill, staring in at her with its beady piss-yellow eyes. It almost reminds her of something she doesn't want to be reminded of, and so she raps on the glass with her knuckles and frightens it away.

12

The old woman named Jackie never comes for her. There's a young boy, instead, fourteen or fifteen, sixteen at the most, his nails polished poppy red to match his rouged lips, and he's dressed in peacock feathers and silk. He opens the door and stands there, very still, watching her, waiting wordlessly. Something like awe on his smooth face, and for the first time Hannah doesn't just feel nude, she feels *naked.*

"Are they ready for me now?" she asks him, trying to sound no more than half as nervous as she is, and then turns her head to steal a last glance at the green fairy in the tall mahogany mirror. But the mirror is empty. There's no one there at all, neither her nor the green woman, nothing but the dusty backroom full of antiques, the pretty hard-candy lamps, the peeling cranberry wallpaper.

"My Lady," the boy says in a voice like broken crystal shards, and then he curtsies. "The Court is waiting to receive you, at your ready." He steps to one side, to let her pass, and the music from the party grows suddenly very loud, changing tempo, the rhythm assuming a furious speed as a thousand notes and drumbeats tumble and boom and chase one another's tails.

"The mirror," Hannah whispers, pointing at it, at the place where her reflection should be, and when she turns back to the boy there's a young girl standing there, instead, dressed in his feathers and make-up. She could be his twin.

"It's a small thing, My Lady," she says with the boy's sparkling, shattered tongue.

"What's happening?"

"The Court is assembled," the girl child says. "They are all waiting. Don't be afraid, My Lady. I will show you the way."

The path, the path through the woods to the well. The path down to the well . . .

"Do you have a name?" Hannah asks, surprised at the calm in her voice; all the embarrassment and unease at standing naked before this child, and the one before, the boy twin, the fear at what she didn't see gazing back at her in the looking glass, all of that gone now.

"My name? I'm not such a fool as that, My Lady."

"No, of course not," Hannah replies. "I'm sorry."

"I will show you the way," the child says again. "Never harm, nor spell, nor charm, come our Lady nigh."

"That's very kind of you," Hannah replies. "I was beginning to think that I was lost. But I'm not lost, am I?"

"No, My Lady. You are here."

"Yes. Yes, I *am* here, aren't I?" and the child smiles for her, showing off its sharp crystal teeth. Hannah smiles back, and then she leaves the dusty backroom and the mahogany mirror, following the child down a short hallway; the music has filled in all the vacant corners of her skull, the music and the heavy living-dying smells of wildflowers and fallen leaves, rotting stumps and fresh-turned earth. A riotous hothouse cacophony of odors—spring to fall, summer to winter—and she's never tasted air so violently sweet.

. . . the path down the well, and the still black water at the bottom.

Hannah, can you hear me? Hannah?

It's so cold down here. I can't see . . .

At the end of the hall, just past the stairs leading back down to St. Mark's, there's a green door, and the girl opens it. Green gets you out.

And all the things in the wide, wide room—the unlikely room that stretches so far away in every direction that it could never be contained in any building, not in a thousand buildings—the scampering, hopping, dancing, spinning, flying, skulking things, each and every one of them stops and stares at her. And Hannah knows that she ought to be frightened of them, that she should turn and run from this place. But it's really nothing she hasn't seen before, a long time ago, and she steps past the child (who is a boy again) as the wings on her back begin to thrum like the frantic, iridescent wings of bumblebees and hummingbirds, red wasps and hungry dragonflies. Her mouth tastes of anise and wormwood, sugar and hyssop and melissa. Sticky verdant light spills from her skin and pools in the grass and moss at her bare feet.

Sink or swim, and so easy to imagine the icy black well water closing thickly over her sister's face, filling her mouth, slipping up her nostrils, flooding her belly, as clawed hands dragged her down.

And down.

And down.

And sometimes, Dr. Valloton says, sometimes we spend our entire lives just trying to answer one simple question.

The music is a hurricane, swallowing her.

My Lady. Lady of the Bottle. *Artemisia absinthium,* Chernobyl, *apsinthion,* Lady of Waking Dreaming, Green Lady of Elation and Melancholy.

I am ruin and sorrow.

My robe is the color of despair.

They bow, all of them, and Hannah finally sees the thing waiting for her on its prickling throne of woven branches and birds' nests, the hulking antlered thing with blazing eyes, that wolf-jawed hart, the man and the stag, and she bows, in her turn.

New York City takes a lot of protecting. Luckily there are mages, like Matthew Szczegielniak, who are there to take care of the more unusual threats . . . like a cockatrice, a creature whose looks kill . . . literally.

CRYPTIC COLORATION

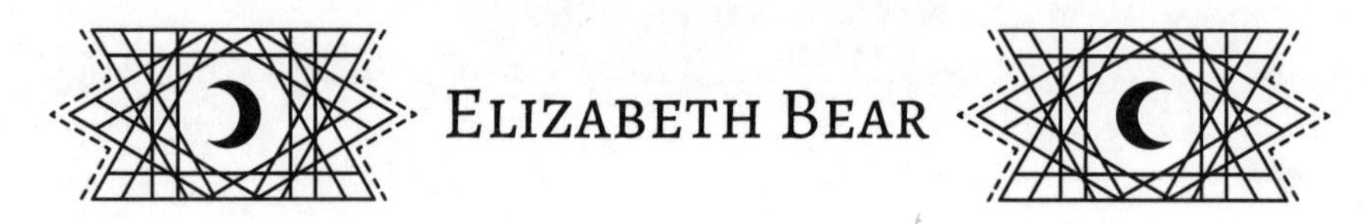

ELIZABETH BEAR

Katie saw him first. The next-best thing to naked, in cutoff camouflage pants and high-top basketball sneakers and nothing else, except the thick black labyrinth of neo-tribal ink that covered his pale skin from collarbones to ankle-bones. He shone like piano keys, glossy-sleek with sweat in a sultry September afternoon.

Katie already had Melissa's sleeve in her hand and was tugging her toward the crosswalk. Gina trailed three steps behind. "We have *got* to go watch this basketball game."

"What?" But then Melissa's line of sight intersected Katie's and she gasped. "Oh my fuck, look at all that ink. Do you think that counts as a shirt or a skin?" Melissa was from Boston, but mostly didn't talk like it.

"Never mind the ink," Katie said. "Look at his *triceps.*"

Little shadowed dimples in the undersides of his arms, and all Katie could think of for a moment was that he wasn't terribly tall, and if she had been standing close enough when he raised his hands to take a pass she could have stood on tiptoe and licked them. The image dried her mouth, heated her face.

Melissa would have thought Katie silly for having shocked herself, though, so she didn't say anything.

Even without the ink, he had the best body on the basketball court. Hard all over, muscle swelling and valleying as he sprinted and sidestepped, chin-length blond hair swinging in his eyes. He skittered left like a boxer, turned, dribbled between his legs—quadriceps popping, calves like flexed cables—caught the ball as it came back up and leaped. Parabolic, sailing. Sweat shook from his elbows and chin as he released.

A three-point shot. A high geometric arch.

Denied when a tall black boy of eighteen or so tipped it off the edge of the basket, jangling the chain, and fired back to half court, but that didn't matter. Katie glanced over her shoulder to make sure Gina was following.

"God," Melissa purred. "I love New York."

Katie, mopping her gritty forehead with the inside of her T-shirt collar, couldn't have agreed more.

So it was mid-September and still too hot to think. So she was filthy just from walking through the city air.

You didn't get anything like the blond boy back home in Appleton.

Melissa was a tall freckled girl who wore her hair in red pigtails that looked like braided yarn. She had a tendency to bounce up on her toes that made her seem much taller, and she craned over the pedestrians as they stepped up onto the far curb. "There's some shade by the—oh, my god would you look at that?"

Katie bounced too, but couldn't see anything except shirts. "Mel!"

"Sorry."

Flanking Gina, two steps ahead of her, they moved on. Melissa was right about the shade; it was cooler and had a pretty good view. They made it there just as the blond was facing off with a white-shirted Latino in red Converse All-Stars that were frayed around the cuffs. "Jump ball," Gina said, and leaned forward between Katie and Melissa.

The men coiled and went up. Attenuated bodies, arching, bumping, big hands splayed. Katie saw dark bands clasping every finger on the blond, and each thumb. More ink, or maybe rings, though wouldn't it hurt to play ball in them?

The Latino was taller; the blond beat him by inches. He tagged the ball with straining fingertips, lofted it to his team. And then he landed lightly, knees flexed, sucked in a deep breath while his elbows hovered back and up, and pivoted.

It wasn't a boy, unless a man in his early thirties counted.

"Holy crap," said Gina, who only swore in Puerto Rican. "Girls, that's *Doctor S.*"

Wednesday at noon, the three mismatched freshman girls who sat in the third row center of Matthew Szczegielniak's 220 were worse than usual. Normally, they belonged to the doe-eyed, insecure subspecies of first-year student, badly needing to be shocked back into a sense of humor and acceptance of their own fallibility. A lot of these young girls reminded Matthew of adolescent cats; trying so hard to look serene and dignified that they walked into walls.

And then got mad at you for noticing.

Really, that was even funnier.

Today, though, they were giggling and nudging and passing notes until he was half-convinced he'd made a wrong turn somewhere and wound up teaching a high school class. He caught the carrot-top mid-nudge while mid-sentence (Byron, Scott), about a third of the way through his introductory forty minutes on the Romantic poets, and fixed her with a glare through his spectacles that could have chipped enamel.

A red tide rose behind her freckles, brightening her sunburned nose. Her next giggle came out a squeak.

"Ms. Martinchek. You have a trenchant observation on the work of Joanna Baillie, perhaps?"

If she'd gone any redder, he would have worried about apoplexy. She stared down at her open notebook and shook her head in tiny quick jerks.

"No, Doctor S."

Matthew Szczegielniak rubbed his nose with the butt of his dry-erase marker, nudging his spectacles up with his thumbnail. He wasn't enough of a problem child to make his students learn his last name—even the simplified pronunciation he preferred—though the few that tried were usually good for endless hours of entertainment.

Besides, Matthew was a Mage. And magic being what it was, he would be hard put to imagine a more counterproductive activity than teaching three hundred undergrads a semester how to pronounce his *name*.

Enough heat of embarrassment radiated from Melissa's body to make Katie lean on her opposite elbow and duck her head in sympathy. She kept sneaking looks at Doctor S., trying to see past the slicked ponytail, the spectacles, the arch and perfectly bitchy precision of his lecturing style to find the laughing half-naked athlete of the day before.

She'd thought he was probably gay.

Sure, books, covers, *whatever*. It was impossible to believe in *him* exultant, shaking sweat from his hair, even though she'd seen it, even though the image fumed wisps of intrigue through her pelvis. Even though she could see the black rings on every finger and each thumb, clicking slightly when he gestured. She couldn't understand how she had never noticed them before. And never noticed the way he always dressed for class, though it was still hotter than Hades; the ribbed soft-colored turtleneck that covered him from the backs of broad hands to the tender flesh under his throat, the camel- or smoke- or charcoal-colored corduroy blazer that hid the shape of his shoulders and the width of his chest.

It was maddening, knowing what was under the clothes. She wondered if the barbaric tattoos extended everywhere, and flushed, herself, at least as bright as Melissa. And then brighter, as she felt the prof's eyes on her, as if he was wondering what she was thinking that so discomfited her.

Oh, lord, but wouldn't that have hurt?

On the other hand, he'd had the insides of his arms done, and the inner thighs. And *that* was supposed to hurt like anything, wasn't it?

And *then* she noticed that his left ear was pierced top to bottom, ten or a dozen rings, and sank down in her chair while she wondered what else he might have had done. And why she'd never noticed any of it—the rings, the earrings, the ink, the muscles—any of it, before.

"Oh, God," she whispered without moving her lips. "I'm never going to make it through this class."

But she did. And leaned up against the wall beside the door afterwards, shoulder-to-shoulder with Melissa while they waited for Gina to come out. Quiet, but if anybody was going to do something crazy or brave or both, it would be her. And right now, she was down at the bottom of the lecture hall, chatting up the professor.

"Oh, God," Katie moaned. "I'm going to have to switch sections. I didn't hear a word he said."

"I did. Oh, God. He knows my name." Melissa blushed the color of her plastic notebook cover all over again. Her voice dropped, developed a mocking precision of pronunciation. "Ms. Martinchek, maybe you can tell me about Joanna Ballyhoo . . . "

"Baillie." Gina, who came up and stood on tiptoe to stick a purple Post-it note to Melissa's tit. "He wrote it down for me. This way you can impress him next week."

Melissa picked the note off her chest and stared at it. "He uses purple Post-it notes?"

"I was right," Katie said. "He's gay."

"Do you want to find out?"

"Oh, and how do you propose we do that? Check the BiGALA membership roster?" Melissa might be scoffing, but her eyes were alight. Katie swallowed.

Gina checked her wristwatch. She had thick brown-black hair swept up in a banana clip, showing tiny curls like inverted devil horns at her pale nape. "He's got office hours until three. I say we grab some lunch and drop off our books, and then when he leaves we see where he goes."

"I dunno." Katie crossed her arms over her notebook. "It's not like playing basketball with your shirt off is a crime . . . "

"It's not like following someone to see where they go is a crime, either," Melissa pointed out. "We're not going to . . . stalk him."

"No, just stalk him."

"Katie!"

"Well, it's true." But Melissa was looking at her, and . . . she had come to Manhattan to have adventures. "What if we get caught?"

"Get caught . . . walking down a public street?"

Right. Whatever. "We could just look him up in the phone book."

"I checked. Not listed, amigas. Maybe it's under his boyfriend's name."

Even Melissa blinked at her this time. "Jesus Christ, Gomez. You're a criminal mastermind."

Those same three girls were holding up the wall when Matthew left the lecture theatre, climbing up the stairs to go out by the top door. He walked past, pretending not to notice them, or the stifled giggles and hiccups that erupted a moment later.

He just had time to grab a sandwich before his office hours. Almost one o'clock; probably nothing left but egg salad.

He needed the protein anyway.

He supplemented the sandwich with two cartons of chocolate milk, a bag of sourdough pretzels and three rip-top packets of French's mustard, and spread the lot out on his desk while he graded papers for his Renaissance drama class. With luck, no students would show up except a lonely or neurotic or favor-currying Ph.D. candidate, and he could get half of the papers done today.

He had twenty-four sophomores and juniors, and of the first ten papers, only two writers seemed to understand that *The Merry Wives of Windsor* was supposed to be funny. One of those was a Sociology major. Matthew was a failure as a teacher. He finished the sandwich, blew crumbs off his desk so he wouldn't leave mayonnaise fingerprints on the essays, and tore open the pretzels before he sharpened his red pencil one more time.

Honey mustard would have been better. He should get some to stick in his desk. Unless it went bad. Honey didn't go bad, and mustard didn't go bad. Logically, an amalgam would reflect the qualities of both.

The spike of ice and acid through the bones of his hands originated from his iron Mage's rings, and it not only made him drop a pretzel—splattering mustard across the scarred wooden desk—but it brought him to his feet before he heard the police sirens start.

He glanced at the clock. Five more minutes. "That which thou hast promised thou must perform," he said, under his breath.

He left his lunch on the desk and found his keys in his pocket on the way to the door.

Their quarry almost ran them over as *they* were on their way in to start stalking him. Katie sidestepped quickly, catching Gina across the chest with a straight left arm. Melissa managed to get herself out of the way.

Doctor S. was almost running. His corduroy jacket flapped along the vent as he skidded between pedestrians, cleared four concrete steps in a bounce, and avoided a meandering traffic jam of students with as much facility as he'd shown on the basketball court. And if Katie had begun to suspect that it was just a bizarre case of mistaken identity, the toreador sidestep around the lady with the baby carriage would have disabused her. Doctor S. moved with a force and grace that were anything but common to academia.

Katie turned to follow him. It was only a small gesture to catch Gina's wrist, and without more urging, Gina trotted along beside her. Which was good, because Gina was strong *and* stubborn, even if she was only three apples high. Melissa took two more beats to get started, but her longer legs soon put her into the lead. "Slow down," Katie hissed, afraid that he would notice them running after him like three fools in a hurry, but frankly, he was getting away.

So when Melissa glared at her, she hustled, like you do. And Gina actually broke into a trot.

Doctor S. strode east on 68th, against traffic, towards the park. He never glanced over his shoulder, but kept rubbing his hands together as if they pained him. Maybe the rings were the magnet kind, for arthritis or something. RSI.

"I can't believe I never noticed he wears all those rings."

"I can't believe I never noticed the muscles," Melissa answered, but Gina said "Rings?"

"On all his fingers?" Melissa was too busy dodging pedestrians to give Gina the *were you born that stupid or do you practice hard?* look, and Katie was as grateful as she could spare breath for. They were disrupting traffic flow, the cardinal sin of New York's secular religion. Katie winced at another glare. Somebody was going to call her a fucking moron any second.

Gina sounded completely bemused. "I never noticed any rings."

Doctor S. continued east on 68th past Park Ave., down the rows of narrow-fronted brick buildings with their concrete window ledges. By the time he crossed Madison Ave., she was sure he was headed for the park. Every so often he actually skipped a step, moving as fast as he possibly could without breaking into a purse-snatcher sprint.

. . . he wasn't going to the park.

Halfway between Park and Fifth Avenue—which, of course, unlike Park, was on the park—traffic was gummed up behind flashing lights and restraining police. Doctor S. slowed as he approached, stuffing his hands back into his pockets—"Would you look at that?" Gina said, and Katie knew she, too, had suddenly noticed the rings—and dropping his shoulders, smallifying himself. He merged with the gawking crowd; Katie couldn't believe how easily he made himself vanish. Like a praying mantis in a rosebush; just one more green thorn-hooked stem.

"Okay," Melissa said, as they edged through bystanders, trying not to shove too many yuppies in the small of the back. "Stabbing?"

"Sidewalk pizza," Gina the Manhattanite said, pointing up. There was a window open on the sixth floor of one of the tenements, and Katie glimpsed a blue uniform behind it.

"Somebody *jumped*?"

"Or was pushed."

"Oh, God."

Gina shrugged, but let her hip and elbow brush Katie's. Solace, delivered with the appearance of nonchalance. And then, watching Doctor S. seem to vanish between people, betrayed only be metallic gleams of light off slick hair. She could pick him out if she knew where to look, if she remembered to look for the tan jacket, the hair. Otherwise, her eyes seemed to slide off him. *Creepy*, she thought. *He's almost not really there.*

And then she thought of something else. And maybe Melissa did too, because Melissa said, "Guys? What's he doing at a crime scene?"

"Or accident scene," Gina said, unwilling to invest in a murder without corroboration.

"Maybe he's a gawker."

"Ew." Katie tugged Gina's sleeve. "We should see if we can get closer. He probably won't notice us." And then she frowned. "How did he know about it?"

"Maybe he has a police scanner in his office?"

"So he's a vulture."

"Maybe he's an investigator. You know. Secret, like."

Katie rolled her eyes. "Right. Our gay college prof is Spiderman."

Gina snorted. "Hey. Everybody knows that Spidey and Peter Parker have a thing."

Melissa hunched down so her head wouldn't stick up so far above the crowd. Her hair was as bad as Doctor S.'s, and she didn't have his knack for vanishing into the scenery. "Gina," she said, "you go up, and tell us what's going on."

"I've seen dead people, chica."

"You haven't seen this one," Melissa said. "Go on. It might be important."

Gina shrugged, rolled her eyes, and started forward. And Melissa was right; a five foot tall Latina in gobs of eyeliner did, indeed, vanish into the crowd. "Criminal mastermind," Melissa said.

Katie grinned, and didn't argue.

This was the part of the job that Matthew liked least. There was no satisfaction in it, no resolution, no joy. The woman on the pavement was dead; face down, one arm twisted under her and the other outflung. She'd bounced, and she hadn't ended up exactly where she'd hit. She'd been wearing a pink blouse. Someone in the crowd beside him giggled nervously.

Matthew figured she hadn't jumped. He checked his wards—pass-unnoticed, which was not so strong as a pass-unseen, and considerably easier to maintain—and the glamours and ghosts that kept him unremarkable.

His hands still ached; he really wished somebody would come up with a system for detecting malevolent magic that didn't leave him feeling like a B-movie bad guy was raking his fingerbones around with a chilled ice pick.

He pulled his cell phone from his pocket, buttoned the middle button on his jacket, and hit speed dial. He was one of five people who had the Promethean archmage's reach-me-in-the-bathtub number; he didn't abuse the privilege.

"Jane Andraste," she said, starting to speak before the line connected. He hadn't heard it ring on his end. "What's going on?"

"Apparent suicide at Fifth and 68th." He checked his watch. "It tickles. I'm on the scene and going to poke around a little. Are any of the responders our guys?"

"One second." Her voice muffled as she asked someone a question; there was a very brief pause, and she was back on the line. "Marla says Marion Thornton is en route. Have you met her?"

"Socially." By which he meant, at Promethean events and rituals. There were about two hundred Magi in the Greater New York area, and like Matthew, most of them held down two jobs: guardian of the iron world by night, teacher or artist or executive or civil servant by day.

They worked hard. But at least none of them had to worry about money. The Prometheus Club provided whatever it took to make ends meet. "I'll look for her."

"She'll get you inside," Jane said. "Any theories yet?"

Matthew crouched amid rubberneckers and bent his luck a little to keep from being stepped on. The crowd moved around him, but never quite squeezed him off-balance. Their shadows made it hard to see, but his fingers hovered a quarter-inch from a dime-sized stain on the pavement, and a chill slicked through his bones. "Not in a crowd," he said, and pulled his hand back so he wouldn't touch the drip accidentally. "Actually, tell Marion to process the inside scene on her own, would you? And not to touch anything moist with her bare hand, or even a glove if she can help it."

"You have a secondary lead?"

"I think I have a trail."

"Blood?"

It had a faint aroma, too, though he wouldn't bend close. Cold stone, guano, moist rancid early mornings full of last winter's rot. A spring and barnyard smell, with an underlying acridness that made his eyes water and his nose run. He didn't wipe his tears; there was no way he was touching his face after being near this.

He dug in his pocket with his left hand, cradling the phone with the right. A moment's exploration produced a steel disk the size of a silver dollar. He spat on the underside, balanced it like a miniature tabletop between his thumb and first two fingers, and then turned his hand over. A half-inch was as close as he dared.

He dropped the metal. It struck the sidewalk and bonded to the concrete with a hiss, sealing the stain away.

"Venom," Matthew said. "I've marked it. You'll need to send a containment team. I have to go."

When he stood, he looked directly into the eyes of one of his giggly freshmen.

"Ms. Gomez," he said. "Fancy meeting you here. Sorry I can't stay to chat."

Gina was still stammering when she came back. "Did you see that? Did you *see* that?"

Katie hadn't. "Just the backs of a bunch of tall people's heads. What happened?"

"I was trying to stay away from him," Gina said. "And he just *appeared* right beside me. Poof. Poof!"

"Or you weren't looking where you were going," Katie said, but Melissa was frowning. "Well?"

"He did just pop up out of nowhere," Melissa said. "I was watching Gina, and he kind of . . . materialized beside her. Like he stood up all of a sudden."

"He's the devil." Gina shook her head, but she sounded half-convinced.

Katie patted her on the shoulder, woven cotton rasping between her fingertips and Gina's flesh. "He could have been tying his shoe."

"Right," Gina said, stepping out from under Katie's hand. She pointed back to the crowd. "Then where did he go?"

Even glamoured, he couldn't run from a murder scene. The magic relied on symbol and focus; if he broke that, he'd find himself stuck in a backlash that would make him the center of attention of every cop, Russian landlady, and wino for fifteen blocks. So instead he walked, fast, arms swinging freely, trying to look as if he was late getting back from a lunch date.

Following the smell of venom.

He found more droplets, widely spaced. In places, they had started to etch asphalt or concrete. Toxic waste indeed; it slowed him, because he had to pause to tag and seal each one.

How it could move unremarked through his city, he did not know. There were no crops here for its steps to blight nor wells for its breath to poison.

Which was not to say it did no harm.

These things—some fed on flesh and some on blood and bone. Some fed on death, or fear, or misery, or drunkenness, or loneliness, or love, or hope, or white perfect joy. Some constructed wretchedness, and some comforted the afflicted.

There was no telling until you got there.

Matthew slowed as his quarry led him north. There were still too many bystanders. Too many civilians. He didn't care to catch up with any monsters in broad daylight, halfway up Manhattan. But as the neighborhoods became more cluttered and the scent of uncollected garbage grew heavy on the humid air, he found more alleys, more byways, and fewer underground garages.

If he were a cockatrice, he thought he might very well lair in such a place. Somewhere among the rubbish and the poison and the broken glass. The cracked concrete, and the human waste.

He needed as much camouflage to walk here undisturbed as any monster might.

His hands prickled ceaselessly. He was closer. He slowed, reinforcing his wards with a sort of nervous tic: checking that his hair was smooth, his coat was buttoned, his shoes were tied. Somehow, it managed to move from its lair to the Upper East Side without leaving a trail of bodies in the street. Maybe it traveled blind. Or underground; he hadn't seen a drop of venom in a dozen blocks. Worse, it might be invisible.

Sometimes . . . often . . . *otherwise* things had slipped far enough sideways that they could not interact with the iron world except through the intermediary of a Mage or a medium. If this had happened to the monster he sought, *then* it could travel unseen. *Then* it could pass by with no more harm done than the pervasive influence of its presence.

But then, it wouldn't drip venom real enough to melt stone.

Relax, Matthew. You don't know it's a cockatrice. It's just a hypothesis, and appearances can be deceptive.

Assuming that he had guessed right could get him killed.

But a basilisk or a cockatrice was what made sense. Except, why would the victim have thrown herself from her window for a crowned serpent, a scaled crow? And why wasn't everybody who crossed the thing's path being killed. Or turned to stone, if it was *that* sort of cockatrice?

His eyes stung, a blinding burning as if he breathed chlorine fumes, etchant. The scent was as much *otherwise* as real; Matthew suffered it more than the civilians, who would sense only the miasma of the streets as they were poisoned. A lingering death.

He blinked, tears brimming, wetting his eyelashes and blurring the world through his spectacles. A Mage's traveling arsenal was both eclectic and specific, but Matthew had never before thought to include normal saline, and he hadn't passed a drugstore for blocks.

How the hell is it traveling?

At last, the smell was stronger, the cold prickle sharper, on his left. He entered the mouth of a rubbish-strewn alley, a kind of gated brick tunnel not tall or wide enough for a garbage truck. It was unlocked, the grille rusted open; the passage brought him to a filthy internal courtyard. Rows of garbage cans—of course, no dumpsters—and two winos, one sleeping on cardboard, one lying on his back on grease-daubed foam reading a two-month-old copy of *Maxim*. The miasma of the cockatrice—if it was a cockatrice—was so strong here that Matthew gagged.

What he was going to do about it, of course, he didn't know.

His phone buzzed. He answered it, lowering his voice. "Jane?"

"The window was unlocked from the inside," she said. "No sign of forced entry. The resident was a fifty-eight-year-old unmarried woman, Janet Stafford. Here's the interesting part—"

"Yes?"

"She had just re-entered secular life, if you can believe this. She spent the last thirty-four years as a nun."

Matthew glanced at his phone, absorbing that piece of information, and put it back to his ear. "Did she leave the church, or just the convent?"

"The church," Jane said. "Marion's checking into why. You don't need to call her; I'll liaise."

"That would save time," Matthew said. "Thank you." There was no point in both of them reporting to Jane *and* to each other if Jane considered the incident important enough to coordinate personally.

"Are you ready to tell me yet what you think it might be?"

Matthew stepped cautiously around the small courtyard, holding onto his don't-notice-me, his hand cupped around the mouthpiece. "I *was* thinking cockatrice," he said. "But you know, now maybe not certain. What drips venom, and can lure a retired nun to suicide?"

Jane's breath, hissing between her teeth, was clearly audible over the cellular crackle. "Harpy."

"Yeah," Matthew said. "But then why doesn't it fly?"

"What are you going to do?"

"Right now? Question a couple of local residents," he said, and moved toward the Maxim-reading squatter.

The man looked up as he approached; Matthew steeled himself to hide a flinch at his stench, the sore running pus down into his beard. A lot of these guys were mentally ill and unsupported by any system. A lot of them *also* had the knack for seeing things that had mostly dropped *otherwise*, as if in being overlooked themselves they gained insight into the half-lit world.

And it didn't matter how he looked; the homeless man's life was still a life, and his only. *You can't save them all. But he had a father and mother and a history and a soul like yours.*

His city, which he loved, dehumanized; Matthew considered it the responsibility that came with his gifts to humanize it right back. It was in some ways rather like being married to a terrible drunk. You did a lot of apologizing. "Hey," Matthew said. He didn't crouch down. He held out his hand; the homeless man eyed it suspiciously. "I'm Matthew. You have absolutely no reason to want to know me, but I'm looking for some information I can't get from just anybody. Can I buy you some food, or a drink?"

Later, over milkshakes, Melissa glanced at Katie through the humidity-frizzled curls that had escaped her braid and said, "I can't believe we lost him."

The straw scraped Katie's lip as she released it. "You mean he gave us the slip."

Melissa snorted. On her left, Gina picked fretfully at a plate of French fries, sprinkling pinched grains of salt down the length of one particular fry and then brushing them away with a fingertip. "He just popped up. Right by me. And then vanished. I never took my eyes off him."

"Some criminal mastermind you turned out to be," Katie said, but her heart wasn't in it. Gina flinched, so Katie swiped one of her fries by way of apology. A brief but giggly scuffle ensued before Katie maneuvered the somewhat mangled fry into her mouth. She was chewing salt and starch when Melissa said, "Don't you guys think this is all a little weird?"

Katie swallowed, leaving a slick of grease on her palate. "No," she said, and slurped chocolate shake to clear it off. Her hair moved on her neck, and she swallowed and imagined the touch of a hand. A prickle of sensation tingled through her, the same excitement she felt at their pursuit of Doctor S., which she had experienced only occasionally while kissing her boyfriend back home. She shifted in her chair. "I think it's plenty weird."

She wasn't going to ask the other girls. Melissa had a boyfriend at Harvard that she traded off weekends with. Gina was . . . Gina. She picked up whatever boy she wanted, kept him a while, put him down again. Katie would rather let them assume that she wasn't all that innocent.

Not that they'd hate her. But they'd laugh.

"What are we going to do about it?" she asked, when Melissa kept looking at her. "I mean, it's not like he did something illegal."

"You didn't see the body up close."

"I didn't. But he didn't kill her. We know where he was when she fell."

Gina's mouth compressed askew. But she nodded, then hid her face in her shake.

Melissa pushed at her frizzing hair again. "You know," she said, "he left in a hurry. It's like a swamp out there."

"So?"

"So. Do you suppose his office door sticks?"

"Oh, no. That *is* illegal. We could get expelled."

"We wouldn't take anything." Melissa turned her drink with the tips of her fingers, looking at them and the spiraling ring left behind on the tabletop, not at Katie's eyes. "Just see if he has a police scanner. And look for his address."

"I'm not doing that," Katie said.

"I just want to see if the door is unlocked."

Melissa looked at Gina. Gina shrugged. "Those locks come loose with a credit card, anyway."

"No. Not just no."

"Oh, you can watch the stairs," Gina said, sharp enough that Katie sat back in her chair. Katie swallowed, and nodded. Fine. She would watch the goddamned stair.

"You want to finish?" she asked.

Gina pushed her mangled but uneaten fries away. "No, baby. I'm done."

The man's name was Henry; he ate an extraordinary amount of fried chicken from a red paper bucket while Matthew crouched on the stoop beside him, breathing shallowly. The acrid vapors of whatever Matthew hunted actually covered both the odor of unwashed man and of dripping grease, and though his eyes still watered, he thought his nose was shutting down in protest. Perversely, this made it easier to cope.

"No," Henry said. He had a tendency to slur his speech, to ramble and digress, but he was no ranting lunatic. Not, Matthew reminded himself, that it would matter if he was. "I mean, okay. I see things. More now than when I got my meds"—he shrugged, a bit of extra crispy coating clinging to his moustache—"I mean, I mean, not that I'm crazy, but you see things out of the corner of your eye, and when you turn? You see?"

He was staring at a spot slightly over Matthew's left shoulder when he said it, and Matthew wished very hard that he dared turn around and look. "All the damned time," he said.

The heat of the cement soaked through his jeans; the jacket was nearly unbearable. He shrugged out of it, laid it on the stoop, and rolled up his sleeves. "Man," Henry said, and sucked soft meat off bones. "Nice ink."

"Thanks," Matthew said, turning his arms over to inspect the insides.

"Hurt much? You don't look like the type."

"Hurt some," Matthew admitted. "What sort of things do you see? Out of the corners of your eyes?"

"Scuttling things. Flapping things." He shrugged. "When I can get a drink it helps."

"Rats? Pigeons?"

"Snakes," Henry said. He dropped poultry bones back into the bucket. "Roosters."

"Not crows? Vultures?"

"No," Henry said. "Roosters. Snakes, the color of the wall."

"Damn." Matthew picked up his coat. "Thanks, Henry. I guess it was a cockatrice after all."

What happened was, Katie couldn't wait on the stairs. Of course she'd known there wasn't a chance in hell that she could resist Melissa. But sometimes it was better to fool yourself a little, even if you knew that eventually you were going to crack.

Instead, she found herself standing beside Gina, blocking a sight line with her body, as Gina knocked ostentatiously on Doctor S.'s door. She slipped the latch with a credit card—a gesture so smooth that Katie could hardly tell she wasn't just trying the handle. She knocked again and then pulled the door open.

Katie kind of thought she was overplaying, and made a point of slipping through the barely opened door in an attempt to hide from passers-by that the room was empty.

Melissa came in last, tugging the door shut behind herself. Katie heard the click of the lock.

Not, apparently, that that would stop anybody.

Katie put her back against the door beside the wall and crossed her arms over her chest to confine her shivering. Gina moved into the office as if entranced; she stood in the center of the small cluttered room and spun slowly on her heel, hands in her hip pockets, elbows awkwardly cocked. Melissa slipped past her—as much as a six foot redhead could slip—and bent over to examine the desk, touching nothing.

"There has to be a utility bill here or something, right? Everybody does that sort of thing at work . . . "

Gina stopped revolving, striking the direction of the bookshelves like a compass needle striking north—a swing, a stick, a shiver. She craned her neck back and began inspecting titles.

It was Katie, after forcing herself forward to peer over Gina's shoulder, who noticed the row of plain black hardbound octavo volumes on one shelf, each with a ribbon bound into the spine and a date penned on it in silver metallic ink.

"Girls," she said, "do you suppose he puts his address in his journal?"

Gina turned to follow Katie's pointing finger and let loose a string of Spanish that Katie was pretty sure would have her toenails smoking if she understood a word. It was obviously self-directed, though, so after the obligatory flinch, she reached past Gina and pulled the most recently dated volume from the shelf.

"Can I use the desk?" The book cracked a little under the pressure of her fingers, and it felt lumpy, with wavy page-edges. If anything was pressed inside, she didn't want to scatter it.

Melissa stood back. Katie laid the book carefully on an uncluttered portion of the blotter and slipped the elastic that held it closed without moving the food or papers. The covers almost burst apart, as if eager to be read, foiling her intention to open it to the flyleaf and avoid prying. The handwriting was familiar: she saw it on the whiteboard twice a week. But that wasn't what made Katie catch her breath.

A pressed flower was taped to the left-hand page, facing a column of text. And in the sunlight that fell in bars through the dusty blind, it shimmered iridescent blue and violet over faded gray.

"Madre de Dios," Gina breathed. "What does it say?"

Katie nudged the book further into the light. "14 October 1995," she read. "Last year, Gin."

"He probably has the new one with him. What does it *say*?"

"It says 'Passed as a ten?' and there's an address on Long Island. Flanagan's, Deer Park Avenue. Babylon. Some names. And then it says 'pursuant to the disappearance of Sean Roberts—flower and several oak leaves were collected from a short till at the under-twenty-one club.' And *then* it says 'Faerie money?' Spelled F-a-e-r-i-e."

"He's crazy," Gina said definitively. "Schizo. Gone."

"Maybe he's writing a fantasy novel." Katie wasn't sure where her stubborn loyalty came from, but she was abruptly brimming with it. "We are reading his private stuff totally out of context. I don't think it's fair to judge by appearances."

Gina jostled her elbow; Katie shrugged the contact off and turned the page. Another record of a disappearance, this one without supporting evidence taped to the page. It filled up six pages. After that, a murder under mysterious circumstances. A kidnapping . . . and then some more pages on the Roberts disappearance. A broken, bronze-colored feather, also taped in, chimed when she touched it. She jerked her finger back.

One word underneath. "Resolved." And a date after Christmastime.

Doctor S., it seemed, thought he was a cop. A special kind of . . . supernatural cop.

"It sounds like *Nick Knight,*" Melissa said. Katie blinked, and realized she had still been reading out loud.

"It sounds like a crazy man," Gina said.

Katie opened her mouth, and suddenly felt as if cold water drained down her spine. She swallowed whatever she had been about to say and flipped the journal to the flyleaf. There was indeed an address, on West 60th. "He's not crazy." *Not unless I am.*

"Why do you say that?" Melissa, gently, but Gina was looking at Katie too—not suspicious, or mocking, anymore, but wide-eyed, waiting for her to explain.

"Guys," Katie said, "He's a magician or something. Remember how he vanished on Gina? Remember the ink that you somehow just don't see? Remember the damned invisible rings?"

Melissa sucked her lower lip in and released it. "So did he kill that woman or not?"

"I don't know," Katie said. "I want him to be a good guy."

Gina patted her shoulder, then reached across to also pat the journal with her fingertips. "I say we go to his apartment and find out."

There were drawbacks to being a member of Matthew's society of Magi. For one thing, nobody else liked them. And with good reason; not only was the Prometheus Club full of snobs, Capitalists, and politicians, but its stated goal of limiting and controlling the influence of wild magic in the world put him in sworn opposition to any hedge-witch, Satanist, purveyor of herbs and simples, houngan, or priest of Santeria he might want to contract with for ritual supplies.

Such as, say, a white, virgin cockerel.

New York City was not bereft of live poultry markets, but given his rather specific needs, Matthew wasn't sure he wanted to trust one of those. He'd hate to find out at the last minute, for example, that his bird had had a few sandy feathers plucked. Or that it was, shall we say, a little more experienced than Matthew was himself.

And then there was the recent influenza scare, which had closed several poultry markets. And what he really needed, now that he thought about it, was an illegal animal; a fighting cock.

He booted his desktop system, entered an IP address from memory, wended his way through a series of logon screens, and asked about it on the Promethean message board.

Fortunately, even if Matthew didn't know something, it was a pretty good bet that *somebody* in Prometheus would.

Before close of business, he was twenty blocks north again, edging through a flaking avocado-green steel door into the antechamber of a dimly lit warehouse that smelled of guano and sawdust and corn and musty feathers. It drove the eyewatering stench of the cockatrice from Matthew's sinuses, finally, and seemed in comparison such a rich, wholesome smell that he breathed it deep and fast. He coughed, sneezed, and waved his hand in front of his face. And then he did it again, feeling as if the inside of his head were clean for the first time in hours.

There was a desk in a cage—not unlike the ones inhabited by the clucking, rustling chickens, but far larger—behind the half-wall at the far end of the dirty, hall-like room. Matthew approached it; a stout woman with her white hair twisted into a bun looked up from her game of solitaire.

He cleared his throat. "I need to buy a cockerel."

"I've got some nice Bantams," she said through the grate. "And a couple of Rhode Island Reds." Not admitting anything; those weren't fighting cocks. "You got a place to keep it? There are zoning things."

"It just needs to be pure white." He hesitated. "Or pure black."

She reached up casually and dropped the shutter in his face. Of course. He sighed, and rapped on the grate, rattling the metal behind it. No answer. He rapped again, and again.

Five minutes later she cracked it up and peered under the bottom, through the little hole for passing papers and money back and forth. He caught a glimpse of bright black eyes and a wrinkled nose. "I'm not selling you any bird for your Satanic rituals, young man."

No, but you'll sell me one for bloodsports? Matthew sighed again and stuck his hand through the slot, nearly getting his fingers up her nose. She jerked back, but he caught the edge of the shutter before she could slide it closed again. His biceps bulged inside his shirt sleeve; his tendons dimpled his wrist. She leaned on the shutter, and couldn't shift him.

"Young man." A level, warning tone. She didn't look intimidated.

Oh, what the hell. "It's for the cockatrice," he said.

Her hand relaxed, and the weight of the shutter lifted. She slid it up; it thumped when it reached the top. "Why didn't you say so? About time somebody took care of that thing. Though I notice you didn't give a shit when it was just in East Harlem."

Matthew glanced aside. The cops were always the last to know.

She hesitated. "You'll need a human virgin too."

"Don't worry," he said, biting the inside of his cheek. "I've got that covered."

When he returned home, there was a woman waiting in his apartment. Not surprising in itself; Jane had a key and the passcode for the locks. But it wasn't Jane. It was the homicide detective, Marion Thornton.

She had an outdoorswoman's squint and silky brown hair that framed her long cheekbones in feathered wings; it made her look like a bright-eyed Afghan hound. She showed him her badge and handed him back the keys before he was fully in the door.

"The victim was an alcoholic," Marion said, re-locking the door as Matthew put his chicken on the counter. It was in a cardboard animal carrier. Occasionally a glossy jet-black beak or a malevolent eye would appear in one of the holes along the top. It scuffed and kicked. He pushed it away from the counter edge and it grabbed at him, as he thought of a line from a Russian fairy tale: *Listen, Crow, crow's daughter! Serve me a certain service—*

"The nun was a drunk?"

"To put it crudely. And we found another possible for the same bogey, about three days ago. Elderly man, never married, lived alone, drank like a fish. We're continuing to check back for others." She flipped pages in her report pad. "Here's something interesting. He was castrated in a farming accident when he was in his teens."

"Oh," Matthew said. "It's always virgins, isn't it?"

"For dragons and unicorns, anyway," Marion answered. "But I'd guess you're correct. And more than that. Heavy drinkers. Possibly with some talent; a link my . . . secular . . . colleagues won't come up with is that Promethean records show that we considered inviting both of these victims for apprenticeship when they were young."

"So they saw things," Matthew said, thinking of Henry, living on the monster's doorstep. If the thing had a preference for sexually inexperienced prey, that would explain why it hadn't eaten him yet. Well, if Matthew was prepared to make a few conjectures. "Do you think it wanted them because they drank, or they drank because they saw things?"

"We operate on the first assumption." Marion picked her way around him, leaned down to peer into the animal carrier. She pulled back as a grabbing beak speared at her eye. "Vicious."

"I sure hope so."

"Jane said you had a possible ID on the bogey?"

He knelt down and began peeling the rug back, starting beside the inside wall of the living room. "The black cock isn't enough of a hint?"

"Basilisk."

"That's a weasel. Cockatrice, I'm guessing. Though how it lured its victim into hurling herself from her window is beyond me. You're describing very specialized prey."

She straightened up and arched, cracking her spine. She picked a spoon off the breakfast bar and turned it, considering the way the light pooled in the bowl. "Call it one in ten thousand? Then the Greater New York metropolitan area has, what, two thousand more just like 'em?"

"Something like that," Matthew said, and pinched the bridge of his nose. A dust bunny was stuck to the heel of his hand; he blew it off. When he opened his eyes, he found her staring at him, tongue-tip peeking between her lips.

"Want to make sure we're safe?" she said, with a grin. The spoon glittered as she turned it beside her face. "I'm off duty. And your chicken won't mind." She held up her left hand and showed him a plain gold band. "No hassles."

He bit his lower lip. Matthew had practice. And years of careful sublimation—which was, of course, the point: sacrifice made power. He also had a trick of flying under the gaydar, of making straight women think he was gay and gay men think he was straight. All just part of the camouflage.

He hated having to say no. "Sorry," he said. "That's a lovely offer. But I need a virgin for the cockatrice already, and it beats having to send out."

She laughed, of course.

They never believed him.

"Come on," he said. "Help me ensorcel this chicken."

Doctor S. lived in Midtown West, on 60th near Columbus Ave. It was kind of a hike, but they got there before sunset. It wouldn't get dark for an hour, but that was only because the afternoons were still long. By the time they paused down the block Katie's stomach was rumbling. That milkshake was only good for so long.

The spot they picked to loiter had a clear view of the front door of Doctor S.'s brown brick apartment building. "Nice place for a junior professor," Melissa said, and for ten seconds she sounded like she was from Boston, all right.

Katie looked at Gina and made big eyes and whimpering noises, but it was Melissa who went and got convenience store hot dogs, Diet Pepsi, and a bag of chips. They ate in the shade on the north side of the building, the heat soaking from the stones, their hair lank and grimy with the city air. Katie scratched her cheek and brought her fingernails away sporting black crescents. "Ew."

"Welcome to New York," Gina said, which was what she said every time Katie complained.

Katie had nearly stopped complaining already. She scratched her nails against her jeans until most of the black came out and finished her hot dog one-handed, then wiped the grime from her face with the napkin before drying her hands. It worked kind of halfway—good enough, anyway, that when Melissa splashed ice water from a sport bottle into everyone's cupped hands and Katie in turn splashed it onto her face, she didn't wind up feeling like she'd faceplanted into a mud puddle.

The second handful, she drank, and only realized she had been carrying a heat headache when the weight of it faded. "All right," she said, and took the bottle from Melissa to squirt some on her hair. "Ready as I'll ever be."

"Unfortunately, apparently Doctor S. isn't," Melissa said, reclaiming the bottle to drink. She tilted her head back, her throat working, and as she lowered it a droplet ran from the corner of her mouth. "No, wait, spoke too soon."

Katie stepped behind the pole of a street lamp—silly, because Doctor S. wasn't even looking in their direction—and caught sight of his stiff little blond ponytail zigzagging through the crowd. He was wearing another sort-of costume—Katie wondered what he wore when he wore what he liked, rather than what suited his role—a well-cut gray suit with a fabulous drape. A woman in a navy pantsuit, whose light flyaway hair escaped its pins around a long narrow face, walked alongside him. Her stride was familiar. She had a white cardboard pet carrier slung from her left hand; Katie could not see what was in it, but it swung as if something was moving slightly inside.

"Isn't that the cop who showed up where the woman jumped?"

Katie glanced at Gina and back at the woman, a stuttering doubletake. It was. Not the same outfit, and her hair was clipped back aggressively now—though it wasn't staying restrained—but the woman was conspicuous. "Well," Katie said, feeling as if she watched the words emerge from a stranger's mouth, "we could follow him and find out where they're going."

Neither Matthew nor Marion was particularly sanguine about attacking on a cockatrice in the dark. They had to take the subway across the island (at least the cockerel was quiet, huddled in the bottom of its carrier) but still ascended to the surface with light to spare. It roused the bird; Matthew heard it shift, and Marion kept her fingers well clear of the air holes. It was, as promised, aggressive.

Matthew shoved down guilt and substantial apprehension. There was no other choice, and power grew out of sacrifices.

They found the courtyard without a problem, that tunnel-like entrance with its broken gate leaving rust on Matthew's clothes as they slipped through. He wasn't wearing his usual patrol clothes, a zipped camouflage jacket and boots enchanted to pass-unnoticed, but a gray silk suit with a linen shirt and a silver, red, and navy tie. A flask in an inside pocket tapped his ribs when he moved. He looked like a dot com paper millionaire on his way to a neck-or-nothing meeting with a crotchety venture capitalist who was going to hate his ponytail.

His clothes today, and the quick preliminary ritual they'd performed in his living room, were not designed to conceal him, to occlude his power, but rather to draw the right attention. If you squinted at him with otherwise eyes, he would shine. And other than his rings and the earrings and the pigment in the ink under his skin, he wasn't wearing any iron, as he might have been if they went to face something Fae.

Iron was of no use against a cockatrice. Except in one particular, and so two steel gaffs wrapped in tissue paper nested in the bottom of Matthew's trouser pocket. He touched them through fabric like a child stroking a favorite toy and drew his hand back when they clinked.

"This is it," he said.

Marion set the carrier down. "Nice place you've got here, Matthew. Decorate it yourself?" From the way her nose was wrinkling, she picked out the acid aroma of the monster as well.

Henry and his comrade at arms were nowhere to be seen. Matthew hoped they had taken his advice and moved on. He hated working around civilians.

Without answering Marion, he kicked aside garbage, clearing a space in the center of the court. The windows overlooking it remained unoccupied, and if for some reason they did not continue so, Marion had a badge.

She helped Matthew sketch a star overlaid on a circle in yellow sidewalk chalk. They left one point open, facing south by Marion's compass. When they were done, Matthew dusted his hands, wiped them on his handkerchief, and reached into his pockets for the spurs, the flask, and something else—a leather hood of the sort used by falconers to quiet their birds.

"Ready?"

She nodded. "Where's the lair?"

He patted himself on the chest—"the s.o.b. comes to us"—and watched her eyes widen. She had thought he was kidding.

They always did.

Well, maybe someday he could catch a unicorn.

"It's okay," he said, when her blush became a stammer. "Let's get the knives on this chicken."

It took both of them, crouched on either side, to open the box and hood the bird without harming it. It exploded into Matthew's grip as Marion pried open the flaps; he caught at it, bungled the grab and got pecked hard for his pains. Somehow he got the bird pressed to his chest, a struggling fury of iridescent black plumage, and caged it in his blunt hands. It felt prickly and slick and hotter than blood under the feathers. He smoothed its wings together and restrained the kicking legs, while Marion dodged the jabbing beak. Once in darkness it quieted, and Marion strapped the three-inch gaffs over its own natural spurs.

When they were done, it looked quite brave and wicked, the gleam of steel on rainbow-black. Marion stroked its back between Matthew's fingers, her touch provoking a tremor when she brushed the back of his hand. "Fucking abomination."

She meant cockfighting, not the bird. Matthew set the cockerel down and moved his hands away. It sat quietly. "How do you think I feel?"

She shrugged. Still crouched, she produced a pair of handcuffs and a silken hood from her tan leather handbag. Matthew bent over to pick up the flask. "God, I hate this part."

He prized it open with his thumb and upended it over his mouth. The fumes of hundred-and-fifty-proof rum made him gasp; he choked down three swallows and stopped, doubled over, rasping.

Matthew didn't often drink.

But that would be enough for the spell.

Light-headed, now, sinuses stinging from more than the reek of the cockatrice, Matthew handed Marion the flask and then his spectacles, feeling naked without them. He wiped his mouth on the back of his hand, fine hairs harsh on his lips. Four steps took him through the open end of the pentagram.

He turned back and faced Marion. With the silk of the hood draped over his forearm, he handcuffed himself—snugly: he did not want his body breaking free while he was not in it.

They weren't replaceable.

He took one more deep breath, closed his eyes on Marion's blurry outline, and with his joined wrists rattling pulled the hood over his head.

In the dark underneath, sounds were muffled. Concentrated rum fumes made his eyes water, but at least he could no longer smell the cockatrice. Chalk grated—Marion closing the pentagram. He heard his flask uncorked, the splash of fluid as she anointed the diagram with the remaining rum. Matthew tugged restlessly against the restraints on his wrists as she began to chant and a deep uneasy curdling sensation answered.

God, too much rum. He wobbled and caught himself, fretting the handcuffs, the tightness on the bones. The sensual thrill of the magic sparking along his nerves was accentuated by the blinding darkness. He wobbled again, or maybe the world did, and gasped at the heat in his blood.

Magic and passion weren't different. It was one reason sublimation worked.

The second gasp came cleaner, no fabric muffling his face, the air cooler if not fresher and the scent of rum less cloying. Marion seemed to have moved, by the sound of her chanting, and somehow the tightness had jumped from Matthew's wrists to his calves. He lay belly-down on rough ground.

He pushed with his arms to try to balance himself to his feet. The chanting stopped, abruptly, and someone was restraining him, folding his arms against his side gently but with massive cautious strength. "Matthew?"

He turned his head, seeking the voice. It echoed. The . . . arms? holding him retreated. "Matthew, if you understand me, flap once."

He extended odd-feeling arms and did so. A moment later, a half-dozen fists, it seemed, were unhooding him. He blinked at dizzy brilliance, and found himself staring into Marion's enormous face from only a few inches away. He hopped back and fouled himself on the gaffs. Fortunately, the needle point slipped between his feathers rather than stabbing him in the wing, and he stopped, precariously balanced, wings half-bent like broken umbrellas.

He clucked.

And flapped hard, surprised to find himself lifting off the ground. He flew the two feet to Marion's shoulder, landed awkwardly, facing the wrong way, and banged her in the eye with his wing. At least he had the sense to turn carefully, keeping the needle-tipped gaffs pointed away from her thin-skinned throat. He crouched on his heels, trying not to prick her with his claws, the alien body's balance far better than his own.

Only if he thought about it did he realize that the warm shoulder he nestled to Marion's warm cheek was feathered, that it was peculiar to be able to feel the beats of her heart through his feet like the footfalls of an approaching predator, that the colors he saw were abruptly so bright and saturated—so discriminate—that he had no names for them. That he balanced on her moving shoulder as easily as he would have roosted on a swaying branch, and that that was peculiar.

"Wow," he said. And heard a soft contemplative cluck. And laughed at himself, which came out a rising, tossing crow.

Marion flinched and put a hand up on his wing. "Matthew, please. My ears."

He ducked his head between his shoulders, abashed, and clucked *sorry*. Maybe she would understand.

His body stood stolidly, restrained, inside a wet circle of chalk and rum. The cockerel wearing it was quieted by the hood and the handcuffs, and Matthew turned his head right and left to center himself in his vision. He failed—he had the peripheral view, and only by turning to see it first with one eye and then the other could he reliably guess how far away it was. Almost no binocular vision, of course. But with a shock, he realized that he could see clearly around to the back of his head.

That was pretty tremendously weird. He'd have to practice that. And think about his small sharp body and its instincts, because the enemy could be along any moment.

Marion was pulling back, stepping into the shadows, an alcove near the gate concealing them. Matthew pressed against her warmth, feeling her heart beating faster. He clucked in her ear.

"Shh."

He hoped the cockatrice would come quickly. This could be very, very awkward to explain if something happened to the glamours. Still, they had brought alcohol, talent, and innocence—symbolically speaking—and left them, special delivery, in the thing's front yard. Wherever it was nesting, it should come to investigate before too long.

He was still thinking that when he heard the singing.

The three of them had been following for a long time, it seemed, when Doctor S. and the woman gave one another a conspiratorial glance and stepped through an archway, past a rusted gate. Gina drew up short, stepping out of the traffic flow into the shelter of a doorway. A moment later, Katie heard glass breaking and something kicked or thrown.

Katie ducked in behind Gina, rubbing her elbow nervously. This wasn't the best neighborhood at all. "That's a dead end, I bet," Gina said, when Melissa came up beside them. "Either they're going inside, or that's where they're going."

"Here?"

Gina winked. "Want to sneak up and peek through the gate?"

Katie and Melissa exchanged a glance, and Melissa angled her head and said, "What the heck." Side by side, the three stepped back out onto the sidewalk, picking their way over chewing gum spots and oily, indeterminate stains. Katie somehow found herself in the lead, as Gina and Melissa fell in single file behind her. She had to glance over her shoulder to make sure they were still with her.

She stopped two feet shy of the broken gate and tried to still her hammering heart. No luck, and so she clenched her hands at her sides and edged forward.

She could see through plainly if she kept her back to the wall and turned her head sideways. She saw Doctor S. and the cop sketch the diagram, saw them pull a black rooster from the box and do something to its head and feet. She flinched, expecting some bloody and melodramatic beheading, but instead Doctor S. went to the center of the star and began chaining himself up, which made her feel distinctly funny inside. And then he blindfolded himself with a hood, and the woman did some more sketching with the chalk and walked around the circle pouring something in between its lines from a flask.

A moment later, the rooster began to struggle, while Doctor S. stood perfectly still. The woman crouched down and unhooded it, and a moment later it flapped onto her shoulder and settled itself.

"This," Melissa whispered, a warm pressure against Katie's side, "is freaking weird."

"Gosh," Gina said, very loudly, "would you listen to that?"

Katie turned to shush her, and heard it herself. She took a deep breath, chest expanding against her shirt, as if she could inhale the music too. It seemed to swell in her lungs and belly, to buoy her. She felt Melissa cringe, and then fingers caught at her shoulder. "Fuck," Melissa said. "What is that?"

"Beautiful." Katie stepped forward, moving out of Melissa's grasp. Into the courtyard, toward the woman and the chicken and the blindfolded English professor. Katie lifted her arms and twirled, her feet light as if she walked on flowers. She strode through a pile of garbage that the magicians had piled up when they cleared the center of the courtyard and her airy foot came down on glass.

A cracked bottle broke further under her foot, shattering and crunching. The soft sole of Katie's tennis sneaker clung to broken glass; she picked it up again and stepped forward, to another crunch.

The noise was almost lost under the music. Rising chorales, crystalline voices.

"It sounds like a rat being shaken to death in a bag of hammers," Melissa groaned, and then sucked in a squeak. "Oh, fuck, Katie, your foot . . ."

There was something slick between her sole and the bottom of the shoe. She must have stepped in a mud puddle. She looked down. Or a puddle of blood.

Well, her foot was already wet. And the singers were over there somewhere. She took one more step, Melissa's fingers brushing her wrist as her friend missed her grab. Behind her, Melissa made funny sobbing noises, as if she'd been running and couldn't get a breath.

Somehow, Gina had gotten ahead of her, and was walking too, kicking rubbish out of the way with her sandaled feet, crunching through more glass, leaving red footsteps. The courtyard was filthy, the buildings moldy-looking, scrofulous: brick black with soot and flaking mortar.

Something moved against the wall. A gleam of brightness, like sun through torn cloth. And then—so beautiful, so bright, oh—a spill of jadevioletandazure, a trailing cloak of feathers, a sort of peacock or bird of paradise emerging like an image reflected in a suddenly lit mirror. Its crested head was thrown back, its long neck swollen with song. Its wings mantled and rays of light cracked from between its feathers.

Gina was still ahead of her, between her and the bird. Katie reached out to push her, but then suddenly she was gone, fallen down, and Katie stepped over her. It was the most beautiful thing she'd ever seen. It was the most beautiful thing she'd ever heard.

And oh, it was blind, the poor thing was blind. Somebody had gouged out its eyes, she saw now. The old wounds were scarred gray, sightless.

And still it sang.

She reached out her hand to touch it, and couldn't understand why Melissa was screaming.

Matthew saw both young women hurry across the glass and stones, faster than he could reach them—not that he could have stopped them. Even though he was airborne, and already on his way.

He saw his body react, too—it hurled itself at the edge of the pentagram, hurled and kept hurling, but the wards they'd so carefully constructed held him, and he bounced from them and slid down what looked like plain still air. So strange, watching himself from the outside. Marion and the red-haired girl both crumpled, Marion with her hands over her ears, belly-crawling determinedly toward the running children; Melissa Martinchek down in a fetal position, screaming.

And he saw the cockatrice.

The movement caught his eye first, a ripple of red like brick and gray like concrete, its hide patterned in staggered courses that blended precisely with the blackened wall behind it. It was bigger than a cock, but not by much, and his rooster's heart churned with rage at its red upright comb and the plumed waterfall of its tail. His wings beat in midair; he exploded after it like a partridge from cover.

It chameleoned from stone to brilliance, colors chasing over its plumage like rainbows over oil. The two girls clutched for it, their feet pierced with unnoticed shards, their hands reaching.

Matthew saw them fall, their bodies curled in around their poisoned hands. He saw the way they convulsed, the white froth dripping from the corners of their mouths.

He shrieked war, wrath, red rage, and oblivion. The spurs were heavy on his shanks; his wings were mighty upon the air. He struck, reaching hard, and clutched at the enemy's neck.

An eruption of rainbow-and-black plumage, a twist and strike and movement like quicksilver on slanted glass. Matthew's gaff slashed the cockatrice's feathers; the cockatrice whipped its head back and forward and struck like a snake. Pearl-yellow droplets flicked from fangs incongruous in a darting beak; the rooster-tail fanned and flared, revealing the gray coils of an adder.

Matthew beat wings to one side; his feathertips hissed where the venom smoked holes through them. He backwinged, slashed for the cockatrice's eye, saw too late that that wound had long ago been dealt it. A black cockerel was immune to a cockatrice's deadly glare, and to the poison of its touch. If he could hit it, he could hurt it.

Except it wasn't a cockatrice, not exactly. Because cockatrices didn't sing like loreleis, and they didn't colorshift for camouflage. Maybe it was hatched by a chameleon rather than a serpent, Matthew thought, beating for altitude, and then reminded himself that now was not the time for theory.

Some kind of hybrid, then.

Just his luck.

And now the thing was airborne, and climbing in pursuit. He dropped—the cockerel was not more than passably aerodynamic—and struck for its back, its wing, its lung. The breast was armored, under the meat, with the anchoring keel bones. His spurs would turn on those. But they might punch through the ribs, from above.

He missed when the monster side-slipped, and the blind cockatrice turned and sank its fangs into his wing. Pain, heat and fire, weld-hot needles sunk into his elbow to the bone. He cackled like a machine gun and fell after the monster; wing-fouled, they tumbled to stone.

It lost its grip at the shock of impact, and Matthew screamed fury and pain. The hurt wing trailed, blood splashing, smoke rising from the envenomed wound. He made it beat anyway, dragged himself up, his spurs scraping and sparking on stone. The cockatrice hissed as he rose; his flight was not silent.

They struck hard, breast to breast, grappling legs and slashing spurs. He had his gaffs; the cockatrice had weight and fangs and a coiling tail like a rubber whip. Wings struck, buffeted, thundered. The cockatrice had stopped singing, and Matthew could hear the weeping now. Someone human was crying.

The cockatrice's talons twined his. Left side, right side. Its wings thumped his head, its beak jabbed. Something tore; blood smeared its beak, his face. He couldn't see on his right side. He ripped his left leg free of its grip and punched, slashed, hammered. The gaff broke skin with a pop; the cockatrice's blood soaked him, tepid, no hotter than the air. A rooster's egg hatched by a serpent.

The cockatrice wailed and thrashed; he ducked its strike at his remaining eye. More blood, pumping, slicking his belly, gumming his feathers to his skin. The blood was venom too. The whole thing was poison; its blood, its breath; its gaze; its song.

The monster fell on top of him. He could turn his head and get his eye out from under it, but when he did, all he saw was Marion, each arm laced under one of Melissa's armpits, holding the redheaded girl on her knees with a grim restraint while Melissa tried to tear herself free, to run to the poisoned bodies of her friends. The bodies were poison too, corrupted by the cockatrice's touch. The very stones soaked by its heart's blood could kill.

It was all venom, all deadly, and there was no way in the world to protect anyone. Not his sacrifice, not the unwitting sacrifice of the black cockerel, made any goddamned difference in the end.

Matthew, wing-broken, one-eyed, his gaff sunk heel-deep in the belly of his enemy, lay on his back under its corpse-weight and sobbed.

The building was emptied, the block closed, the deaths and the evacuations blamed on a chemical spill. Other Prometheans would handle the detox. Matthew, returned to his habitual body, took the shivering black cockerel to a veterinarian with Promethean sympathies, who—at Matthew's insistence and Jane's expense—amputated his wing and cleaned and sewed shut his eye. Spared euthanasia, he was sent to a farm upstate to finish his days as a lopsided, piratical greeter of morning. He'd live long, with a little luck, and father many pullets.

Matthew supposed there were worse deaths for a chicken.

Marion did the paperwork. Matthew took her out to dinner. She didn't make another pass, and they parted good friends. He had a feeling he'd be seeing her again.

There were memorial services for his students, and that was hard. They were freshmen, and he hadn't known them well; it seemed . . . presumptuous to speak, as if his responsibility for their deaths gave him some claim over their lives. He sat in the back, dressed in his best black suit, and signed the guest book, and didn't speak.

Katherine Berquist was to be buried in Appleton, Wisconsin; Matthew could not attend. But Regina Gomez was buried in a Catholic cemetery in Flushing, her coffin overwhelmed with white waxy flowers, her family swathed in black crepe and summer-weight worsted, her friends in black cotton or navy. Melissa Martinchek was there in an empire-waisted dress and a little cardigan. She gave Matthew a timid smile across the open grave.

The scent of the lilies was repellent; Matthew vomited twice on the way home.

Melissa came to see him in the morning, outside of his regular office hours, when he was sitting at his desk with his head in his heads. He dragged himself up at the knock, paused, and sat heavily back down.

Thirty seconds later, the locked door clicked open. It swung on the hinges, and Melissa stepped inside, holding up her student ID like a talisman. "The lock slips," she said. "Gina showed me how. I heard, I heard your chair."

Gina's name came out a stammer too.

"Come in," Matthew said, and gestured her to a dusty orange armchair. She locked the door behind her before she fell into it. "Coffee?"

There was a pot made, but he hadn't actually gotten up and fetched any. He waved at it vaguely, and Melissa shook her head.

He wanted to shout at her—*What were you thinking? What were you* doing *there?*—and made himself look down at his hands instead. He picked up a letter opener and ran his thumb along the dull edge. "I am," he said, when he had control of his voice again, "so terribly sorry."

She took two sharp breaths, shallow and he could hear the edge of the giggle under them. Hysteria, not humor. "It wasn't your fault," she said. "I mean, I don't know what happened." She held up her hand, and his words died in his open mouth. "I don't . . . I don't *want* to know. But it wasn't your fault."

He stood up. He got himself a cup of coffee and poured one for her, added cream and sugar without asking. She needed it. Her eyes were pink-red around the irises, the lower lids swollen until he could see the mucous membrane behind the lashes. She took it, zombie-placid.

"I was safe inside the circle," he said. "I was supposed to be the bait. Gina and Katie were unlucky. They were close enough to being what it wanted that it took them, instead. As well. Whatever."

"What did . . . it want?"

"Things feed on death." He withdrew on the excuse of adding more sugar to his coffee. "Some like a certain flavor. It might even. . . ."

He couldn't say it. It might even have been trying to lure Matthew out. That would explain why it had left its safe haven at the north end of the island, and gone where Prometheus would notice it. Matthew cringed. If his organization had some wardens in the bad neighborhoods, it might have been taken care of years ago. If Matthew himself had gone into its court unglamoured that first time, it might just have eaten him and left the girls alone.

A long time, staring at the skim of fat on the surface of her coffee. She gulped, then blew through scorched lips, but did not lift her eyes. "Doctor S.—"

"Matthew," he said. He took a breath, and made the worst professional decision of his life. "Go home, Ms. Martinchek. Concentrate on your other classes; as long as you show up for the mid-term and the final in mine, I will keep your current grade for the semester."

Cowardice. Unethical. He didn't *want* to see her there.

He put his hand on her shoulder. She leaned her cheek against it, and he let her for a moment. Her skin was moist and hot. Her breath was, too.

Before he got away, he felt her whisper, "Why not me?"

"Because you put out," he said, and then wished he'd just cut his tongue out when she jerked, slopping coffee across her knuckles. He retreated behind the desk and his own cup, and settled his elbows on the blotter. Her survivor guilt was his fault, too. "It only wanted virgins," he said, more gently. "Send your boyfriend a thank-you card."

She swallowed, swallowed again. She looked him in the eyes, so she wouldn't have to look past him, at the memory of her friends. Thank God, she didn't ask. But she drank the rest of her too-hot coffee, nerved herself, licked her lips, and said, "But Gina—Gina was . . ."

"People," he replied, as kindly as he could manage with blood on his hands, "are not always what they want you to think. Or always what you think they ought to be."

When she thanked him and left, he retrieved the flask from his coat pocket and dumped half of it into his half-empty coffee mug. Later, a TA told him it was his best lecture ever. He couldn't refute her; he didn't remember.

Melissa Martinchek showed up for his next Monday lecture. She sat in the third row, in the middle of two empty desks. No one sat beside her.

Both Matthew and she survived it, somehow.

The Brooklyn Bridge was dubbed "The Eighth Wonder of the World" when it opened in 1883. It is made of more than granite, steel, and concrete. The men who built it sacrificed sweat, blood, health, and even lives to build it. But perhaps one builder gained something very special indeed.

CAISSON

KARL BUNKER

The first time I saw Mischke was in the winter of 1871, and he was on his knees making cooing noises at a baby. The baby was on the lap of its mother, a plump young woman whose expression made it clear she didn't know quite what to make of the oversized bear of a man who was tickling her infant's cheek with a calloused finger. The woman had entered the noisy tavern a few moments prior, and had sat at one of the tables after speaking a few sharp words to the barkeep. Her presence had attracted some attention, as it was a rare thing to see a woman in one of these New York taverns. But the man on his knees hardly seemed to notice her; he was only interested in the baby. For its part, the infant seemed quite happy with his new friend, laughing and flailing a fat little arm as he tried to catch the finger tickling his face. After a few attempts he succeeded, his hand clamping down on a great log of a forefinger it could only half encircle. At this the man's enthusiasm redoubled, and he launched into an excited monologue that included a few phrases of Polish along with the clucking nonsense syllables. I recognized the eastern drawl of Kresy dialect, close enough to the Mazovian Polish I grew up with to give me a sudden ache of homesickness. Then another man approached. He looked down at the Pole with disapproval, but immediately the woman launched into a tirade at him, snapping out a string of angry words in Irish-accented English that was too fast for me to follow. The couple left, and the big Pole got to his feet.

I was new to this country, and I felt always on the edge of being overwhelmed by the strangeness of everything. I slept in one of the many small rooms above the Nassau Avenue tavern I was in, and five other men shared the room with me. We were all strangers to one another, and it was clearly the tradition that we continue to treat each other as strangers, even as we unrolled our sleeping pallets side-by-side, so close they almost touched. Indeed, it sometimes seemed that being strangers to each other was the rule for all people of America. The Greenpoint neighborhood of Brooklyn where I lived was largely a mix of German and Irish immigrants, with a few Poles like myself, and a dozen or so other nationalities beginning to sprinkle in. So everywhere I turned there were people not like myself, and I felt like a small fish tossed into an alien sea.

And this new man, in spite of the familiarity of his language, was a strange-looking figure even in a country of strangers. Like the crude wooden tables and chairs around us, he looked like something banged together by a peasant carpenter. He was coarsely chopped and chiseled and sawn, the various mismatched pieces of him held together with pegs and nails. His nose was crooked, and one eye was always open wider than the other. He hadn't shaved recently, and his hair looked like it was hacked off with a pocketknife. His face was craggy and lined in a way that made it impossible to guess his age.

I was sitting at a long table a few feet from where the Irish girl had sat to wait for her husband. As the man I'd been watching stood, I called out to him in Polish, shouting over the background noise. "I think you must have a well loved little baby of your own at home."

I knew before the words were fully out of my mouth that I'd made a terrible mistake. The man looked down at me, and while his face was as immobile as stone, he seemed to turn gray and crumple in on himself as I watched. He pulled out the empty chair across the table from me and sat down slowly. For a long time he stared at me with an expression I found frightening, until I realized he wasn't truly looking at me at all, or at anything else in this world. Finally he made a hunching, rolling gesture with his huge shoulders, as if throwing off some great weight. Then he turned and bellowed out to the bartender, calling him by name and asking for vodka and a bowl of cabbage soup. When the bottle and a glass were delivered to the table Mischke poured the little glass full and then emptied it in two swallows. Only then did he look at me—*really* looking at me now—his eyes scanning my face. *"Mazowsze,"* he said, guessing the general region of my origin from my accent as I'd done with him. "Warsaw?"

"Kutno," I corrected, and then I stuck out my hand in the American fashion. "Stephan Dudek."

He took my hand. "Mischke," he said. In all the time I knew him, I never learned his first name.

A bowl of soup and a slab of bread were brought to the table, and Mischke began to eat. A few minutes passed without him speaking or looking at me, and I began to wonder if he'd forgotten about my existence—if the few words he'd shared with me were all I would ever get from him.

But then he looked up, his eyes meeting mine. He jabbed a finger in the direction of his soup bowl. "I showed the cook here how to make *kapusniak*," he said. "It's not bad." He twisted around in his chair and yelled the bartender's name again, demanding another bowl of soup "for my countryman." Then he looked me over, examining what he could see of my body as well as my face. "You work in the docks?"

I nodded.

"You look like a strong man, and healthy." He'd switched to English, and I got the feeling he was repeating something he'd heard in that language. He refilled his vodka glass and took a sip from it—an oddly delicate gesture on a man of his size. "You want to make two dollars and twenty-five cents a day?" he asked. "Come with me tomorrow, I'll get you a job working on the bridge."

My face must have taken on a silly expression, because Mischke broke into a ragged grin. Two dollars and twenty-five cents was far more than I earned on the docks, but . . . "You mean on the towers?" I asked. I was thinking of the dizzying height of the Brooklyn tower, only half-finished, I'd heard, and already it was taller than any other man-made thing I'd ever seen.

"Nah!" Mischke growled. His voice was full of disdain, as if he considered wrestling huge blocks of granite into place hundreds of feet in the air to be work for boys. "Not the towers. The caissons! The Brooklyn side is all done, but on the New York side there's still months of work."

"The caissons!" I echoed.

"You've heard about them?"

"I've heard a little," I said, not adding that what I'd heard sounded both terrifying and incomprehensible. "But I don't understand it too well. Something about working under the water?"

"Yes!" Mischke said with a kind of wild delight in his eyes. "Under the water, but not *in* the water! I'll explain." He took hold of his soup bowl with both hands and slid it toward me a few inches. "It's like this: Here is Brooklyn." He stabbed his thick forefinger down on the table between himself and his soup bowl. "And here is New York." His finger thumped down on the opposite side of the bowl. Then he pointed into the bowl. "The soup here is the East River; a big, wide river, you know. So. To build a bridge this big, first you need two towers, one on each side, but both of them *in* the river, not back here on the shore. The towers will hold up the bridge, okay? Aha! But how to build a stone tower that has its foundation deep down in the water of the river?" He held two fingers together and poked them into his soup, down to the flat bottom of the bowl. "That's the problem!"

When you order vodka from a bar in America, they give you a little doll-sized glass to drink it out of. Mischke picked up his glass and emptied it into his mouth. Then he held it upside down over his soup, lowering it slowly toward the surface. "Imagine this is made of wood," he said, tapping the glass with a finger of his left hand. "Imagine it is big. Very, very big. But it floats, see?" He held the glass so it was just skimming the surface of his soup. "Now. You float this out to the right place in the river, and then you start laying blocks of stone on top of it. More and more stone. You start building your tower. You know what happens? This thing"—he pointed at the glass—"it sinks. The more stone you add to the top, the lower it sinks in the river. Enough stone, it goes down to the bottom of the river." He pushed the glass down to the bottom of his soup bowl.

"Clever," I said.

He leaned closer to me suddenly, glaring with his mismatched eyes. "Wrong!" he said. "Not clever, because that's not the end of it." The wider of his eyes relaxed, while the narrower one kept up a skeptical squint. "What's at the bottom of a river, Dudek? Mud, that's what! These towers that will hold up the bridge, they're going to be tall, huge! Taller than the Trinity Church when they're done! You want to build something like that on mud?"

I was new to New York, and hadn't seen Trinity Church yet.

Mischke's voice changed to a gravelly whisper and he smiled like someone making a sly joke. "This is where it gets interesting, young Dudek. This is where *you* come in. You and me, and the job we do." Again he pointed down at the glass he was holding up-ended in his soup. "This thing, that's the *caisson*. That's French for *box*, because that's what it is, a big wooden box, open at the bottom. It has air in it, right? I push it down into the river, the soup, but the air is still in it, right? Hah?"

"Right," I said. "Air."

"So what they do, what Colonel Roebling does—he's the boss, the big boss, the chief engineer, they call him—what Colonel Roebling does, he makes it so men can go down inside here." He tapped the little glass. "Men go down in there, and they dig. They breathe the air that's pumped down and they dig and dig, and all the dirt they dig is hauled up and out from inside the caisson, and it—the caisson—it goes down into the mud at the bottom of the river. The men dig out the mud and dirt and rocks from all around the floor of the caisson, and down and down it goes, into the earth, while up top they keep laying on more and more stone blocks. The caisson goes down more, and more, and more . . . until it is on bedrock." He thumped his fist on the table. "Solid."

I peered down at Mischke's upside-down vodka glass, sitting in the bowl of murky soup. "Inside . . . that box . . . under the water . . . under the *bottom* of the river . . . That's where you go? To dig?"

He was grinning at me, his big yellow teeth showing. "Inside, Dudek! That is the job I got for you. Me, I already worked on the Brooklyn caisson. Now you and me, we go work on the New York side. We go in there and we dig, dig, dig." He put his free hand near the glass, extended the first two fingers and made waggling motions with them, like the scratching, digging legs of a rodent. "There is more," he said, his grin becoming uncertain. "Much more for you to know, to learn, to find out. But that is enough for now. You know more now than I did when I started."

I had a dozen questions, and probably there were a hundred more that I didn't know enough to ask, but I said nothing. It was a job, and a job that paid well. Two dollars and twenty-five cents a day was more than any other job I'd ever heard of.

The next morning I was standing on a sea of stone, half a city block in size. Scattered here and there were huge boom derricks, steam engines spewing out black coal smoke and white steam, and everywhere men busy at a myriad of different tasks. Mischke and I worked the first shift, so the start of our day came at six in the morning. We were in a cluster of about a hundred men grouped around a small opening in the center of the stone plateau. Most of these men had an easy slouch that showed they were familiar with the setting, but a few of us were what the foreman called new guys. "You new guys come with me," he said. "I'll lock in with you."

"Lock in?" I asked Mischke, not sure I liked the sound of it.

"It means go in through the air lock. You'll see." The foreman led us through the crowd of workers and then down a long spiral staircase. When the steps ended, the outside world had been reduced to a small disk of light above us, and we were standing on an iron deck the size of a big room, surrounded by walls of stone. There was a square hatch built into the floor, and the foreman went over to this, opened it and climbed down through it, calling up to us to follow. One by one we went through the door and down a ladder and found ourselves in a smaller room, this one cylindrical and walled with more iron. There were about ten of us in our group, but there was space enough in the room for at least twice that many. The foreman climbed back up the ladder and closed the door we'd come through, and then called out to Mischke, "Open the valve, Mickey!"

Mischke turned a thing like an oversized faucet handle, and the room was filled with a howling roar. Air was rushing through the valve, bringing with it a stifling flood of heat and humidity. After a short time I felt a piercing pain in my ears, and it was obvious that others of us "new guys" were feeling it too. The foreman was yelling an English word at us over and over, but I was distracted by the pain and I couldn't think of the word's meaning. "Swallow!" Mischke translated, shouting at me. "Swallow, swallow!" Some minutes later the roaring stopped, and the foreman opened another hatch at our feet. Again there was a ladder leading down, and again the foreman went first, then Mischke, then the rest of us.

It could have been another world, a world out of a fever dream.

It had been explained to us that the caisson was divided by timber walls into six lengthwise sections, and we were in one of these sections. So the width of the chamber was not so great, but the length seemed interminable, the far wall invisible in the misty gloom. The roof was three or four feet above our heads, and the ground we stood on was hard-packed dirt and gravel. At intervals along the walls there were blazing white lights, so bright that it hurt to look at them. But as bright as the individual lamps were, the steamy air seemed to swallow up the light before it had gone any distance. I could see that the walls had been whitewashed at one time, but months of spattering mud had blackened all but the uppermost few feet.

One of the men standing near me swore in English, and his voice was so strangely thin and weak that we all turned to look at him. He repeated the word, listening to himself, and then laughed, saying that he sounded like his own mother. The foreman spoke to us then, and his voice too was transformed into a thin, wheezing treble.

We new guys were directed to a shelf where we could stow our lunch pails, and to pegs where we could hang our jackets and shirts. I saw then that the men who had "locked in" before us were all stripped to the waist. Outside it was a chilly November morning, but in this place it was miserably hot and humid.

And the air . . . I'd been distracted by my surroundings, but now I realized that I was panting as if I'd been running for miles. The air was thick and sluggish; it took effort to pull it into my lungs and then force it out again, like breathing water. I felt a flicker of panic nudging at the back of my mind: the panic of drowning. Mischke thumped his hand on my back. "It's best not to think about the air," he said. "Just breathe the stuff, and you'll be okay." Even Mischke's voice, as big as he was, became weak and feminine in this place. I was about to make a joke to him about this, but the foreman was yelling at us—as well as he could in his enfeebled voice. It was time for us to work, he said.

The work was digging. Just as Mischke had described it with his soup bowl and vodka glass, we were to dig out the dirt from under our feet, and from underneath the walls of the massive structure we were inside. Shovelful by shovelful, we dug. We filled wheelbarrows with dirt and emptied them into a water-filled depression at the center of the caisson. A huge pipe ran from this pool up through the ceiling and on to the surface above, and inside this pipe was a clamshell device that lifted the dirt up to the outside world. Rocks too big to be lifted out in this way were broken up by men with picks. Boulders too big for men with picks were blasted apart with gunpowder. But for me and most of the men in the caisson, all we did was dig. Plunge your shovel into the sandy soil, lift it, dump out the soil. Then do it again, and again, and a thousand more times. It seemed absurd, what we were being asked to do—a few dozen men using the strength of their arms to create an inverse mountain, to lower this monster structure of wood and stone into the earth, like a farmer pounding a fence-post into the ground. But Mischke told me that the caisson was measured to sink a few inches every day, perhaps a foot in a week, a few feet in a month, and by these degrees the job would be done. The tower would have its foundation, the bridge would have its tower, and in time, the river would have its bridge.

So we shoveled.

At our lunch break Mischke went and sat on a bench that was against one of the outside walls of the caisson. Holding a gigantic slab of a sandwich in one hand, he banged on the wall behind us with the beer bottle in his other fist. It clanged metallically. "The inside is covered with sheet iron," he said. "They didn't know to do that with the Brooklyn caisson, so it was just wood. One day—it was when the digging in the caisson was almost done—a worker held a candle too close to the calking fiber between the timbers, up near the roof, and it started to burn. Nobody noticed the fire for a while, and by the time they did, it had eaten out a void inside the wood." He leaned closer to me, looking into my eyes. "Things do not behave down here like they do up in the world. And fire . . . fire is one thing that behaves *very* differently." He pointed up at the ceiling over our heads. "You know the walls and the roof of this caisson are thick, right? Layer on layer of the heaviest timbers, so the roof is fifteen feet thick. Well, that was a good thing, because the fire was burning through all of that. The place where the fire started was a small hole, no bigger than my hand. But inside the timbers of the ceiling, it was like a living thing, eating away more and more of the wood, hollowing out a big chamber. But that wasn't the strangest thing, or the worst. Once that fire got started, it seemed that nothing would put it out. We used buckets of water at first, then they brought in a big hose and a pump, blasting water into the hole the fire had made. But always as soon as the water stopped, the fire would begin again. It seemed like it would soon eat away the whole top of the caisson, and all the stone of the tower above us and all the water of the East River would come down on our heads." Mischke paused to chuckle, and I knew it was the sickly expression on my face that was making him laugh.

"So Colonel Roebling, the boss, the chief engineer," Mischke continued, "he comes down. He has carpenters drill holes to see how far the fire has gone into the wood. They drill here, there, there . . . and they find live, burning coals two feet deep in the wood, three feet deep, four feet . . ."

Mischke had finished his first sandwich, and he took the second out of his lunch pail and made a swooping gesture with it. He was eating a huge amount, even for a man of his size, and he'd emptied two of the four bottles of beer that were in his pail. "Finally Colonel Roebling decides to flood the caisson. He gets all of us out, and then he lets all the air out so that the river floods in, and the whole caisson is full of water. He didn't want to do this, because he was afraid the water crashing in might wreck the caisson. But there was no choice; the fire would not die any other way. You understand? *The fire would not die.* Not down here. Not with this air." Mischke waved his hand through the thick, heavy air between us.

"And it worked?" I asked. "Flooding the caisson put out the fire?"

"Of course! The colonel, he's a smart man; he knows what he's doing. They flooded it, and left it full of water for two days. That finally put the fire out. And the caisson wasn't damaged by the water at all. Once they pumped the water out again, we went back in and had the Brooklyn caisson down to bedrock in two weeks." He looked at me with a crooked grin of pride. "Forty-five feet below the bottom of the river we dug that thing." The gong ending our allotted time for lunch sounded, and we stood up to go back to our shoveling. Mischke caught my arm. "You have to understand," he said, putting his face close to mine again. "It's different down here." He stabbed a finger in the direction of his lunch pail. "You see how much I eat? We are all like that down here—you will be too in a day or so. The air does something to you, to your insides, so you burn through food like that fire burned through wood. Everything is different down here. Life is different, fire is different. Even the stones are different!"

I looked at him, not sure what he meant. "The stones?" I asked, but too late; he had turned to pick up his shovel and was walking away to his assigned digging station.

We shoveled. Our shift ended, and we went home and came back the next day and the next and the next. As Mischke predicted, my appetite while in the caisson became as outsized as his. And at the end of each day, as we "locked out" and climbed the spiral stairs to the outside world of afternoon sun and cold November air, a crushing weight of exhaustion descended on me, out of any proportion to the work I had done. I would have been ashamed at my feebleness as I staggered up those steps, but I saw that all the men around me were in the same condition. There was something about leaving the air of the caisson that made the energy drain out of you like water being poured from a jug.

Then one afternoon as we were waiting for the boat that would ferry us to shore, one of the men near me suddenly made a strange yelping sound, crouching in on himself and grabbing at his stomach. A moment later he dropped to his knees, his face screwed up in agony.

"Agh," Mischke grunted beside me. "It's caisson disease—the Grecian Bends."

His words confirmed my guess. I'd heard of this disease that struck caisson workers, though this was the first time I'd seen it. Like any disease, this one seemed to be random and inexplicable. There was no guessing who would fall sick from it, or when. They said that sometimes a big, muscular man would become ill after his first day in the caisson, while a puny man would work day after day for months. Even the form the disease took was random. It might be a pain in the knee or elbow, or agonizing stomach cramps, or a temporary paralysis of the legs, or sudden fainting and unconsciousness. They also said that at another place in America, where a bridge was being built across the Mississippi river, caisson workers had died of the disease.

Soon two men came along and helped the sick worker to his feet. They seemed to be friends of his, and they got him onto the ferry and sat on either side of him for the ride back to shore. Perhaps he would be back at work the next day, or perhaps not.

A few days after we saw the man get sick, Mischke came to me at lunch, drawing me over to his favorite bench in a corner of one of the interior partitions. "Look at this," he said when we were sitting down. He pulled a stone a little smaller than a fist out of his pocket and handed it to me. At first I saw nothing but a rock, but at Mischke's "Look, look!" I peered closer. Embedded into the stone and only partially revealed was the skull of a small animal, showing a pointed jaw with many teeth. Except for the teeth it looked like the skull of a bird, but I guessed it to be some kind of lizard.

"Colonel Roebling," Mischke said, "he calls these stone bones 'fossils,' and says they have been here for a long, long time, since before there was even a river here. He also tells me that in some parts of the world they find bones like these that are huge, bones from giant monsters that died out long ago. Around here there are only these smaller ones, but still, it's strange to think about, eh?" He took the stone back from me and stared down at it himself. "I find a lot of these. I keep my eyes open while I dig, and I find them. Sometimes when the colonel comes down here he asks me if I have any good ones, and he buys them from me."

He hesitated for a time, and then looked up at me. "You want to see something else, young Dudek? Look here." He moved toward me so that we were huddling together over the stone in his hand. "Up there, in the regular air of the world, these things, these fossils, they are like stone. Stone in the shape of bones, but just stone. But down here . . . as long as they stay down here, in this air . . ." Cupping the stone in one hand, he slowly drew the thumbnail of his other hand across the edge of the jaw. Bits of stone flaked away under the pressure of his nail, revealing a line of white.

"You see?" He lifted the thing closer to my face. "It is still bone, as if this little animal died a year ago, even less! Down here, in this air. . ." He paused, squinting at me so that the narrower of his mismatched eyes closed down to nothing. "Things don't die so easy, so *completely*. Like the fire in the Brooklyn caisson that wouldn't die. And now, here, we are deeper than the Brooklyn caisson ever went."

"Mischke," I said slowly. "What are you saying? Do you think these bones aren't dead?" I didn't know whether to be embarrassed for my friend or if he was making a joke. I'd found that Americans often like to tease us "fresh off the boat" immigrants, telling us wild, silly stories just to see what we'll believe. Perhaps Mischke was playing this sort of game with me.

"No, I'm not saying that," he answered. "This thing is dead. It was dead before it even got covered up in the ground. I know when something is dead, Dudek, have no doubts about that." With that he turned away from me, putting the stone back in his pocket.

Mischke didn't speak to me much over the next few weeks. In the vast, six-chambered space of the caisson, it's easy enough for a man to keep to himself, even with over a hundred men down there with you. I worked. I shoveled dirt, I cracked boulders with a pickaxe, I learned how to drill holes for gunpowder in the larger boulders. And at the end of each day I drank, I ate, I slept, I missed my home.

Then Mischke came to me one afternoon as we were lining up at the airlock at the end of our shift. "Dudek, I need to ask for something from you. A favor. I need to ask for a favor." He said the word as if it was something shameful.

"Of course, Mischke," I said. "What can I do?"

"I want you to ask them to put you on second shift. You see . . ." His eyes shifted around uncertainly, which was something I'd never seen in him before. "I watch out for it on first shift," he said. "You can keep your eye on it in second shift, and third shift, at night . . . well, there's not so many men down here then, and they don't work so hard. That foreman is drunk most of the time, so we just have to hope . . ."

I waited, not wanting to annoy Mischke with a flurry of confused questions. Finally he seemed to notice my silence and uncomprehending expression. "I . . . I found something," he said. "Maybe it's nothing. Probably it's nothing. But I have to see, I have to try, to find out . . ."

"What did you find, Mischke?"

He regarded me silently for a time, and then brought one of his big hands up to the level of his chest, his fingers curled as if holding an imaginary object the size of an apple. "An egg!" he said after another pause. "I was digging, and there were fossil bones first, and then three eggs. One smashed in, one cracked . . . and one . . . perfect. No cracks . . . just smooth, clean, perfect. I think . . . I think maybe it is not dead, Dudek. I think . . . if I take care of it, keep it warm . . . I think maybe it will hatch!"

Where I come from, people believe many things that I'm told the educated people of America do not believe. The evil eye that can spoil a baby's heart and make it die, the bit of red string to protect the baby, the danger of black cats, of spilled salt, and a hundred other things our grandmothers tell us of the hidden ways the world works. But this was not like one of those things that might be or might not. This was something that made me feel bad for Mischke. Once I started looking, I had seen many of these fossil bones that Mischke had shown me, and they were all nothing but stone; rocks in the shape of bones. Even if one of them was in the shape of an egg, it could no more hatch than any other stone. I avoided Mischke's eyes, not knowing what to say.

"I keep it hidden," he went on, "in a tin box I keep on the shelf where I put my lunch pail, covered up with a rag. It has to be up out of the ground so the air can get at it. And it's up high, so it stays warm. That's important. You understand? But the air . . . that's what's most important. It has to stay down here in this air until it's ready. If someone finds it and takes it up, takes it outside, that will kill it for sure!"

"So what do you want me to do, Mischke?"

"Just watch! Make sure nobody goes poking around in my stuff! That nobody moves the tin or tries to look inside! Put your lunch pail up on the shelf next to where I leave the tin, so it will look like it belongs to you."

It seemed vastly unlikely to me that anyone among the caisson laborers would touch, much less steal, anything that belonged to another worker, but I didn't argue the point. The more Mischke talked about this thing, the wilder his eyes got and the sadder I felt.

So I asked to be put on second shift, and the bosses agreed. They had a hard time finding men to work in the caissons; once men got a taste of how hard the work was, how strange the environment was, how terrifying it was if you let your imagination go, many of them left after their first day. Every week there were new faces in the crew, and after only a couple of months I was considered one of the "old hands" among the men.

As Mischke had said, on his corner of a shelf there was a bunched-up rag, and under the rag was a tobacco tin with a few holes punched into it. I didn't look into the tin, or even touch it. I just did my work and left at the end of my shift.

Again I barely saw Mischke for a few weeks. When I did encounter him, it was in the caisson, during the second shift. "Hullo, Mischke!" I called out. "You've switched to the afternoon shift?"

"Yes," he grumbled, and then took me by the arm and led me to an empty corner. "Listen, Dudek. I need some food. I haven't had anything since . . . Can I have some of yours? I'll pay you back."

Puzzled almost beyond speaking, I said "Of course!" then fetched my lunch pail and handed it to him. "Take whatever you like."

He fished around, took out one of my two thick sandwiches, unwrapped the paper to look at it, and apparently satisfied, tore off half of it and put the rest back in the pail. "Thanks, Dudek," he said, already turning his back to me. He walked away, holding the piece of sandwich as if it was precious to him in some way that had nothing to do with hunger.

I saw him again as the shift was close to ending. "Can you bring more food tomorrow?" he asked. He stood crookedly, as if he was too exhausted to straighten his back.

"Mischke, what's wrong? Why can't you get your own food?"

"I'm not coming out. I have to stay down here for . . . I don't know, a little longer. Maybe a few days. It's not ready . . . I mean, I don't think it should come out yet. It might not be strong enough yet. And I have to feed it!"

I felt certain I knew what "it" was, or what Mischke thought it was, and that certainty made me feel sick. I couldn't bring myself to try to confirm my guess, and in any case I doubted that Mischke would answer me if I did. "You can't just stay down here around the clock, Mischke," I said. "The foremen will notice—"

He put his hand on my arm. "Please! I just need food for a few days! Do this for me, Dudek!" It was strange, beyond strange, to see this big man, whose strength and toughness had once seemed limitless to me, reduced to pleading; and pleading not even for himself, but for . . .

"Of course, Mischke," I said. "I'll bring extra food tomorrow."

Things stayed like that for three days. During that time I saw that Mischke had taken one of the empty gunpowder boxes for his own. These were sturdy little wooden crates that the men often used as stools to sit on while eating. Mischke had whittled a few holes in the box, and had tied the lid on with a crisscross of rope. Watching him from a shadowy distance, I saw him dropping bits of food in through the holes. When I left the caisson at the end of the shift each day Mischke would stay behind, hiding in one of the far partitions so the foreman wouldn't notice.

On the morning of the fourth day, a man approached me as I was eating breakfast. It was an Irishman named Quinn, who worked the evening shift and who I'd shared a few drinks with recently. "They caught your crazy friend Mickey," he began. From the story that followed I gathered that Mischke had been noticed as he tried yet again to stay behind in the caisson as the work shifts changed. The foreman had called him a dozen foul names and ordered him into the airlock and off of the jobsite. "So he came up with the rest of us," Quinn said, "but as soon as he was out in the air you could see he was sick—sick with caisson disease. He walked a few steps, and then he was on the ground, like a dead man. They took him to the company hospital on the dock."

Asking after Mischke at the hospital, I was led to a room where there were six men, all lying in narrow beds that were lined up along one wall. More and more men had been getting the disease as the caisson went deeper under the bottom of the river, and there was space in the room for many additional beds.

"Young Dudek," Mischke said to me as I approached, making a weak smile. His head was propped up with pillows, but his body was so limp it looked as if he had been crushed into the mattress by a great weight. "Who would think that I would get the Grecian Bends, eh? I've been down there as long as anyone, and never had even a twinge before." He attempted another smile, and then just lay breathing for a time. "Not a good disease, Dudek. I can barely move. My legs are like dead sticks of wood. They say I will get better, but they don't know. . . . Some get better, some don't." I couldn't think of anything to say that wouldn't have been an insult to Mischke. We both knew that two men had died from the bends in the past few weeks.

Then Mischke's eyes sharpened, fixing on me. "Listen Dudek. I need your help. My box—what I have in the box—I need you to . . ." He stopped, perhaps because of something I allowed to show on my face. Another span of time passed in silence, and I had the feeling that Mischke was gathering himself for some effort. But when he finally spoke again, it seemed that he was changing the subject.

"They have some nurses here," he said, shifting his eyes to the doors of the big room. "Nice women, very good and kind. But they keep talking to me about prayer; they will pray for me, they want me to pray for myself. Do you pray, Dudek?"

"Not often."

"I used to. I used to feel close to God, sometimes, like he was . . ." with painful effort, he lifted one arm, vaguely indicating a space somewhere beside him. "Like he was right there, with me. I thought about becoming a priest when I was a boy. Then I grew up, I got a wife, and we . . . we had . . ."

Mischke's face was stony, showing no emotion, but he couldn't seem to finish the sentence. Finally he lifted both arms from the bed, bringing his hands near each other, as if cradling something. "When you see death, Dudek, when you see it and hold it, hold it as a *thing* in your hands, and you know it for what it is, something as solid and real as a stone, something that is black and terrible and is always there, always with us, eating out the insides of life . . ." He sighed and slowly lowered his trembling arms. "When a man sees that, Dudek, he does not pray any more."

He lay very still then, so quiet and still that I found myself checking whether he was still breathing. His voice was soft when he spoke again. "But now I have seen something else, Dudek. Something alive, something alive that shouldn't be alive. Something beautiful, and like nothing else in the world. It stands on two legs like a bird, but it's not a bird. And always it looks at me, following me with its eyes. When I take the lid off the box it looks up at me with those eyes and . . . it *sees* me. It sees me as a fellow living being, and its eyes say to me, 'I am alive, Mischke. I am alive like you, and you are alive like me.' Do you understand, Dudek?" Again he raised one arm, reaching toward me, but he was too weak and his arm dropped, hanging off the side of the bed until I moved it back onto the mattress for him. A tear was making a slow trek down the left side of his face, following a deep crease that ran from the corner of his eye almost to his ear.

"What do you want me to do, Mischke?" I asked.

"Just feed it. Put some food through the holes in the box. Some bread, soft meat, maybe boiled egg. Just keep it fed! When I get down there again, I'll take it out. Out of the caisson. I don't know if it's strong enough yet for the outside, but we have to take our chances, eh? It and me both, we'll just have to see."

On my next shift in the caisson I found Mischke's box, pushed into a corner and apparently undisturbed. Mischke had written his name on the side of it with charcoal, the letters rough and almost illegible. The lid was still tied on with rope. I stood looking at it for a long time. In the dim light there was little hope of peering through the holes to see if anything was inside it, and I didn't try. I could have untied the rope and taken the lid off, but I didn't do that either. I just stood looking into the shadowy corner until the foreman yelled at me to get to work. At my lunch break I got down in a squat in front of the box with my back to the nearest group of men. Quickly and furtively I tore up half a sandwich and stuffed the pieces through the holes in the lid of the box. No sound came from inside, but I kept jamming in pieces of bread and meat as fast as I could and then walked away.

I repeated this ritual for three days, and on the fourth day the box was gone. I went to the man nearest me, and then another and another, asking each one if he knew anything about the box. Finally one answered with something other than a blank stare: "Sure, the big guy, Mickey, he had it under his arm when he locked out this morning. He was right there at the shift change—didn't you see him?"

When my shift ended I went to the boarding house where Mischke lived. He wasn't there, and the men he shared a room with said he had packed all his belongings and left that morning. I didn't see him again until four years later.

It was one of the first warm days in the summer of 1876. Though the great bridge itself was still years from completion, the New York caisson was long finished. The vast space that Mischke and I and hundreds of others had toiled inside of was now filled up solid with concrete, and the huge tower of countless tons of stone had been built on top of it. But all of that was behind me. I worked at a bookbinder's now, and I was walking in Central Park, on my way to a concert at the Naumburg bandstand. I had just passed a couple without really looking at them, only vaguely noticing that the woman was carrying a young child on her hip. But after I'd gone a few steps further I heard a gruff voice calling my name. I realized who it was before I'd even turned around.

"Mischke!"

"Young Dudek," he answered, grinning at me.

For a moment, I could only stare dumbly at him. I knew it was Mischke I was looking at, but he was a man transformed. The rough, irregular features were still there, but his face was softer, cleanly shaven and pink. His hair was neatly trimmed and oiled, his clothes clean. Even his eyes seemed less mismatched, and far less imposing. I realized I was seeing Mischke as a happy man, and even as that thought occurred to me he was introducing me to the woman at his side as "My wife Rosalie." The tenderness in his voice left no doubt about the source of his happiness. "And my little one, Anna!" he added, touching his hand to the cheek of the toddler in her mother's arms. "Who could believe I would have such a beautiful family? Eh? Who could believe?" The pride glowed from him like heat from a fire.

For a few minutes we stood there among the trees and grass of the park, talking of our time in the caisson, the progress of the bridge, and about our lives now. Mischke told me he'd used his savings from his caisson wages to purchase half-ownership in a grocer's shop, and had met Rosalie as one of his customers. "She kept telling me how to run the business," he said, "so I told her she better marry me so she can run things herself!" He laughed, and his wife rolled her eyes with an expression that told me this was an old joke between them. Neither of us made any mention of Mischke's last days in the caisson or of the box he took away from it.

As we talked, Mischke's daughter began to squirm in her mother's arms. She pointed down the path to one of the sausage-vendor carts that had recently begun appearing in Central Park. "Ma, Pa," she said excitedly, "get sau'ge for J'zurkie? Get sau'ge for J'zurkie?"

Mischke smiled over at his daughter. "Jaszczurkie has plenty of other food, Anna," he said. You can feed him when we get home, okay?"

"But sau'ges are his favorite!" Anna protested, but then her mother set her down on the gravel path, and after a few soft words took her hand and strolled out onto the grass with her.

I realized then that the word that was puzzling me was a diminutive of *jaszczurka*, the Polish for *lizard*. But already Mischke was continuing our conversation, asking me where I was living now and whether I'd met "a nice girl" yet. Distracted, I stammered out an answer. Mischke's only acknowledgement of my befuddled, questioning expression was to give me the briefest of winks before turning to look at his wife and daughter walking hand in hand on the grass. Somehow I knew that was all the answer I would ever get.

We parted a short time later, and I walked on alone. The sun was warm on my face, and the breeze was sweet with the smell of life.

In the world of Seanan McGuire's Incryptid series, the waheela hail from Canada's Northwest Territories where the thaw never comes and the cold needs no name. They tend to lose their tempers and eat whatever happens to be vexing them. But Istas, like many young human women, has left her provincial family to live in New York City.

RED AS SNOW

SEANAN MCGUIRE

"Flesh is temporary; flesh will end. Ice is forever. Remember this, and choose your steps with caution."

—Waheela proverb.

The Freakshow, a highly specialized nightclub
somewhere in Manhattan
Now

"Istas!"

I studied my reflection in the small mirror set into my locker door for a moment more, trying to figure out what I could do differently with my eye makeup, before yawning and turning toward the sound of my name. Looking was a courtesy, nothing more: even if I could not recognize the sound of my employer's voice, I would have known the smell of her, a mixture of cream foundation, overheated velvet, and the curious pheromone stew of her sweat.

"Yes?" I closed my locker as I turned. It was one in a row of twenty, matching three other free-standing rows, all arranged like this was some sort of gymnasium, and not the changing room of a popular strip club turned burlesque show.

Kitty Smith, owner and operator of the Freakshow—the aforementioned strip club turned burlesque show, which had been founded by her uncle—folded her arms and scowled at me. This took several seconds; bogeymen have very long arms. That, along with their grayish skin and the extra joints in their fingers, is all that visibly distinguishes them from the humans. She even wore her long black hair curled in the human style, framing her pointed, inhuman face. "You're supposed to be on the floor. What are you doing back here?"

"I am not supposed to be on the floor," I replied, picking up my parasol. It opened into a pleasing bloom of pink and black lace, which went perfectly with my puff-sleeved, pink and black satin dress. It had taken me weeks to sew the alternating tiers of pink and black petticoats, but the effect was worth the effort, especially once I had dyed pink streaks into my naturally black hair. "If you check the schedule, you will see that I was scheduled to end my labors at nine o'clock. It is now nine-fifteen. I am done for the evening."

"That schedule was made before Candy went on maternity leave," protested Kitty.

"My request for time off was not dependent on the status of Candy's gestation." I gave my parasol a lazy twirl. "Ryan and I will be having a pleasant evening involving courtship activities, food, and coitus."

There was a pause before Kitty asked, "You're going out for dinner and dancing before you go back to his place for sex?"

I frowned. "I believe I just said that."

"No, honey, you didn't." Ryan sounded amused and exasperated at the same time, a combination that I have become intimately familiar with since we began our relationship. I turned, smiling, to see him standing in the doorway of the women's locker room. He shook his head, smiling back. "Remember what I said about sounding like a dictionary? It confuses people."

"Refrain from discussion of carnage and how many colors are inside a person, try not to sound like a dictionary . . . this is why waheela don't talk to people, you know. It's far too difficult."

People might be difficult, but Ryan was easy. Tall, with dark hair, dark eyes, and golden skin, Ryan Yukimura was the first man of any species who had thought to ask me if I was in search of a mate. He was not human—his species, the tanuki, originated in Japan—but as I was not human either, that did not present a significant barrier. Both of us were shapeshifters, and as such looked perfectly human when we saw the need.

"It has its rewards." Ryan looked past me to Kitty. "My shift's up. Angel's got the bar. See you tomorrow night, ma'am?"

Kitty threw her hands in the air. "Oh, sure, you leave, too. My best bartender and my most productive waitress. Why isn't there a law against employees dating?"

"Because your uncle wanted to hit on the cocktail waitresses," said Ryan amiably. "Come on, Istas, or we'll miss our table."

"Coming." I picked up my clutch purse, bobbed my head at Kitty, and followed Ryan out of the dressing room. He looped his arm through mine. Normally, he was taller than I was, but I was wearing high heeled boots, and we were almost the same height. Side-by-side, we strolled away.

I was born in a place that has no name, so high in the Canadian tundra that the permafrost never melted, no matter the season. There were five pups in my litter. I was third-born, large enough to fight off my siblings, small enough not to seem like an attractive mouthful to my father. The largest of us did not survive the winter. Neither did the smallest, and when the first green of springtime came, only three of us remained. I think of those days often, when I am frustrated with the crush and chaos of Manhattan, or when the stupidity of the humans I have surrounded myself with seems too much to bear. Those were my happiest days, cradled in the love of my siblings, protected by the instincts of my mother. And if those days were the best that my homeland has to offer . . . is it any wonder that I have no intent to ever, ever go back?

Ryan kept his arm looped through mine as we walked along the sidewalk toward our destination, as much a restraint as a show of ownership for the people around us. He didn't want me departing from the path that we had charted for our evening. A pity. There were some lovely-smelling rats in the nearby alley, and I had yet to eat.

"We're almost there, Izzy," he said, still pulling me along.

"Anyone else who called me by such a diminutive would find themselves searching the gutters for their arms," I said, amiably enough.

Ryan grinned. "Good thing I'm not anyone else, then, isn't it."

"Yes."

We walked a few blocks more, finally stopping in a pizza parlor that smelled amazing enough to make up for the fact that it was essentially a dark cavern carved from the wall. I frowned. Ryan tapped my shoulder and pointed to a sign in the window.

SUNDAY ONLY—ALL YOU CAN EAT, NINE TO MIDNIGHT.

"I love you," I breathed.

He grinned. "Yes, you do."

To be waheela is to be a creature of endless appetite, as hungry as the winter wind which blows from the north. After consuming the better part of three large pizzas with everything and an entire medium pizza with ham and pineapple, I began to wonder if the north wind had been going about things the wrong way for all these years. Maybe it just needed to visit a nice Italian restaurant and eat until it wanted to vomit.

Not that this was technically a "nice" Italian restaurant. It was narrow, and dark, with walls that had once been white, and were now a dingy shade of cream. I would have thrown away any article of clothing as visibly stained as those walls. The furniture was old, full of splinters and scarred by inexpert repairs. None of which mattered; the food was plentiful, and that was the end of my concern.

Ryan reached for one of the last slices of pizza. I growled briefly, reminding him that the food was mine, before leaning back in my seat and allowing him to take it. Ryan grinned.

"I take it you approve?"

"I do." I nudged him under the table with my toe. "How did you discover this venue?"

"I told some friends that I needed somewhere to take my lady where they wouldn't look at us funny for eating everything in sight. This place," he gestured to the restaurant around us, "does all-you-can-eat Sunday once a month, at which point it winds up packed with college kids, competitive eaters, and lots of other folks who are more interested in eating than they are in judging."

"Excellent." I scanned the room, taking note of the wide variety of people who had crammed themselves into the narrow space. I was most definitely the best dressed of the lot, or at least the only one who had bothered to coordinate my earrings with my vertically striped stockings.

Most waheela do not care for crowds. I do not care for crowds. But I am very fond of watching fashion trends, and this has required me to learn to be still even when surrounded. It was not an easy lesson.

One of the waitresses wove through the crowd with an easy grace that I admired, putting a small dessert pizza down between us. It was grated chocolate and sliced strawberries on cinnamon bread, and I appreciated the artistry of it, even as I felt no desire to continue eating.

"We didn't order this," said Ryan, sounding puzzled.

"Compliments of the chef," said the waitress. "You're tonight's big eaters!" Her announcement drew a round of applause from the tables around us.

"Oh. Well, thanks." Ryan looked back to me and shrugged. "I guess we should try it. To be polite."

"Your weakness for chocolate will be your undoing one day," I said, and sighed, and reached for the pizza. If there is one thing I have learned since leaving the cave of my fathers, it is how to be polite.

There was a bitter taste lurking beneath the sweetness of the treat, like bones sleeping under snow. I paused in the act of chewing my first mouthful, trying to figure out why I knew that flavor—and more, what it was doing in my food.

Then Ryan's eyes rolled up in his head, and he fell, face-first, into his plate. I threw my slice of pizza aside, reaching for him. Someone in the crowd protested. I swallowed my half-chewed mouthful in order to snarl at her. The protests stopped.

My hand never reached my boyfriend's shoulder. Cold swept over me like the cruel north wind, and I barely felt my own head hit the table.

I snapped awake. The pizza parlor was gone, replaced by a dark, cold room and a metal chair beneath me. Something held me in place. I tensed, testing my bonds. Metal chains, with a smell I did not recognize. No common alloy, then. They were wrapped around my body half a dozen times, holding me down, torso, arms, and legs. If I changed forms, and the chains did not snap . . .

I have seen stronger than I killed by their own foolish bravado, believing they could transform their way out of any trap or trouble. I calmed my breathing and was still.

The scent of Ryan hung in the room, but I did not know whether it meant my boyfriend was present or whether I was simply smelling my own clothing until he groaned off to my left, and said, "I don't think that pizza was a good idea."

"Shh," I cautioned, despite my relief. "We are unlikely to be alone here."

"I know, but they wouldn't have put us together if they didn't want us talking. Can you change?"

"The chains are too tight. I fear I would break myself. Can you?"

"No. Same." Ryan sighed. "They're too tight for me to get bigger, and too complicated for me to get smaller. Even if I shrank, I'd be all tangled up."

"Ah." Waheela have two shapes that we choose to wear: the one I was chained in, and my great-form, which was ten feet tall and difficult to buy shoes for. Tanuki have three common shapes—man, beast-man, and beast. It was a pity that none of them were currently available to us. "Is there a length of chain between your legs?"

"Yeah, and it's, um, a little closer to the boys than I really appreciate."

"Is there direct constriction of your testicles?"

I could virtually hear Ryan's wince. "No, but it's close."

"Hmm." I looked around the darkened room again. My eyes were adjusting to the dark, allowing me to pick out some small details, such as the location of the nearest walls. I considered rocking back and forth until I fell over, but dismissed the idea as impractical. I would injure myself well before I did anything to damage either the chains or the chair, and I would probably rip my stockings in the process. That was unacceptable.

"So honey? Do you smell anything that might tell us where we are?"

"I smell you. I smell metal. I smell cold. We are near something refrigerated. I do not smell anything that would indicate why we are here, or how we have been brought here." As I said the last words, I froze. There was one thing that would explain how we had been brought here without our captors leaving any scent hanging in the air to warn me of their natures.

Ryan realized it, too. The silence stretched between us for what felt like an age before he said, "Waheela smell like cold."

"Yes," I agreed. "We do."

It is hard to be a predator in any world, but harder still in a world where all is ice and snow and cold, forever. The waheela grew large, to fight off all who would challenge us, and then, when that was not enough, we grew difficult to track, to confound those who we would hunt. The scent of a waheela in human form is indistinguishable from fresh-fallen snow. Even in our great hunting forms, we leave behind meaningful scent trails only when we are wounded. We had been taken;

we were in a room where the only abiding smell was the smell of the cold. It was thus clear that we had been taken by waheela.

"Ryan?" My voice was suddenly brittle in the cold, dark air, like ice that was on the verge of breaking.

"Yeah, Istas?"

"I have been very fond of you, and am glad to have entered into a casual mating relationship, despite the differences in our species and cultural backgrounds. I hope that you have not regretted your time with me."

"What? Of course not. Istas—" Confusion and burgeoning panic sharpened his voice to a killing edge.

In some stories of the waheela, we can grab the wind itself to use as a weapon, when the need is upon us. If only all stories were true. I sat up taller in my chair, as tall as the chains allowed, and wished that I had my parasol. I have always felt braver when properly accessorized.

"We are ready for you," I said. "You have toyed with your prey sufficiently, don't you think?"

A rectangle of light opened at the far end of the room, not so bright as to be blinding, but enough to sting my eyes, which had long since adjusted to the dark. Three figures made their way inside, and they smelled of nothing, nothing but the cold. Their steps were soft as they walked across the room; predator's steps, designed to make as little noise as possible. I had stopped walking like a predator long ago, preferring shoes that politely announced my presence to the potential victims around me.

The three waheela walked until they had come to the very edge of where the light reached, and stopped, silently waiting to see what I would do next. They were all male, with dark hair and eyes, and brown skin. Waheela could pass for Canada's First People, when we had to, and in a way, I suppose that was not a lie. We had been there longer than most after all, as cold and unchanging as the glaciers.

I cocked my head. "Hello, Father."

The tallest of the three figures nodded in return. "Hello, eldest of my daughters."

I was not the firstborn female of my litter, but the dead are not the family of the living. After my sister was eaten, I became eldest. I looked at the shadowed figures behind him, and asked, "Why have you come here with my brothers? Why have you followed me down into the human lands? I went into exile of my own volition."

"Your mother is dead," he said calmly. "You are the eldest of my daughters."

In the land of the waheela, the words he had just uttered made perfect sense. But this was the land of the humans, and I had been living here for a very long time. It took me a moment to realize what he was saying, what the words really meant beyond the thin veneer of his civility. They would have been easier in great-form, where nothing has two meanings: everything is only ever what it is, as cold and unforgiving as the snow.

Clarity did not come easy, but it came. I stiffened in my chair. "No," I said. "I refuse. I am in exile."

"You have exiled yourself."

"But if Mother is dead, then I have the authority to exile myself. I am in exile. You must find another."

My father growled. Even in man-form, it was a chilling, primal sound, commanding obedience from the tip of my head to the toes of my feet—my feet, which were still clad in my fine black boots with the heels that clattered when I walked. I rapped one of them against the floor, relishing the sound it made. I was Istas. I had run very far to become her, and I was not letting her go that easily.

"No," I said, calmly. "I will not go with you."

"Izzy?" Ryan sounded confused. I managed not to wince—showing weakness was beneath me, and here and now, I was my father's daughter, whether I desired to be or no. "What's going on?"

Even in the dark, I could see my father baring his teeth in a smile. "You refuse me, but you forget that you are not the only thing we hold. How loudly will your little toy scream, eldest daughter? How many limbs must we remove before you will see reason?"

I opened my mouth to answer, and then paused, rapping my heel against the floor again. It made a sharp, almost hollow sound. "Father, are we on the second floor?"

"Third," he said smugly. "No one will overhear the screaming."

"Ah. That is pleasing. Ryan?"

"Um, yeah, Izzy?"

"Are you ready to rock?"

Ryan's surprised laugh was followed by the sound of a large, heavy object crashing through the wooden floorboards. My brothers shouted, rushing past me toward the hole that had suddenly opened up in the floor. My father snarled. I bared my teeth in a smile.

"I believe you have lost a prisoner," I said. "Pity, that. Now what are you going to do to entice me?"

He grabbed the front of my dress, jerking me toward him until I heard the seams starting to give. Nose only inches from mine, he whispered, "I'll think of something."

This time, I couldn't stop myself from flinching.

Waheela are not unthinking beasts, to be ruled by instinct. We are very thoughtful monsters, ruled by tradition, which is like instinct, only crueler. Once, it may have made sense for the eldest to rule in all things; once, it may have been fair to drag back runaway children and force them to rejoin a family they had chosen to leave. Those times are far behind us, lost in the distance of the past.

My father's hand gripped my jaw, forcing me to look at him as he studied me. His lip curled in a sneer when he considered my ponytails. "You dress like a human," he spat.

"You are wearing human clothing," I countered. My brothers were gone, descending into the abandoned building as they searched for my missing boyfriend. I wished them all the luck in the world, including the greatest luck of all: if they were lucky, they would not find him. A fall from this height would doubtless have broken the chair that kept his chains in position. He would be loose. And most of all, he would be angry.

Tanuki are therianthropes, like waheela: shapeshifters whose power comes from within, unlike the poor, diseased wretches infected with lycanthropy. Ryan could transform his body in a variety of ways, including convincing his flesh that it was a type of stone far denser than lead. He could not move when in statue-form, but he could do a remarkable amount of damage to things like non-load-bearing floors.

"I am dressed for the sake of blending in," said my father. "You are groomed. You have embraced the mockery they continue to pretend serves as a culture."

I blinked at him, startled. And then I laughed. "Truly? You call human culture a mockery? Our culture is a hole in the ground! Our culture is your teeth in my sister's throat! How did Mother die? Hunters? A blizzard? Or you, coming in the night with claws bared and temper blazing? We don't have a culture, Father! We have a war that we've been fighting against our own kind for centuries, and there will never be a winner!"

His hand was hard against my cheek. I glared at him. He glared back, showing me his teeth.

"You will come home," he said. "I do not care what you want. Desires are for the warm lands."

"I left the cold."

"The cold never leaves you." This time, his hand against my cheek was a caress. "You are never going to be as warm as they are."

I turned my head, fast as a striking snake, and sunk my teeth into his fingers. How he howled! And his blood was as warm as any mammal's. There was nothing of the cold in him at all.

He yanked himself away from me, snarling. "Insolent bitch!"

"I told you, Father. I will not come home with you. You'll have to kill me first."

"So be it, then." He primly removed his overcoat, tossing it off to the side. Then, without another word, he began to swell, human features first distorting, and finally vanishing beneath the onrushing force of the battle-form. He unfolded, shirt and trousers tearing away, until a great wolf-bear stood before me, fully eleven feet in height, with bearlike paws and claws the length of my palm. He roared, and it was the sound of an avalanche crashing down upon an empty valley. All the cold of Canada was in his bellowed declaration of dominance.

I looked at him calmly. "Yes," I said. "I know. But what can you do?"

He stepped forward, barely bipedal, all-too-aware that the floor would barely support his weight; Ryan had made that very clear. Almost gentle now, he wrapped his paw around my chin, claws pricking the flesh of my cheek. He looked at me. I looked back.

"How did Mother die?" I asked.

His answer would no doubt have involved teeth and claws and a rather unpleasant death, both for me, and for my dress, which was not designed to deal with that much blood. Instead, he was hit from the side by a beast almost his size, differentiated only by paler fur and a long striped tail. Father roared. Ryan roared back.

I frowned. "This is very inconvenient." I turned my head in the direction Ryan had arrived from. The younger of my brothers was standing where a door had not been previously, his shirt torn and stained with blood. "You. Release me. I am the eldest female now, and I command it."

Instinct is weak where tradition is strong. My brother knew that I was to be chained, and that Father would be unhappy if I were free.

But as Father was in the process of having his head slammed into the wall by an angry tanuki, I was the only eldest in our family currently in a position to give orders. He grabbed Father's overcoat from the floor; as I expected, the key was in the pocket. What other reason would someone so dismissive of human culture have for being careful of his clothes?

My brother moved to kneel behind me, fumbling with the chains. When they fell away I stood, not thanking him, and began undoing the buttons on my dress as quickly as I could without damaging anything. It was time for this to end, and I was going to be the one to end it.

Waheela have two forms: man-form and great-form. Neither is superior to the other. Both have strengths and weaknesses, and if I miss the animal grace of my great-form when I am in man-form, I miss the thumbs and fashion opportunities of my man-form when I am in great-form. Still. Great-form is well-suited to anger, and as I stepped out of my stockings, I allowed my anger to run free.

Ryan looked up as I raced on all four paws toward the tangled mass of fur and teeth that was his clench with Father. He let go, rolling out of the way just before I slammed into my father's chest, teeth seeking and finding his throat. He roared, claws scrabbling to find purchase on my back, but all he found was fur, thicker and more luxurious than any waheela who does not have regular access to quality hair care products could hope to grow.

I bit harder, slamming my father into the floor, and held him there, putting as much pressure as I could against his throat. Eventually, his thrashing stilled, and he lay limp.

Instinct told me to bite down, to end him. Tradition said the same. But I am stronger than both. I have learned to wear high-heeled shoes, and to walk among men without eating them. I released my hold, straightening and shrinking at the same time, until I was in my man-form once more.

"Izzy?"

"Did you kill my other brother?" I asked curiously, turning toward Ryan. He was naked, and had no doubt shredded his clothing when he transformed. No matter. We would take my father's overcoat, and the taxi drivers of New York had seen stranger things.

Ryan shook his head. "I didn't think you'd like that. He's passed out in the basement."

"Good." I turned to my brother. He took a step backward. "I will not harm you, but I will not be so merciful a second time. Tell Father this is my territory. No waheela are welcome here; none save me. Come again, and I will kill you. Do you understand?"

"I do," he said, and tilted his head back, showing me his throat.

I walked forward, resting my hand against the exposed skin. "Find a name, brother," I murmured. "Find something stronger than tradition. And for the love of the north wind, find better trousers. Those are very unattractive."

Then I gathered my clothing and my boyfriend, and left.

Ryan put Father's overcoat on, shoving his hands into the pockets, and hung back while I flagged down a cab. By the time the driver realized he had picked up a half-naked man to go with the half-naked woman, it was already too late to drive past.

I snuggled against Ryan in the backseat, trying to finger-comb my hair back into a semblance of order.

"So," he said finally. "That was your family."

"Yes," I agreed. "Let's meet your family next. I am sure it will be equally enlightening." My stomach growled. I frowned. "But perhaps we should have more pizza first. I have burned a great many calories this evening."

Ryan's laughter had a hysterical edge to it. He kissed the top of my head, and said, "Let's do that, honey."

As he gave the address to the driver, I smiled. It had been a good night. I was stronger than tradition, stronger than the call of the cold.

So long as that is true, I can stay.

Fairy tales come true in New York, but one should always remember fairy tale justice is sure, if not always swift, and the punishment is appropriate.

A HUNTSMAN PASSING BY

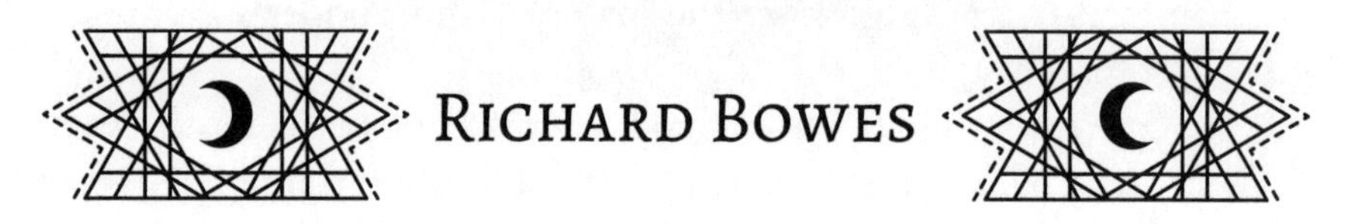

RICHARD BOWES

1

Good evening! Here I am back working the door at an exclusive event. Like old times. It's been a while since we met. I'm not sure anyone else can see you in your coat of moonlight. Or what any of them would understand if they did.

The secret behind my being able to recognize you is dyslexia. It's how I found my identity and my job, how I got married and had kids. If I'd been able to read, God knows where I'd be now.

My not being able to write things down is why my memory got good. It's why, even though I haven't done doors for a few years, I can still remember every face and name on the Lower Manhattan art circuit.

Tonight they're celebrating the memory of the late seventies. And back then no Downtown event was complete without me. So when they organized the party for the release of Victor Sparger's *Raphael!* I was asked to provide security for old time's sake.

The idea of this event bothered me and I wasn't going to do it. Then something I read to my kids recently made me change my mind. That and something my wife told me. (My wife, when we were wondering if you'd be here, told me to say hello.)

Raphael! is one painter directing a film about another. People say that's kind of a culmination of that whole scene. The movie's set downtown thirty years ago when the art world was the buzz in New York's ear. Big money changed hands. Large reputations got made. Victor Sparger was "in" right from the start. Painter and sculptor, very smart and pretty talented, he knew all the right names: Picasso and Braque, Warhol and Geldzahler. He was and is a prudent man. He invested his earnings, cultivated his image, bought real estate. Then out of nowhere came Louis Raphael. And in magazine articles about the scene Victor Sparger suddenly looked like a footnote.

In this film, Sparger gives the world a movie about Louis Raphael. He intends that people interested in Raphael will find out about him through Sparger. It's not exactly crooked or illegal. But it's unjust in some way that's beyond the reach of human law.

That kind of thing only gets resolved in fairy tales. Which I take it is why you are here before me in that blue and silver dress on this Bowery sidewalk. And why I bow you into Ling's Fortune Cookie. You're on everybody's guest list whether they know it or not.

The Fortune Cookie is new since the last time you were around. Back then the site was still an upscale gay baths. Now it's a Chinese restaurant with waitresses who happen to be Asian guys. Drag is the gimmick of the moment.

From inside the door we get to see the aging, slightly raddled survivors of the Mudd Club plus their younger tricks and camp followers. The walls are hung with shots from the movie.

Some of the stills are of Raphael's paintings. Out of backgrounds of dark carnival colors, Caribbean faces stare. Like they're looking out of a deep, rich night into this bright room. Not angry. Not happy. Glaring not at but right through the viewer. And scrawled on the canvases are phrases in Spanglish and pidgin French, slogans that—when you decipher them—are like bizarre ads. "Breathe Oxygen Every Day," that one over there says.

Raphael, of course, is dead. And Sparger has yet to make his dramatic entrance. It's uncool to turn and stare at new arrivals. So everybody glances out of the corner of their eyes as the door opens. It's obvious from their reactions that they see nothing but me surveying the room. I alone am aware of you. Everyone goes back to watching the murderers.

Two of them are in the room. For an event this big, the jealous sculptor who threw his wife out the thirty-story window and the coke-crazed art dealer who tortured and butchered the fashion design student—both showed up. They arrived separately and alone. Once each realized the other was here, they tried to stay as far apart as possible. Like both are afraid of guilt by association.

It's the chance to witness this kind of encounter that brings out the crowds. Alert as forest animals, they watch a wife killer/sculptor powerful enough to throw almost anybody out a window, a sadist/gallery owner, sleek and taut, who could be at any throat in a moment. But those things won't happen. Not to people who have survived Max's Kansas City, The Factory, and Studio 54. The craziest part is that I'm here to keep out dangerous riff-raff.

In the mundane world, justice is a contest between bad luck and cold cash. The sculptor walked free, the dealer only served time for tax evasion. I almost feel sorry for the murderers. Compared to some of the guests, they seem pathetic. And theirs isn't the kind of wrong that concerns the Huntsman.

Fairy tale justice is sure, if not always swift, and the punishment is appropriate. My only question is which tale gets told tonight. You smile at the question and there's a glimmer like gold, like sun-fire when you do.

Seeing that, I remember how I found my place in the world. The place where I got brought up was in the Five Towns out on Long Island. Kind of a surprise right? But I was the tough, poor kid in the soft, rich town. In school, I got kept back once or twice. And I was big to start with.

Dyslexia, as I say, was the problem. My oldest girl has it too. Now they can actually do something. Back then when I reached ninth grade, they sent me to this old lady who sat in a little office in the cellar of the school. Just her and me.

She'd have me read and correct me. Stupid stuff. Not Dick and Jane but very simple sentences. It didn't seem to help and I hated her at first. Eventually I worked my way up to a book by the Grimm brothers. Those stories stuck with me. Maybe because I'd never read anything else. Or maybe because the old lady was a witch. No disrespect intended, in case you belong to the same union or something.

The characters I liked weren't the princes or princesses. In fairy tales, they're a dime a dozen. You can't tell them apart. Poor tailors and honest woodcutters didn't do it for me either. I knew what it was like to be poor if not honest.

The out-of-work soldiers, sly, smart and smoky, making deals with the devil, caught me first. Like a prophecy, you know. Because rich kids get into as much trouble as ones in the ghetto. Drugs, stolen cars, breaking and entering: whatever they did they wanted me along as protection.

But the rules are different for rich kids. When trouble came down, they all went into counseling. Forty years ago, poor kids went in the army. Right then that meant 'Nam. I did my tour in a bad time. When it was over, I became a discharged soldier, every bit as bent and nasty and bitter as the ones in the stories. It happened the devil wasn't signing deals for souls at that moment or I would have gone that way.

Instead, I bummed around for a couple of years then started to contact old friends. A lot of them had finished college, taken their time about it, and ended up in New York. So I followed them to this city with nothing but a duffle bag with my clothes and the only book I ever read.

But everything was in that book. New York was full of frog cabbies who were actually actor princes under a cruel spell. Cinderella waited tables in every bar. Acquaintances had started their own little kingdoms: clubs and restaurants and galleries. Sometimes those places weren't in the best neighborhoods, or the patrons forgot their good manners, or the wrong kind of people wanted to come inside. They started calling me.

Maybe a tiny bit wiser, I put the idea of the discharged soldier behind me. There's another kind of guy in a lot of the stories. He never has the major role. But I didn't want stardom. He gets different titles: forester, game keeper, the hunter. He plays key parts. And I have the feeling he's around even when he's not talked about. Every king or queen needs a royal huntsman. That at least is how it worked in the dark woods of Manhattan.

2

That's my secret identity. It's because of Rinaldo Baupre that I discovered it. And it's because of him that I first saw you in action. Rinaldo is standing over there looking, as always, like he's in pain. No the years have not been kind to him. Drug treatment. Mental hospitals. It's like something's been tearing Mr. Baupre in two.

Sometimes with celebrities, it's amazing how much smaller they are in real life than in the media. With Rinaldo it's the opposite. I'm always surprised that he's average height and build. On first meeting, he seems pretty creepy but in no way misshapen. Inside, though, he's a dwarf, a troll.

Mr. Baupre wrote the script for *Raphael!* And he's treated his own part in Louis' life very sympathetically. It turns out he was the kid's mentor and inspiration. Lots of amazing changes have gotten rung on history.

Rinaldo was a fixture of the downtown scene, a poet, a sponger, a scene maker. And he had a legend. I mean, the name demanded one. So he was the illegitimate son of a French Resistance fighter who abandoned him and a minor Mexican muralist who died young.

Rinaldo is a critic. Thirty years ago, the art magazines kind of used him to keep watch at the crossroads where art and the underground intersected. People were starting to pay attention to the downtown scene. Victor Sparger had started getting hot. Victor had gone through a careful rebellion, done graffiti, nailed broken glass onto boards. Rinaldo Baupre had a small part in his rise. But mostly Victor managed himself.

By then I'd met Louis Raphael through a young photographer, Norah Classon. Norah loved Louis like he was a little brother. He was this skinny, Caribbean kid, living on the street, bumming money and cigarettes and a couch to crash on.

I'm supposed to say I got knocked out the first time I looked at his work. Like everyone else apparently did. And that I could kick myself for not having the fifty bucks or whatever he was charging for a painting. In reality, the first time Norah talked me into letting Louis stay at my place I was pissed off because he got paint on my walls. And he was apologetic and cleaned it up. That was shortly before Rinaldo discovered Raphael. Like Columbus finding America is how my wife described it. That is, America was always there, big and rich and unexploited. A lot of Indians knew about America. But Columbus talked it up where it counted.

Rinaldo was the same way. Others had the goods. But he had the contacts. And a talent for spinning. Most people can't do it. Publicity is the magic that spins gold. And once Mr. Baupre had done that for you, he never let you forget it. Rinaldo was always real nice with me. He was too smart to insult headwaiters or gate keepers. To our faces. And I was always polite enough. But I'd gotten to see him in action with Norah Classon.

To give him credit, he saw what she had done and made sure that others noticed too. Of course, then he wanted her first born. For Norah in the days before she had children, that meant her work. And he claimed a major chunk. "Oh, this is beautiful! Darling, I must have it!" That kind of thing. He told people that he hadn't just discovered Norah Classon, he had shaped her art.

Norah I were stepping out back then. She had gotten a one woman Soho show. He wrote the auction catalog and wanted his name bigger than hers. When she objected, he decided to sink the whole deal.

One night in the packed bathroom at the Mudd Club, I was trying to fight my way through to the can. And I heard the unmistakable voice of Mr. Baupre saying, "I'm the only hose in this hick town gas station. You want fuel baby, you line up here. The spot right where you're standing is where I discovered Louis Raphael. You don't know who he is!"

Someone said something I couldn't make out, a couple of other people got mentioned. Then I heard Norah's name and Rinaldo said, "Not if she begged. Ms. Classon is over and done. She's screwing doormen now. The next step is busboys."

And, yeah, I saw red. But I knew that decking Rinaldo wouldn't help Norah. These days I've got a private investigator license. I'm entitled to carry a gun if I ever want to. But a Swiss Army knife is about all I usually pack.

Back then, I was still learning. I already knew enough, though, to stand aside and wait.

As Rinaldo made his way out of the room, he looked at something in his hand, grimaced and threw it aside. Curious, I recovered it and stepped out of the club. Under a light on Milk Street, I unfolded a matchbook for the Thunder Ranch Bar and Grill in Wilkes-Barre. Thinking it was a joke or a camp, I was ready to toss it aside.

And this figure appeared, a radiant being, I guess I'd say. My first thought was that you were an acid flashback from the sixties. Then you spoke one word. What you said was,

Rumplestiltskin.

I didn't remember any hunter in that story. But I went home and re-read it slowly, taking my time with every word like always. The girl whose future depends on her weaving straw into gold and the little man who appears and does it for her fit perfectly. She becomes queen but he's going to take her child if she can't guess his name. I still didn't see where I fit in. Then I reached the part where the queen sends out a messenger to scour the countryside for the secret name.

He's the one who comes back just before the little man appears to claim the baby and says, "At the edge of the forest where the fox and the hare say good night to each other . . ."

What he goes on to tell her is that he's seen a bonfire and a little man dancing and heard the song with the name *Rumplestiltskin* in it. But that stuff about the fox and the rabbit gives him away. He's a hunter. It makes sense. Who else would she have sent out to comb the woods?

So I made a couple of calls, took a little trip down to Pennsylvania. I found the trailer park outside Wilkes-Barre where a certain Mona Splevetsky lived.

Oh, there was a dance and a song all right. Thursday was polka night at the Thunder Ranch and I got her drunk and she boogied and told me all about her son Marvin.

For people like Rinaldo their most important creation is themselves. With anyone else I would have called it the old and sorry tale of an unhappy kid who leaves his past behind. But I wasted little sympathy on Mr. Baupre.

Unlike Rumplestiltskin, Rinaldo didn't put his foot through the floor when Norah Classon said the name Marvin Splevetsky. He was real angry. But it had so much power over him that he begged her to keep it secret and gave her back her career.

3

A reminder of my next case is also here at Ling's Fortune Cookie tonight. That scary looking lady waiting for Victor Sparger to appear is Edith Crann, the producer of *Raphael!* The guy with her is an Italian industrialist. Her fourth husband. Edith's face is amazing, tragic but unlined, pained but cold, crazy but contained.

Bankrolling the film was a way of enhancing her investments. Edith Crann was the first important buyer of Louis' work. She had no idea of why it was good. But Rinaldo advised her and took a commission.

In the movie, Rinaldo and Victor have turned Edith into Louis Raphael's muse. It seems that the tragedy of losing her daughter is supposed to have made her sensitive to the plight of a kid thrown out on the street by his family.

Back at the time their daughter disappeared, I worked for Edith and her first husband, Harris Crann. I had been hired as a body-guard-chauffeur for young Alycia. It didn't take me long to recognize Mrs. Crann.

Everyone around knew she was an evil queen or a wicked stepmother. The only question was which story. Cinderella? Hansel and Gretel? I heard bartenders and waitresses, people who had worked for her, actually discuss this.

Alycia was seven years old when we met. Her picture was in the papers all the time. She attended Broadway openings. She was at Met galas. Any little girl likes to dress up. All children are thrilled to be out late at night. Little twitches of adulthood. But mostly kids have childhood. Missing that is death as sure as having your lungs and liver cut out.

One day I heard Mrs. Crann talk about her daughter to an interviewer. "We have long discussions about what she's going to wear. I never push her. This is what she wants." And the kid said nothing. Just looked at herself in the mirror, tried on a little powder, as if she didn't hear.

As a huntsman, I watched the animals. Like in the tales, they spoke the truth while people lied. Mr. Jimbo was the springer spaniel, brown and white that followed the kid around. Alycia had named him when she was three. Whenever the mother put her hand on her daughter's mass of careful curls, the dog tensed. I understood what he was saying: he had taken on a job that made him feel bad inside.

Another time Mrs. Crann told someone, "I talk to Alycia in ways I never had anyone talk to me. It's amazing. I come into her room the first thing in the morning and we discuss what she has scheduled for that day." Queen Milly was the Persian cat. She got up from Alycia's lap where she was sitting and slunk out of the room. I understood: even the cat couldn't stand to listen to this.

The parakeet actually spoke, of course. "Hi gorgeous!" it said to Edith Crann.

She gave her scariest smile and asked, "Who's the fairest in the land?"

"You are!" said the parakeet. "Lady. You are!"

Then the bird flew into the next room and lighted on the little girl's shoulder. "Hi gorgeous," it said and whistled.

"Fairest . . . " it started to say and fell silent as the mother appeared. Her face was like a mask. But the eyes behind it were wild with anger.

Two things finally did it for me. First was seeing Alycia trying to skip like every seven year old does. Except she was wearing high heels and tripped. The second was the picture of her in a leather outfit. She was posed in what was supposed to be a worldly and sophisticated way. The idea, maybe, was to be cute. But her eyes under false lashes looked lost and desperate.

In fairy tales, everyone's a prince or a princess. Step-mothers move in to perform wicked deeds. In real life, no one's a princess and parents do their own dirty work. The parts of the stories are just that, parts. They're all shaken up and reassembled when you actually encounter them.

What Edith Crann was doing was stealing her daughter's most precious possession, her childhood. Seeing her parents, I knew that Edith herself probably hadn't had one. They were a loveless pair of sticks. I almost felt sorry for Edith. Alycia didn't like those grandparents either. I know because we talked all the time in the car. She sat up front with me. Going to her mother's parents, she'd fall silent. They'd look at her and wouldn't crack a smile.

With her father's side of the family it was different. Harris Crann's family had gotten bigger and dumber with each generation. Harris was six foot tall and Ivy League. Waspy and stiff as a board. If he saw what was being done to his kid, he never let on.

His parents were, maybe, five-foot-six, but big on museum and opera boards. And they had established a charitable foundation. In the city, they had this huge co-op up on Riverside Drive, several floors, countless rooms. Kind of pretentious. But when they saw their grand-daughter, their eyes lit up.

Once I took her up there and they weren't home. Alycia smiled which she didn't do a lot and beckoned me down a hall like she was showing me this great secret. We went up some stairs and into this whole separate apartment within the larger one. That's where I met her great-grandparents.

Theodore and Heddy Kranneki were ancient and tiny. They had founded the family fortune long ago. They spent part of the year in the Homeland. They had done lots of work for the independence movement there. Probably they were little to start with but now they were no bigger than their grand-daughter. They were entertaining some friends equally old and small. And smart still, with amazingly bright eyes behind bifocals. They looked at the kid in her leather outfit as she tottered on heels to hug them. Their eyes met mine and we all understood exactly what had to happen.

So now we had the wicked step-mother and the magic little people in place. And the huntsman. That's all the identity the story gives. He's a royal employee, as I see it. One day he's told to take the little girl out in the woods, kill her and bring back her liver and lungs as proof he's done it.

The boss's wife has given him the orders. But he looks at the little girl and she's so beautiful he can't. Thinking that the wild animals will kill her, the huntsman lets her go and brings back a young boar's liver and lungs. These the queen has the cook boil in salted water then eats. I'll be fair to Edith Crann, she was into more sophisticated dining.

The day came when I was supposed to drive Alycia up to the Hotel Pierre. Edith's parents were going to meet her and take her on vacation. Alycia wasn't looking forward to that at all.

Under everything her mother had done to her, she had the beauty that's given to all kids, however the world may bend and warp it. When we were in the car together, we used to sing songs like I do with my own kids now. Old corny stuff. "Singing in the Rain" when it was raining. "A Little Help from My Friends," when one of us was down. Or I'd tell her stories.

That particular day I told her "Snow White." Not because she didn't know the story, but for the same reason I'm telling you: to make it clear in my own mind what led up to this situation and what will happen afterwards.

Alycia understood. She was crying when I came to the part about the huntsman and the woods. We got up to the Pierre and there was a delivery truck broken down right in front of the hotel just as I'd been told there would be. As instructed, I parked down the block. The kid got out and stood on the curb while I went around to get her bags out of the trunk. In their prime, Ted and Heddy Kranneki must really have been something. I turned away and on a grey morning there was a flash like sunlight reflecting on a passing rearview mirror. Magic. When I turned back, Alycia was gone.

It was THE hot New York story for a couple of weeks. Cops grilled me. Reporters wanted my story. The question was whether I was an idiot or an accomplice. I had expected that. Alycia's picture was in the papers and on TV. Posters were everywhere. The thing was, Edith Crann couldn't help herself. The picture she used showed the kid in a slinky dress and a tortured expression.

People began to wonder about little Alycia's home life. That summer there was a nasty mayoral primary and a racial killing in Brooklyn, the Mets arose from the dead and ran for the pennant, someone named

Louis Raphael came out of nowhere and took the art world by storm. Rumors circulated that Alycia had been seen in various places. But no new leads appeared. The Crann kidnapping story quietly died.

That summer also, Norah Classon and I both started going out with other people. Somehow, it didn't make me as happy as I thought it was going to. And it didn't give her more time for her career as she thought it would. I heard that she was having booze troubles. Probably the same stories were going around about me. A couple, friends of us both, invited me out to the Hamptons for the weekend because Norah was staying nearby. But when I dropped around to see her, she had left for Fire Island. When I took the ferry over there, she was gone.

There is no tale where we see the huntsman get his rewards. Believe me, I've looked and I know. But that Sunday evening I took the late train back to Penn Station. Walking underground along the platform of the Long Island Railway, I wasn't paying much attention to what went on. In the gloom and humidity, I saw a figure of light. And when I looked your way, you pointed at the window of a car on the train I'd just gotten off.

Inside was a commotion, a bunch of conductors and nosy citizens standing over a sleeping woman. She looked vulnerable, beautiful, her hair long and loose. I got right onto the car, told them I knew her. They seemed doubtful. So I bent over Norah and kissed her. She woke up, put her arms around my neck and said, "Prince!" And I picked her up and carried her off the train, up all the stairs, and back home.

Who's to say that the huntsman didn't get to marry above his station and have three beautiful kids? What tale says he didn't form a nice, discreet little security business, or that his wife hasn't had a good career showing her work, teaching.

When our oldest kid was little. I told her that story with certain things edited out. But I did mentioned the lady in the moonlight dress. When my daughter asked me who you were, I said to ask her mother.

My wife also was raised on fairy tales. Maybe that's what the marriage has going for it. But the book she had as a kid is different. French. There aren't a whole lot of fairies in Grimm, in spite of the title. The French stories are choked with them. Fairy godmothers especially. Even when they're not mentioned, you figure they're operating behind the scene.

For a long while Norah wouldn't tell me much about her fairy godmother. Lately, though, she's said a couple of things about you. She loved Louis, like I say, and this film has bothered the hell out of her. Which brings us to the matter at hand. People are stirring. Victor Sparger is about to make his entrance.

4

Louis Raphael got a lot of money very fast. It's too bad. He was basically a sweet kid at the start. His stuff grows on me, like that life size picture in the movie still on the wall. The staring face is almost familiar, the words are like slogans you heard in dreams. He came out of nowhere and caught the attention of the world. Everyone wanted to be his friend. Then something else caught their attention and he was left strung out, crazy and deep in the hole. Nobody wanted to know him. Then he was dead, way shy of thirty. Now everyone wants to be his friend again.

That particular scene is now history. The boat has sailed, the balloons have gone up, the reputations have all been made. And anyone in the future who wants to set a movie in New York in 1980 will make it look like a Louis Raphael painting. Like they use Gershwin tunes when they want to say it's 1930.

The downtown ethic is that if you're not moving, you're meat. Enter Victor Sparger. Victor was the artist who had made all the right choices, been in the right places, said the right things, donated to the right charity, bought property at the right moment. In life he had been no friend to Raphael. As a rival, he was nowhere.

But with Louis dead, Victor saw his chance to swallow him whole. He could make sure that anyone interested in Louis Raphael would have to go through Victor Sparger.

That's when his real talents came into play. He tied up all the rights to Louis' life. He enlisted the help of Rinaldo Baupre and Edith Crann. He oversaw Rinaldo's script. And in it he is Louis best friend, his big brother, his mentor in bad times. The fact that back then Victor was busy jumping on the fingers of everybody who tried to crawl out of the hole, disappears from history.

Rumplestiltskin, after they guess his name, stamps so hard he puts his foot through the floor and rips himself in two trying to pull himself free. Watching Rinaldo Baupre tonight, I remember his mother telling me how Marvin Splevetsky went to New York to become a poet, a famous writer. Instead he's a supporting player the story of others' lives. And it's tearing him apart.

Owning Louis Raphael's work has given Edith Crann a certain claim to existence. She is the sum of her possessions. She accumulates because she can't help herself. In that same way she once tried to collect the soul of a child.

A short time after Alycia disappeared, Mrs. Crann started sporting a nasty little smile. It reminded me of poison apples and long comas. I worried about the kid. Tonight, though, Edith seems nervous. In the story, the queen's spell is broken, Snow White wakes up and falls in love. The Wicked Queen is invited to her wedding and can't refuse to go. For the wedding, iron slippers get heated over a fire. When the queen sees them, she can't help herself. She puts them on and dances until her heart bursts. Did today's mail bring Edith her invitation to Alycia's wedding? Norah and I just got ours.

Like I said, my wife grew up with a different book. Sometimes the stories are different versions of the ones I know. I've been reading them to my kids. As much of an education for me as for them. The other night, I sat down with the four-year-old and read him one I'd never looked at before, the French "Little Red Riding Hood." In the story I remember, she was Little Red Cap.

I'd already been asked to do this gig and certain things about it bothered me. But I couldn't have told you what. As I read, though, I began to understand exactly what was wrong. Then I got to the end of the story and there was no huntsman who happens to be passing by. He's the one who rushes in, cuts open the belly of the wolf and saves the kid and her grandmother. In my wife's book, they get eaten and stay eaten.

It's one of the big hunter parts in the stories and it's not in the French book. All they have is some piece of smart-ass poetry telling us not to talk to strangers.

That bothered me until I remembered that no fairy godmother appeared dropping clues in "Rumplestiltskin." But you were there. You're not in "Little Red Riding Hood" either. So I figure since you showed up today it may mean there's a place for me in this version of the story.

Now there's a buzz in the room. Victor Sparger, unshaven to just the fashionable degree, walks among us in a two thousand-dollar workman's jumpsuit. He's smiling and sleek. The way you look, I guess, after you've swallowed someone whole. And I don't know how I'm going to cut open this particular beast.

See him one way and Louis Raphael was no innocent child. He'd come off the street and that part of his life never left him. Another way of looking at it, though, is that nobody is more trusting than a street person who puts his life in strangers' hands again and again. Or than the artist who shows everybody in the world his riches. Almost asking to be eaten whole.

As I think about that, your hand moves, a wand flashes like a laser. Something moves behind Victor and I realize the eyes in the Raphael painting have shifted. They stare, haunted, trapped, at Victor Sparger. The graffiti now says, "In Prison There Is Nothing to Breathe." And the face is Louis Raphael's.

Everyone: Rinaldo and Edith, the murderers and the Chinese drag waitresses, the battle hardened Downtown circuit riders who you can bet have seen a lot, turn toward Sparger and say things like, "Oh Victor, what a big film you've got!"

Sparger smiles, false modesty and vindictive triumph on his face. And he replies, "All the better to eat you with." Or words to that effect.

Then people see the staring face, read the words on the the picture above Victor's head. You nod to me that this is the moment and I reach into my pocket. They say that a Swiss Army Knife can kill in a dozen ways. I've made it a point to learn none of them. But for this it's perfect. I step forward and make a single cut across the front of the still. And, simple as magic, out leaps the one trapped inside.

Even in his cursed form, the man recognized New York as a city of the mad. Living there—thriving there—took a particular form of acceptable madness.

PAINTED BIRDS AND SHIVERED BONES

KAT HOWARD

The white bird flew through the clarion of the cathedral bells, winging its way through the rich music of their tolling to perch in the shelter of the church's walls. The chiming continued, marking time into measured, holy hours.

Maeve had gone for a walk, to clear her head and give herself the perspective of something beyond the windows and walls of her apartment. She could feel the sensation at the back of her brain, that almost-itch that meant a new painting was ready to be worked on. Wandering the city, immersing herself in its chaos and beauty would help that back of the head feeling turn into a realized concept.

But New York had been more chaos than beauty that morning. Too much of everything and all excess without pause. Maeve felt like she was coming apart at the seams.

In an effort to hold herself together, Maeve had gone to the Cathedral of St. John the Divine. There, she could think, could sit quietly, could stop and breathe without people asking what was wrong.

Midwinter was cold enough to flush her cheeks as she walked to the cathedral, but Maeve couldn't bear being inside—large as the church was, she could feel the walls pressing on her skin. Instead, she perched on a bench across from the fallen tower, and pulled her scarf higher around her neck.

Maeve sipped her latte, and leaned back against the bench, then sat up. She closed her eyes, then opened them again.

There was a naked man crouched on the side of the cathedral.

She dug in her purse for her phone, wondering how it was possible that such a relatively small space always turned into a black hole when she needed to find anything. Phone finally in hand, she sat up.

The naked man was gone.

In his place was a bird. Beautiful, white feathers trailing like half-remembered thoughts. Impressive, to be sure, especially when compared to the expected pigeons of the city. But bearing no resemblance to a man, naked or otherwise.

Maeve let her phone slip through her fingers, back into her bag, and sat up, shaking her head at herself. "You need to cut down on your caffeine."

"You thought what?" Emilia laughed. "Oh, honey. The cure for thinking that you see a naked man at the cathedral isn't giving up caffeine, it's getting laid."

"Meeting men isn't really a priority for me." Maeve believed dating to be a circle of Hell that Dante forgot.

"Maeve, you don't need to meet them. Just pick one." Emilia gestured at the bar.

Maeve looked around. "I don't even know them."

"That's exactly my point." Emilia laughed again. "Take one home, send him on his way in the morning, and I can guarantee your naked hallucinations will be gone."

"Fine." Maeve sipped her bourbon. "I'll take it under advisement."

Surprising precisely no one, least of all the woman who had been her best friend for a decade, Maeve went home alone, having not even attempted to take one of the men in the bar with her. She hung up her coat, and got out her paints.

Dawn was pinking the sky when she set the brush down and rolled the tension from her neck and shoulders.

The canvas was covered in birds.

Madness is easier to bear with the wind in your feathers. Sweeney flung himself into the currents of the air, through bands of starlight that streaked the sky, and winged toward the cloud-coated moon.

Beneath Sweeney, the night fell on the acceptable madness of the city. Voices cried out to each other in greeting or curse. Tires squealed and horns blared. Canine throats raised the twilight bark, and it was made symphonic by feline yowls, skitterings of smaller creatures, and the songs of more usual birds.

Not Sweeney's.

Silent Sweeney was borne on buffeting currents over the wild lights of the city. Over the scents of concrete and of rot, of grilling meat and decaying corners, of the blood and love and dreams and terrors of millions.

And of their madness as well.

Even in his bird form, Sweeney recognized New York as a city of the mad. Not that one needed to be crazy to be there, or that extended residency was a contributing factor to lunacy of some sort, but living there—thriving there—took a particular form of madness.

Or caused it. Sweeney had not yet decided which.

He had not chosen his immigration, but had been pulled over wind and salt and sea by the whim of a wizard. Exiled from his kingdom in truth, though there were no kings in Ireland anymore.

On he flew, through a forest of buildings built to assault the sky. Over bridges, and trains that hurtled from the earth as if they were loosed dragons. Over love and anger and countless anonymous mysteries.

Sweeney tucked his wings, and coasted to the ground at the Cathedral of St. John the Divine. The ring of church bells set the madness on him, sprang the feathers from his skin, true. But madness obeyed rules of its own devising, and the quietness of the cathedral grounds soothed him. He roosted in the ruined tower, and fed on seed scattered on the steps after weddings.

He had done so for years, making the place a refuge. There had been a woman, Madeleine, he thought her name was, who smelled of paper and stories. She had been kind to him, kind enough that he had wondered sometimes if she could see the curse beneath the feathers. She scattered food, and cracked the window of the room she worked in so that he might perch just inside the frame, and watch her work among the books.

Yes. Madeleine. He had worn his man shape to her memorial, there at the cathedral, found and read her books, with people as out of time as he was. She had been kind to him, and kindness was stronger even than madness was.

Maeve stood in front of the canvas, and wiped the remnants of sleep from her eyes with paint-smeared fingers.

It was good work. She had gotten the wildness of the feathers, and the way a wing could obscure and reveal when stretched in flight. She could do a series, she thought.

"I mean, it's about time, right?" she asked Brian, her agent, on the phone. "Be ambitious, move out of my comfort zone, all those things you keep telling me I need to do."

"Yes, but birds, Maeve?"

"Not still lifes, or landscapes, if that's what you're worried about."

"Well, not worried exactly . . . Look, send me pictures of what you're working on. I'll start looking for a good venue to show them. If it doesn't work, we'll call this your birdbrained period."

It hadn't been the resounding endorsement of her creativity that Maeve had been hoping for, but that was fine. She would paint now, and enthusiasm could come later.

She could feel her paintings, the compulsion to create, just beneath the surface of her skin. She gathered her notebook and pencils, and went out into the city to sketch.

Sweeney perched on a bench in Central Park, plucking feathers from his arms. He had felt the madness creeping back for days this time before the feathers began appearing. Sure, he knew it was the madness. His blood itched, and unless that was the cursed feathers being born beneath his skin, itchy blood meant madness.

Itchy blood had meant madness and feathers for close to forever now, hundreds of years since the curse had first been cast. Life was long, and so were curses.

Though when he thought about it, Sweeney suspected curses were longer.

Pigeons cooed and hopped about near the bench's legs, occasionally casting their glinting eyes up at him. Sweeney thumbed a nail beneath a quill, worried at it until he could get a good grip. The feather emerged slowly, blood brightening its edges. He sighed as it slid from his skin. Sweeney flicked the feather to the ground, and the pigeons scattered.

"Can't blame you. I don't like the fucking things, either." Sweeney tugged at the next feather, one pushing through the skin at the bend of his elbow. Plucking his own feathers wouldn't stop the change, or even slow it, but it gave him something to do.

"The curse has come upon me," he said. Blood caked his nails, and dried in the whorls and creases of his fingers.

And it would. The curse would come upon him, as it had time and time again, an ongoing atonement. He might be occasionally mad, and sometimes a bird with it, but Sweeney was never stupid. He knew the metamorphosis would happen. A bell would ring, and his skin would grow too tight around his bones, and he would bend and crack into bird shape.

Sooner, rather sooner indeed than later, if the low buzz at the back of his skull was any indication.

"But just because something is inevitable, doesn't mean that we resign ourselves to it. No need to roll over and show our belly, now." Sweeney watched the pigeons as they skritched about in the dirt.

There were those who might say that Sweeney's stubbornness had gone a long way to getting him into the fix he was currently in. Most days, Sweeney would agree with them, and on the days he wouldn't, well, those days he didn't need to, as his agreement was implied by the shape he wore.

You didn't get cursed into birdhood and madness because you were an even-tempered sort of guy.

"You guys all really birds, there beneath the feathers?" Sweeney asked the flock discipled at his feet.

The pigeons kept their own counsel.

Then the bells marked the hour, and in between ring and echo, Sweeney became a bird.

Dusk was painting the Manhattan skyline in gaudy reds and purples when Maeve looked up from her sketchbook. She had gotten some good studies, enough to start painting the series. She scrubbed her smudged hands against the cold-stiffened fabric of her jeans. She would get take out—her favorite soup dumplings—and then go home and paint.

The bird winged its way across her sightlines as she stood up. Almost iridescent in the dying light, a feathered sweep of beauty at close of day. Watching felt transcendent—

"Oh, fuck, not again." In the tree not a bird, but a man, trying his best to inhabit a bird-shaped space.

Maeve closed her eyes, took a deep breath, opened them again. Still: Man. Tree. Naked.

"Okay. It's been a long day. You forgot to eat. You have birds on the brain. You're just going to go home now"—she tapped the camera button on her phone—"and when you get there, this picture of a naked man is going to be a picture of a bird."

It wasn't.

Sweeney watched the woman pick up her paintbrush, set it down. Pick up her phone, look at it, clutch her hair or shake her head, then set the phone down and walk back to her canvas. She had been repeating a variation of this pattern since he landed on the fire escape outside of her window.

He had seen her take the picture, and wanted to know why. The people who saw him were usually quite good at ignoring his transformations, in that carefully turned head, averted eyes, and faster walking way of ignoring. Most people didn't even let themselves see him. This woman did. Easy enough to fly after her, once he was a bird again.

Sweeney wondered if perhaps she was mad, too, this woman who held the mass of her hair back by sticking a paintbrush through it, and who talked to herself as she paced around her apartment.

She wasn't mad now though, not that he could tell. She was painting. Sweeney stretched his wings, and launched himself into the cold, soothing light of the stars.

In the center of the canvas was a man, and feathers were erupting from his skin.

"Oh, yes. Brian is going to love it when you tell him about this. 'That series of paintings you didn't want me to do? Well, I've decided that the thing it really needed was werebirds.'"

It was good, though, she thought. The shock of the transformation as a still point in the chaos of the city that surrounded him.

The transformation had been a shock. The kind of thing you had to see to believe, and even then, you doubted. Such a thing should have been impossible to see.

And maybe that was the thread for the series, Maeve thought. Fantasy birds, things that belonged in fairy tales and medieval bestiaries, feathered refugees from mythology and legend scattered throughout a modern city that refused to see them there.

She could paint that. It would be a series of paintings that would let her do something powerful if she got them right.

Maeve sat at her computer, and began compiling image files of harpy and cockatrice, phoenix and firebird. There were, she thought, so many stories of dead and vengeful women returning as ghost birds, but nothing about men who did so. Not that she thought what she had seen was a ghost, or that she was trying some form of research-based bibliomancy to discern the story behind the bird (the man) she kept seeing, but she wouldn't have turned away an answer.

"And would it have made you feel better if you had found one? Because hallucinating a ghost bird in Manhattan is so much better than if you're just seeing a naked werebird? Honestly." She shook her head.

Though it wasn't a hallucination. Not with the picture on her phone. Why it was easier to think she was losing her mind than to accept that she had seen something genuinely impossible was something Maeve didn't understand.

She printed out reference photos for all the impossible birds she hadn't yet seen, and taped them over the walls.

In the beginning, when the curse's claws still bled him, and Sweeney had nothing to recall him to himself or his humanity, he would fly after Eorann, who had been his wife, before he was a bird. She was the star to his wanderings.

Eorann had loved Sweeney, and so she had tried, at the beginning, to break the curse. Unspeaking, she wove garments from nettles and cast them over Sweeney like nets, in the hopes that pain and silence spun together might force a bird back into a man's shape. Even had one perfect wing lingered as a reminder of his past and his errors, it would have been change enough. More, it would have been stasis, a respite from the constant and unpredictable change that, Sweeney discovered, was the curse's true black heart.

When that did not work, she had shoes made from iron, and walked the length and breadth of Ireland in an attempt to wear them out. But she was already east of the sun and west of the moon, the true north of her compass set to once upon a time. Such places are not given to the wearing out of iron shoes.

Eorann spun straw into gold, then spun the gold into thread that flexed and could be woven into a dress more beautiful than the sun, the moon, and the stars. She uncurdled milk, and raised from the dead a cow that gave it constantly, without needing food nor drink of its own.

If there were a miracle, a marvel, or a minor wonder that Eorann could perform in the hopes of breaking Sweeney's curse, she did so.

Until the day she didn't.

"A wife's role may be many things, Sweeney. But it is not a wife's job to break a husband's curse, not when he is the one who has armored himself in it."

Those were the last words that Eorann had spoken to him. From the distance of time, Sweeney could admit now that she was right. Still, from the height of the unfeeling sky, he wished that she had been the saving of him.

"Well, they're different. That's certain," Brian said, walking between the canvases.

"If different means crap, just say so. I'm too tired to parse euphemisms."

Maeve only had one completed canvas—the man transforming into a bird. But she had complete studies of two others—a phoenix rising out of the flame of a burning skyline, and a harpy hovering protectively over a woman.

"They're darker than your usual thing, but powerful." Brian stepped back, walked back and forth in front of the canvas.

"They're good. I've a couple galleries in mind—I'll start making calls.

"You'll come to the opening, of course."

"No," Maeve said. "Absolutely not. Nonnegotiable."

"Look, the reclusive artist thing was fine when you were starting out, because you didn't matter enough for people to care about you. But we can charge real money for these. People who pay real money for their art aren't just buying a decoration for their wall, they're buying the story that goes with it."

Maeve was pretty sure no one wanted to buy the story of the artist who had a panic attack at her own opening. No, scratch that. She was absolutely sure someone would want to buy that story. She just didn't want to sell her paintings badly enough to give it to them.

"Well, then how about the story is I am a recluse. A crazy bird lady instead of a crazy cat lady. I live with the chickens. Whatever you need to say. But I don't interact with the people buying my work, and I don't go to openings."

"You're lucky I'm good at my job, Maeve."

"I'm good at mine, too."

Brian sighed. "Of course you are. I didn't mean to suggest otherwise. But I don't understand why you don't just buy yourself a pretty dress, and have fun letting rich people buy you drinks and tell you how wonderful you are.

"Let yourself celebrate a little. It's the fun part of the job, Maeve."

It wasn't, not for her. Of course, Brian wouldn't understand that. Maeve worked too hard to keep her panic attacks hidden. She had an entire portfolio of tricks to keep them manageable, and out of view.

Out of the apartment was fine, as long as she didn't have to interact with too many people. Crowds were okay as long as she had someone she knew with her, and she didn't have to interact with the people she didn't know. When she had to meet new people, she did so in familiar surroundings, either one on one, or in a group of people she already knew and felt comfortable with. Even then, she usually needed a day at home, undisturbed, after, in order to rest and regain her equilibrium.

A party where everyone would be strangers who wanted to pay attention to her, who wanted her to interact with them, with no safety net of friends that she could fall onto, was impossible.

Even after Eorann had told Sweeney that she could not save him, it took him some time to realize that he would need to be the saving of himself. More time still, an infinity of church bells, of molting feathers, to understand that saving himself did not necessarily include lifting the curse.

In search of himself, of answers, of peace, long and long ago, Sweeney had undertaken a quest.

A quest is a cruel migration. This is the essence of a quest, no matter who undertakes it. But Sweeney had not known what to look for, save for the longing to see something other than what he was.

The Sangréal had been found once already, and though lost again, it was the kind of thing where the first finding mattered. The dragons were all in hiding, and Sweeney had never particularly thought they needed to be slain.

Nor had he known the map with which to travel by, save for one that would take him to a place other than where he was. He took wing. Over sea and under stone and then over the sea to sky.

Maeve saw the bird at the Cathedral of St. John the Divine again.

Cathedrals, churches, museums, libraries, they were useful sorts of places for her. When the walls of her apartment pressed too tightly, these were places she could go, and sit, and think, and not have to worry about people insisting that she interact with them in order to justify her presence.

"I came here for peace and quiet, you know. Not because I'm hoping to catch a glimpse of you naked."

The bird did not seem to have an opinion on that.

When she sat, Maeve specifically chose a bench that did not have a line of sight to the bird's current perch. Not like it couldn't fly, but it was the principle of the thing. And she really didn't want to see it become a naked man again.

Stories about artistic inspiration that came to life and then interacted with the artist were only interesting if they were stories. When they were your life, they were weird.

The bird landed next to her on the bench.

Maeve looked at her bird, at her sketchbook, and back at the bird.

"Fine. Fine. But do not turn into a man. Not in front of me. Just don't. If you think you're going to, leave. Please." She tore off a chunk of her croissant and set it on the bird's side of the bench. "Okay?"

Maeve was relieved when the bird did not answer.

There was a package from Brian waiting for her when she got home. The card read, "For the crazy bird lady."

Inside was a beautiful paper bird. A crane, but not the expected origami. Paper-made sculpture, not folded. Feathers and wings and beak all shaped from individual pieces of brightly colored paper. It was a gorgeous fantasy of practicality and feathers.

Maeve tucked it on a shelf, where she could see it while she painted.

He hadn't answered her today, the red-haired painter.

Sweeney could speak in bird form—he was still a man, even when feather-clad—but he had learned, finally, the value of silence.

This had not always been so. It had been speaking that had first called his curse down upon him.

He had called out an insult to Ronan. Said something he should not have, kept speaking when he should have driven a nail through his tongue to hold his silence.

Ronan had spoken then, too. Spoken a word that burnt the sky, and shifted the bones of the earth. A curse, raw and dire. That was the first time the madness fell upon Sweeney. The madness, and the breaking of himself into the too-light bones that made up a bird's wing.

When it came down to it, it was pride that cursed Sweeney into his feathers as sure as pride had melted Icarus out of his. Pride, and a too-quick temper, faults that dwelt in any number of people without changing their lives and their shapes, without sending them on a path of constant migration centered on a reminder of error.

Curses didn't much care that there were other people they could have landed on, just as comfortably. They fell where they would, then watched the aftermath unfold.

Some days were good days, days when Maeve could walk through her life and not be aware of any of the adjustments she performed to make it livable.

Tuesday was not one of those days.

She had taken the subway, something she did only rarely, preferring to walk. But a sudden hailstorm had driven her underground, and sent what seemed like half of the city after her.

Maeve got off at the second stop, not even sure what street it was. Her pulse had been racing so fast that her vision had gone grey and narrow. If she hadn't gotten out, away from all those people she would have collapsed.

Her notebook, her most recent sketches for her paintings, was left behind on the Uptown 2 train. It had to have been the train where it went missing. She had been sure it was in her bag when she left her apartment, and it was clearly not among the bag's upended contents now.

Forty-five minutes on the phone with MTA lost and found had done no more than she expected, and reassured her the odds of its return were small.

And though it had smelled fine—she had checked—the milk with which she had made the hot chocolate that was supposed to make her feel better had instead made her feel decidedly worse.

The floor of the bathroom was cool against her cheek. Exhausted and sick, Maeve curled in on herself, and fell into tear-streaked sleep.

The bird was in her dream, and that was far from the weirdest thing about it.

The sky shaded to lavender, the clouds like ink splotches thrown across it.

Then a head sailed across the waxing moon.

Sweeney cocked his own head, and shifted on the branch.

Another head described an arc across the sky, a lazy rise and fall.

Sweeney looked around. He could not tell where the heads were launching from, nor could he hear any sounds of distress.

Three more heads, in rapid succession, and Sweeney was certain he was mad again. He wished he were in his human form, so that he might throw back his own head and howl.

Five heads popped up in front of Sweeney, corks popping to the surface of the sea.

Identical, each to each, the world's strangest set of brothers.

They looked, Sweeney thought, cheerful. Certainly more cheerful than he would be, were he suddenly disconnected from the neck down.

Each head had been neatly severed. Or no. Not severed. They looked as if they were heads that had never had bodies at all. Smiling, clean-shaven, bright-eyed. No dangling veins or spines, no ragged skin. No blood.

Sweeney supposed the fact that the heads were levitating was no more remarkable than the fact that they were not bleeding. Still, it was the latter that seemed truly strange.

"Hail."

"And."

"Well."

"Met."

"Sweeney," said the heads.

"Er, hello," said Sweeney.

"A."

"Fine."

"Night."

"Isn't."

"It?" Their faces were the picture of benevolence.

"Indeed it is," said Sweeney.

"We."

"Would."

"Speak."

"With."

"You."

As they seemed to be doing that already, Sweeney simply bobbed his head.

"Do."

"You."

"Not."

"Remember."

"Us?" The heads circled around Sweeney.

He tried to focus, to imagine them with bodies attached. Nothing about them seemed familiar. He could not see past their duplicated strangeness. "Please forgive me, gentlemen, but I don't."

"We."

"So."

"Often."

"Forget."

"Ourselves."

"Or."

"Perhaps."

"We."

"Haven't."

"Met." They slid into line in front of him again, the last one bumping its left-side neighbor, and setting him gently wobbling.

"Can you read the future, then?" It seemed the most likely explanation, though nothing about this encounter was at all likely.

"Yes."

"And."

"No."

"Only."

"Sometimes."

Sweeney appreciated the honesty of the answer almost as much as he appreciated the thoroughness.

"Listen."

"Now."

"Sweeney."

"Listen."

"Well."

"No.

"One."

"Chooses."

"His."

"Quest."
"It."
"Is."
"Chosen."
"For."
"Him."
"All.
"Quests."
"End."
"In."
"Death."
"So does life," said Sweeney.
"Then."
"Choose."
"Yours."
"Well."
"Sweeney."

The heads cracked their jaws so wide, Sweeney wondered if they would swallow themselves. Then they began to laugh, and while laughing, whirled themselves into a small cyclone. Faster and faster it spun, until the heads were nothing but a laughing blur, and then were gone.

Sweeney, contemplative, watched the empty sky until dawn.

Maeve sat up, her head and neck aching from sleeping on the tile, her mouth tasting as if she had licked the subway station she fled from earlier that day.

Legs still feeling more like overcooked noodles than functioning appendages, she staggered into the kitchen, and poured the milk down the sink. It was a largely symbolic sort of gesture, performed only to make her head feel better—it certainly wouldn't undo the food poisoning or the resulting fucked up dream, but seeing the milk spiral down the drain was still a relief.

Talking heads flying around Central Park and conversing with a bird who was sometimes a man. It was like something out of a Henson movie, except without the good soundtrack.

Becoming involved enough in her work to dream about it was, on balance, a good thing. But there were limits. She was not putting disembodied heads into her paintings.

Maeve painted a tower, set into the Manhattan skyline. A wizard's tower, dire and ancient, full of spirals and spires, held together with spells and impossibility.

She hung the surrounding sky with firebirds, contrails of flame streaking the clouds.

Dawn came, but it was neither rebirth nor respite. Sweeney was still befeathered. He turned to the glow of the rising sun, and the tower that appeared there, as if painted on the sky.

Every wizard had a tower, even in twenty-first century New York. It was the expected, required thing, and magic had rules and bindings more powerful than aught else. It had to, made as it was out of words and will and belief. Certain things had to be true or the magic crumbled to dust and nothingness.

Sweeney cracked open his beak, and tore at the promise-crammed air.

A wizard's tower is protected by many things, but the most puissant are the wizard's own words of power. Even after they have cast their spells and done their work, the words of a wizard retain tracings of magic. Their echoes continue to cast and recast the spells, for as long as sound travels.

The words do not hang idle in the air. Power recognizes power, and old spells linger together like former lovers. Though the connections are no longer as bright as the crackle and spark of that first magic, they can never be entirely erased. They gather, each to each, and in their greetings, new magics are made.

Ronan had been a wizard for centuries now, perhaps millennia. A few very important years longer than Sweeney had been a bird.

He had fled Ireland in the coffin ships, with the rest of the decimated, starving population. His magic, the curse's binding, had pulled Sweeney along in his wake.

In the years since his arrival, magic had wrapped itself around Ronan's tower like fairy tale thorns, a threat, a protection, and a guarantee of solitude. A locus of power that sang, siren-like, to Sweeney, though he knew it was never what he sought.

Sweeney flew around the tower three times, then three, then three again, in the direction of unraveling. The curse, as it always had, remained.

"How many paintings do you have finished?"

"Five."

"How long will it take you to do, say, five or maybe seven more?"

"Why?"

"Drowned Meadow will give you gallery space, but I think these new pieces are strong enough you'd be better served if you had enough finished work to fill the gallery, rather than being part of a group showing."

"When would I need them finished by?"

Brian's answer made her wince, and mourn, once again, the loss of the sketchbook, and the studies it contained. Still.

"It's a good space. I'll get the pieces done."

"Excellent. I'll email you the contracts."

"Wait, that's what the naked bird guy looks like?" Emilia stood in front of the first painting in the series, the man transforming into a bird. "No wonder you keep seeing him around the city. He's hot."

"He's usually a bird."

"Still, yum. And is that drawn to scale?"

Maeve snorted. "Fine. The next time I see him, if he's being a person, I'll give him your number."

Emilia laughed, but she looked sideways at Maeve while she did. "So, are you seeing all of the things from your paintings?"

Emilia had moved to the newest painting in the series, a cockatrice among the tents at Bryant Park's Fashion Week, models turned to statues under its gaze.

"Do you think I would be here with you, discussing the attractiveness of a werebird, after having consumed far too much Ethiopian food, if I had really encountered a bird that can turn people to stone just by looking at them?"

Maeve looked at Emilia again. "Or no. It's not actually that you think that. You're just doing the sanity check."

"I don't think you're crazy. But you know you don't always take care of yourself before a show. And this one did start with you thinking that you saw a bird turn into a naked guy."

"Which, I admit, sounds odd. But you don't need to worry that I've started the New York Chapter of the Phoenix Watching Club."

"That sounds very Harry Potter. You haven't seen any wizards wandering around the city, have you? I mean, other than the guys who like to get out their wands on the subway." Emilia twisted her face into an expression of repulsed boredom.

"And you wonder why I don't like to leave the house."

"No wizards?"

"No wizards."

There were wizards in New York City, nearly everywhere. War mages, who changed history over games of speed chess. Chronomancers who stole seconds from the subway trains. And the city built on dreams was rife with onieromancers channeling desires between sleep and waking.

Even the wizard who had set the curse on Sweeney looked out over the speed and traffic of the city as he spoke his spells, shiftings and transformations, covering one thing in some other's borrowed skin, whether they will or no.

But though Ronan was here, and had been, he was not the direction to which Sweeney looked to break his curse. Wizards did not, under any but the most extreme circumstances, undo their own magic. Magic, magic that is practiced and cast, is at odds with entropy. Not only does it reshape order out of chaos, but it wrenches the rules for order sideways. It rewrites the laws, so that a man might be shifted to a bird, and back again, no matter how physics wails.

To make such a thing happen, though it might seem the work of an incantation and an arcane gesture, is the marriage of effort and will. And will, once wielded in such fashion, is not lightly undone.

But just because the wizard would not lift his curse did not mean that the spell might never be broken.

It just meant it would require a magic stronger than wizardry to break it.

Maeve's apartment was full of birds. Photographs papered the walls, layered over each other in collage, Escheresque spirals of wings that had never flown together fell in cascading recursive loops of impossible birds.

The statue from Brian was a carnival fantasy among articulated skeletons in shadowboxes, shivered bones set at precise angles of flight.

Her own bones ached as if wings mantled beneath the surface of her skin and longed to burst forth from her back.

The canvas before her was enormous, six feet in height and half again as wide, the largest she had ever painted. On it, a murmuration of starlings arced and turned across a storm-tossed sky.

Among the starlings were other birds. Bird of vengeance, storm-called, and storm-conjuring. The Erinyes.

The Kindly Ones.

More terrible than lightning, they harried the New York skyline.

Cramps spasmed Maeve's hands around her brushes, and her eyes burned, but still she layered color onto the canvas.

It was a kind of madness, she thought, the way it felt to finish a painting. The muscle-memory knowledge of exactly where the brush strokes went, even though this was nothing she had painted before. The fizzing feeling at the top of her head that told her what she was painting was right, was true. The adrenaline that flooded her until she couldn't sit, or sleep, or eat until it was finished.

Madness, surely. But a madness of wings, and of glory.

The skies of New York had grown stranger. Sweeney was used to the occasional airborne mystery. It wasn't as if he had ever thought himself the only sometimes-bird on the wing.

But a flock of firebirds had taken up residence in Central Park, and an exaltation of larks had begun exalting in Mandarin in the bell tower of St. Patrick's Cathedral.

He thought he had seen the phoenix, but perhaps it had only been a particularly gaudy sunset.

Magic all unasked for, and stuck about with feathers.

Though perhaps not magic unconjured.

Sweeney paged through a notebook, not lost on a train but slid from a messenger bag. He had wanted, he supposed, to see how she saw him.

Of course, he was in none of the sketches.

But its pages crawled with magic. It was rife in the shadows and shadings and lines of the sketches. Sweeney didn't know if it was wizardry or not, what he was looking at, but there was power in her drawings.

Perhaps enough power to unmake a curse.

"You're sure I can't convince you to come to the opening?" Brian asked. "Because I think people are really going to want to talk to you about these paintings, and Maeve, do not say 'my art speaks for itself.'"

"You have to admit, you pretty much asked me to."

"Maeve."

"They'll sell better if I'm not there."

"What would make you think that?"

Because if I'm there, I'll spend the entire evening locked in the bathroom, occasionally vomiting from panic, she thought. "Because if I'm not there, you can spin me as mysterious. Or better yet, perfect. Tell them what they want to hear without the risk that I'll show up with paint still in my hair."

"I have never once seen you with paint in your hair. And even if I had, artists are supposed to be absent-minded and eccentric. It's part of your charm."

"You told me I wasn't allowed to be absent-minded and eccentric anymore, remember? Not in this gallery. Not at these prices."

"I suppose I did. Still, this is your night, Maeve. If you want to be here, even if there is paint in your hair, you should come."

"I can assure you, Brian, I won't want to."

Sweeney could, if he concentrated enough, prevent the shift in form from man to bird from happening. Usually, he didn't bother—the change came when it would, and after all of these years, he had made peace with his spontaneous wings.

But he wanted to see the paintings. To see, captured in pigment and brushstroke the birds that Maeve had made a space for in New York's skies.

He wanted to see her, just once, in the guise and costume of a normal man.

More, he wanted to see if the magic that crackled across the pages of her notebook was in the paintings as well, to see if she could paint him free. A request that might allow him to once again be a normal man, instead of what he was: a creature cursed into loneliness and the wrong skin, whose only consolation was the further loneliness of flight.

Sweeney's difficulty was that while he could, by force of will, hold himself in human form, it let the madness push further into his consciousness. The longer he fought the transformation, the more he struggled to be shaped like a man, they less he thought like one.

Sweeney slid on his jacket. He checked to make sure his buttons matched, his fly was up, and his shoes were from the same pair. He hailed a cab, and hoped for the best.

On the night of the opening, Maeve was not at the gallery. She had been there earlier in the day to double-check the way the paintings had been hung, to see to all the last minute details, and to tell Brian, one more time, that she was absolutely not coming to the opening.

"Fine. Then at least put on a nice dress at home and have some champagne with a friend so I don't get depressed thinking about you."

"If that's what will make you happy, of course I will," she lied, offering a big smile, and accepting Brian's hug.

As the show opened, Maeve was wearing a T-shirt with holes in it, and eating soup dumplings. Which she toasted with a glass of the very fine champagne that Brian had sent over. Emilia had texted from the gallery that the "paintings are your best thing ever. So proud of you!" Comfort and celebration and a friend, even if far from what Brian imagined.

Strange to think that this show, which Brian thought could be big enough to change her career, began with seeing a bird turn into a naked man. Which was certainly the one story she could never tell when asked what inspired her work.

She hadn't seen the bird for a while now. Or, thankfully, the naked man. Some parts of the strangeness of the city were better left unexplained.

Too many answers killed the magic, and Maeve wanted the magic. Its possibilities were what made up for the discomfort and worry of every day life.

The lights were too bright and there were too many people. Sweeney bit the insides of his cheeks and walked through the gallery as if its floor were shattering glass.

The paintings. He thought they were beautiful, probably, or that they would be if he could ever stand still long enough to really look at them, to see them as more than blurs as he circled the gallery. He felt too hot, his skin ill-fitting, his heart racing like a bird's.

Sweeney clenched his fists, digging his nails into his palms, and forced his breath in and out until it steadied.

There.

Almost comfortably human.

Sweeney walked the room slowly this time, giving himself space to step back and look at the canvases.

Feathers itched and crawled beneath his skin.

And there he was.

The still point at the center of the painting, and feathers were bursting from his skin there, too, but there, it didn't look like madness, it looked like transcendence.

Sweeney heaved in a breath.

"It does have that effect on people."

Sweeney glanced at the man standing next to him, the man who hadn't seemed to realize it was Sweeney in the painting hanging before them.

"Are you familiar with Maeve's work? Maeve Collins, the artist, I mean," Brian said.

"Ah. A bit. Only recently. Is she here tonight?"

"Not yet, though I hope she'll make an appearance later. But if you're interested in the piece, I'd be happy to assist you with it."

"If I buy it, can I meet her?"

"I can understand why you'd make the request, but that's not the usual way art sales work."

And now the man standing next to him did step back and look at Sweeney. "Wait. Wait. You're the model for the painting. Oh, this is fantastic."

Feathers. Feathers unfurling in his blood.

"But of course you'd know Maeve already then."

"I don't." Sweeney braceleted his wrist, his left wrist, downed with white feathers, with his right hand. "But I think I need to."

He unwrapped his fingers, and extended his feathered hand to the man in the gallery, beneath the painting that was and wasn't him.

Brian looked down at the feathers. "I'll call her."

"I don't care how good the party is, Brian, I'm not coming."

"Your model is here, and he would like to meet you."

"How many vodka tonics have you had? That doesn't even make sense. I didn't use any models in this series."

"Not even the guy with feathers coming out of his skin? Because he's standing right in front of the painting, and it certainly looks like him, not to mention this thing where I'm watching him grow feathers on his arms, and what the fuck is going on here, Maeve?"

"What did you say?" The flesh on her arms rose up in goose bumps.

"You heard me. You need to get here.

"Now."

Maeve took a cab, and went in through the service entrance, where she had loaded the paintings earlier that week.

"Brian, what is—you!"

"Yes," Sweeney said, and in an explosion of feathers and collapsing clothes, turned into a bird.

Maeve sat with the bird while the celebration trickled out of the gallery. She had gathered up the clothes he had been wearing, and folded them into precise piles, stuffing his socks into the toes of the shoes, spinning the belt into a coil.

At one point, Brian had brought back a mostly empty bottle of vodka, filched from the bar. Maeve took a swig, and thought of taking another before deciding that some degree of sobriety was in order to counterbalance the oddity of the night.

The bird didn't seem interested in drinking either.

Maeve dropped her head into her hands, and scraped her hair back into a knot. When she sat up again, Sweeney was pulling on his pants.

"I am sorry about before. Stress makes me less capable of interacting with people."

Maeve laughed under her breath. "I can relate."

Brian walked back. "Oh, good. You're, ah, dressed again. Have you two figured out what's going on?"

"I am under a curse," Sweeney said. "And I think Maeve can paint me free of it. There is some kind of power in her work, something that I would call magic. I'd like to commission a painting from her to see if this is possible."

"That's—" Maeve bit down hard on the next word.

"Mad? Impossible?" Sweeney met her eyes. "So am I."

"I'm not magic," Maeve said.

"That may be. After all this time and change, I am not a bird, though I sometimes have the shape of one. Magic reshapes truth."

Maeve could see the bird in the lines of the man, in the way he held his weight, in the shape of the almost-wings the air made space for.

She could see the impossibility, too, of what was asked.

"Please," said Sweeney. "Try."

"I'll need you," Maeve said, "to pose for me."

"This has got to be the weirdest contract I have ever negotiated."

"Brian. You negotiated with a guy who had been a bird for a significant part of the evening. Even if it had been straight up sign here boilerplate, it still would have been the weirdest contract you ever negotiated."

"True."

"I'm surprised he didn't ask for a deadline." Maeve picked up one of the white feathers from the floor, ran it through her fingers. "Some way of marking whether this will work or not, rather than just waiting to find out."

"You say whether like you genuinely believe it's a possibility, Maeve.

"And yes, this has been a night of strangeness, but magic is not what happens at the end. The way this ends is that you're going to wind up painting a very nice picture for a guy who is, I don't know how, sometimes a bird, and he is still going to be sometimes a bird after it is signed and framed, and once it is, we will never speak of this again because it is just too weird.

"You're good, Maeve. But you're not a magician. So stop worrying about whether there's magic in your painting, because there isn't."

"You said people don't buy paintings just because of what's on the canvas, they buy the story they think the painting tells," Maeve said.

Brian nodded.

"Sweeney bought a story where magic might be what happens at the end. He's bought that hope.

"And that much, I can paint."

Maeve took a sketchbook and went back to the Cathedral of St. John the Divine. It seemed like the right place to start, even if she didn't put the church itself into her painting. Full circle, somehow, to try and end the transformation in the same place she had first witnessed it.

Spring had come early, the buds on the trees beginning to limn the branches with a haze of green. The crocuses unfurled their purples in among the feet of the trees, and an occasional bold daffodil waved yellow.

And this was transformation, too, Maeve thought. More regular, less astonishing than a man suddenly enfeathered, but change all the same.

Maeve sat beneath a branch of birdsong, and cleared her mind of the magic she had been asked to make. If the bird—if Sweeney was correct, it would be there anyway.

She opened her sketchbook, and began to draw.

Sweeney walked the streets of his city. It wasn't often that he wandered on foot, preferring to save his peregrinations for when he wore wings. But tonight, he did not want to be above the grease and char scents of food cooking on sidewalk carts, of the crunch of shattered glass beneath his shoes.

He wanted the pulse and the press of people he had never quite felt home among. They would be his home, if Maeve succeeded. Perhaps then he would feel as if he belonged.

He should have, perhaps, spent his night on the wing, the flight a fragment to shore against the ruin of his days once he could no longer fly. He would miss, every day of his life he would miss the sensation of the air as his feathers cut through it. But he would have a life.

Sweeney bought truly execrable coffee in an "I Love NY" cup, because at that moment, with every fiber of his being, Sweeney did.

"Can I ask," Maeve hesitated.

"How this happened," Sweeney said.

She looked up from her sketchbook. "Well, yes. I don't want to be rude, or ask you to talk about something that's hurtful, but maybe I'll know better how to paint you out of being a bird if I know how you became one in the first place."

"It was a curse."

"I thought that was the kind of thing that only happened in fairy tales."

Sweeney shrugged, then apologized.

"That's fine. I don't need you to hold the pose . . . And I'll stop interrupting." Maeve bent back to her sketchbook.

"It is like something from a fairy tale. I was angry. I spoke and acted without thought, and, in the way of these things, it was a wizard I insulted. He cursed me for what I had done.

"For over a thousand years since, this has been my life."

"I'm sorry. Even if it was your fault, over a thousand years of vengeance seems cruel."

Tension rippled over Sweeney's skin. He shrank in on himself, fingers curling to claws.

"What is it?"

Sweeney extended his arm. Feathers downed its underside. "I had hoped this wouldn't happen."

"Does it hurt?"

"Only in my pride. Which was the point of the thing, after all." He schooled his breathing, and Maeve watched him relax, muscle by muscle. Except for a patch near his wrist, the feathers fell from Sweeney's skin.

"May I?" Maeve asked.

Sweeney nodded.

Maeve stroked her hand over the feathers, feeling the softness, and the heat of Sweeney's skin beneath. Heart racing like a bird's she stepped closer and kissed him.

A beat passed, and then another.

Sweeney's hand fisted in her hair, and he shuddered a breath into her mouth. She struggled out of her clothes, not wanting to break the kiss, or the contact.

Feathers alternated with skin under Maeve's hands, and Sweeney traced the outlines of her shoulder blades as if she, too, had wings.

As they moved together, Sweeney was neither feathered nor mad. Maeve did not feel the panic of a body too close, only the joy of a body exactly close enough.

White feathers blanketed the floor beneath them.

Maeve looked at Sweeney. "I don't think the painting is going to work."

"Why?" He tucked her hair behind her ear.

"I mean, I think it will be a good painting. But I don't think it will be magic."

"I'm no worse than I am now if it isn't. All I ask is for a good painting, Maeve. Anything beyond that would be," he smiled, "magic."

The parcel arrived in Wednesday's post. Inside, the sketchbook Maeve had lost. In the front cover, a scrawled note: "Forgive me my temporary theft. It's long past time that I returned this. —S." There was also a white feather.

She flipped through the pages and wondered what Sweeney had seen that convinced him her art was magic, the kind of magic that could help him. Whatever that thing had been, she couldn't see it.

Maeve kept the feather, but she slid the notebook into a fresh envelope to return it to Sweeney. Even if she couldn't give him freedom, she could give him this.

That done, Maeve took down all of the reference photos of mystical, fantastic birds that she had printed out and hung on her walls while painting the show for the gallery. She closed the covers of the bestiaries, and slid feathers into glassine envelopes, making bright kaleidoscopes of fallen flight.

She packed away the shadow boxes, the skeletons, the figurines, reshelved the fairy tales.

The return of the sketchbook had reminded her of one thing. If there were any magic she could claim, it was hers, pencil on a page, pigment on canvas. It came from her, not from anywhere else.

The only things Maeve left in sight were a white feather, a photo she had downloaded from her phone of a naked man perched in a tree, and the sketches she had made of Sweeney. Finally, she hung the recent sketches from the cathedral. She would have to go back there, she thought, before this was finished, but not yet. Not until the end.

At first, Sweeney thought it was the madness come upon him again. His skin itched as if there were feathers beneath it, but they were feathers he could neither see nor coax out of his crawling skin.

His bones ground against each other, too light, the wrong shape, shivering, untrustworthy. Not quite a man, not wholly a bird and uncertain what he was supposed to be.

The soar of flight tipped over the edge into vertigo, and he landed with an abrading slap of his hands against sidewalk.

And then he knew.

Maeve was painting. Painting his own, and perhaps ultimate, transformation.

Dizzy, he ran to where he had first seen her, the Cathedral of St. John the Divine.

Maeve hated painting in public. Hated it. People stood too close, asked grating questions, offered opinions that were neither solicited nor useful, and offered them in voices that were altogether too loud.

The quiet space in her head that painting normally gave here became the pressure of voices, the pinprick texture of other people's eyes on her skin.

She hated it, but this was the place she had to paint, to finish Sweeney's commission here at the cathedral. The end was the beginning.

On the canvas: the shadow of Sweeney rising to meet him, a man-shape grayed and subtle behind a bird. Sweeney, feathers raining around him as he burst from bird to man. A white bird, spiraling in flight, haunting the broken tower of the cathedral, a quiet and stormy ruin.

The skies behind Maeve filled with all manner of impossible birds. On the cathedral lawn, women played chess, and when one put the other in check, a man in a far away place stood up from a nearly negotiated peace.

Behind Maeve, Sweeney gasped, stumbled, fell. And still, she painted.

This time, it felt like magic.

The pain was immense. Sweeney could not speak, could not think, could barely breathe as he was unmade. Maeve was not breaking his curse, she was painting a reality apart from it.

Feathers exploded from beneath his skin, roiling over his body in waves, and disappearing again.

He looked up at the canvas, watched Maeve paint, watched the trails of magic in her brush strokes. In the trees were three birds with the faces and torsos of women, sirens to sing a man to his fate.

The church bells rang out, a sacred clarion, a calling of time, and Sweeney knew how this would end.

It was not what he had anticipated, but magic so rarely was.

Maeve set her brush down, and shook the circulation back into her hands. A white bird streaked low across her vision, and perched in front of one of the clerestory windows.

"Maeve."

She turned, and Sweeney the man lay on the ground behind her. "Oh, no. This isn't what I wanted."

She sat next to him, took his hand. "What can I do?"

"Just sit with me, please."

"Did you know this would happen, when you commissioned the painting?"

"I considered the possibility. I had to. Without the magic binding me into one spell or the next, the truth is I have lived a very long time, and I knew that death might well be my next migration."

Sweeney's next words were quieter, as if he was remembering them. "No one chooses his quest. It is chosen for him."

Sweeney closed his eyes. "This is just another kind of flight."

Maeve hung the finished painting on her wall. Outside, just beyond the open window, perched a white bird.

Unusual companions join an older Cubano musician at his nighttime gig at a children's care facility.

SALSA NOCTURNA

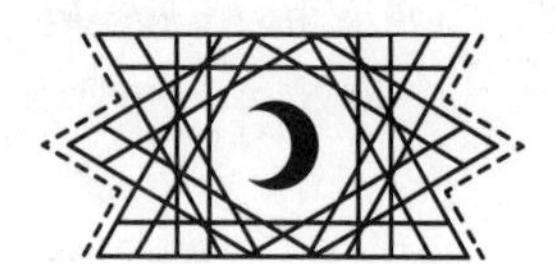

Daniel José Older

People say that all musical geniuses die in the gutter, and I've made my peace with that, but this is ridiculous. Anyway, it's a boiler room, but let me start at the beginning: the whole gigging around at late night bars and social clubs really began drying up right around the time the great white flight did a great white about-face. Mosta my main night spots shut down or started serving cappuccino instead of El Presidente. Two of my guys moved to Philly. Things were looking kinda grim, to be honest with you. I mean, me, I knew it'd work out in the long run—it's not that I'm an optimist, there's just certain things I do know—but meanwhile, the short run was kicking my ass. Kicking all our asses really.

So when my son's girl Janey came to me about this gig at the overnight center, I had to pay her some mind. Janey's a special kid, I gotta say. I couldn't ask for a better woman for Ernesto either. She keeps him in line, reminds him, I think, where he is from, that he's more than that fancy suit he puts on every morning. And she makes us all laugh with that mouth of hers too. Anyway, she comes to me one morning while I'm taking my morning medicina with my café con leche and bacon, eggs and papas fritas. I always take my high blood pressure pills with a side of bacon or sausage, you know, for balance.

"Gordo," she says. My name is Ernesto too, just like my son, but everyone calls me Gordo. It's not 'cause I'm fat. Okay, it's 'cause I'm fat. "Gordo," she says, "I want you to come interview at this place I work on

Lorimer." You see what she did? She made it look like I would be doing her the favor. Smart girl, Janey.

I eyed her coolly and put some more bacon in me.

"They need someone to watch the kids at night and later on maybe you can teach music in the mornings."

"Kids?" I said. "What makes you think I want to have anything to do with kids?"

There's two kinds of people that really are drawn to me: kids and dead people. Oh yeah, and crackheads on the street but that hardly counts because they obviously have an agenda. Kids seek me out like I'm made of candy. They find me and then they attach themselves to me and they don't let go. Maybe it's because I don't really buy into that whole "Aren't they cute" shit, I just take 'em as they come. If I walk onto a playground, and I swear to you I'm never the instigator, it's like some memo goes out: Drop whatever game you're playing and come chase the fat guy. Family events and holidays? Forget it. I don't really mind it because I hate small talk, and if there's one thing about kids, they give it to you straight: "Tío Gordo why you so big?"

And I get real serious looking. "Because I eat so many children," I say.

Then they run off screaming and usually, I give chase until I start wheezing.

It beats *How's the music business?* and *Oh, really? How interesting!* Because really and truly, I don't care how everyone's little seed is doing at CUNY or whatever.

I'm not bragging but even teenagers like me. They don't admit it most of the time, but I can tell. They're just like overgrown, hairy five year olds anyway. Also, notoriously poor small talkers.

Janey told me exactly how it would go down and exactly what to say. She's been doing this whole thing for a while now, so she speaks whitelady-ese like a pro. She had this Nancy lady down pat too, from the extra-extra smile to the cautious handshake to the little sing-song apologies dangling off every phrase. Everything went just like she said it would. The words felt awkward in my mouth, like pieces of food that're too big to chew, and I thought that Nancy was on to me right up until she says—*That sounds terrific, Mr. Cortinas.*

You can call me Gordo, I say.

It's called a non-profit but everyone at the office is obviously making a killing. The kids are called *minority* and *emotionally challenged* but there's a lot more of them and they show a lot more emotions than the staff. It's a care facility but the windows are barred. The list goes on and on, but still, I like my job. The building's one of these old gothic type numbers on the not-yet-gentrified end of Lorimer. Used to be an opera house or something, so it's still got all that good run-down music hall juju working for it. I show up at nine p.m. on the dot, because Janey said my sloppy Cuban time won't cut it here so just pretend I'm supposed to be there at eight and I'll be alright. And it works.

They set up a little desk for me by a window on the fifth floor. Outside I can see the yard and past that a little park. I find that if I smoke my Malagueñas in the middle of the hallway, the smell lingers like an aloof one-night stand till the morning and I get a stern/apologetic talking to from Nancy and then a curse-out from Janey. So, I smoke out the window.

It's a good thing that most of the kids are already sleeping by the time I arrive, because even as it is I can feel my presence course through the building like an electrical current. I can't help it. Occasionally a little booger will get up to make a number one or number two and not want to go back to bed. I make like I'm gonna slap 'em and they scatter back to their rooms. Soon they'll be on to me though.

A little after midnight, the muertos show up. They're always in their Sunday best, dressed to the nines, as they say, in pinstriped suits and fancy dresses. Some of them even have those crazy Spanish flamenco skirts on. They wear expensive hats and white gloves. While the children sleep, the muertos gather around my little desk on the fifth floor foyer and carry on. Mostly they dance, but a few of them bring instruments: old wooden guitars and basses, tambores, trumpets. Some of them show up with strange ones that I've never seen before—African, I think—and then I have to figure out how to transpose whatever-it-is into the piano/horn section arrangement I'm used to.

Look, their music is close enough to what I'd write anyway, so either they're some part of my subconscious or it's a huge supernatural coincidence—really, what are the chances? So either way I don't feel bad jotting down the songs. Besides, I started bringing my own little toy store carry-along keyboard and accompanying them. Course I keep the volume low so as not to wake up the little ones.

There's a jangle to the music of the dead. I mean that certain something that's so happy and so sad at the same time. The notes almost make a perfect harmony but don't. Then they do but quickly crash into dissonance. They simmer in that sweet in-between, rhythm section rattling along all the while. Chords collapse chaotically into each other, and just when you think the whole thing's gonna spill into total nonsense, it stands back up and comes through sweet as a lullaby on your mami's lips. Songs that'll make people tap their feet and drink melancholically but not realize the twisting genius lurking within until generations later. That's the kind of music I make, and the dead do too. We make it together.

Tonight was different, though. The muertos didn't show up. They never scared me. If anything they kept me company in those wee hours. But this, this silence, made me shiver and feel like I was both being watched by a thousand unfriendly eyes and all alone in the world. I looked down that empty hallway. Tried to imagine my brand-new-long-lost friends making their shadowy way up towards me, but it remained empty.

Just to have something to do, I made the rounds. Each troubled young lump in its curled up spot. Some nights when I don't feel like doing my music, I read their files. Their twisted little sagas unwind through evaluation forms and concerned emails. Julio plays with himself at meal times. Devon isn't allowed near mirrors on the anniversary of his rape. Tiffany hides knives in case the faceless men come back for her. But night after night, they circle into themselves like those little curlup bugs and drift off into sleep.

One bed, though, was empty. The cut out construction paper letters on the door spelled MARCOS. A little Ecuadorian kid, if I remembered his file right. Untold horrors. Rarely spoke. The muertos being gone was bad in a supernatural, my-immortal-soul kind of way and Marcos being gone was bad in a frowning-Nancy-in-the-morning, lose-my-job kind of way, and I wasn't really sure which was worse. I turned and walked very quickly back down the hallway. First I spot-checked all the rooms I'd already passed just in case little man was crouching in one of the corners unnoticed. But I knew he wasn't. I knew wherever Marcos was, there would be a whole lot of swaying shrouds with him. Remember I told you sometimes I just know stuff? This was one of those things. Besides, I don't believe in coincidence. Not when kids and the dead are involved.

When I got to the end of the hallway, I stood still and just panted and sweated for a minute. That's when I heard the noise coming from one of the floors below. It was just barely there, a ghost of a sound really, and kept fading away and coming back. Like the little twinkling of a music box, far, far away.

To the untrained eye, I appear bumbling. You can see my blood vessels strain tight to support my girth. My hands are ungainly and callused. For a man who makes such heart-wrenching, subtle melodies, I am not delicate. But if you were to watch me in slow-mo, you would then understand that really I am a panther. A slow, overweight panther, perhaps, but still, there is a fluidity to me—a certain poise. I flowed, gigantic and cat-like, down the five flights of stairs to the lobby, pausing at each landing to catch my breath and check for signs of stroke or heart attack. *Infarto*, in Spanish, so that in addition to perhaps dying you have the added discomfort of it sounding like you were laid low by a stinky shot of gas.

The lobby is covered in posters that are supposed to make the children feel better about having been abused and discarded. Baby animals snuggle amidst watercolor nature drawings. It's a little creepy.

The noise was still coming from somewhere down below, definitely the basement. I wasn't thrilled about this, was hoping the muertos had simply gathered in the lobby (perhaps to enjoy the inspirational artwork) but can't say I was surprised either. I opened the old wooden door that leads down the last flight of stairs and took a deep breath. Each step registered my presence unenthusiastically. At the bottom, I reached into the darkness till my hand swatted a dangling chain. The bulb was dim. It cast an uneven, gloomy light on a cluttered universe of broken furniture, file cabinets and forgotten papier-mâché projects.

I followed the noise through the shadows. I could now make it out definitively to be a melody, a lonely, minor key melody, beautiful like a girl with one eye standing outside a graveyard. I rounded a corner and then held perfectly still. Before me hovered all my friends, the muertos, with their backs turned to me. I tried to see past them but they were crowded together so densely it was impossible. Ever so quietly, I crept forward among them, their chilly undead shadows sending tiny earthquakes down my spine.

The muertos were gathered around a doorway. I entered and found myself in this dank boiler room. At the far end, little Marcos sat calmly in a niche of dusty pipes and wiring. He held my carry-along in his lap. His eyes were closed and his fingers glided up and down the keys. Between myself and Marcos, about thirty small muertos, muertocitos, bobbed up and down, their undivided attention on the boy. You know—I never think much about those who die as children—what their wandering souls must deal with. Who watches over them, checks on those small, curly-bug lumps at night? The ghost children were transfixed; I could feel their love for this boy and his music as surely as I felt the pulse pounding in my head.

And, to be quite honest with you, at first I too found myself lost in the swirling cascade of notes coming from my little keyboard. It is rare that I feel humbled, rarer still that it would happen because of a ten year old, but I'm not above admitting it. The song filled the heavy boiler room air, so familiar and so brand-new. It was a mambo, but laced with the saddest melody I've ever heard—some unholy union of Mozart and Perez Prado that seemed to speak of so many drunken nights and whispered promises. It tore into me, devoured me and pieced me back together a brand new man.

But now the song has ended, breaking the quiet reverie we had all fallen into and ripping open a great painful vacancy where it once had been. The rapture is over and we are just in a boiler room, which is about as good as a gutter when it comes to places to die.

I'm strong, and not the addictive type, so I shake my head and welcome myself back to the strange silence. But the muertocitos are not so quick to move on. A furious rustling ripples through their ranks, and the small, illuminated shadows nudge towards Marcos. The boy looks up finally, and turns to me, eyes wide. He starts to play the song again, but he's afraid now. His heart's not in it and the ghostlings can tell. They continue their urgent sway, a tough crowd, and begin to edge closer to him.

I carry a few saints with me and I find more often than not, they do their part. They tend to really come through when my more basic human instincts, like caution, fail. This is definitely one of those times. I surge (cat-like) through the crowd of wily young ghosts. Their cool tendrils cling to me like cobwebs but I keep moving. I scoop up little man and his living body feels so warm against me compared to all that death. He's still clutching the keyboard. Eyes squeezed shut. His little heart sends a pitter-patter pulse out like an S-O-S.

I decide if I pause to consider the situation around me, I may come to my senses, which would definitely mean an icy, uncomfortable death for myself and Marcos. So I make like a linebacker—fake left, swerve right (slowly, achingly, but—gracefully) and then just plow down the middle. They're more ready for me this time, and angrier. The air is thick with their anger; any minute the wrong molecule might collide and blow the whole place up. Also, I didn't gain quite the momentum I'd hoped to. I can feel all that stillness reach far inside me, penetrate my most sacred places, throw webs across my inner shrines, detain my saints. It is seriously holding me up.

But there is more music to write. I won't be around to see my legacy honored properly but I have a few more compositions in me before I can sleep peacefully. Also, I enjoy my family and Saturday nights playing dominos with the band after rehearsal and my morning café con leche, bacon, eggs, papas fritas, and sometimes sausage. Young Ernesto who's not so young and whatever crazy creation him and Janey will come up with in their late night house-rocking—there are still things I would like to see. Plus, this little fellow in my arms seems like he may have a long, satisfying career ahead of him. A little lonely perhaps, but musical genius can be an all-consuming friend until you know how to tame her. I have room under my wing here, I realize as I plow through this wee succubus riot, and many things to tell young Marcos. Practical things—things that they don't teach about you in books or grad school.

Is trundle a word? It should be. I trundle through those creatures, tearing their sloppy ice tentacles from my body. The door comes up on me quicker than I thought it would, catches me a little off guard and I'm so juiced up thinking of all the beautiful and sad truths I will tell Marcos when we survive that I just knock it out of my way. I don't stop to see how the mama and papa muertos feel about the situation; I move through them quick.

At the corner I glance back. An intervention of some kind seems to be taking place. The muertos have encircled their young. I can only suppose what must be happening, but I'd like to believe it's a solid scolding, an ass beating like the one I would've gotten from Papi (God rest his troubled soul) if I'd trapped one of my younger brothers in the basement and made like I was gonna end them.

When we reach the c'mon-get-happy lobby, I notice that dawn is edging out onto the streets. Marcos's song must've been longer than I realized. I put the boy down, mostly because I'm losing feeling in the lower half of my body and my shirt is caked in sweat. Wrap my fat hand around the banister and slowly, languidly, huff and puff up the stairs behind him. I pause on the landing, listen to the quick, echoing tak-tak-tak of his footfall bound up the next three flights. He will be curled in his bed by the time I reach the second floor, asleep by sunrise.

At six, the morning crew will come in, smiles first, and I will chuckle with them nonchalantly about the long, uneventful night. Tomorrow evening, as I show my new student a few tricks to keep his chops up, my friends will return. In their Sunday best, they will slither as always from the shadows of the fifth floor hallway. And this time, they will bring their young along with them.

Peter S. Beagle revisits the Van Cortlandt Park of his 1950s Bronx childhood with one of his oldest friends. He'll swear on his grave that this "really did happen just like this, back when Phil Sigunick and I were thirteen. Some things you can't make up."

THE ROCK IN THE PARK

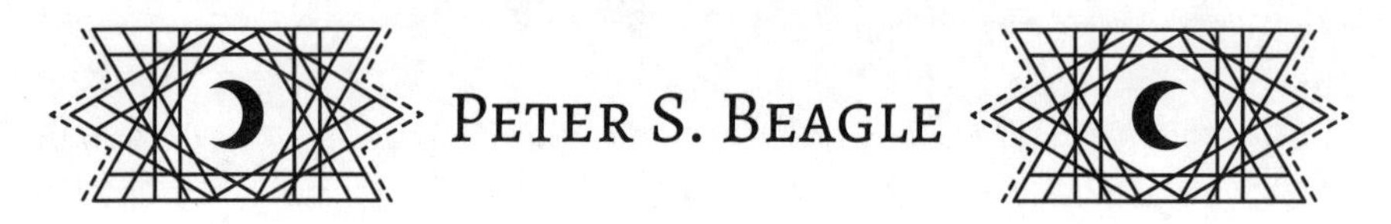

PETER S. BEAGLE

Van Cortlandt Park begins a few blocks up Gunhill Road: past the then-vacant lot where us neighborhood kids fought pitched battles over the boundaries of our parents' Victory Gardens; past Montefiore Hospital, which dominates the entire local skyline now; past Jerome Avenue, where the IRT trains still rattle overhead, and wicked-looking old ladies used to sit out in front of the kosher butcher shops, savagely plucking chickens. It's the fourth-largest park in New York City, and on its fringes there are things like golf courses, tennis courts, baseball diamonds, bike and horse trails, a cross-country track and an ice-skating rink—even a cricket pitch. That's since my time, the cricket pitch.

But the heart of Van Cortlandt Park is a deep old oak forest. Inside it you can't hear the traffic from any direction—the great trees simply swallow the sound—and the place doesn't seem to be in anybody's flight path to JFK or LaGuardia. There are all sorts of animals there, especially black squirrels, which I've never seen anywhere else; and possums and rabbits and raccoons. I saw a coyote once, too. Jake can call it a dog all he likes. I know better.

It's most beautiful in fall, that forest, which I admit only grudgingly now. Mists and mellow fruitfulness aren't all that comforting when bloody school's starting again, and no one's ever going to compare the leaf-changing season in the Bronx to the shamelessly flamboyant dazzle of October New Hampshire or Vermont, where the trees seem to turn overnight to glass, refracting the sunlight in colors that actually hurt your eyes and confound your mind. Yet the oak forest of Van Cortlandt Park invariably, reliably caught fire every year with the sudden *whoosh* of a building going up, and it's still what I remember when someone says the word *autumn,* or quotes Keats.

It was all of Sherwood to me and my friends, that forest.

Phil and I had a rock in Van Cortlandt that belonged to us; we'd claimed it as soon as we were big enough to climb it easily, which was around fourth grade. It was just about the size and color of an African elephant, and it had a narrow channel in its top that fit a skinny young body perfectly. Whichever one of us got up there first had dibs: the loser had to sit beside. It was part of our private mythology that we had worn that groove into the rock ourselves over the years, but of course that wasn't true. It was just another way of saying *get your own rock, this is ours.* There are whole countries that aren't as territorial as adolescent boys.

We'd go to our Rock after school, or on weekends—always in the afternoons, by which time the sun would have warmed the stone surface to a comfortable temperature—and we'd lie on our backs and look up through the leaves and talk about painters Phil had just discovered, writers I was in love with that week, and girls neither of us quite knew how to approach. We never fixated on the same neighborhood vamp, which was a good thing, because Phil was much more aggressive and experienced than I. Both of us were highly romantic by nature, but I was already a *princesse lointaine* fantasist, while Phil had come early to the understanding that girls were human beings like us. I couldn't see how that could possibly be true, and we argued about it a good deal.

One thing we never spoke of, though, was our shared awareness that the oak forest was magic. Not that we ever expected to see fairies dancing in a ring there, or to spy from our warm, safe perch anything like a unicorn, a wizard or a leprechaun. We knew better than *that*: as a couple of New Yorkers, born and bred, cynicism was part of our bone marrow. Yet even so, in our private hearts we always expected something wild and extraordinary from our Rock and our forest. And one hot afternoon in late September, when we were thirteen, they delivered.

That afternoon, I had been complaining about the criminal unfairness of scheduling a subway World Series, between the Yankees and the Dodgers, during school hours, except for the weekend, when there would be no chance of squeezing into little Ebbets Field. Phil, no baseball fan, dozed in the sun, grunting a response when absolutely required ("Love to do a portrait of Casey Stengel; *there's* a face!"). I was spitballing ways to sneak a portable radio and earpiece into class, so I could follow the first game, when we heard the hoofbeats. In itself, that wasn't unusual—there was a riding stable on the western edge of the Park—but there was a curious hesitancy and wariness about the sound that had us both sitting up on our Rock, and me saying excitedly, "Deer!"

These days, white-tail deer dropping by to raid your vegetable garden are as common in the North Bronx as rabbits and squirrels. Back then, back when I knew Felix Salten's *Bambi* books by heart, they were still an event. But Phil shook his head firmly. "Horse. You don't hear deer."

True enough: like cats, deer are just *there,* where they weren't a moment before. And now that it was closer it didn't sound like a deer to my city ears—nor quite like a horse, either. We waited, staring toward a grove of smaller trees, young sycamores, where something neither of us could quite make out was moving slowly down the slope. Phil repeated, "Horse—look at the legs," and lay back again. I was just about to do the same when the creature's head came into view.

It didn't register at first; it couldn't have done. In that first moment what I saw—what I allowed myself to see—was a small boy riding a dark-bay horse not much bigger than a colt. Then, somewhere around the time that I heard myself whisper "Jesus *Christ,*" I realized that neither the boy nor the horse was *that* small, and that the boy wasn't actually riding. The two of them were *joined,* at the horse's shoulders and just below the boy's waist. In the Bronx, in Van Cortlandt Park, in the twentieth century—in our little lives—a centaur.

They must operate largely on sight, as we do, because the boy only became aware of us just after we spotted him. He halted instantly, his expression a mix of open-mouthed curiosity and real terror—then whirled and was gone, out of sight between the great trees. His hoofbeats were still fading on the dead leaves while we stared at each other.

Phil said flatly, "Just leave me out of your hallucinations, okay? You got weird hallucinations."

"This from a person who still thinks Linda Darnell's hot stuff? You know what we saw."

"I never. I wasn't even here."

"Okay. Me neither. I got to get home." I slid down off the Rock, picking up my new schoolbook bag left at its base. Less than a month, and already my looseleaf notebook looked as though I'd been teething on it.

Phil followed. "Hell, no, it was your figment, you can't just leave it on a doorstep and trust to the kindness of strangers." We'd seen the Marlon Brando *Streetcar Named Desire* a year earlier, and were still bellowing "STELLA!!!" at odd moments in the echoing halls of Junior High School 80. "You saw it, you saw it, I'm gonna tell—Petey saw a centaur—*nyaahh, nyaahh,* Petey saw a centaur!" I swung the book bag at him and chased him all the way out of the Park.

On the phone that evening—we were theoretically doing our biology homework together—he asked, "So what do the Greek myths tell you about centaurs?"

"Main thing, they can't hold their liquor, and they're mean drunks. You don't ever want to give a centaur that first beer."

"I'll remember. What else?"

"Well, the Greeks have two different stories about where they came from, but I can't keep them straight, so forget it. In the legends they're aggressive, always starting fights—there was a big battle with the Lapiths, who were some way their cousins, except human, don't ask, and I think most of the centaurs were killed. I'm not sure. But some of them were really good, really noble, like Cheiron. Cheiron was the best of the lot, he was a healer and an astrologer and a teacher—he was the tutor of people like Odysseus, Achilles, Hercules, Jason, Theseus, all those guys." I paused, still thumbing through the worn Modern Library Bulfinch my father had given me for my tenth birthday. "That's all I know."

"Mmmff. Book say anything about centaurs turning up in the Bronx? I'll settle for the Western Hemisphere."

"No. But there was a shark in the East River, a couple of years back, you remember? Cops went out in a boat and shot at it."

"Not the same thing." Phil sighed. "I still think it's your fault, somehow. What really pisses me off, I didn't have so much as a box of Crayolas to draw the thing with. Probably never get another chance."

But he did: not the next day, when, of course, we cut PE and hurried back to the Park, but the day after that, which was depressingly chilly, past pretending that it was still Indian Summer. We didn't talk much: I was busy scanning for centaurs (I'd brought my Baby Brownie Special camera and a pair of binoculars), and Phil, mumbling inaudibly to himself, kept rummaging through his sketch pads and colored pencils, pastels, gouaches, charcoals and crayons. I made small jokes about his equipment almost crowding me off the Rock, and he glared at me in a way that made me uneasy about that "almost."

I don't remember how long we waited, but it must have been close to two hours. The sun was slanting down, the Rock's surface temperature was actually turning out-and-out cold, and Phil and I were well past conversation when the centaurs came. There were three of them: the young one we had first seen, and the two who were clearly his parents, to judge by the way they stood together on the slope below the sycamore grove. They made no attempt to conceal themselves, but looked directly at us, as we stared back at them. After a long moment, they started down the slope together.

Phil was shaking with excitement, but even so he was already sketching as they came toward us. I was afraid to raise my camera, for fear of frightening the centaurs away. They had a melancholy dignity about them, even the child, that I didn't have words for then: I recall it now as an air of royal exile, of knowing where they belonged, and knowing, equally, that they could never return there. The male—no, the *man*—had a short, thick black beard, a dark, strong-boned face, and eyes of a strange color, like honey. The woman . . .

Remember, all three of them were naked to the waist, and Phil and I were thirteen years old. For myself. I'd seen nude models in my uncles' studios since childhood, but this woman, this *centauride* (I looked the word up when I got home that night), was more beautiful than anyone I knew. It wasn't just a matter of round bare breasts: it was the heartbreaking grace of her neck, the joyous purity of the line of her shoulders, the delicacy of her collarbones. Phil had stopped sketching, which tells you more than I can about what we saw.

The boy had freckles. Not big ones, just a light golden dusting. His hair was the same color, with a kind of reddish undercoloring, like his mother's hair. He looked about ten or eleven.

The man said, "Strangers, of your kindness, might either of you be Jersey Turnpike?"

He had a deep, calm voice, with absolutely no horsiness in it—nothing of a neigh or a whinny, or anything like that. Maybe a slight sort of funny gurgle in the back of the throat, but hardly noticeable—you'd really have to be listening for it. When Phil and I just gaped, the woman said, "We have never come this way south before. We are lost."

Her voice was low, too, but it had a singing cadence to it, a warm off-beat lilt that entranced and seduced both of us even beyond her innocent nudity. I managed to say, "South . . . you want to go south . . . um, you mean south like down south? Like *south* south?"

"Like Florida?" Phil asked. "Mexico?"

The man lifted his head sharply. "Mexico, yes, that was the name, I always forget. It is where we go, all of us, every year, when the birds go. *Mexico*."

"But we set out too late," the woman explained in her soft, singing voice. "Our son was ill, and we traveled eastward to seek out a healer, and by the time we were ready to start, all the others were gone—"

"And Father took the wrong road," the boy broke in, his tone less accusatory than excited. "We have had such adventures—"

His mother quelled him with a glance. Embarrassment didn't sit easily on the man's powerful face, but he flushed and nodded. "More than one. I do not know this country, and we are used to traveling in company. Now I am afraid that we are completely lost, except for that one name someone gave me—Jersey Turnpike. Can Jersey Turnpike lead us to Mexico?"

We looked at each other. Phil said, "Jersey Turnpike isn't a person, it's a road, a highway. You can go south that way, but not to Mexico—you're way off course for Mexico. I'm sorry."

The boy mumbled, "I *knew* it," but not in a triumphant, wise-ass sort of way; if anything, he appeared suddenly very weary of adventures. The man looked utterly stricken. He bowed his head, and the color seemed to fade visibly from his bright chestnut coat. The woman's manner, on the other hand, hardly altered with Phil's news, except that she moved closer to her husband and pressed her light-gray flank against his, in a gesture of silent trust and confidence.

"You're too far east," I said. "You have to cut down through Texas." They stared uncomprehendingly. I said, "Texas—I *think* you'd go by way of Pennsylvania, Tennessee, maybe Georgia . . . " I stopped, because I couldn't bear the growing fatigue and bewilderment in their three faces, nor in the way their shining bodies sagged a little more with each state name. I told them, "What you need is a map. We could bring you one tomorrow, easy." But their expressions did not change. The man said, "We cannot read."

"Not now," the woman said wistfully. "There was a time when our folk were taught the Greek in colthood, every one, and some learned the Roman as well, when it became necessary. But that was in another world that is no more . . . and learning unused fades with long years. Now only a few of our elders know letters enough to read such things as maps in your tongue—the rest of us journey by old memory and starlight. Like the birds."

Her own eyes were different from her husband's honey-colored eyes: more like dark water, with deep-green wonder turning and glinting far down. Phil never could get them right, and he tried for a long time.

He said quietly now, "I could draw you a picture."

I can't say exactly how the centaurs reacted, or how they looked at him. I was too busy gawking at him myself. Phil said, "Of your route, your road. I could draw you something that'll get you to Mexico."

The man started to speak, but Phil anticipated him. "Not a map. I said a *picture*. No words." I remember that he was sitting cross-legged on the Rock, like our idea of a swami or a yogi; and I remember him leaning intensely forward, toward the centaurs, so that he seemed almost to be joined to the Rock, growing out of it, as they were joined to their horse bodies. He was already drawing invisible pictures with his right forefinger on the palm of his left hand, but I don't think he knew it.

I opened *my* mouth then, but he cut me off too. "It'll take me all day tomorrow, and most likely all night too. You'll be okay till the day after tomorrow?"

The woman said to Phil, "You can do this?"

He grinned at her with what seemed to me outrageous confidence. "I'm an artist. Artists are always drawing people's journeys."

I said, "You could wait right here, if you like. We hardly ever see anybody but us in this part of the park. I mean, if it would suit you," for it occurred to me that I had no idea what they ate, or indeed how they survived in the twentieth century. "I guess we could bring you food."

The man's teeth showed white and large in his black beard. "The forage here is most excellent, even this late in the year."

"There are lots of acorns," the boy said eagerly. "I love acorns."

His mother turned her dark gaze to me. "Can you also make such pictures?"

"Never," I said. "But I could maybe write you a poem." I wrote a lot of poems for girls when I was thirteen. She seemed pleased.

Phil was gathering his equipment and scrambling off the Rock, imperiously beckoning me to follow. "Quit fooling around, Beagle. We got work to do." Standing among them, the size and sheer presence of all three centaurs was, if not intimidating, definitely daunting. Even the boy looked down at us, and we barely came up to the shoulders of his parents' horse-bodies. I've always enjoyed the smell of horses—in those days, they were among the very few animals I wasn't allergic to—but centaurs in groups smell like thunder, like an approaching storm, and it left me dizzy and a bit disoriented. Phil repeated briskly, "Day after tomorrow, right here."

We were halfway up the slope when he snapped his fingers, said, "Ah, *shit*!", dropped his equipment and went running back toward the centaurs. I waited, watching as he moved swiftly between the three of them; but I couldn't, for the life of me, make out what he was doing. He came back almost as quickly, and I noticed then that he was tucking something into his shirt pocket. When I asked what it was, he told me it was nothing I needed to trouble my pretty little head about. You couldn't do anything with him in those tempers, so I left it alone.

He didn't say much else on the walk home, and I managed to keep my curiosity in check until we were parting at my apartment building. Then I burst out with it: "Okay, you're going to draw them a picture that's going to get a family of migrating centaurs all the way to Mexico. This, excuse me, I want to hear." His being on the hook meant, as always, us being on the hook, so I felt entitled to my snottiness.

"I can do it. It's been done." His jaw was tight, and his face had the ferocious pallor that I associated entirely with street fights, usually with fat Stewie Hauser and Miltie Mellinger, who never tired of baiting him. "Back in the Middle Ages, I read about it—Roger Bacon did it, somebody like that. But you have to get me some maps, as many as you can. A ton of maps, a shitload of maps, covering every piece of ground between here—right here, your house—and the Texas border. You got that? Maps. Also, you should stop by Bernardos and see can you borrow that candle of his mothers. He says she got it from a *bruja*, back in San Juan, what could it hurt?"

"But if they can't read maps—"

"Beagle, I have been extraordinarily lenient about that two bucks—"

"Maps. Right. Maps. You think they came down from Canada? Summer up north, winter in Mexico? I bet that's what they do."

"*Maps*, Beagle."

The next day was Saturday, and he actually called me around seven in the morning, demanding that I get my lazy ass on the road and start finding some maps for him. I said certain useful things that I had picked up from Angel Salazar, my Berlitz in such affairs, and was at the gas station up the block by 7:30. By 10:00, I'd hit every other station I could reach on my bike, copped my parents' big Rand McNally road atlas, and triumphantly dumped them all—Bernardo's mother's witch-candle included—on Phil's bed, demanding, "Now what, fearless leader?"

"Now you take Dusty for her morning walk." He had his favorite easel set up, and was rummaging through his paper supplies. "Then you go away and write your poem, and you come back when it's time to take Dusty for her evening walk. Then you go away again. All well within your capacities." Dusty was his aged cocker spaniel, and the nearest thing I had to the longed-for dog of my own. I went home after tending to her, and sat down at the desk in my bedroom to write the poem I'd promised to the centaur mother. I still remember the first lines:

If I were a hawk,
I would write you letters—
featherheaded jokes,
scribbled on the air.
If I were a dog
I would do your shopping.
If I were a cat
I would brush your hair.
If I were a bear,
I would build your fires,
bringing in the wood,
breaking logs in two.
If I were a camel I'd take out the garbage.
If I were a fox I would talk to you . . .

There was more and sillier, but never mind. I was very romantic at thirteen, on very short notice, and I had never seen beauty like hers.

Okay, a little bit extra, because I do like the way it ended:

If I were a tiger,
I would dance for you.
If I were a mouse,
I would dance for you.

If I were a whale,
I would dance for you . . .

When I came back in the evening to walk Dusty again, Phil was working in his bedroom with the door closed, and an unattended dinner plate cooling on the sill. His parents were more or less inured to his habits by now, but it fretted at them constantly, just as my unsociability worried my mother, who would literally bribe Phil and Jake to get me out of the house. I reassured them, as I always did, that he was working on a really demanding, really challenging project, then grabbed up dog and leash and was gone. It was dark when I brought her back, but Phil's door was still shut.

As it was the next morning, and remained until mid-afternoon, when he called me to say, "Done. Get over here."

He sounded awful.

He looked worse. His eyes were smudgy red pits in a face so white that his own small freckles stood out, and he moved like an old man, as though no part of his body could be trusted not to hurt. He said, "Let's go."

"You're kidding. You wouldn't make it to Lapin's." That was the candy-and-newspaper store across the street. "Take a nap, for God's sake, we'll go when you wake up."

"Now." When he cleared his throat, it sounded exactly like my father's car trying to start on a cold morning.

He was holding a metal tube that I recognized as a tennis-ball can. I reached for it, but he snatched it away. "You'll see it when they see it." Just then, he didn't look like anyone I'd ever known.

So we trudged to Van Cortlandt Park, which seemed to take the rest of the afternoon, as slowly as Phil was walking. He had clearly been sitting in more or less the same position for hours and hours on end, and the cramps weren't turning loose without a fight. Now and then he paused to shake his arms and legs violently, and by the time we reached the Park, he was moving a little less stiffly. But he still hardly spoke, and he clung to that tennis-ball can as though it were a cherished trophy, or a life raft.

The centaurs were waiting at the Rock. The boy, a little way up the forest slope from his parents, saw us first, and called out, "They're here!" as he galloped to meet us. But he turned shy midway, as children will, and ran back to the others as we approached. I remember that the man had his arms folded across his chest, and that there were a couple of dew-damp patches on the centauride's coat, the weather having turned cloudy. They said nothing.

Phil said, "I brought it. What I promised. Here, I'll show you."

They moved close, plainly careful not to crowd him with their bodies, as he opened the airtight can and took out a roll of light, flexible drawing paper. He handed the free end to the man, saying, "See? There you are, all three of you. And there's your road to Mexico."

Craning my neck, I could see a perfectly rendered watercolor of the oak forest, so detailed that I saw not only our Rock with its long groove along the top surface, but also such things as the bird's nest in the upper branches of the tallest sycamore and its family of occupants. I couldn't tell what sort of birds they were, but I knew past doubt that Phil knew. The centaurs in the painting, on the other hand, were not done in any detail beyond the generic, except for relative size, the boy being obviously smaller than the other two. They might have been pieces in a board game.

The man said slowly, not trying to conceal his puzzlement, "This is very pretty, I can see that it is pretty. But it is not our road."

"No, you don't understand," Phil answered him. "Look, take both ends, so." He handed the whole roll to the centaur. "Now . . . hold it up so you can watch it, and walk straight ahead. Just walk."

The man moved slowly forward, his eyes fixed on the image of the very place where he stood. He had not gone more than a few paces when he cried out, "But it moves! It moves!"

His wife and son—and I—pressed close now, and never mind who stepped on whose feet. The watercolor had changed, though not by much; only a few paces' worth. Now it showed a distinctly marked path in front of the centaur's feet: the path we ourselves took, coming and going in the oak forest. He said again, this time in a near-whisper, "It *moves* . . . "

"And we too," the woman said. "The little figures—as we move, so do they."

"Not always." Phil's voice was sounding distinctly fuller and stronger. "Go left now, walk off the path—see what happens."

The man did as directed—but the figures remained motionless in the watercolor, reproving him with their stillness. When he returned to the path and stepped along it, they moved with him again, sliding like the magnet-based toys we had then. I noticed for the first time that each one's painted tail had a long, coarse hair embedded in the pigment: chestnut, gray, dark-bay.

Almost speechless, the man turned to Phil, holding up the roll to stare at it. "And all our journey is in this picture, truly? And all we need do is follow these . . . poppets of ourselves?"

Phil nodded. "Just pay attention, and they won't let you go wrong. I fixed it so they'll guide you all the way to Nogales, Texas—that's right on the Mexican border. You'll know the way from there." He looked up with weary seriousness at the proud, bearded face above him. "It's a very long way—almost two thousand miles. I'm sorry."

"We have made longer journeys, and with no such guide." The man was still moving forward and back, watching in fascination as the little images mimicked his pacing. "Nothing to compare," he murmured, "not in all my life . . . " He halted and faced Phil again. "One with the wisdom to create this for us is also wise enough to know that there is no point in even trying to show our gratitude properly. Thank you."

Phil reached up to take the proffered hand. "Just go carefully, that's all. Stay off the main roads—the way I drew it, you shouldn't ever have to set foot on a highway. And don't ever let that picture out of your sight. Definitely a one-shot deal."

He climbed up onto the Rock and instantly fell asleep. The man seemed to doze on his feet, as horses do, while the boy embarked on one last roundup of every last acorn in the area. For myself, I spent the time saying my poem over and over to the centauride, until she had it perfectly memorized, and could repeat it back to me, line for line. "Now I will never forget it," she told me. "The last time anyone wrote a poem for me, it was in the Greek, the oldest Greek that none speak today." She recited it to me, and while I understood not one word, I would know it if I heard it again.

Phil was still asleep when the centaurs left at twilight. I did try to wake him to bid them farewell, but he only blinked and mumbled, and was gone again. I watched them out of sight among the oaks: the man in the lead, intently following the little moving images on Phil's painting; the boy trotting close behind, exuberant with adventure, for good or ill. The woman turned once to look back at us, and then went on.

I don't remember how I finally got Phil on his feet and home; only that it was late, and that both sets of parents were mad at us. The next day was school, and after that I had a doctors appointment, and Phil had flute lessons, and what with one family thing or another, we had almost no time together until close to the end of the week. We didn't go to the Rock—the weather had turned too grim even for us—rather we sat shivering on the front stoop of my apartment building, like winter birds on a telephone line, and didn't say much of anything. I asked if Phil thought they'd make it all the way to Mexico, and he shrugged and answered, "We'll never know." After a moment, he added, "All I know, I got a roomful of stupid maps, and my whole body hurts. Never again, boy. You and your damn hallucinations."

I said, "I didn't know you could do stuff like that. Like what you made for them."

He turned to stare intently into my face. "You saw those hairs in those little figures? I saw you seeing them." I nodded. "Well, each was from one of their tails—Mom, Pop, or the Kid. And I plucked a few more hairs, wove those into my brushes. That was the magic part: centaurs may have a lousy sense of direction, but they're still magic. Wouldn't have worked for a minute without that." I stared, and he sighed. "I keep telling you, the artist isn't the magic. The artist is the *sight,* the artist is someone who knows magic when he sees it. The magic doesn't care whether it's seen or not—that's the artist's business. My business."

I tried earnestly, stumblingly, to absorb what he was telling me. "So all that—I mean, the painting moving and guiding them, and all . . . "

Phil gave me that crooked, deceptively candid grin he's had since we were five years old. "I'm a good artist. I'm really good. But I ain't *that* good."

We sat in silence for a while, while the leaves blew and tumbled past us, and a few sharp, tiny raindrops stung our faces. By and by Phil spoke again, quietly enough that I had to lean closer to hear him. "But we were magic too, in our way. You rounding up every single map between here and Yonkers, and me . . . " He hunched over, arms folded on his knees, the way he still does without realizing it. "Me at that damn easel, brush in one hand, gas-station map in the other, trying to make art out of the New Jersey Turnpike. Trying to make all those highways and freeways and Interstates and Tennessee and Georgia come alive for a family of mythological, nonexistent . . . hour after goddam miserable, backbreaking, cockamamie hour, and that San Juan candle dropping wax everywhere . . . "

His voice trailed off into the familiar disgusted mumble. "I don't know how I did it. Beagle. Don't ask me. All I knew for sure was, you can't let centaurs wander around lost in the Bronx—you can't, it's all wrong—and there I was."

"It'll get them to Mexico," I said. "I know it will."

"Yeah, well." The grin became a slow, rueful smile, less usual. "The weird thing, it's made me . . . I don't know *better*, but just *different*, some way. I'm never going to have to do anything like that again, thank God—and I bet I couldn't. But there's other stuff, things I never thought about trying before, and now it's all I'm doing in my head, right now—my head's full of stuff I have to do, even if I can't ever get it right. Even *though*." The smile faded, and he shrugged and looked away. "That's them. They did that."

I turned my coat collar up around my face. I said, "I read a story about a boy who draws cats so well that they come to life and fight off demons for him."

"Japanese," Phil said. "Good story. Listen, don't tell anybody, not even Jake and Marty. It gets out, they'll want me to do all kinds of stuff, all the time. And magic's not an all-the-time thing, you're not ever *entitled* to magic—not ever, no matter how good you are. Best you can do—all you can do—is make sure you're ready when it happens. If."

His voice had grown somber again, his eyes distant, focusing on nothing that I could recognize. Then he brightened abruptly, saying, "Still got the brushes, anyway. There's that. Whatever comes next, there's the brushes."

Weston offers customized insider tours of New York, but he never wants to take the tourists down to the unfinished city projects—tunnels, aborted subway stations, abandoned spaces—underneath the city he loves.

WESTON WALKS

KIT REED

When your life gets kicked out from under you like a chair you thought you were standing on, you start to plan. You swear: *Never again.* After the funeral Lawrence Weston sat in a velvet chair that was way too big for him while the lawyer read his parents' will out loud. He didn't care about how much he was getting; he only knew what he had lost and that he would do anything to keep it from happening again.

He was four.

Like a prince in the plague years, he pulled up the drawbridge and locked his heart against intruders. Nobody gets into Weston's tight, carefully furnished life, and nobody gets close enough to mess up his heart.

Now look.

When your money makes money you don't have to do anything—so nothing is what Weston ordinarily does, except on Saturdays, when he comes out to show the city to you. It isn't the money—don't ask how much he has—he just needs to hear the sound of a human voice. He lives alone because he likes it, but at the end of the day that's exactly what he is. Alone.

It's why he started Weston Walks.

He could afford an LED display in Times Square but he sticks to three lines in *The Village Voice*: "New York: an intimate view. Walk the city tourists never see."

He'll show you things you'll never find spawning upstream at Broadway and Forty-second Street or padding along Fifth Avenue in your puffy coats. This is *the insider's walking tour.*

Nobody wants to be an outsider, so you make the call. It's not like he will pick up. His phone goes on ringing in some place you can't envision, coming as you do from out of town. You hang on the phone, humming "pick up, pick up, pick up." When his machine takes your message, you're pathetically grateful. Excited, too. You are hooked by Weston's promise: *Tailored to your desires.*

What these are, he determines on the basis of a preliminary interview conducted over coffee at Balthazar, on him—or at Starbucks, on you—depending on how you are dressed, and whether he likes you well enough to spend the day with you, in which case he'll let you pay. He is deciding whether to take you on. No matter how stylish your outfit—or how tacky—if he doesn't like what he hears, he will slap a hundred or a twenty on the table at Balthazar or Starbucks, depending, and leave you there. It's not his fault he went to schools where you learn by osmosis what to do and what not to wear. It's not your fault that you come from some big town or small city where Weston would rather die than have to be. Whatever you want to see, Weston can find, and if you don't know what that is and he decides for you, consider yourself lucky. This is an insider tour!

You're itching to begin your Weston Walk, but you must wait until the tour is filled, and that takes time. Weston is very particular. At last! You meet on the designated street corner. You're the ones with the fanny packs, cameras, monster foam fingers, Deely Bobbers, Statue of Liberty crowns on the kids—unless you're the overdressed Southerner or one of those razor-thin foreigners in understated black and high-end boots. Weston's the guy in black jeans and laid-back sweater, holding the neatly lettered sign.

He is surprisingly young. Quieter than you'd hoped. Reserved, but in a good way. Nothing like the flacks leafleting in Times Square or bellowing from tour buses on Fifth Avenue or hawking buggy rides through Central Park. He will show you things that you've never seen before, from discos and downtown mud baths nobody knows about to the park where your favorite stars rollerblade to the exclusive precincts of the Academy of Arts and Letters—in the nosebleed district, it's so far uptown—to the marble grand staircase in the Metropolitan Club, which J. P. Morgan built after all the best clubs in the city turned him down.

Notice that at the end Weston says good-bye in Grand Central, at Ground Zero, or the northeast corner of Columbus Circle—some public place where he can shake hands and fade into the crowd. You may want to hug him, but you can't, which is just as well because he hates being touched. By the time you turn to ask one last question and sneak in a thank-you slap on the shoulder, he's gone.

He vanishes before you know that you and he are done.

You thought you were friends, but for all he knows, you might follow him home and rip off his Van Gogh or trash his beautiful things; you might just murder him, dispose of the body, and move into his vacant life. Don't try to call; he keeps the business phone set on silent. It's on the Pugin table in his front hall, and if you don't know who Pugin was, you certainly don't belong in his house.

The house is everything Weston hoped. Meticulously furnished, with treasures carefully placed. A little miracle of solitude. Leaving the upper-class grid at venerable St. Paul's and Harvard was like getting out of jail. No more roommates' clutter and intrusions, no more head-on collisions with other people's lives. He sees women on a temporary basis; he'll do anything for them, but he never brings them home, which is why it always ends. It's not Weston's fault he's fastidious. Remember, he's an orphaned only child. To survive, he needs everything perfect: sunlight on polished mahogany in his library, morning papers folded and coffee ready and housekeeper long gone, no outsiders, no family to badger him; they all died in that plane crash when he was four.

He spends days at his computer, although he deletes more than he types, lunches at a club even New Yorkers don't know about, hunts treasure in art galleries and secondhand bookstores, can get the best table wherever he wants, but girls?

He's waiting for one who cares about all the same things.

Too bad that Wings Germaine, and not the first tourist he booked, the one with the lovely phone voice, whom he loved on sight at the interview, shows up for the last-ever Weston Walking Tour. While thirteen lucky tourists gather at the subway kiosk on Seventy-second at Broadway, Wings is waiting elsewhere and for unstated reasons—down there.

Weston has no idea what's ahead. It's a sunny fall Saturday, light breeze, perfect for the classic Central Park walk, so what could be easier or more convenient? It's a half block from his house.

All he has to do is collect his group outside the kiosk, where they are milling with vacant smiles. They light up at the sight of his neatly lettered placard. Grinning, he stashes it in the back of his jeans, to be used only when for some unforeseen reason he loses one of them.

A glance tells him this is a Starbucks bunch. With their cameras and sagging fanny packs, they wouldn't be comfortable at chic old Café des Artistes, which is right around the corner from his house. It's not their fault their personal styles are, well, a bad match. But they are. He's one short, which bothers him. Where is that girl he liked so much? Too bad he has to move on, but maybe she'll catch up. *Nice day, nice enough people,* he thinks—with the possible exception of the burly tourist in the black warm-up jacket with the Marine Corps emblem picked out in gold, who walks with his shoulders bunched, leaning into a scowl.

Never mind. It's a beautiful day, and Weston is in charge. Happy and obedient, his tourists trot past the spot where John Lennon died and into the park on a zigzag, heading for the east side, where the Metropolitan Museum bulks above the trees like a mastodon lumbering away. He keeps up a lively patter, spinning stories as his people smile blandly and nod, nod, nod, all except the man with the scowl, who keeps looking at his watch.

Weston looks up: *Ooops.* Like a cutting horse, his ex-marine has the herd heading into a bad place.

Time to get out of here. He'll walk them south on Fifth, point out houses owned by people he used to know. "All right," he says brightly, "time to see how the rich people live."

"Wait." The big marine fills the path like a rhino bunched to charge. "You call this the insider tour?"

Smile, Weston. "Didn't I just . . . "

He points to a gap in the bushes; Weston knows it too well. "TAKE US THE FUCK INSIDE."

No! Behind those bushes, a gash in the rocks opens like a mouth. He can't go back! Weston struggles for that tour-guide tone. "What would you like to see?"

"Tunnels."

The ground underneath the park is laced with unfinished city projects—tunnels, aborted subway stations, all closed to them; Weston has researched, and he knows. "Oh," he says, relieved, "then you want City Spelunking Tours. I have their number and . . . "

"Not those. The ones real people dug. Nam vets. Old hippies."

"There aren't any—"

The big man finishes with a disarming grin. "Crazies like me. I have buddies down there."

"There's nothing down there." Weston shudders. *He's a client; don't offend.* "That's just urban legend, like a lot of other things you think you know. Now, if you like legends, I can take you to Frank E. Campbell's, where they have all the famous funerals, or the house where Stanford White got shot by Harry K. Thaw. . . . "

"No. DOWN!" The renegade tourist roars like a drill sergeant, and the group snaps to like first-day recruits. "Now. Moving out!"

Weston holds up his placard, shouting, "Wait!"

Too late. Like a pack of lemmings, the last-ever Weston Walking Tour falls in behind the big man.

They are heading into a very bad place. No, Weston doesn't want to talk about it. He waves his arms like signal flags. "Wrong way! There's nothing here!"

The marine whirls, shouting, "You fucking well know it's here."

The hell of it is, Weston does. He is intensely aware of the others in his little group: the newlyweds, the dreary anniversary couple, the plump librarian and the kid in the Derek Jeter shirt, the others are watching with cool, judgmental eyes. In spite of their cheap tourist claptrap and bland holiday smiles, they are not stupid people; they're fixed on the conflict, eager to see something ordinary tourists don't see. The authority of their guide is at issue. They are waiting to see how this plays out. There is an intolerable pause.

"Well?"

One more minute and the last Weston Walking Tour will die of holding its breath.

If you knew what Weston knew, you would be afraid.

His only friend at St. Paul's vanished on their senior class trip to the city. One minute weird Ted Bishop was hunched on the steps of the Museum of Natural History, shivering under a long down coat that was brown and shiny as a cockroach's shell and zipped to the chin on the hottest day of the year. Then he was gone.

Last winter Weston ran into Bishop on Third Avenue, with that same ratty coat leaking feathers and encrusted with mud. It was distressing; he did what he could. He took him into a restaurant and bought him hot food, looked away when his best friend stuffed everything he couldn't devour into his pockets with the nicest smile. "I went crazy. I hid because I didn't want you to know."

"I wouldn't have minded." Weston's stomach convulsed.

"At first I was scared but then, Weston. Oh!"

It was terrifying, all that naked emotion, so close. He shrank, as if whatever Ted had was catching.

"Then they found me." Bishop's pale face gleamed. "Man, there's a whole world down there. I suppose you think I'm nuts."

"Not really." Weston reached for a gag line. "I thought you'd gotten a better offer."

"I did!" Ted lit up like an alabaster lamp. "One look and I knew: *These are my people. And this is my place!* You have to see!"

"I'll try." He did; he followed the poor bastard to the entrance—it's right behind these bushes, he knows—and stopped. . . . "Wait."

. . . and heard Ted's voice overlapping, "Wait. I have to tell them you're coming. You *will* wait for me, right?"

Weston wanted to be brave, but he could not lie. "I'll try."

He couldn't stop Ted, either. The tunnel walls shifted behind his friend as if something huge had swallowed him in its sleep. Its foul breath gushed out of the hole; Weston heard the earth panting, waiting to swallow him. Forgive him, he fled.

Awful place, he vowed never to . . . But they are waiting. "Okay," he says finally, plunging into the bushes like a diver into a pool full of sharks. "Okay."

With the others walking up his heels, Weston looks down into the hole. It's dark as death. Relieved, he looks up. "Sorry, we can't do it today. Not without flashlights. Now—"

"Got it covered." The veteran produces a bundle—halogen miner's lamps on headbands. Handing them out, he says the obvious, "Always . . ."

Weston groans. "Prepared."

He stands by as his tourists drop into the tunnel, one by one. If they don't come out, what will he tell their families? Will they sue? Will he go to jail? He's happy to stand at the brink mulling it, but the marine shoves him into the hole. "Your turn."

He drops in after Weston, shutting out daylight with his bulk. The only way they can go is down.

All his life since his parents died, Lawrence Weston has taken great pains to control his environment. Now he is in a place he never imagined. Life goes on, but everything flies out of control. He is part of *this* now, blundering into the ground.

Weston doesn't know what he expects: rats, lurking dragons, thugs with billy clubs, a tribe of pale, blind mutants, or a bunch of gaudy neo-hippies in sordid underground squats. In fact, several passages fan out from the main entrance, rough tunnels leading to larger caverns with entrances and exits of their own; the underground kingdom is bigger than he feared. He had no idea it would be so old. Debris brought down from the surface to shore up the burrow sticks out of the mud and stone like a schoolchild's display of artifacts from every era. The mud plastering the walls is studded with hardware from the streetcar/gaslight 1890s, fragments of glass and plastic from the Day-Glo skateboard 1990s, and motherboards, abandoned CRTs, bumpers from cars that are too new to carbon date. The walls are buttressed by four-by-fours, lit by LED bulbs strung from wires, but Weston moves along in a crouch, as though the earth is just about to collapse on his head—which might be merciful, given the fumes. Although fresh air is coming in from somewhere, there is the intolerable stink of mud and small dead things, and although to his surprise this tunnel, at least, is free of the expected stink of piss and excrement, there is the smell that comes of too many people living too close together, an overpoweringly human fug.

At first Weston sees nobody, hears nothing he can make sense of, knows only that he can't be in this awful place.

Dense air weighs on him so he can hardly breathe—the effluvia of human souls. Then a voice rises in the passage ahead, a girl's bright, almost-festive patter running along ahead of his last-ever Weston Walking Tour, as though she and the hulking marine, and not Weston, are in charge.

Meanwhile the mud walls widen as the path goes deeper. The tunnels are lined with people, their pale faces gleaming wherever he flashes his miner's lamp, and it is terrifying. The man who tried so hard to keep all the parts of his life exactly where he put them has lost any semblance of control; the orphan who lived alone because it was safest is trapped in the earth, crowded—no, surrounded—by souls, dozens, perhaps hundreds of others with their needs, their grief and sad secrets and emotional demands.

The pressure of their hopes staggers him.

All at once the lifelong solo flier comprehends what he read in Ted Bishop's face that day, and why he fled. Educated, careful, and orderly and self-contained as Lawrence Weston tries so hard to be, only a tissue of belief separates him from them.

Now they are all around him.

I can't. Every crease in his body is greased with the cold sweat of claustrophobia. *I won't.*

He has forgotten how to breathe. One more minute and . . . He doesn't know. Frothing, he wheels, cranked up to fight the devil if he has to, anything to get out of here: he'll tear the hulking veteran apart with teeth and nails, offer money, do murder or, if he has to, die in the attempt—anything to escape the dimly perceived but persistent, needy humanity seething underground.

As it turns out, he doesn't have to do any of these things. The bulky vet lurches forward with a big-bear rumble. *"Semper Fi."*

In the dimness ahead, a ragged, gravelly chorus responds: *"Semper Fi."*

The marine shoulders Weston aside. "Found 'em. Now, shove off. Round up your civilians and move 'em out."

Miraculously, he does. He pulls the WESTON WALKS placard out of the back of his jeans and raises it, pointing the headlamp so his people will see the sign. Then he blows the silver whistle he keeps for emergencies and never had to use.

It makes the tunnels shriek.

"Okay," he says with all the force he has left in his body. "Time to go! On to Fifth Avenue and . . . " He goes on in his best tour-guide voice; it's a desperation move, but Weston is desperate enough to offer them anything. "The Russian Tea Room! I'll treat. Dinner at the Waldorf, suites for the night, courtesy of Weston Walking Tours."

Oddly, when they emerge into fresh air and daylight—*dear God, it's still light*—the group is no smaller, but it is different. It takes Weston a minute to figure out what's changed. The bulky ex-marine with an agenda is gone, an absence he could have predicted, but when he lines them up at the bus stop (yes, he is shaking quarters into the coin drop on a city bus!), he still counts thirteen. Newlyweds, yes; anniversary couple; librarian; assorted bland, satisfied middle Americans, yes; pimply kid. The group looks the same, but it isn't. He is too disrupted, troubled, and distracted to know who . . .

Safe at last in the Russian Tea Room, he knows which one she is, or thinks he knows, because unlike the others, she looks perfectly comfortable here: lovely woman with tousled hair, buff little body wrapped in a big gray sweater with sleeves pulled down over her fingertips; when she reaches for the samovar with a gracious offer to pour he is startled by a flash of black-rimmed fingernails. Never mind; maybe it's a fashion statement he hasn't caught up with.

Instead of leading his group to Times Square or Grand Central for the ceremonial send-off so he can fade into the crowd, he leaves them at the Waldorf, all marveling as they wait at the elevators for the concierge to show them to their complimentary suites.

Spent and threatened by his close encounter with life, Weston flees.

The first thing he does when he gets home is pull his ad and trash the business phone. Then he does what murderers and rape victims do in movies, after the fact: He spends hours under a hot shower, washing away the event. It will be days before he's fit to go out. He quiets shattered nerves by numbering the beautiful objects in the ultimate safe house he has created, assuages grief with coffee and the day's papers in the sunlit library, taking comfort from small rituals. He needs to visit his father's Turner watercolor, stroke the smooth flank of the Brancusi marble in the foyer, study his treasure, a little Remington bronze.

When he does go out some days later, he almost turns and goes back in. The sexy waif from the tour is on his front steps. Same sweater, same careless toss of the head. The intrusion makes his heart stop and his belly tremble, but the girl who poured so nicely at the Russian Tea Room greets him with a delighted smile.

"I thought you'd never come out."

"You have no right, you have no *right*. . . ." She looks so pleased that he starts over. "What are you doing here?"

"I live in the neighborhood." She challenges him with that gorgeous smile.

How do you explain to a pretty girl that she has no right to track you to your lair? How can you tell any New Yorker that your front steps are private, specific only to you? How can you convince her that your life is closed to intruders, or that she is one?

He can't. "I have to go!"

"Where are you—"

Staggered by a flashback—tunnel air repeating like something he ate—Weston is too disturbed to make polite excuses, beep his driver, manage any of the usual exit lines. "China!" he blurts, and escapes.

At the corner he wheels to make sure he's escaped and gasps: "Oh!"

Following him at a dead run, she smashes into him with a stirring little *thud* that splits his heart, exposing it to the light. Oh, the chipped tooth that flashes when she grins. "Um, China this very minute?"

Yes, he is embarrassed. "Well, not really. I mean. Coffee first."

She tugs down the sweater sleeves, beaming. "Let's! I'll pay."

By the time they finish their cappuccinos and he figures out how to get out without hurting her feelings, he's in love.

How does a man like Weston fall in love?

Accidentally. Fast. It's nothing he can control. Still he manages to part from Wings Germaine without letting his hands shake or his eyes mist over; he must not do anything that will tip her off to the fact that this is the last good time. He even manages to hug good-bye without clinging, although it wrecks his heart. "It's been fun," he says. "I have to go."

"No big. Nothing is forever," she says, exposing that chipped tooth.

Dying a little, he backs away with a careful smile. To keep the life he's built so lovingly, he has to, but it's hard. "So, bye."

Her foggy voice curls around him and clings. "Take care."

They're friends now, or what passes for friends, so he trusts her not to follow. Even though it's barely four in the afternoon he locks his front door behind him, checks the windows, and sets the alarm.

That beautiful girl seemed to be running ahead of his thoughts so fast that when they exchanged life stories she saw the pain running along underneath the surface of the story he usually tells. Her triangular smile broke his heart. "I'm so sorry," she said.

"Don't be," he told her. "It's nothing you did."

"No," she said. "Oh, no. But I've been there, and I know what it's like."

Orphaned, he assumed. *Like me,* he thinks, although she is nothing like him. Named in honor of her fighter-pilot father, she said. Art student, she said, but she never said when. Mystifyingly, she said, "You have some beautiful stuff." Had he told her about the Calder maquette and forgotten, or mentioned the Sargent portrait of his great-grandfather or the Manet oil sketch? He has replayed that conversation a dozen times today and he still doesn't know.

At night, even though he's secured the house and is safely locked into his bedroom, he has a hard time going to sleep. Before he can manage it, he has to get up several times and repeat his daytime circuit of the house. He patrols rooms lit only by reflected streetlights, padding from one to the next in T-shirt and pajama bottoms, touching table tops with light fingers, running his hands over the smooth marble flank of the Brancusi, because every object is precious and he needs to know that each is in its appointed place.

Day or night, Weston is ruler of his tight little world, secure in the confidence that although he let himself be waylaid by a ragged stranger today, although he ended up doing what she wanted instead of what he intended, here, at least, he commands the world.

Then why can't he sleep?

The fourth time he goes downstairs in the dark he finds her sitting in his living room. At first he imagines his curator has moved a new Degas bronze into the house in the dead of night. Then he realizes it's Wings Germaine, positioned like an ornament on his ancestral brocade sofa, sitting with her arms locked around her knees.

"What," he cries, delighted, angry and terrified. "What!"

Wings moves into his arms so fluidly that the rest flows naturally, like a soft, brilliant dream. "I was in the neighborhood."

They are together in a variety of intense configurations until Weston gasps with joy and falls away from her, exhausted. Drenched in sense memory, he plummets into sleep.

When the housekeeper comes to wake him in the morning, Wings is gone.

By day Weston is the same person; days pass in their usual sweet order, but his nights go by in that fugue of images of Wings Germaine, who hushes his mouth with kisses whenever he tries to ask who she is and how she gets in or whether what they have together is real or imagined. No matter how he wheedles, she doesn't explain; "I live in the neighborhood," she says, and the pleasure of being *this close* quiets his heart. He acknowledges the possibility that the girl is, rather, only hallucination and—astounding for a man so bent on control—he accepts that.

As long as his days pass in order, he tells himself, as long as nothing changes, he'll be okay. He thinks.

When Wings arrives she does what she does so amazingly that he's never quite certain what happened, only that it leaves him joyful and exhausted; then she leaves. His nights are marvels, uncomplicated by the pressure of the usual lover's expectations, because they both know she will be gone before the sun comes up. She always is. He wakes up alone, to coffee and the morning paper, sunlight on mahogany. Their nights are wild and confusing, but in the daytime world that Weston has spent his life perfecting, everything is reassuringly the same.

Or so he tells himself. It's what he has to believe. If he saw any of this for what it is, he'd have to act, and the last thing Weston wants right now is for his dizzy collisions in the night to end.

Until today, when he hurtles out of sleep at 4:00 A.M. Panic wakes him, the roar of blood thundering in his ears. His synapses clash in serial car crashes; the carnage is terrible. He slides out of bed in the gray dawn and bolts downstairs, lunging from room to room, shattered by the certain knowledge that something has changed.

Unless everything has changed.

What, he wonders, running a finger over tabletops, the rims of picture frames, the outlines of priceless maquettes by famous sculptors, all still in place, reassuringly *there*. What?

Dear God, his Picasso plates are missing. Treasures picked up off the master's studio floor by Great-grandfather Weston, who walked away with six signed plates under his arm, leaving behind a thousand dollars and the memory of his famous smile. Horrified, he turns on the light. Pale circles mark the silk wallpaper where the plates hung; empty brackets sag, reproaching him.

He doesn't mention this to Wings when she comes to him that night; he only breathes into her crackling hair and holds her closer, thinking, *It can't be her. She couldn't have, it couldn't be Wings.*

Then he buries himself in her because he knows it is.

Before dawn she leaves Weston drowsing in his messy bed, dazed and grateful. His nights continue to pass like dreams; the rich orphan so bent on life without intrusions welcomes the wild girl in spite of certain losses; love hurts, but he wants what he wants. Their time together passes without reference to the fact that when Weston comes down tomorrow his King George silver service will be missing, to be followed by his Kang dynasty *netsuke,* and then his best Miró. *I love her too much,* he tells himself as objects disappear daily. *I don't want this to stop.*

He inspects. All his external systems remain in place. Alarms are set; there's no sign of forcible entry or exit. It is as though things he thought he prized more than any woman have dropped into the earth without explanation.

He can live without these things, he tells himself. He can! Love is love, and these are only objects.

Until the Brancusi marble goes missing.

In a spasm of grief, his heart empties out.

Wings won't know when they make love that night that her new man is only going through the motions—unless she does know, which straightforward Weston is too new at deception to guess. He does the girl with one eye on the door, which is how he assumes she exits once she's pushed him off the deep end into sleep—which she has done nightly, vanishing before he wakes up.

Careful, Wings. Tonight will be different.

To him, Wings is a closed book.

He needs to crack her open like a piñata and watch the secrets fall out.

Guilty and terrible as he feels about doubting her, confused because he can't bear to lose *one more thing,* he can't let this go on. With Wings still in his arms he struggles to stay awake, watching through slitted eyes for what seems like forever. She drowses; he waits. The night passes like a dark thought, sullenly dragging its feet. Waiting is terrible. By the time a crack of gray light outlines his bedroom blackout shades, he's about to die of it. The girl he loves sighs and delicately disengages herself. Grieving, he watches through slitted eyes, and when she goes, he counts to twenty and follows.

He knows the house better than Wings; she'll take the back stairs, so he hurries down the front. When she sneaks into the central hall and silences the alarm so she can escape with another of his treasures, he'll spring. Sliding into the niche behind the Brancusi's empty pedestal, he crouches until his joints crack, echoing in the silent house. He has no idea how she escaped.

Damn fool, he thinks, and does not know which of them he's mad at, himself or elusive Wings Germaine.

When they lie down together after midnight, Weston's fears have eased: of being caught following—the tears of regret, the recriminations—unless his greatest fear was that she wasn't coming back because she knew.

Did she know he followed? Does she?

She slides into his arms in the nightly miracle that he has come to expect, and he pulls her close with a sigh. What will he do after he ends this? What will she steal from him tonight, and what will she do when he confronts her? He doesn't know, but it's long overdue. When she slips out of bed before first light, he gives her time to take the back stairs and then follows. Like a shadow, he drifts through darkened rooms where the girl moves so surely that he knows she must linger here every night, having her way with his treasured things.

With the swift, smooth touch of a child molester, she strokes his family of objects but takes nothing.

Damn! Is he waiting for her to steal? What is she waiting for? Why doesn't she grab something so he can pounce and finish this?

Empty-handed, she veers toward the darkened kitchen.

Weston's back hairs rise and tremble as Wings opens the door to the smoky stone cellar and starts down.

His heart sags. Is that all she is? A generic homeless person with a sordid squat in a corner of his dank basement? When Wings Germaine comes to his bed at night she is freshly scrubbed; she smells of wood smoke and rich earth, and in the part of his head where fantasies have moved in and set up housekeeping, Weston wants to believe that she's fresh from her own rooftop terrace or just in from a day on her country estate.

Idiot.

He has two choices here. He can go back to bed and pretend what he must in order to keep things as they are in spite of escalating losses—or he can track her to her lair.

But, oh! The missing furniture of his life, the art. His Brancusi! What happened to them? Has she sneaked his best things out of the house and fenced them, or does she keep them stashed in some secret corner of his cellar for reasons she will never explain? Is his treasured Miró safe? Is anything? He has to know.

Oh, lover. It is a cry from the heart. *Forgive me.*

He goes down.

The cellar is empty. Wings isn't anywhere. He shines his caretaker's flashlight in every corner and underneath all the shelves and into empty niches in Great-grandfather's wine rack, but there is no sign. It takes him all morning to be absolutely certain, hours in which the housekeeper trots around the kitchen overhead making his breakfast, putting his coffee cup and the steaming carafe, his orange juice and cinnamon toast—and a rose, because roses are in season—on his breakfast tray. He times the woman's trips back and forth to the library where he eats, her visit to his bedroom where she will change his sheets without remarking, because she does it every day; he waits for her to finish, punch in the code, and leave by the kitchen door. Then he waits another hour.

When he's sure the house is empty, Weston goes back upstairs for the klieg lights his folks bought for a home tour the year they died.

Bright as they are, they don't show him much. There are cartons of books in this old cellar, bundles of love letters that he's afraid to read. His parents' skis, the ice skates they bought him the Christmas he turned four, the sled—all remnants of his long-lost past. This is the sad but ordinary basement of an ordinary man who has gone through life with his upper lip stiffer than is normal and his elbows clamped to his sides. It makes him sigh.

Maybe he imagined Wings Germaine.

Then, when he's just about to write her off as a figment of his imagination, and the missing pieces, up to and including the Brancusi, as the work of his housekeeper or the guy who installed the alarms, he sees that the floor in front of the wine rack is uneven and that there are fingerprints on one stone.

Very well. He could be Speke, starting out after Burton, or Livingstone, heading up the Zambezi. The shell Weston has built around himself hardens so that only he will hear his heart crack as he finishes: *Alone.*

When she comes back too long after midnight, he is waiting: provisioned this time, equipped with pick and miner's light—because he thinks he knows where Wings is going—handcuffs, and a length of rope. He will follow her down. Never mind what Weston thinks in the hours while he crouches in his own basement like a sneak thief, waiting; don't try to parse the many heartbroken, reproachful, angry escalating to furious, ultimately threatening speeches he writes and then discards.

The minute that stone moves, he'll lunge. If he's fast enough, he can grab her as she comes out; if she's faster and drops back into the hole, then like a jungle cat, he will plunge in after her and bring her down. Then he'll kneel on the woman's chest and pin her wrists and keep her there until she explains. He already knows that eventually he'll soften and give her one more chance, but it will be on his terms.

She'll have to pack up her stuff and move into his handsome house and settle down in his daytime life, because he is probably in love with her. Then he'll have every beautiful thing that he cares about secured in the last safe place.

And, by God, she'll bring all his stuff back. She will!

He's been staring at the stone for so long that he almost forgets to douse the light when it moves. He manages it just as the stone scrapes aside like a manhole cover and her head pops up.

"Oh," she cries, although he has no idea how she knows he is crouching here in the dark. "Oh, fuck."

It's a long way to the bottom. The fall is harder than he thought. By the time he hits the muddy floor of the tunnel underneath his house, Wings Germaine is gone.

He is alone in the narrow tunnel, riveted by the possibility that it's a dead end and there's no way out.

He's even more terrified because a faint glow tells him that there is. To follow Wings, he has to crawl on and out, into the unknown.

Weston goes along on mud-caked hands and slimy knees for what seems like forever before he comes to a place big enough to stand up in. It's a lot like the hole where the runaway tourist stampeded him, but it is nothing like it. The man-made grotto is wired and strung with dim lights; the air is as foul as it was in the hole where Ted Bishop disappeared, but this one is deserted. He is at a rude crossroads. Access tunnels snake out in five directions, and he has to wonder which one she took and how far they go.

Stupid bastard, he calls, "Wings?"

There is life down here, Weston knows it; *she* is down here, but he has no idea which way she went or where she is hiding or, in fact, whether she is hiding from him. A man in his right mind, even a heartbroken lover, would go back the way he came, haul himself up and station his caretaker by the opening with a shotgun to prevent incursions until he could mix enough concrete to fill the place and cement the stone lid down so no matter what else happened in his house, she would never get back inside.

Instead he cries, "Wings. Oh, Wings!"

He knows better than to wait. If anything is going to happen here, he has to make it happen.

The idea terrifies him. Worse. There are others here.

For the first time in his well-ordered life, careful Weston, who vowed never to lose anybody or anything he cared about, is lost.

The chamber is empty for the moment, but there is life going on just out of sight; he hears the unknown stirring in hidden grottoes, moving through tunnels like arteries—approaching, for all he knows. The knowledge is suffocating. The man who needs to be alone understands that other lives are unfolding down here; untold masses are deep in their caverns doing God knows what. A born solitary, he is staggered by the pressure of all those unchecked lives raging out of sight and beyond the law or any of the usual agencies of control.

Encroaching. *God!*

Trembling, he tries, "Wings?"

As if she cares enough to answer.

The tunnels give back nothing. He wants to run after her but he doesn't know where. Worse, she may see him not as a lover in pursuit but a giant rat scuttling after food. He should search but he's afraid of what he will find. Much as he misses his things, he's afraid to find out what Wings has done with them and who she is doing it with.

Overturned, he retreats to the mouth of the tunnel that leads to his house and hunkers down to think.

There are others out there—too many! Accustomed now, Weston can sense them, hear them, smell them in the dense underground air, connected by this tunnel to the treasures he tries so hard to protect. The labyrinth is teeming with life, but he is reluctant to find out who the others are or how they are. They could be trapped underground like him, miserable and helpless, snapped into fetal position in discrete pits they have dug for themselves. They could be killing each other out there, or lying tangled in wild, orgiastic knots doing amazing things to each other in communal passion pits, or thinking great thoughts, writing verse or plotting revolution, or they could be locked into lotus position in individual niches, halfway to Nirvana or—no!—they could be trashing his stolen art. He doesn't want to know.

It is enough to know that for the moment, he is alone at a dead end and that, in a way, it's a relief.

Surprise. For the first time since the runaway tourist forced him underground and Wings flew up to the surface and messed up his life, Weston has nothing to hope for and no place to go. And for the first time since he was four years old, he feels safe.

After a time he takes the pick he had strapped to his backpack in case and begins to dig.

In the hours or days that follow, Weston eats, he supposes: By the time the hole is big enough to settle down in, his supply of granola bars is low and the water in his canteen is almost gone, but he is not ready to go back into his house. In between bouts of digging, he probably sleeps.

Mostly he thinks and then stops thinking, as his mind empties out and leaves him drifting in the zone. What zone, he could not say. What he wants and where this will end, he is too disturbed and disrupted to guess.

Then, just when he has adjusted to being alone in this snug, reassuringly tight place, when he is resigned to the fact that he'll never see her again, she comes, flashing into life before him like an apparition and smiling that sexy and annoying, enigmatic smile.

"Wings!"

Damn that wild glamour, damn the cloud of tousled hair, damn her for saying with that indecipherable, superior air, "What makes you think I'm really here?"

The girl folds as neatly as a collapsible tripod and sits cross-legged on the floor of the hole Weston has dug, fixed in place in front of him, sitting right here where he can see her, waiting for whatever comes next.

It's better not to meet her eyes. Not now, when he is trying to think. It takes him longer than it should to frame the question.

"What have you done with my stuff?"

Damn her for answering the way she does. "What do you care? It's only stuff."

Everything he ever cared about simply slides away.

They sit together in Weston's tight little pocket in the earth. They are quiet for entirely too long. She doesn't leave but she doesn't explain, either. She doesn't goad him and she doesn't offer herself. She just sits there regarding him. It's almost more than he can bear.

A question forms deep inside Weston's brain and moves slowly, like a parasite drilling its way to the surface. Finally it explodes into the still, close air. "Are you the devil, or what?"

This makes her laugh. "Whatever, sweetie. What do you think?"

"I don't know," he shouts. "I don't know!"

"So get used to it."

But he can't. He won't. More or less content with his place in the narrow hole he has dug for himself, Weston says, "It's time for you to go," and when she hesitates, wondering, he pushes Wings Germaine outside and nudges her along the access tunnel to the hub, the one place where they can stand, facing. She gasps and recoils. To his astonishment, he is brandishing the pick like a club. Then he clamps his free hand on her shoulder, and with no clear idea what he will do when this part is done or what comes next, he turns Wings Germaine in his steely grip and sends her away. Before he ducks back into his territory Weston calls after her on a note that makes clear to both of them that they are done. "Don't come back."

Behind him, the cellar waits, but he can't know whether he wants to go back to his life. He is fixed on what he has to do. Resolved, relieved because he know this at least, he sets to work on the exit where he left her, erasing it with his pick.

In the alternate universe of Wild Cards, reality diverged from ours on September 15, 1946, when an alien virus was released in the skies over Manhattan, and spread across an unsuspecting Earth. Of those infected, 90% died horribly, drawing the black queen, 9% were twisted and deformed into jokers, while a lucky 1% gained extraordinary and unpredictable powers that made them aces.

SHELL GAMES

GEORGE R. R. MARTIN

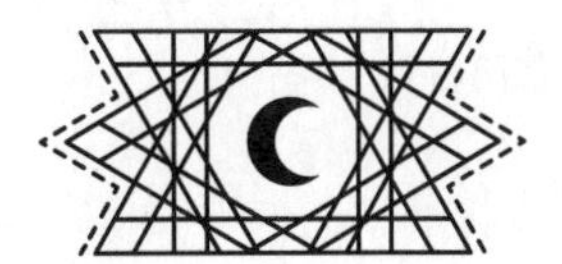

When he'd moved into the dorm back in September, the first thing that Thomas Tudbury had done was tack up his signed photograph of President Kennedy, and the tattered 1944 *Time* cover with Jetboy as Man of the Year.

By November, the picture of Kennedy was riddled with holes from Rodney's darts. Rod had decorated his side of the room with a Confederate flag and a dozen *Playboy* centerfolds. He hated Jews, niggers, jokers, and Kennedy, and didn't like Tom much either. All through the fall semester, he had fun; covering Tom's bed with shaving cream, short-sheeting him, hiding his eyeglasses, filling his desk drawer with dog turds.

On the day that Kennedy was killed in Dallas, Tom came back to his room fighting to hold the tears. Rod had left him a present. He'd used a red pen. The whole top of Kennedy's head was dripping blood now, and over his eyes Rod had drawn little red Xs. His tongue was sticking out of the corner of his mouth.

Thomas Tudbury stared at that for a long, long time. He did not cry; he would not allow himself to cry. He began to pack his suitcases.

The freshman parking lot was halfway across campus. The trunk on his '54 Mercury had a broken lock, so he tossed the bags into the seat. He let the car warm up for a long time in the November chill. He must have looked funny sitting there; a short, overweight guy with a crew cut and horn-rim glasses, pressing his head against the top of the steering wheel like he was going to be sick.

As he was driving out of the lot, he spied Rodney's shiny Olds Cutlass.

Tom shifted to neutral and idled for a moment, considering. He looked around. There was no one in sight; everybody was inside watching the news. He licked his lips nervously, then looked back at the Oldsmobile. His knuckles whitened around the wheel. He stared hard, furrowed his brow, and *squeezed.*

The door panels gave first, bending inward slowly under the pressure. The headlights exploded with small pops, one after the other. Chrome trim clattered to the ground, and the rear windshield shattered suddenly, glass flying everywhere. Fenders buckled and collapsed, metal squealing in protest. Both rear tires blew at once, the side panels caved in, then the hood; the windshield disintegrated entirely. The crankcase gave, and then the walls of the gas tank; oil, gasoline, and transmission fluid pooled under the car. By then Tom Tudbury was more confident, and that made it easier. He imagined he had the Olds caught in a huge invisible fist, a *strong* fist, and he squeezed all the harder. The crunch of breaking glass and the scream of tortured metal filled the parking lot, but there was no one to hear. He methodically mashed the Oldsmobile into a ball of crushed metal.

When it was over, he shifted into gear and left college, Rodney, and childhood behind forever.

Somewhere a giant was crying.

Tachyon woke disoriented and sick, his hangover throbbing in time to the mammoth sobs. The shapes in the dark room were strange and unfamiliar. Had the assassins come in the night again, was the family under attack? He had to find his father. He lurched dizzily to his feet, head swimming, and put a hand against the wall to steady himself.

The wall was too close. These weren't his chambers, this was all wrong, the smell . . . and then the memories came back. He would have preferred the assassins.

He had dreamed of Takis again, he realized. His head hurt, and his throat was raw and dry. Fumbling in the darkness, he found the chain-pull for the overhead light. The bulb swung wildly when he yanked, making the shadows dance. He closed his eyes to still the lurching in his gut. There was a foul taste at the back of his mouth. His hair was matted and filthy, his clothing rumpled. And worst of all, the bottle was empty. Tachyon looked around helplessly. A six-by-ten on the second floor of a lodging house named ROOMS, on a street called the Bowery. Confusingly, the surrounding neighborhood had once been called the Bowery too—Angelface had told him that. But that was before; the area had a different name now. He went to the window, pulling up the shade. The yellow light of a streetlamp filled the room. Across the street, the giant was reaching for the moon, and weeping because he could not grasp it.

Tiny, they called him. Tachyon supposed that was human wit. Tiny would have been fourteen feet tall if only he could stand up. His face was unlined and innocent, crowned with a tangle of soft dark hair. His legs were slender, and perfectly proportioned. And that was the joke: slender, perfectly proportioned legs could not begin to support the weight of a fourteen-foot-tall man. Tiny sat in a wooden wheelchair, a great mechanized thing that rolled through the streets of Jokertown on four bald tires from a wrecked semi. When he saw Tach in the window, he screamed incoherently, almost as though he recognized him. Tachyon turned away from the window, shaking. It was another Jokertown night. He needed a drink.

His room smelled of mildew and vomit, and it was very cold. ROOMS was not as well heated as the hotels he had frequented in the old days. Unbidden, he remembered the Mayflower down in Washington, where he and Blythe . . . but no, better not to think of that. What time was it anyway? Late enough. The sun was down, and Jokertown came to life at night.

He plucked his overcoat from the floor and slipped it on. Soiled as it was, it was still a marvelous coat, a lovely rich rose color, with fringed golden epaulets on the shoulders and loops of golden braid to fasten the long row of buttons. A musician's coat, the man at the Goodwill had told him. He sat on the edge of his sagging mattress to pull on his boots.

The washroom was down at the end of the hall. Steam rose from his urine as it splashed against the rim of the toilet; his hands shook so badly that he couldn't even aim right. He slapped cold, rust-colored water on his face, and dried his hands on a filthy towel.

Outside, Tach stood for a moment beneath the creaking ROOMS sign, staring at Tiny. He felt bitter and ashamed. And much too sober. There was nothing to be done about Tiny, but he could deal with his sobriety. He turned his back on the weeping giant, slid his hands deep into the pockets of his coat, and walked off briskly down the Bowery.

In the alleys, jokers and winos passed brown paper bags from hand to hand, and stared with dull eyes at the passersby. Taverns, pawnbrokers, and mask shops were all doing a brisk trade. The Famous Bowery Wild Card Dime Museum (they still called it that, but admission was a quarter now) was closing for the day. Tachyon had gone through it once, two years ago, on a day when he was feeling especially guilt-ridden; along with a half-dozen particularly freakish jokers, twenty jars of "monstrous joker babies" floating in formaldehyde, and a sensational little newsreel about the Day of the Wild Card, the museum had a waxworks display whose dioramas featured Jetboy, the Four Aces, a Jokertown Orgy . . . and him.

A tour bus rolled past, pink faces pressed to the windows. Beneath the neon light of a neighborhood pizza parlor, four youths in black leather jackets and rubber facemasks eyed Tachyon with open hostility. They made him uneasy. He averted his eyes and dipped into the mind of the nearest: *mincing pansy looka that hair dye-job fershure thinks he's inna marching band like to beat his fuckin' drums but no wait shit there's better we'll find us a good one tonight yeah wanna get one that squishes when we hit it.* Tach broke the contact with distaste and hurried on. It was old news, and a new sport: come down to the Bowery, buy some masks, beat up a joker. The police didn't seem to care.

The Chaos Club and its famous All-Joker Revue had the usual big crowd. As Tachyon approached, a long gray limo pulled up to the curb. The doorman, wearing a black tuxedo over luxuriant white fur, opened the door with his tail and helped out a fat man in a dinner jacket. His date was a buxom teenager in a strapless evening gown and pearls, her blonde hair piled high in a bouffant hairdo.

A block farther on, a snake-lady called out a proposition from the top of a nearby stoop. Her scales were rainbow-colored, glistening. "Don't be scared, Red," she said, "it's still soft inside." He shook his head.

The Funhouse was housed in a long building with giant picture windows fronting the street, but the glass had been replaced with oneway mirrors. Randall stood out front, shivering in tails and domino.

He looked perfectly normal—until you noticed that he never took his right hand out of his pocket. "Hey, Tacky," he called out. "Whattaya make of Ruby?"

"Sorry, I don't know her," Tachyon said.

Randall scowled. "No, the guy who killed Oswald."

"Oswald?" Tach said, confused. "Oswald who?"

"Lee Oswald, the guy who shot Kennedy. He got killed on TV this afternoon."

"Kennedy's dead?" Tachyon said. It was Kennedy who'd permitted his return to the United States, and Tach admired the Kennedys; they seemed almost Takisian. But assassination was part of leadership. "His brothers will avenge him," he said. Then he recalled that they didn't do things that way on Earth, and besides, this man Ruby had already avenged him, it seemed. How strange that he had dreamed of assassins.

"They got Ruby in jail," Randall was saying. "If it was me, I'd give the fucker a medal." He paused. "He shook my hand once," he added. "When he was running against Nixon, he came through to give a speech at the Chaos Club. Afterward, when he was leaving, he was shaking hands with everybody." The doorman took his right hand out of his pocket. It was hard and chitinous, insectile, and in the middle was a cluster of swollen blind eyes. "He didn't even flinch," Randall said. "Smiled and said he hoped I'd remember to vote."

Tachyon had known Randall for a year, but he had never seen his hand before. He wanted to do what Kennedy had done, to grasp that twisted claw, embrace it, shake it. He tried to slide his hand out of the pocket of his coat, but the bile rose in the back of his throat, and somehow all he could do was look away, and say, "He was a good man." Randall hid his hand again. "Go on inside, Tacky," he said, not unkindly. "Angelface had to go and see a man, but she told Des to keep your table open."

Tachyon nodded and let Randall open the door for him. Inside, he gave his coat and shoes to the girl in the checkroom, a joker with a trim little body whose feathered owl mask concealed whatever the wild card had done to her face. Then he pushed through the interior doors, his stockinged feet sliding with smooth familiarity over the mirrored floor. When he looked down, another Tachyon was staring back up at him, framed by his feet; a grossly fat Tachyon with a head like a beach ball.

Suspended from the mirrored ceiling, a crystal chandelier glittered with a hundred pinpoint lights, its reflections sparkling off the floor tiles and walls and mirrored alcoves, the silvered goblets and mugs, and even the waiters' trays. Some of the mirrors reflected true; the others were distorting mirrors, funhouse mirrors. When you looked over your shoulder in the Funhouse, you could never tell what you'd find looking back. It was the only establishment in Jokertown that attracted jokers and normals in equal numbers. In the Funhouse the normals could see themselves twisted and malformed, and giggle, and play at being jokers; and a joker, if he was very lucky, might glance in the right mirror and see himself as he once had been.

"Your booth is waiting, Doctor Tachyon," said Desmond, the maître d'. Des was a large, florid man; his thick trunk, pink and wrinkled, curled around a wine list. He lifted it, and beckoned for Tachyon to follow with one of the fingers that dangled from its end. "Will you be having your usual brand of cognac tonight?"

"Yes," Tach said, wishing he had some money for a tip.

That night he had his first drink for Blythe, as always, but his second was for John Fitzgerald Kennedy.

The rest were for himself.

At the end of Hook Road, past the abandoned refinery and the import/export warehouses, past the railroad sidings with their forlorn red boxcars, beneath the highway underpass, past the empty lots full of weeds and garbage, past the huge soybean-oil tanks, Tom found his refuge. It was almost dark by the time he arrived, and the engine in the Merc was thumping ominously. But Joey would know what to do about that.

The junkyard stood hard on the oily polluted waters of New York Bay. Behind a ten-foot-high chain-link fence topped with three curly strands of barbed wire, a pack of junkyard dogs kept pace with his car, barking a raucous welcome that would have terrified anyone who knew the dogs less well. The sunset gave a strange bronze cast to the mountains of shattered, twisted, rusted automobiles, the acres of scrap metal, the hills and valleys of junk and trash. Finally Tom came to the wide double gate. On one side a metal sign warned TRESPASSERS KEEP OUT; on the other side another sign told them to BEWARE OF THE DOGS. The gate was chained and locked.

Tom stopped and honked his horn.

Just beyond the fence he could see the four-room shack that Joey called home. A huge sign was mounted on top of the corrugated tin roof, with yellow spotlights stuck up there to illuminate the letters. It said DI ANGELIS SCRAP METAL & AUTO PARTS. The paint was faded and blistered by two decades of sun and rain; the wood itself had cracked, and one of the spots had burned out. Next to the house was parked an ancient yellow dump truck, a tow truck, and Joey's pride and joy, a blood-red 1959 Cadillac coupe with tail fins like a shark and a monster of a hopped-up engine poking right up through its cutaway hood.

Tom honked again. This time he gave it their special signal, tooting out the *Here-he-comes-to-save-the-daaaay!* theme from the *Mighty Mouse* cartoons they'd watched as kids.

A square of yellow light spilled across the junkyard as Joey came out with a beer in either hand.

They were nothing alike, him and Joey. They came from different stock, lived in different worlds, but they'd been best friends since the day of the third-grade pet show. That was the day he'd found out that turtles couldn't fly; the day he realized what he was, and what he could do.

Stevie Bruder and Josh Jones had caught him out in the schoolyard. They played catch with his turtles, tossing them back and forth while Tommy ran between them, red-faced and crying. When they got bored, they bounced them off the punchball square chalked on the wall. Stevie's German shepherd ate one. When Tommy tried to grab the dog, Stevie laid into him and left him on the ground with broken glasses and a split lip.

They would have done worse, except for Junkyard Joey, a scrawny kid with shaggy black hair, two years older than his classmates, but he'd already been left back twice, couldn't hardly read, and they always said he smelled bad on account of his father, Dom, owned the junkyard. Joey wasn't as big as Stevie Bruder, but he didn't care, that day or any day. He just grabbed Stevie by the back of his shirt and yanked him around and kicked him in the balls. Then he kicked the dog too, and he would have kicked Josh Jones, except Josh ran away. As he fled, a dead turtle floated off the ground and flew across the schoolyard to smack him in the back of his fat red neck.

Joey had seen it happen. "How'd you do that?" he said, astonished. Until that moment, even Tommy hadn't realized that *he* was the reason his turtles could fly.

It became their shared secret, the glue that held their odd friendship together. Tommy helped Joey with his homework and quizzed him for tests. Joey became Tommy's protector against the random brutality of playground and schoolyard. Tommy read comic books to Joey, until Joey's own reading got so much better that he didn't need Tommy. Dom, a grizzled man with salt-and-pepper hair, a beer belly, and a gentle heart, was proud of that; he couldn't read himself, not even Italian. The friendship lasted through grammar school and high school and Joey's dropping out. It survived their discovery of girls, weathered the death of Dom DiAngelis, and Tom's family moving off to Perth Amboy. Joey DiAngelis was still the only one who knew what Tom was.

Joey popped the cap on another Rheingold with the church key that hung around his neck. Under his sleeveless white undershirt a beer belly like his father's was growing. "You're too fucking smart to be doing shitwork in a TV repair shop," he was saying.

"It's a job," Tom said. "I did it last summer, I can do it full time. It's not important what kind of job I have. What's important is what I do with my, uh, talent."

"Talent?" Joey mocked.

"You know what I mean, you dumb wop." Tom set his empty bottle down on the top of the orange crate next to the armchair. Most of Joey's furnishings weren't what you'd call lavish; he scavenged them from the junkyard. "I been thinking about what Jetboy said at the end, trying to think what it meant. I figure he was saying that there were things he hadn't done yet. Well, shit, I haven't done *anything*. All the way back I asked what I could do for the country, y'know? Well, fuck, we both know the answer to that one."

Joey rocked back in his chair, sucking on his Rhcingold and shaking his head. Behind him, the wall was lined with the bookshelves that Dom had built for the kids almost ten years ago. The bottom row was all men's magazines. The rest were comic books. Their comic books. *Supermans* and *Batmans, Action Comics* and *Detective,* the *Classics Illustrateds* that Joey had mined for all his book reports, horror comics and crime comics and air-war comics, and best of all, their treasure—an almost complete run of *Jetboy Comics.*

Joey saw what he was looking at. "Don't even think it," he said, "you're no fuckin' Jetboy, Tuds."

"No," said Tom, "I'm more than he was. I'm—"

"A dork," Joey suggested.

"An ace," he said gravely. "Like the Four Aces."

"They were a colored doo-wop group, weren't they?"

Tom flushed. "You dumb wop, they weren't singers, they—"

Joey cut him off with a sharp gesture. "I know who the fuck they were, Tuds. Gimme a break. They were dumb shits, like you. They all went to jail or got shot or something, didn't they? Except for the fuckin' snitch, whatsisname." He snapped his fingers. "You know, the guy in *Tarzan!*'

"Jack Braun," Tom said. He'd done a term paper on the Four Aces once. "And I bet there are others, hiding out there. Like me. I've been hiding. But no more."

"So you figure you're going to go to the *Bayonne Times* and give a fucking show? You asshole. You might as well tell 'em you're a commie. They'll make you move to Jokertown and they'll break all the goddamned windows in your dad's house. They might even draft you, asswipe."

"No," said Tom. "I've got it scoped out. The Four Aces were easy targets. I'm not going to let them know who I am or where I live." He used the beer bottle in his hand to gesture vaguely at the bookshelves. "I'm going to keep my name secret. Like in the comics."

Joey laughed out loud. "Fuckin' A. You gonna wear long Johns too, you dumb shit?"

"Goddamn it," Tom said. He was getting pissed off. "Shut the fuck up." Joey just sat there, rocking and laughing. "Come on, big mouth," Tom snapped, rising. "Get off your fat ass and come outside, and I'll show you just how dumb I am. C'mon, you know so damned much." Joey DiAngelis got to his feet. "This I gotta see."

Outside, Tom waited impatiently, shifting his weight from foot to foot, breath steaming in the cold November air, while Joey went to the big metal box on the side of the house and threw a switch. High atop their poles, the junkyard lights blazed to life. The dogs gathered around, sniffing, and followed them when they began to walk. Joey had a beer bottle poking out of a pocket of his black leather jacket.

It was only a junkyard, full of garbage and scrap metal and wrecked cars, but tonight it seemed as magical as when Tommy was ten. On a rise overlooking the black waters of New York Bay, an ancient white Packard loomed like a ghostly fort. That was just what it had been, when Joey and he had been kids; their sanctum, their stronghold, their cavalry outpost and space station and castle rolled all in one. It shone in the moonlight, and the waters beyond were full of promise as they lapped against the shore. Darkness and shadows lay heavy in the yard, changing the piles of trash and metal into mysterious black hills, with a maze of gray alleys between them. Tom led them into that labyrinth, past the big trash heap where they'd played king-of-the-mountain and dueled with scrap-iron swords, past the treasure troves where they'd found so many busted toys and hunks of colored glass and deposit bottles, and once even a whole cardboard carton full of comic books.

They walked between rows of twisted, rusty cars stacked one on another; Fords and Chevys, Hudsons and DeSotos, a Corvette with a shattered accordion hood, a litter of dead Beetles, a dignified black hearse as dead as the passengers it had carried. Tom looked at them all carefully. Finally he stopped. "That one," he said, pointing to the remains of a gutted old Studebaker Hawk. Its engine was gone, as were its tires; the windshield was a spiderweb of broken glass, and even in the darkness they could see where rust had chewed away at the fenders and side panels. "Not worth anything, right?"

Joey opened his beer. "Go ahead, it's all yours."

Tom took a deep breath and faced the car. His hands became fists at his sides. He stared hard, concentrating. The car rocked slightly. Its front grille lifted an unsteady couple of inches from the ground.

"Whooo-eeee," Joey said derisively, punching Tom lightly in the shoulder. The Studebaker dropped with a clang, and a bumper fell off. "Shit, I'm impressed," Joey said.

"Damn it, keep quiet and leave me alone," Tom said. "I can do it, I'll show you, just shut your fuckin' mouth for a minute. I've been practicing. You don't know the things I can do."

"Won't say a fuckin' word," Joey promised, grinning. He took a swig of his beer.

Tom turned back to the Studebaker. He tried to blot out everything, forget about Joey, the dogs, the junkyard; the Studebaker filled his world. His stomach was a hard little ball. He told it to relax, took several deep breaths, let his fists uncurl. *Come on, come on, take it easy, don't get upset, do it, you've done more than this, this is easy, easy.*

The car rose slowly, drifting upward in a shower of rust. Tom turned it around and around, faster and faster. Then, with a triumphant smile, Tom threw it fifty feet across the junkyard. It crashed into a stack of dead Chevys and brought the whole thing down in an avalanche of metal.

Joey finished his Rheingold. "Not bad. A few years ago, you could barely lift me over a fence."

"I'm getting stronger all the time," Tom said.

Joey DiAngelis nodded, and tossed his empty bottle to the side. "Good," he said, "then you won't have any problem with me, willya?" He gave Tom a hard push with both hands.

Tom staggered back a step, frowning. "Cut it out, Joey."

"Make me," Joey said. He shoved him again, harder. This time Tom almost lost his footing.

"Damn it, *stop* it," Tom said. "It's not funny, Joey."

"No?" Joey said. He grinned. "I think it's fuckin' hilarious. But hey, you can stop me, can't you? Use your damn power." He moved right up in Tom's face and slapped him lightly across the cheek. "Stop me, ace," he said. He slapped him harder. "C'mon, Jetboy, stop me." The third slap was the hardest yet. "Let's go, supes, whatcha waitin' for?" The fourth blow had a sharp sting; the fifth snapped Tom's head half around. Joey stopped smiling; Tom could smell the beer on his breath.

Tom tried to grab his hand, but Joey was too strong, too fast; he evaded Tom's grasp and landed another slap. "You wanna box, ace? I'll turn you into fuckin' dogmeat. Dork. Asshole." The slap almost tore Tom's head off, and brought stinging tears to his eyes. "*Stop me,* jagoff," Joey screamed. He closed his hand, and buried his fist in Tom's stomach so hard it doubled him over and took his breath away.

Tom tried to summon his concentration, to grab and push, but it was the schoolyard all over again, Joey was everywhere, fists raining down on him, and it was all he could do to get his hands up and try to block the blows, and it was no good anyway, Joey was much stronger, he pounded him, pushed him, screaming all the while, and Tom couldn't think, couldn't focus, couldn't do anything but hurt, and he was retreating, staggering back, and Joey came after him, fists cocked, and caught him with an uppercut that landed right on his mouth with a crack that made his teeth hurt. All of a sudden Tom was lying on his back on the ground, with a mouth full of blood.

Joey stood over him frowning. "Fuck," he said. "I didn't mean to bust your lip." He reached down, took Tom by the hand, and yanked him roughly to his feet.

Tom wiped blood from his lip with the back of his hand. There was blood on the front of his shirt too. "Look at me, I'm all messed up," he said with disgust. He glared at Joey. "That wasn't fair. You can't expect me to do anything when you're pounding on me, damn it."

"Uh-huh," Joey said. "And while you're concentrating and squinting your eyes, you figure the fuckin' bad guys are just gonna leave you alone, right?" He clapped Tom across the back. "They'll knock out all your fuckin' teeth. That's if you're lucky, if they don't just shoot you. You ain't no Jetboy, Tuds." He shivered. "C'mon. It's fuckin' cold out here."

When he woke in warm darkness, Tach remembered only a little of the binge, but that was how he liked it. He struggled to sit up. The sheets he was lying on were satin, smooth and sensual, and beneath the odor of stale vomit he could still smell a faint trace of some flowery perfume.

Unsteady, he tossed off the bedclothes and pulled himself to the edge of the four-poster bed. The floor beneath his bare feet was carpeted. He was naked, the air uncomfortably warm on his bare skin. He reached out a hand, found the light switch, and whimpered a little at the brightness. The room was pink-and-white clutter with Victorian furnishings and thick, soundproofed walls. An oil painting of John F. Kennedy smiled down from above the hearth; in one corner stood a three-foot-tall plaster statue of the Virgin Mary.

Angelface was seated in a pink wingback chair by the cold fireplace, blinking at him sleepily and covering her yawn with the back of her hand.

Tach felt sick and ashamed. "I put you out of your own bed again, didn't I?" he said.

"It's all right," she replied. Her feet were resting on a tiny footstool. Her soles were ugly and bruised, black and swollen despite the special padded shoes she wore. Otherwise she was lovely. Unbound, her black hair fell to her waist, and her skin had a flushed, radiant quality to it, a warm glow of life. Her eyes were dark and liquid, but the most amazing thing, the thing that never failed to astonish Tachyon, was the warmth in them, the affection he felt so unworthy of. With all he had done to her, and to all the rest of them, somehow this woman called Angelface forgave, and cared.

Tach raised a hand to his temple. Someone with a buzz saw was trying to remove the back of his skull. "My head," he groaned. "At your prices, the least you could do is take the resins and poisons out of the drinks you sell. On Takis, we—"

"I know," Angelface said. "On Takis you've bred hangovers out of your wines. You told me that one already."

Tachyon gave her a weary smile. She looked impossibly fresh, wearing nothing but a short satin tunic that left her legs bare to the thigh. It was a deep, wine red, lovely against her skin. But when she rose, he glimpsed the side of her face, where her cheek had rested against the chair as she slept. The bruise was darkening already, a purple blossom on her cheek. "Angel . . . " he began.

"It's nothing," she said. She pushed her hair forward to cover the blemish. "Your clothes were filthy. Mal took them out to be cleaned. So you're my prisoner for a while."

"How long have I slept?" Tachyon asked.

"All day," Angelface replied. "Don't worry about it. Once I had a customer get so drunk he slept for five months." She sat down at her dressing table, lifted a phone, and ordered breakfast: toast and tea for herself, eggs and bacon and strong coffee with brandy for Tachyon. With aspirin on the side.

"No," he protested. "All that food. I'll get sick."

"You have to eat. Even spacemen can't live on cognac alone."

"Please . . ."

"If you want to drink, you'll eat," she said brusquely. "That's the deal, remember?"

The deal, yes. He remembered. Angelface provided him with rent money, food, and an unlimited bar tab, as much drink as he'd ever need to wash away his memories. All he had to do was eat and tell her stories. She loved to listen to him talk. He told her family anecdotes, lectured about Takisian customs, filled her with history and legends and romances, with tales of balls and intrigues and beauty far removed from the squalor of Jokertown.

Sometimes, after closing, he would dance for her, tracing the ancient, intricate pavanes of Takis across the nightclub's mirrored floors while she watched and urged him on. Once, when both of them had drunk far too much wine, she talked him into demonstrating the Wedding Pattern, an erotic ballet that most Takisians danced but once, on their wedding night. That was the only time she had ever danced with him, echoing the steps, hesitantly at first, and then faster and faster, swaying and spinning across the floor until her bare feet were raw and cracked and left wet red smears upon the mirror tiles. In the Wedding Pattern, the dancing couple came together at the end, collapsing into a long triumphant embrace. But that was on Takis; here, when the moment came, she broke the pattern and shied away from him, and he was reminded once again that Takis was far away.

Two years before, Desmond had found him unconscious and naked in a Jokertown alley. Someone had stolen his clothing while he slept, and he was fevered and delirious. Des had summoned help to carry him to the Funhouse. When he came to, he was lying on a cot in a back room, surrounded by beer kegs and wine racks. "Do you know what you were drinking?" Angelface had asked him when they'd brought him to her office. He hadn't known; all he recalled was that he'd needed a drink so badly it was an ache inside him, and the old black man in the alley had generously offered to share. "It's called Sterno," Angelface told him. She had Des bring in a bottle of her finest brandy. "If a man wants to drink, that's his business, but at least you can kill yourself with a little class." The brandy spread thin tendrils of warmth through his chest and stopped his hands from shaking. When he'd emptied the snifter, Tach had thanked her effusively, but she drew back when he tried to touch her. He asked her why. "I'll show you," she had said, offering her hand. "Lightly," she told him. His kiss had been the merest brush of his lips, not on the back of her hand but against the inside of her wrist, to feel her pulse, the life current inside her, because she was so very lovely, and kind, and because he wanted her.

A moment later he'd watched with sick dismay as her skin darkened to purple and then black. *Another one of mine,* he'd thought.

Yet somehow they had become friends. Not lovers, of course, except sometimes in his dreams; her capillaries ruptured at the slightest pressure, and to her hypersensitive nervous system even the lightest touch was painful. A gentle caress turned her black and blue; lovemaking would probably kill her. But friends, yes. She never asked him for anything he could not give, and so he could never fail her.

Breakfast was served by a hunchbacked black woman named Ruth who had pale blue feathers instead of hair. "The man brought this for you this morning," she told Angelface after she'd set the table, handing across a thick, square packet wrapped in brown paper. Angelface accepted it without comment while Tachyon drank his brandy-laced coffee and lifted knife and fork to stare with sick dismay at the implacable bacon and eggs.

"Don't look so stricken," Angelface said.

"I don't think I've told you about the time the Network starship came to Takis, and what my great-grandmother Amurath had to say to the Ly'bahr envoy," he began.

"No," she said. "Go on. I like your great-grandmother."

"That's one of us. She terrifies me," Tachyon said, and launched into the story.

Tom woke well before dawn, while Joey was snoring in the back room. He brewed a pot of coffee in a battered percolator and popped a Thomas' English muffin into the toaster. While the coffee perked, he folded the hide-a-bed back into a couch. He covered his muffins with butter and strawberry preserves, and looked around for something to read. The comics beckoned.

He remembered the day they'd saved them. Most had been his, originally, including the run of *Jetboy* he got from his dad. He'd loved those comics. And then one day in 1954 he'd come home from school and found them gone, a full bookcase and two orange crates of funny books vanished. His mother said some women from the PTA had come by to tell her what awful things comic books were. They'd shown her a copy of a book by a Dr. Wertham about how comics turned kids into juvenile delinquents and homos, and how they glorified aces and jokers, and so his mother had let them take Tom's collection. He screamed and yelled and threw a tantrum, but it did no good.

The PTA had gathered up comic books from every kid in school. They were going to burn them all Saturday, in the schoolyard. It was happening all over the country; there was even talk of a law banning comic books, or at least the kinds about horror and crime and people with strange powers.

Wertham and the PTA turned out to be right: that Friday night, on account of comic books, Tommy Tudbury and Joey DiAngelis became criminals.

Tom was nine; Joey was eleven, but he'd been driving his pop's truck since he was seven. In the middle of the night, he swiped the truck and Tom snuck out to meet him. When they got to the school, Joey jimmied open a window, and Tom climbed on his shoulders and looked into the dark classroom and concentrated and grabbed the carton with his collection in it and lifted it up and floated it out into the bed of the truck. Then he snatched four or five other cartons for good measure. The PTA never noticed; they still had plenty to burn. If Dom DiAngelis wondered where all the comics had come from, he never said a word; he just built the shelves to hold them, proud as punch of his son who could read. From that day on, it was their collection, jointly.

Setting his coffee and muffin on the orange crate, Tom went to the bookcase and took down a couple of issues of *Jetboy Comics.* He reread them as he ate, *Jetboy on Dinosaur Island, Jetboy and the Fourth Reich,* and his favorite, the final issue, the true one, *Jetboy and the Aliens.* Inside the cover, the title was "Thirty Minutes Over Broadway." Tom read it twice as he sipped his cooling coffee. He lingered over some of the best panels. On the last page, they had a picture of the alien, Tachyon, weeping. Tom didn't know if that had happened or not. He closed the comic book and finished his English muffin. For a long time he sat there thinking.

Jetboy was a hero. And what was he? Nothing. A wimp, a chickenshit. A fuck of a lot of good his wild card power did anybody. It was useless, just like him.

Dispiritedly, he shrugged into his coat and went outside. The junkyard looked raw and ugly in the dawn, and a cold wind was blowing. A few hundred yards to the east, the bay was green and choppy. Tom climbed up to the old Packard on its little hill. The door creaked when he yanked it open. Inside, the seats were cracked and smelled of rot, but at least he was out of that wind. Tom slouched back with his knees up against the dash, staring out at sunrise. He sat unmoving for a long time; across the yard, hubcaps and old tires floated up in the air and went screaming off to splash into the choppy green waters of New York Bay. He could see the Statue of Liberty on her island, and the hazy outlines of the towers of Manhattan off to the northeast.

It was nearly seven-thirty, his limbs were stiff, and he'd lost count of the number of hubcaps he'd flung, when Tom Tudbury sat up with a strange expression on his face. The icebox he'd been juggling forty feet from the ground came down with a crash. He ran his fingers through his hair and lifted the icebox again, moved it over twenty yards or so, and dropped it right on Joey's corrugated tin roof. Then he did the same with a tire, a twisted bicycle, six hubcaps, and a little red wagon.

The door to the house flew open with a bang, and Joey came charging out into the cold wearing nothing but boxer shorts and a sleeveless undershirt. He looked real pissed. Tom snatched his bare feet, pulled them out from under him, and dumped him on his butt, hard. Joey cursed.

Tom grabbed him and yanked him into the air, upside down. "Where the fuck are you, Tudbury?" Joey screamed. "Cut it out, you dork. Lemme down."

Tom imagined two huge invisible hands, and tossed Joey from one to the other. "When I get down, I'm going to punch you so fuckin' hard you'll eat through a straw for the rest of your life," Joey promised.

The crank was stiff from years of disuse, but Tom finally managed to roll down the Packard's window. He stuck his head out. "Hiya, kids, hiya, hiya, hiya," he croaked, chortling.

Suspended twelve feet from the ground, Joey dangled and made a fist. "I'll pluck your fuckin' magic twanger, shithead," he shouted. Tom yanked off his boxer shorts and hung them from a telephone pole. "You're gonna die, Tudbury," Joey said.

Tom took a big breath and set Joey on the ground, very gently. The moment of truth. Joey came running at him, screaming obscenities. Tom closed his eyes, put his hands on the steering wheel, and *lifted.*

The Packard shifted beneath him. Sweat dotted his brow. He shut out the world, concentrated, counted to ten, slowly, backward.

When he finally opened his eyes, half expecting to see Joey's fist smashing into his nose, there was nothing to behold but a seagull perched on the hood of the Packard, its head cocked as it peered through the cracked windshield. He was floating. He was flying.

Tom stuck his head out of the window. Joey stood twenty feet below him, glaring, hands on his hips and a disgusted look on his face. "Now," Tom yelled down, smiling, "what was it you were saying last night?"

"I hope you can stay up there all day, you son of a bitch," Joey said. He made an ineffectual fist, and waved it. Lank black hair fell across his eyes. "Ah, shit, what does this prove? If I had a gun, you'd still be dead meat."

"If you had a gun, I wouldn't be sticking my head out the window," Tom said. "In fact, it'd be better if I didn't have a window." He considered that for a second, but it was hard to think while he was up here. The Packard was heavy. "I'm coming down," he said to Joey. "You, uh, you calmed down?"

Joey grinned. "Try me and see, Tuds."

"Move out of the way. I don't want to squash you with this damn thing."

Joey shuffled to one side, bare-ass and goose-pimpled, and Tom let the Packard settle as gently as an autumn leaf on a still day. He had the door half open when Joey reached in, grabbed him, yanked him up, and pushed him back against the side of the car, his other hand cocked into a fist. "I oughtta—" he began. Then he shook his head, snorted, and punched Tom lightly in the shoulder. "Gimme back my fuckin' drawers, ace," he said.

Back inside the house, Tom reheated the leftover coffee. "I'll need you to do the work," he said as he made himself some scrambled eggs and ham and a couple more English muffins. Using his teke always gave him quite an appetite. "You took auto shop and welding and all that shit. I'll do the wiring."

"Wiring?" Joey said, warming his hands over his cup. "What the fuck for?"

"The lights and the TV cameras. I don't want any windows people can shoot through. I know where we can get some cameras cheap, and you got lots of old sets around here, I'll just fix them up." He sat down and attacked his eggs wolfishly. "I'll need loudspeakers too. Some kind of PA system. A generator. Wonder if I'll have room for a refrigerator in there?"

"That Packard's a big motherfucker," Joey said. "Take out the seats and you'll have room for three of the fuckers."

"Not the Packard," Tom said. "I'll find a lighter car. We can cover up the windows with old body panels or something."

Joey pushed hair out of his eyes. "Fuck the body panels. I got armor plate. From the war. They scrapped a bunch of ships at the Navy base in '46 and '47, and Dom put in a bid for the metal, and bought us twenty goddamn tons. Fuckin' waste a money—who the fuck wants to buy battleship armor? I still got it all, sitting way out back rusting. You need a fuckin' sixteen-inch gun to punch through that shit, Tuds. You'll be safe as—fuck, I dunno. Safe, anyhow."

Tom knew. "Safe," he said loudly, "as a turtle in its shell!"

Only ten shopping days were left until Christmas, and Tach sat in one of the window alcoves, nursing an Irish coffee against the December cold and gazing through the one-way glass at the Bowery. The Funhouse wouldn't open for another hour yet, but the back door was always unlocked for Angelface's friends. Up on stage, a pair of joker jugglers who called themselves Cosmos and Chaos were tossing bowling balls around. Cosmos floated three feet above the stage in the lotus position, his eyeless face serene. He was totally blind, but he never missed a beat or dropped a ball. His partner, six-armed Chaos, capered around like a lunatic, chortling and telling bad jokes and keeping a cascade of flaming clubs going behind his back with two arms while the other four flung bowling balls at Cosmos. Tach spared them only a glance. As talented as they were, their deformities pained him.

Mal slid into his booth. "How many of those you had?" the bouncer demanded, glaring at the Irish coffee. The tendrils that hung from his lower lip expanded and contracted in a blind wormlike pulsing, and his huge, malformed blue-black jaw gave his face a look of belligerent contempt.

"I don't see that it's any of your business."

"You're no damn use at all, are you?"

"I never claimed I was."

Mal grunted. "You're worth 'bout as much as a sack of shit. I don't see why the hell Angel needs no damn pantywaist spaceman hanging round the place sopping up her booze. . . ."

"She doesn't. I told her that."

"You can't tell that woman nothin'," Mal agreed. He made a fist. A very large fist. Before the Day of the Wild Card, he'd been the eighth-ranked heavyweight contender. Afterward, he had climbed as high as third . . . until they'd banned wild cards from professional sports, and wiped out his dreams in a stroke. The measure was aimed at aces, they said, to keep the games competitive, but there had been no exceptions made for jokers. Mal was older now, sparse hair turned iron gray, but he still looked strong enough to break Floyd Patterson over his knee and mean enough to stare down Sonny Liston. "Look at that," he growled in disgust, glaring out the window. Tiny was outside in his chair. "What the hell is he doing here? I told him not to come by here no more." Mal started for the door.

"Can't you just leave him alone?" Tachyon called after him. "He's harmless."

"Harmless?" Mal rounded on him. "His screamin' scares off all the fuckin' tourists, and who the hell's gonna pay for all your free booze?"

But then the door pushed open, and Desmond stood there, overcoat folded over one arm, his trunk half-raised. "Let him be, Mal," the *maitre d'* said wearily. "Go on, now." Muttering, Mal stalked off.

Desmond came over and seated himself in Tachyon's booth. "Good morning, Doctor," he said.

Tachyon nodded and finished his drink. The whiskey had all gone to the bottom of the cup, and it warmed him on the way down. He found himself staring at the face in the mirrored tabletop: a worn, dissipated, *coarse* face, eyes reddened and puffy, long red hair tangled and greasy, features distorted by alcoholic bloat. That wasn't him, that couldn't be him, he was handsome, clean-featured, distinguished, his face was—

Desmond's trunk snaked out, its fingers locking around his wrist roughly, yanking him forward. "You haven't heard a word I've said, have you?" Des said, his voice low and urgent with anger. Blearily, Tach realized that Desmond had been talking to him. He began to mutter apologies.

"Never mind about that," Des said, releasing his grip. "Listen to me. I was asking for your help, Doctor. I may be a joker, but I'm not an uneducated man. I've read about you. You have certain—abilities, let us say."

"No," Tach interrupted. "Not the way you're thinking."

"Your powers are quite well documented," Des said.

"I don't . . . " Tach began awkwardly. He spread his hands. "That was then. I've lost—I mean, I can't, not anymore." He stared down at his own wasted features, wanting to look Des in the eye, to make him understand, but unable to bear the sight of the joker's deformity.

"You mean you won't," Des said. He stood up. "I thought that if I spoke to you before we opened, I might actually find you sober. I see I was mistaken. Forget everything I said."

"I'd help you if I could," Tach began to say.

"I wasn't asking for me," Des said sharply.

When he was gone, Tachyon went to the long silver-chrome bar and got down a full bottle of cognac. The first glass made him feel better; the second stopped his hands from shaking. By the third he had begun to weep. Mal came over and looked down at him in disgust. "Never knew no man cried as much as you do," he said, thrusting a dirty handkerchief at Tachyon roughly before he left to help them open.

He had been aloft for four and a half hours when the news of the fire came crackling over the police-band radio down by his right foot. Not very *far* aloft, true, only about six feet from the ground, but that was enough—six feet or sixty, it didn't make all that much difference, Tom had found. Four and a half hours, and he didn't feel the least bit tired yet. In fact, he felt *sensational.*

He was strapped securely into a bucket seat Joey had pulled from a mashed-up Triumph TR-3 and mounted on a low pivot right in the center of the VW The only light was the wan phosphor glow from an array of mismatched television screens that surrounded him on all sides. Between the cameras and their tracking motors, the generator, the ventilation system, the sound equipment, the control panels, the spare box of vacuum tubes, and the little refrigerator, he hardly had space to swing around. But that was okay. Tom was more a claustrophile than a claustrophobe anyway; he liked it in here. Around the exterior of the gutted Beetle, Joey had mounted two overlapping layers of thick battleship armor. It was better than a goddamned tank. Joey had already pinged a few shots off it with the Luger that Dom had taken off a German officer during the war. A lucky shot might be able to take out one of his cameras or lights, but there was no way to get to Tom himself inside the shell. He was better than safe, he was *invulnerable,* and when he felt this secure and sure of himself, there was no limit on what he might be able to do.

The shell was heavier than the Packard by the time they'd gotten finished with it, but it didn't seem to matter. Four and a half hours, never touching ground, sliding around silently and almost effortlessly through the junkyard, and Tom hadn't even worked up a sweat.

When he heard the report over the radio, a jolt of excitement went through him. *This is it!* he thought. He ought to wait for Joey, but Joey had driven to Pompeii Pizza to pick up dinner (pepperoni, onion, and extra cheese) and there was no time to waste; this was his chance.

The ring of lights on the bottom of the shell threw stark shadows over the hills of twisted metal and trash as Tom pushed the shell higher into the air, eight feet up, ten, twelve. His eyes flicked nervously from one screen to the next, watching the ground recede. One set, its picture tube filched from an old Sylvania, began a slow vertical roll. Tom played with a knob and stopped it. His palms were sweaty. Fifteen feet up, he began to creep forward, until the shell reached the shoreline. In front of him was darkness; it was too thick a night to see New York, but he knew it was there, if he could reach it. On his small black-and-white screens, the waters of New York Bay seemed even darker than usual, an endless choppy ocean of ink looming before him. He'd have to grope his way across, until the city lights came into sight. And if he lost it out there, over the water, he'd be joining Jetboy and J.F.K. a lot sooner than he planned; even if he could unscrew the hatch quick enough to avoid drowning, he couldn't swim.

But he *wasn't* going to lose it, Tom thought suddenly. Why the fuck was he hesitating? He wasn't going to lose it ever again, was he? He had to believe that.

He pressed his lips together, pushed off with his mind, and the shell slid smoothly out over the water. The salt waves beneath him rose and fell. He'd never had to push against water before; it felt different. Tom had an instant of panic; the shell rocked and dropped three feet before he caught hold of himself and adjusted. He calmed himself with an effort, shoved upward, and rose. *High,* he thought, he'd come in high, he'd *fly* in, like Jetboy, like Black Eagle, like a fucking *ace.* The shell moved out, faster and faster, gliding across the bay with swift serenity as Tom gained confidence. He'd never felt so incredibly powerful, so good, so goddamned *right.*

The compass worked fine; in less than ten minutes, the lights of the Battery and the Wall Street district loomed up before him. Tom pushed still higher, and floated uptown, hugging the shoreline of the Hudson. Jetboy's Tomb came and went beneath him. He'd stood in front of it a dozen times, gazing up at the face of the big metal statue out front. He wondered what that statue might think if it could look up and see him tonight.

He had a New York street map, but tonight he didn't need it; the flames could be seen almost a mile off. Even inside his armor Tom could feel the heat waves licking up at him when he made a pass overhead. He carefully began a descent. His fins whirred, and his cameras tracked at his command; below was chaos and cacophony, sirens and shouting, the crowd, the hurrying firemen, the police barricades, and the ambulances, big hook-and-ladder trucks spraying water into the inferno. At first no one noticed him, hovering fifty feet above the sidewalk—until he came in low enough for his lights to play on the walls of the building. Then he saw them looking up, pointing; he felt giddy with excitement.

But he had only an instant to relish the feeling. Then, from the corner of an eye, he saw her in one of his screens. She appeared suddenly in a fifth-floor window, bent over and coughing, her dress already afire. Before he could act, the flames licked at her; she screamed and jumped.

He caught her in midair, without thinking, without hesitating, without wondering whether he could do it. He just *did* it, caught her and held her and lowered her gently to the ground. The firemen surrounded her, put out her dress, and hustled her into an ambulance. And now, Tom saw, *everyone* was looking up at him, at the strange dark shape floating high in the night, with its ring of shining lights. The police band was crackling; they were reporting him as a flying saucer, he heard. He grinned.

A cop climbed up on top of his police car, holding a bullhorn, and began to hail him. Tom turned off the radio to hear better over the roar of the flames. He was telling Tom to land and identify himself, asking who he was, what he was.

That was easy. Tom turned on his microphone. "I'm the Turtle," he said. The VW had no tires; in the wheel wells, Joey had rigged the most humongous speakers they could find, powered by the largest amp on the market. For the first time, the voice of the Turtle was heard in the land, a booming "I'M THE TURTLE" echoing down the streets and alleys, a rolling thunder crackling with distortion. Except what he said didn't sound quite right. Tom cranked the volume up even higher, injected a little more bass into his voice. *"I AM THE GREAT AND POWERFUL TURTLE,"* he announced to them all.

Then he flew a block west, to the dark polluted waters of the Hudson, and imagined two huge invisible hands forty feet across. He lowered them into the river, cupped them full, and lifted. Rivulets of water dribbled to the street all the way back. When he dropped the first cascade on the flames, a ragged cheering went up from the crowd below.

"*Merry Christmas,*" Tach declared drunkenly when the clock struck midnight and the record Christmas Eve crowd began to whoop and shout and pound on the tables. On stage, Humphrey Bogart cracked a lame joke in an unfamiliar voice. All the lights in the house dimmed briefly; when they came back up, Bogart had been replaced by a portly, round-faced man with a red nose. "Who is he now?" Tach asked the twin on his left.

"W.C. Fields," she whispered. She slid her tongue around the inside of his ear. The twin on the right was doing something even more interesting under the table, where her hand had somehow found a way into his trousers. The twins were his Christmas gift from Angelface. "You can pretend they're me," she'd told him, though of course they were nothing like her. Nice kids, both of them, buxom and cheerful and absolutely uninhibited, if a bit simpleminded; they reminded him of Takisian sex toys. The one on the right had drawn the wild card, but she wore her cat mask even in bed, and there was no visible deformity to disturb the sweet pleasure of his erection.

W.C. Fields, whoever he was, offered some cynical observation, about Christmas and small children. The crowd hooted him off the stage. The Projectionist had an astonishing array of faces, but he couldn't tell a joke. Tach didn't mind; he had all the diversion he needed.

"Paper, Doc?" The vendor thrust a copy of the *Herald Tribune* across the table with a thick three-fingered hand. His flesh was blue-black and oily-looking. "All the Christmas news," he said, shifting the clumsy stack of papers under his arm. Two small curving tusks protruded from the corners of his wide, grinning mouth. Beneath a porkpie hat, the great bulge of his skull was covered with tufts of bristly red hair. On the streets they called him the Walrus.

"No thank you, Jube," Tach said with drunken dignity. "I have no desire to wallow in human folly tonight."

"Hey, look," said the twin on the right. "The Turtle!"

Tachyon looked around, momentarily befuddled, wondering how that huge armored shell could possibly have gotten inside the Funhouse, but of course she was referring to the newspaper.

"You better buy it for her, Tacky," the twin on the left said, giggling. "If you don't she'll pout."

Tachyon sighed. "I'll take one. But only if I don't have to listen to any of your jokes, Jube."

"Heard a new one about a joker, a Polack, and an Irishman stuck on a desert island, but just for that I'm not going to tell it," the Walrus replied with a rubbery grin.

Tachyon dug for some coins, found nothing in his pockets but a small, feminine hand. Jube winked. "I'll get it from Des," he said. Tachyon spread the newspaper out on the table, while the club erupted in applause as Cosmos and Chaos made their entrance.

A grainy photograph of the Turtle was spread across two columns. Tachyon thought it looked like a flying pickle, a big lumpy dill covered with little bumps. The Turtle had apprehended a hit-and-run driver who had killed a nine-year-old boy in Harlem, intercepting his flight and lifting the car twenty feet off the ground, where it floated with its engine roaring and its tires spinning madly until the police finally caught up. In a related sidebar, the rumor that the shell was an experimental robot flying tank had been denied by an Air Force spokesman.

"You'd think they'd have found something more important to write about by now," Tachyon said. It was the third big story about the Turtle this week. The letter columns, the editorial pages, everything was Turtle, Turtle, Turtle. Even television was rabid with Turtle speculation. Who was he? What was he? How did he do it?

One reporter had even sought out Tach to ask that question. "Telekinesis," Tachyon told him. "It's nothing new. Almost common, in fact." Teke had been the single ability most frequently manifested by virus victims back in '46. He'd seen a dozen patients who could move paper clips and pencils, and one woman who could lift her own body weight for ten minutes at a time. Even Earl Sanderson's flight had been telekinetic in origin. What he did not tell them was that teke on *this* scale was unprecedented. Of course, when the story ran, they got half of it wrong.

"He's a joker, you know," whispered the twin on the right, the one in the silver-gray cat mask. She was leaning against his shoulder, reading about the Turtle.

"A joker?" Tach said.

"He hides inside a shell, doesn't he? Why would he do that unless he was really awful to look at?" She had taken her hand out of his trousers. "Could I have that paper?"

Tach pushed it toward her. "They're cheering him now," he said sharply. "They cheered the Four Aces too."

"That was a colored group, right?" she said, turning her attention to the headlines.

"She's keeping a scrapbook," her sister said. "All the jokers think he's one of them. Stupid, huh? I bet it's just a machine, some kind of Air Force flying saucer."

"He is not," her twin said. "It says so right here." She pointed to the sidebar with a long, red-painted nail.

"Never mind about her," the twin on the left said. She moved closer to Tachyon, nibbling on his neck as her hand went under the table. "Hey, what's wrong? You're all soft."

"My pardons," Tachyon said gloomily. Cosmos and Chaos were flinging axes, machetes, and knives across the stage, the glittering cascade multiplied into infinity by the mirrors around them. He had a bottle of fine cognac at hand, and lovely, willing women on either side of him, but suddenly, for some reason he could not have named, it did not feel like such a good night after all. He filled his glass almost to the brim and inhaled the heady alcoholic fumes. "Merry Christmas," he muttered to no one in particular.

Consciousness returned with the angry tones of Mal's voice. Tach lifted his head groggily from the mirrored tabletop, blinking down at his puffy red reflection. The jugglers, the twins, and the crowd were long gone. His cheek was sticky from lying in a puddle of spilled liquor. The twins had jollied him and fondled him and one of them had even gone under the table, for all the good it did. Then Angelface had come to the tableside and sent them away. "Go to sleep, Tacky," she'd said.

Mal had come up to ask if he should lug him back to bed. "Not today," she'd said, "you know what day this is. Let him sleep it off here." He couldn't recall when he'd gone to sleep.

His head was about to explode, and Mal's shouting wasn't making things any better. "I don't give a flyin' fuck *what* you were promised, scumbag, you're not seeing her," the bouncer yelled. A softer voice said something in reply. "You'll get your fuckin' money, but that's all you'll get," Mal snapped.

Tach raised his eyes. In the mirrors he saw their reflections darkly: odd twisted shapes outlined in the wan dawn light, reflections of reflections, hundreds of them, beautiful, monstrous, uncountable, his children, his heirs, the offspring of his failures, a living sea of jokers. The soft voice said something else. "Ah, kiss my joker ass," Mal said. He had a body like a twisted stick and a head like a pumpkin; it made Tach smile. Mal shoved someone and reached behind his back, groping for his gun.

The reflections and the reflections of the reflections, the gaunt shadows and the bloated ones, the round-faced ones and the knife-thin ones, the black and the white, they moved all at once, filling the club with noise; a hoarse shout from Mal, the crack of gunfire. Instinctively Tach dove for cover, cracking his forehead hard on the edge of the table as he slid down. He blinked back tears of pain and lay curled up on the floor, peering out at the reflections of feet while the world disintegrated into a sharp-edged cacophony. Glass was shattering and falling, mirrors breaking on all sides, silvered knives flying through the air, too many for even Cosmos and Chaos to catch, dark splinters eating into the reflections, taking bites out of all the twisted shadow-shapes, blood spattering against the cracked mirrors.

It ended as suddenly as it had begun. The soft voice said something and there was the sound of footsteps, the crunch of glass underfoot. A moment later, a muffled scream from off behind him. Tach lay under the table, drunk and terrified. His finger hurt: bleeding, he saw, sliced open by a sliver of mirror. All he could think of were the stupid human superstitions about broken mirrors and bad luck. He cradled his head in his arms so the awful nightmare would go away. When he woke again, a policeman was shaking him roughly.

Mal was dead, one detective told him; they showed him a morgue photo of the bouncer lying in a pool of blood and a welter of broken glass. Ruth was dead too, and one of the janitors, a dim-witted cyclops who had never hurt anyone. They showed him a newspaper. The Santa Claus Slaughter, that was what they called it, and the lead was about three jokers who'd found death waiting under the tree on Christmas morning.

Miss Fascetti was gone, the other detective told him, did he know anything about that? Did he think she was involved? Was she a culprit or a victim? What could he tell them about her? He said he didn't know any such person, until they explained that they were asking about Angela Fascetti and maybe he knew her better as Angelface. She was gone and Mal was shot dead, and the most frightening thing of all was that Tach did not know where his next drink was coming from.

They held him for four days, questioning him relentlessly, going over the same ground again and again, until Tachyon was screaming at them, pleading with them, demanding his rights, demanding a lawyer, demanding a drink. They gave him only the lawyer. The lawyer said they couldn't hold him without charging him, so they charged him with being a material witness, with vagrancy, with resisting arrest, and questioned him again.

By the third day, his hands were shaking and he was having waking hallucinations. One of the detectives, the kindly one, promised him a bottle in return for his cooperation, but somehow his answers never quite satisfied them, and the bottle was not forthcoming. The bad- tempered one threatened to hold him forever unless he told the truth. I thought it was a nightmare, Tach told him, weeping. I was drunk, I'd been asleep. No, I couldn't see them, just the reflections, distorted, multiplied. I don't know how many there were. I don't know what it was about. No, she had no enemies, everyone loved Angelface. No, she didn't kill Mal, that didn't make sense, Mal loved her. One of them had a soft voice. No, I don't know which one. No, I can't remember what they said. No, I don't know if they were jokers or not, they looked like jokers, but the mirrors distort, some of them, not all of them, don't you see? No, I couldn't possibly pick them out of a lineup, I never really saw them. I had to hide under the table, do you see, the assassins had come, that's what my father always told me, there wasn't anything I could do.

When they realized that he was telling them all he knew, they dropped the charges and released him. To the dark streets of Jokertown and the cold of the night.

He walked down the Bowery alone, shivering. The Walrus was hawking the evening papers from his newsstand on the corner of Hester. "Read all about it," he called out. "Turtle Terror in Jokertown." Tachyon paused to stare dully at the headlines. POLICE SEEK TURTLE, the *Post* reported. TURTLE CHARGED WITH ASSAULT, announced the *World-Telegram*. So the cheering had stopped already. He glanced at the text. The Turtle had been prowling Jokertown the past two nights, lifting people a hundred feet in the air to question them, threatening to drop them if he didn't like their answers. When police tried to make an arrest last night, the Turtle had deposited two of their black-and-whites on the roof of Freakers at Chatham Square. CURB THE TURTLE, the editorial in the *World-Telegram* said.

"You all right, Doc?" the Walrus asked.

"No," said Tachyon, putting down the paper. He couldn't afford to pay for it anyway.

Police barriers blocked the entrance to the Funhouse, and a padlock secured thc door. CLOSED INDEFINITELY, the sign said. He needed a drink, but the pockets of his bandleader's coat were empty.

He thought of Des and Randall, and realized that he had no idea where they lived, or what their last names might be.

Trudging back to ROOMS, Tach climbed wearily up the stairs. When he stepped into the darkness, he had just enough time to notice that the room was frigidly cold; the window was open and a bitter wind was scouring out the old smells of urine, mildew, and drink. Had he done that? Confused, he stepped toward it, and someone came out from behind the door and grabbed him.

It happened so fast he scarcely had time to react. The forearm across his windpipe was an iron bar, choking off his scream, and a hand wrenched his right arm up behind his back, hard. He was choking, his arm close to breaking, and then he was being shoved toward the open window, running at it, and Tachyon could only thrash feebly in a grip much stronger than his own. The windowsill caught him square in the stomach, knocking the last of his breath right out of him, and suddenly he was falling, head over heels, locked helplessly in the steel embrace of his attacker, both of them plunging toward the sidewalk below.

They jerked to a stop five feet above the cement, with a wrench that elicited a grunt from the man behind him.

Tach had closed his eyes before the instant of impact. He opened them as they began to float upward. Above the yellow halo of the streetlamp was a ring of much brighter lights, set in a hovering darkness that blotted out the winter stars.

The arm across his throat had loosened enough for Tachyon to groan. "You," he said hoarsely, as they curved around the shell and came to rest gently on top of it. The metal was icy cold, its chill biting right through the fabric of Tachyon's pants. As the Turtle began to rise straight up into the night, Tachyon's captor released him. He drew in a shuddering breath of cold air, and rolled over to face a man in a zippered leather jacket, black dungarees, and a rubbery green frog mask. "Who . . . ?" he gasped.

"I'm the Great and Powerful Turtle's mean-ass sidekick," the man in the frog mask said, rather cheerfully.

"DOCTOR TACHYON, I PRESUME," boomed the shell's speakers, far above the alleys of Jokertown. "I'VE ALWAYS WANTED TO MEET YOU. I READ ABOUT YOU WHEN I WAS JUST A KID."

"Turn it down," Tach croaked weakly.

"OH. SURE. Is that better?" The volume diminished sharply. "It's noisy in here, and behind all this armor I can't always tell how loud I sound. I'm sorry if we scared you, but we couldn't take the chance of you saying no. We need you."

Tach stayed just where he was, shivering, shaken. "What do you want?" he asked wearily.

"Help," the Turtle declared. They were still rising; the lights of Manhattan spread out all around them, and the spires of the Empire State Building and the Chrysler Building rose uptown. They were higher than either. The wind was cold and gusting; Tach clung to the shell for dear life.

"Leave me alone," Tachyon said. "I have no help to give you. I have no help to give anybody."

"Fuck, he's crying," the man in the frog mask said.

"You don't understand," the Turtle said. The shell began to drift west, its motion silent and steady. There was something awesome and eerie about the flight. "You have to help. I've tried on my own, but I'm getting nowhere. But you, your powers, they can make the difference." Tachyon was lost in his own self-pity, too cold and exhausted and despairing to reply. "I want a drink," he said.

"Fuck it," said Frog-face. "Dumbo was right about this guy, he's nothing but a goddamned wino."

"He doesn't understand," said the Turtle. "Once we explain, he'll come around. Doctor Tachyon, we're talking about your friend Angelface."

He needed a drink so badly it hurt. "She was good to me," he said, remembering the sweet perfume of her satin sheets, and her bloody footprints on the mirror tiles. "But there's nothing I can do. I told the police everything I know."

"Chickenshit asshole," said Frog-face.

"When I was a kid, I read about you in *Jetboy Comics*," the Turtle said. "'Thirty Minutes Over Broadway,' remember? You were supposed to be as smart as Einstein. I might be able to save your friend Angelface, but I can't without your powers."

"I don't do that any longer. I *can't*. There was someone I hurt, someone I cared for, but I seized her mind, just for an instant, for a good reason, or at least I thought it was for a good reason, but it . . . destroyed her. I can't do it again."

"Boohoo," said Frog-face mockingly. "Let's toss 'im, Turtle, he's not worth a bucket of warm piss." He took something out of one of the pockets of his leather jacket; Tach was astonished to see that it was a bottle of beer.

"Please," Tachyon said, as the man popped off the cap with a bottle-opener hung round his neck. "A sip," Tach said. "Just a sip." He hated the taste of beer, but he needed something, anything. It had been days. "Please."

"Fuck off," Frog-face said.

"Tachyon," said the Turtle, "you can make him."

"No I can't," Tach said. The man raised the bottle up to green rubber lips. "I can't," Tach repeated. Frog-face continued to drink. "No." He could hear it gurgling. "Please, just a little."

The man lowered the beer bottle, sloshed it thoughtfully. "Just a swallow left," he said.

"Please." He reached out, hands trembling.

"Nah," said Frog-face. He began to turn the bottle upside down. "Course, if you're really thirsty, you could just grab my mind, right? *Make* me give you the fuckin' bottle." He tipped the bottle a little more. "Go on, I dare ya, try it."

Tach watched the last mouthful of beer dribble down onto the Turtle's shell and run off into empty air.

"Fuck," said the man in the frog mask. "You got it bad, don't you?" He pulled another bottle from his pocket, opened it, and handed it across. Tach cradled it with both hands. The beer was cold and sour, but he had never tasted anything half so sweet. He drained it all in one long swallow. "Got any other smart ideas?" Frog-face asked the Turtle.

Ahead of them was the blackness of the Hudson River, the lights of Jersey off to the west. They were descending. Beneath them, overlooking the Hudson, was a sprawling edifice of steel and glass and marble that Tachyon suddenly recognized, though he had never set foot inside it: Jetboy's Tomb. "Where are we going?" he asked.

"We're going to see a man about a rescue," the Turtle said.

Jetboy's Tomb filled the entire block, on the site where the pieces of his plane had come raining down. It filled Tom's screens too, as he sat in the warm darkness of his shell, bathed in a phosphor glow. Motors whirred as the cameras moved in their tracks. The huge flanged wings of the tomb curved upward, as if the building itself was about to take flight. Through tall, narrow windows, he could see glimpses of the full-size replica of the JB-1 suspended from the ceiling, its scarlet flanks aglow from hidden lights. Above the doors, the hero's last words had been carved, each letter chiseled into the black Italian marble and filled in stainless steel. The metal flashed as the shell's white-hot spots slid across the legend:

I CANT DIE YET,
I HAVEN'T SEEN *THE JOLSON STORY*

Tom brought the shell down in front of the monument, to hover five feet above the broad marble plaza at the top of the stairs. Nearby, a twenty-foot-tall steel Jetboy looked out over the West Side Highway and the Hudson beyond, his fists cocked. The metal used for the sculpture had come from the wreckage of crashed planes, Tom knew. He knew that statue's face better than he knew his father's.

The man they'd come to meet emerged from the shadows at the base of the statue, a chunky dark shape huddled in a thick overcoat, hands shoved deep into his pockets. Tom shone a light on him; a camera tracked to give him a better view. The joker was a portly man, round-shouldered and well-dressed. His coat had a fur collar and his fedora was pulled low. Instead of a nose, he had an elephant's trunk in the middle of his face. The end of it was fringed with fingers, snug in a little leather glove.

Dr. Tachyon slid off the top of the shell, lost his footing and landed on his ass. Tom heard Joey laugh. Then Joey jumped down too and pulled Tachyon to his feet.

The joker glanced down at the alien. "So you convinced him to come after all. I'm surprised."

"We were real fuckin' persuasive," Joey said.

"Des," Tachyon said, sounding confused. "What are you doing here? Do you know these people?"

Elephant-face twitched his trunk. "Since the day before yesterday, yes, in a manner of speaking. They came to me. The hour was late, but a phone call from the Great and Powerful Turde does pique one's interest. He offered his help, and I accepted. I even told them where you lived."

Tachyon ran a hand through his tangled, filthy hair. "I'm sorry about Mal. Do you know anything about Angelface? You know how much she meant to me."

"In dollars and cents, I know quite precisely," Des said.

Tachyon's mouth gaped open. He looked hurt. Tom felt sorry for him. "I wanted to go to you," he said. "I didn't know where to find you."

Joey laughed. "He's listed in the fuckin' phone book, dork. Ain't that many guys named Xavier Desmond." He looked at the shell. "How the fuck is he gonna find the lady if he couldn't even find his buddy here?"

Desmond nodded. "An excellent point. This isn't going to work. Just look at him!" His trunk pointed. "What good is he? We're wasting precious time."

"We did it your way," Tom replied. "We're getting nowhere. No one's talking. He can get the information we need."

"I don't understand any of this," Tachyon interrupted.

Joey made a disgusted sound. He had found a beer somewhere and was cracking the cap.

"What's happening?" Tach asked.

"If you had been the least bit interested in anything besides cognac and cheap tarts, you might know," Des said icily.

"Tell him what you told us," Tom commanded. When he knew, Tachyon would surely help, he thought. He *had* to.

Des gave a heavy sigh. "Angelface had a heroin habit. She hurt, you know. Perhaps you noticed that from time to time, Doctor? The drug was the only thing that got her through the day. Without it, the pain would have driven her insane. Nor was hers an ordinary junkie's habit. She used uncut heroin in quantities that would have killed any normal user. You saw how minimally it affected her. The joker metabolism is a curious thing. Do you have any idea how expensive heroin is, Doctor

Tachyon? Never mind, I see that you don't. Angelface made quite a bit of money from the Funhouse, but it was never enough. Her source gave her credit until she was in far over her head, then demanded . . . call it a promissory note. Or a Christmas present. She had no choice. It was that or be cut off. She hoped to come up with the money, being an eternal optimist. She failed. On Christmas morning her source came by to collect. Mal wasn't about to let them have her. They insisted."

Tachyon was squinting in the glare of the lights. His image began to roll upward. "Why didn't she tell me?" he said.

"I suppose she didn't want to burden you, Doctor. It might have taken the fun out of your self-pitying binges."

"Have you told the police?"

"The police? Ah, yes. New York's finest. The ones who seem so curiously uninterested whenever a joker is beaten or killed, yet ever so diligent if a tourist is robbed. The ones who so regularly arrest, harass, and brutalize any joker who has the poor taste to live anywhere outside of Jokertown. Perhaps we might consult the officer who commented that raping a joker woman is more a lapse in taste than a crime." Des snorted. "Doctor Tachyon, where do you think Angelface bought her drugs? Do you think any ordinary street pusher would have access to uncut heroin in the quantities she needed? The police *were* her source. The head of the Jokertown narcotics squad, if you care to be precise. Oh, I'll grant you that it's unlikely the whole department is involved. Homicide may be conducting a legitimate investigation. What do you think they'd say if we told them that Bannister was the murderer? You think they'd arrest one of their own? On the strength of my testimony, or the testimony of any joker?"

"We'll make good her note," Tachyon blurted. "We'll give this man his money or the Funhouse or whatever it is he wants."

"The promissory note," Desmond said wearily, "was not for the Funhouse."

"Whatever it was, give it to him!"

"She promised him the only thing she still had that he wanted," Desmond said. "Herself. Her beauty and her pain. The word's out on the street, if you know how to listen. There's going to be a very special New Year's Eve party somewhere in the city. Invitation only. Expensive. A unique thrill. Bannister will have her first. He's wanted that for a long time. But the other guests will have their turn. Jokertown hospitality."

Tachyon's mouth worked soundlessly for a moment. "The *police*?" he finally managed. He looked as shocked as Tom had been when Desmond told him and Joey.

"Do you think they love us, Doctor? We're freaks. We're *diseased.* Jokertown is a hell, a dead end, and the Jokertown police are the most brutal, corrupt, and incompetent in the city. I don't think anyone planned what happened at the Funhouse, but it happened, and Angelface knows too much. They can't let her live, so they're going to have some fun with the joker cunt."

Tom Tudbury leaned toward his microphone. "I can rescue her," he said. "These fuckers haven't seen anything like the Great and Powerful Turtle. But I can't *find* her."

Des said, "She has a lot of friends. But none of us can read minds, or make a man do something he doesn't want to."

"I *can't,*" Tachyon protested. He seemed to shrink into himself, to edge away from them, and for an instant Tom thought the little man was going to run away. "You don't understand."

"What a fuckin' candy-ass," Joey said loudly.

Watching Tachyon crumble on his screens, Tom Tudbury finally ran out of patience. "If you fail, you fail," he said. "And if you don't try, you fail too, so what the fuck difference does it make? Jetboy failed, but at least he *tried.* He wasn't an ace, he wasn't a goddamned *Takisian,* he was just a guy with a jet, but he did what he could."

"I want to. I . . . just . . . *can't.*"

Des trumpeted his disgust. Joey shrugged.

Inside his shell, Tom sat in stunned disbelief. He wasn't going to help. He hadn't believed it, not really. Joey had warned him, Desmond too, but Tom had insisted, he'd been sure, this was *Doctor Tachyon,* of course he'd help, maybe he was having some problems, but once they explained the situation to him, once they made it clear what was at stake and how much they needed him—he *had* to help. But he was saying no. It was the last goddamned straw.

He twisted the volume knob up all the way. "YOU SON OF A BITCH," he boomed, and the sound hammered out over the plaza. Tachyon flinched away. "YOU NO-GOOD FUCKING LITTLE ALIEN CHICKENSHIT!" Tachyon stumbled backward down the stairs, but the Turtle drifted after him, loudspeakers blaring. "IT WAS ALL A LIE, WASN'T IT? EVERYTHING IN THE COMIC BOOKS, EVERYTHING IN THE PAPERS, IT WAS

ALL A STUPID LIE. ALL MY LIFE THEY BEAT ME UP AND THEY CALLED ME A FUCKING WIMP AND A COWARD BUT *YOU'RE* THE COWARD, YOU ASSHOLE, YOU SHITTY LITTLE WHINER, YOU WON'T EVEN TRY, YOU DON'T GIVE A DAMN ABOUT ANYBODY, ABOUT YOUR FRIEND ANGELFACE OR ABOUT KENNEDY OR JETBOY OR ANYBODY, YOU HAVE ALL THESE FUCKING POWERS AND YOU'RE *NOTHING,* YOU WON'T DO ANYTHING, YOU'RE WORSE THAN OSWALD OR BRAUN OR ANY OF THEM." Tachyon staggered down the steps, hands over his ears, shouting something unintelligible, but Tom was past listening. His anger had a life of its own now. He lashed out, and the alien's head snapped around and reddened with the force of the slap. *"ASSHOLE!"* Tom was shrieking. *"YOU'RE THE ONE IN A SHELL."* Invisible blows rained down on Tachyon in a fury. He reeled, fell, rolled a third of the way down the stairs, tried to get back to his feet, was bowled over again, and bounced down to the street head over heels. "ASSHOLE!" the Turtle thundered. "RUN, YOU SHITHEAD. GET OUT OF HERE, OR I'LL THROW YOU IN THE DAMNED RIVER! RUN, YOU LITTLE WIMP, BEFORE THE GREAT AND POWERFUL TURTLE REALLY GETS UPSET! RUN, DAMN IT! YOU'RE THE ONE IN THE SHELL! YOU'RE THE ONE IN THE SHELL!"

And he ran, dashing blindly from one streetlight to the next, until he was lost in the shadows. Tom Tudbury watched him vanish on the shell's array of television screens. He felt sick and beaten. His head was throbbing. He needed a beer, or an aspirin, or both. When he heard the sirens coming, he scooped up Joey and Desmond and set them on top of his shell, killed his lights, and rose straight up into the night, high, high up, into darkness and cold and silence.

That night Tach slept the sleep of the damned, thrashing about like a man in a fever dream, crying out, weeping, waking again and again from nightmares, only to drift back into them. He dreamt he was back on Takis, and his hated cousin Zabb was boasting about a new sex toy, but when he brought her out it was Blythe, and he raped her right there in front of him. Tach watched it all, powerless to intervene; her body writhed beneath his and blood flowed from her mouth and ears and vagina. She began to change, into a thousand joker shapes each more horrible than the last, and Zabb went right on raping them all as they screamed and struggled. But afterward, when Zabb rose from the corpse covered with blood, it wasn't his cousin's face at all, it was his own, worn and dissipated, a *coarse* face, eyes reddened and puffy, long red hair tangled and greasy, features distorted by alcoholic bloat or perhaps by a Funhouse mirror.

He woke around noon, to the terrible sound of Tiny weeping outside his window. It was more than he could stand. It was all more than he could stand. He stumbled to the window and threw it open and screamed at the giant to be quiet, to stop, to leave him alone, to give him peace, please, but Tiny went on and on, so much pain, so much guilt, so much shame, why couldn't they let him be, he couldn't take it anymore, no, shut up, shut up, *please shut up,* and suddenly Tach shrieked and reached out with his mind and plunged into Tiny's head and shut him up.

The silence was thunderous.

The nearest phone booth was in a candy store a block down. Vandals had ripped the phone book to shreds. He dialed information and got the listing for Xavier Desmond on Christie Street, only a short walk away. The apartment was a fourth-floor walkup above a mask shop. Tachyon was out of breath by the time he got to the top.

Des opened the door on the fifth knock. "You," he said.

"The Turtle," Tach said. His throat was dry. "Did he get anything last night?"

"No," Desmond replied. His trunk twitched. "The same story as before. They're wise to him now, they know he won't really drop them. They call his bluff. Short of actually killing someone, there's nothing to do."

"Tell me who to ask," Tach said.

"You?" Des said.

Tach could not look the joker in the eye. He nodded.

"Let me get my coat," Des said. He emerged from the apartment bundled up for the cold, carrying a fur cap and a frayed beige raincoat.

"Put your hair up in the hat," he told Tachyon, "and leave that ridiculous coat here. You don't want to be recognized." Tach did as he said. On the way out, Des went into the mask shop for the final touch.

"A chicken?" Tach said when Des handed him the mask. It had bright yellow feathers, a prominent orange beak, a floppy red coxcomb on top.

"I saw it and I knew it was you," said Des. "Put it on."

A large crane was moving into position at Chatham Square, to get the police cars off Freakers' roof. The club was open. The doorman was a seven-foot-tall hairless joker with fangs. He grabbed Des by the arm as they tried to pass under the neon thighs of the six-breasted dancer who writhed on the marquee. "No jokers allowed," he said brusquely. "Get lost, Tusker."

Reach out and grab his mind, Tachyon thought. Once, before Blythe, he would have done it instinctively. But now he hesitated, and hesitating, he was lost.

Des reached into his back pocket, pulled out a wallet, extracted a fifty-dollar bill. "You were watching them lower the police cars," he said. "You never saw me pass."

"Oh, yeah," the doorman said. The bill vanished in a clawed hand. "Real interesting, them cranes."

"Sometimes money is the most potent power of all," Des said as they walked into the cavernous dimness within. A sparse noontime crowd sat eating the free lunch and watching a stripper gyrate down a long runway behind a barbed-wire barrier. She was covered with silky gray hair, except for her breasts, which had been shaved bare. Desmond scanned the booths along the far wall. He took Tach's elbow and led him to a dark corner, where a man in a peacoat was sitting with a stein of beer. "They lettin' jokers in here now?" the man asked gruffly as they approached. He was saturnine and pockmarked.

Tach went into his mind. *Fuck what's this now the elephant man's from the Funhouse who's the other one damned jokers anyhow gotta lotta nerve.* "Where's Bannister keeping Angelface?" Des asked.

"Angelface is the slit at the Funhouse, right? Don't know no Bannister. Is this a game? Fuck off, joker, I ain't playing." In his thoughts, images came tumbling: Tach saw mirrors shattering, silver knives flying through the air, felt Mal's shove and saw him reach for a gun, watched him shudder and spin as the bullets hit, heard Bannister's soft voice as he told them to kill Ruth, saw the warehouse over on the Hudson where they were keeping her, the livid bruises on her arm when they'd grabbed her, tasted the mans fear, fear of jokers, fear of discovery, fear of Bannister, the fear of *them.* Tach reached out and squeezed Desmond's arm.

Des turned to go. "Hey, hold it right there," the man with the pockmarked face said. He flashed a badge as he unfolded from the booth. "Undercover narcotics," he said, "and you been using, mister, asking asshole junkie questions like that." Des stood still as the man frisked him down. "Well, looka this," he said, producing a bag of white powder from one of Desmond's pockets. "Wonder what this is? You're under arrest, freak-face."

"That's not mine," Desmond said calmly.

"The hell it ain't," the man said, and in his mind the thoughts ran one after another *little accident resisting arrest what could i do huh? jokers'll scream but who listens to a fuckin' joker only whatymi gonna do with the other one?* and he glanced at Tachyon. *Jeez looka the chickenman's shaking maybe the fucker IS using that'd be great.*

Trembling, Tach realized the moment of truth was at hand.

He was not sure he could do it. It was different than with Tiny; that had been blind instinct, but he was awake now, and he knew what he was doing. It had been so easy once, as easy as using his hands. But now those hands trembled, and there was blood on them, and on his mind as well . . . he thought of Blythe and the way her mind had shattered under his touch, like the mirrors in the Funhouse, and for a terrible, long second nothing happened, until the fear was rank in his throat, and the familiar taste of failure filled his mouth.

Then the pockfaced man smiled an idiot's smile, sat back down in his booth, laid his head on the table, and went to sleep as sweetly as a child.

Des took it in stride. "Your doing?"

Tachyon nodded.

"You're shaking," Des asked. "Are you all right, Doctor?"

"I think so," Tachyon said. The policeman had begun to snore loudly. "I think maybe I am all right, Des. For the first time in years." He looked at the joker's face, looked past the deformity to the man beneath. "I know where she is," he said. They started toward the exit. In the cage, a full-breasted, bearded hermaphrodite had started into a bump-and-grind. "We have to move quickly."

"In an hour I can get together twenty men."

"No," Tachyon said. "The place they're holding her isn't in Jokertown."

Des stopped with his hand on the door. "I see," he said. "And outside of Jokertown, jokers and masked men are rather conspicuous, aren't they?"

"Exactly," Tach said. He did not voice his other fear, of the retribution that would surely be enacted should jokers dare to confront police, even police as corrupt as Bannister and his cohorts. He would take the risk himself, he had nothing left to lose, but he could not permit them to take it. "Can you reach the Turtle?" he asked.

"I can take you to him," Des replied. "When?"

"Now," Tach said. In an hour or two, the sleeping policeman would awaken and go straight to Bannister. And say what? That Des and a man in a chicken mask had been asking questions, that he'd been about to arrest them but suddenly he'd gotten very sleepy? Would he dare admit to that? If so, what would Bannister make of it? Enough to move Angelface? Enough to kill her? They could not chance it.

When they emerged from the dimness of Freakers, the crane had just lowered the second police car to the sidewalk. A cold wind was blowing, but behind his chicken feathers, Doctor Tachyon had begun to sweat.

Tom Tudbury woke to the dim, muffled sound of someone pounding on his shell.

He pushed aside the frayed blanket and bashed his head sitting up. "Ow, goddamn it," he cursed, fumbling in the darkness until he found the map light. The pounding continued, a hollow *boom boom boom* against the armor, echoing. Tom felt a stab of panic. The police, he thought, they've found me, they've come to drag me out and haul me up on charges. His head hurt. It was cold and stuffy in here. He turned on the space heater, the fans, the cameras. His screens came to life.

Outside was a bright cold December day, the sunlight painting every grimy brick with stark clarity. Joey bad taken the train back to Bayonne, but Tom had remained; they were running out of time, he had no other choice. Des found him a safe place, an interior courtyard in the depths of Jokertown, surrounded by decaying five-story tenements, its cobblestones redolent with the smell of sewage, wholly hidden from the street. When he'd landed, just before dawn, lights had blinked on in a few of the dark windows, and faces had come to peer cautiously around the shades; wary, frightened, not-quite-human faces, briefly seen and gone as quickly, when they decided that the thing outside was none of their concern.

Yawning, Tom pulled himself into his seat and panned his cameras until he found the source of the commotion. Des was standing by an open cellar door, arms crossed, while Doctor Tachyon hammered on the shell with a length of broom handle.

Astonished, Tom flipped open his microphones. "YOU."

Tachyon winced. "Please."

He lowered the volume. "Sorry. You took me by surprise. I never expected to see you again. After last night, I mean. I didn't hurt you, did I? I didn't mean to, I just—"

"I understand," Tachyon said. "But we've got no time for recriminations or apologies now."

Des began to roll upward. Damn that vertical hold. "We know where they have her," the joker said as his image flipped. "That is, if Doctor Tachyon can indeed read minds as advertised."

"Where?" Tom said. Des continued to flip, flip, flip.

"A warehouse on the Hudson," Tachyon replied. "Near the foot of a pier. I can't tell you an address, but I saw it clearly in his thoughts. I'll recognize it."

"Great!" Tom enthused. He gave up on his efforts to adjust the vertical hold and whapped the screen. The picture steadied. "Then we've got them. Let's go." The look on Tachyon's face took him aback. "You are coming, aren't you?"

Tachyon swallowed. "Yes," he said. He had a mask in his hand. He slipped it on.

That was a relief, Tom thought; for a second there, he'd thought he'd have to go it alone. "Climb on," he said.

With a deep sigh of resignation, the alien scrambled on top of the shell, his boots scrabbling at the armor. Tom gripped his armrests tightly and pushed up. The shell rose as easily as a soap bubble. He felt elated. This was what he was meant to do, Tom thought; Jetboy must have felt like this.

Joey had installed a monster of a horn in the shell. Tom let it rip as they floated clear of the rooftops, startling a coop of pigeons, a few winos, and Tachyon with the distinctive blare of *Here-I-come-to-save-the-daaaaaay.*

"It might be wise to be a bit more subtle about this," Tachyon said diplomatically.

Tom laughed. "I don't believe it, I got a man from outer space who mostly dresses like Pinky Lee riding on my back, and he's telling me I ought to be subtle." He laughed again as the streets of Jokertown spread out all around them.

They made their final approach through a maze of waterfront alleys. The last was a dead end, terminating in a brick wall scrawled over with the names of gangs and young lovers. The Turtle rose above it, and they emerged in the loading area behind the warehouse. A man in a short leather jacket sat on the edge of the loading dock. He jumped to his feet when they hove into view. His jump took him a lot higher than he'd anticipated, about ten feet higher. He opened his mouth, but before he could shout, Tach had him; he went to sleep in midair. The Turtle stashed him atop a nearby roof.

Four wide loading bays opened onto the dock, all chained and padlocked, their corrugated metal doors marked with wide brown streaks of rust. TRESPASSERS WILL BE PROSECUTED said the lettering on the narrow door to the side.

Tach hopped down, landing easily on the balls of his feet, his nerves tingling. "I'll go through," he told the Turtle. "Give me a minute, and then follow."

"A minute," the speakers said. "You got it."

Tach pulled off his boots, opened the door just a crack, and slid into the warehouse on purple-stockinged feet, summoning up all the stealth and fluid grace they'd once taught him on Takis. Inside, bales of shredded paper, bound tightly in thin wire, were stacked twenty and thirty feet high. Tachyon crept down a crooked aisle toward the sound of voices. A huge yellow forklift blocked his path. He dropped flat and squirmed underneath it, to peer around one massive tire.

He counted five altogether. Two of them were playing cards, sitting in folding chairs and using a stack of coverless paperbacks for a table. A grossly fat man was adjusting a gigantic paper-shredding machine against the far wall. The last two stood over a long table, bags of white powder piled in neat rows in front of them. The tall man in the flannel shirt was weighing something on a small set of scales. Next to him, supervising, was a slender balding man in an expensive raincoat. He had a cigarette in his hand, and his voice was smooth and soft. Tachyon couldn't quite make out what he was saying. There was no sign of Angelface.

He dipped into the sewer that was Bannister's mind, and saw her. Between the shredder and the baling machine. He couldn't see it from under the forklift; the machinery blocked the line of sight, but she was there. A filthy mattress had been tossed on the concrete floor, and she lay atop it, her ankles swollen and raw where the handcuffs chafed against her skin.

"... FIFTY-EIGHT HIPPOPOTAMI, FIFTY-NINE HIPPOPOTAMI, *SIXTY* HIPPOPOTAMI," Tom counted.

The loading bays were big enough. He squeezed, and the padlock disintegrated into shards of rust and twisted metal. The chains came clanking down, and the door rattleded upward, rusty tracks screeching protest. Tom turned on all his lights as the shell slid forward. Inside, towering stacks of paper blocked his way. There wasn't room to go between them. He shoved them, *hard,* but even as they started to collapse, it occurred to him that he could go above them. He pushed up toward the ceiling.

"What the fuck," one of the cardplayers said, when they heard the loading gate screech open.

A heartbeat later, they were all moving. Both cardplayers scrambled to their feet; one of them produced a gun. The man in the flannel shirt looked up from his scales. The fat man turned away from the shredder, shouting something, but it was impossible to make out what he was saying. Against the far wall, bales of paper came crashing down, knocking into neighboring stacks and sending them down too, in a chain reaction that spread across the warehouse.

Without an instant's hesitation, Bannister went for Angelface. Tach took his mind and stopped him in mid-stride, with his revolver half-drawn.

And then a dozen bales of shredded paper slammed down against the rear of the forklift. The vehicle shifted, just a little, crushing Tachyon's left hand under a huge black tire. He cried out in shock and pain, and lost Bannister.

Down below, two little men were shooting at him. The first shot startled him so badly that Tom lost his concentration for a split second, and the shell dropped four feet before he got it back. Then the bullets were *ping*ing harmlessly off his armor and ricocheting around the warehouse. Tom smiled. "I AM THE GREAT AND POWERFUL TURTLE," he announced at full volume, as stacks of paper crashed down all around. "YOU ASSHOLES ARE UP SHIT CREEK. SURRENDER NOW"

The nearest asshole didn't surrender. He fired again, and one of Tom's screens went black. "OH, FUCK," Tom said, forgetting to kill his mike. He grabbed the guy's arm and pulled the gun away, and from the way the jerk screamed he'd probably dislocated his shoulder too, goddammit. He'd have to watch that. The other guy started running, jumping over a collapsed pile of paper. Tom caught him in mid-jump, took him straight up to the ceiling, and hung him from a rafter. His eyes flicked from screen to screen, but one screen was dark now and the damned vertical hold had gone again on the one next to it, so he couldn't make out a fucking thing to that side. He didn't have time to fix it. Some guy in a flannel shirt was loading bags into a suitcase, he saw on the big screen, and from the corner of his eye, he spied a fat guy climbing into a forklift . . . .

His hand crushed beneath the tire, Tachyon writhed in excruciating pain and tried not to scream. Bannister—had to stop Bannister before he got to Angelface. He ground his teeth together and tried to will away the pain, to gather it into a ball and push it from him the way he'd been taught, but it was hard, he'd lost the discipline, he could feel the shattered bones in his hand, his eyes were blurry with tears, and then he heard the forklift's motor turn over, and suddenly it was surging forward, rolling right up his arm, coming straight at his head, the tread of the massive tire a black wall of death rushing toward him . . . and passing an inch over the top of his skull, as it took to the air.

The forklift flew nicely across the warehouse and embedded itself in the far wall, with a little push from the Great and Powerful Turtle. The fat man dove off in midair and landed on a pile of coverless paperbacks. It wasn't until then that Tom happened to notice Tachyon lying on the floor under the place the forklift had been. He was holding his hand funny and his chicken mask was all smashed up and dirty, Tom saw, and as he staggered to his feet he was shouting something. He went running across the floor, reeling, unsteady. Where the fuck was he going in such a hurry?

Frowning, Tom smacked the malfunctioning screen with the back of his hand, and the vertical roll stopped suddenly. For an instant, the image on the television was clear and sharp. A man in a raincoat stood over a woman on a mattress. She was real pretty, and there was a funny smile on her face, sad but almost accepting, as he pressed the revolver right up to her forehead.

Tach came reeling around the shredding machine, his ankles all rubber, the world a red blur, his shattered bones jabbing against each other with every step, and found them there, Bannister touching her lightly with his pistol, her skin already darkening where the bullet would go in, and through his tears and his fears and a haze of pain, he reached out for Bannister's mind and seized it . . . just in time to feel him squeeze the trigger, and wince as the gun kicked back in his mind. He heard the explosion from two sets of ears.

"Noooooooooooooooooo!" he shrieked. He closed his eyes, sunk to his knees. He made Bannister fling the gun away, for what good it would do, none at all, too late, again he'd come too late, *failed, failed,* again, Angelface, Blythe, his sister, everyone he loved, all of them gone. He doubled over on the floor, and his mind filled with images of broken mirrors, of the Wedding Pattern danced in blood and pain, and that was the last thing he knew before the darkness took him.

He woke to the astringent smell of a hospital room and the feel of a pillow under his head, the pillowcase crisp with starch. He opened his eyes. "Des," he said weakly. He tried to sit, but he was bound up somehow. The world was blurry and unfocused.

"You're in traction, Doctor," Des said. "Your right arm was broken in two placcs, and your hand is worse than that."

"I'm sorry," Tach said. He would have wept, but he had run out of tears. "I'm so sorry. We tried, I . . . I'm so sorry, I—"

"Tacky," she said in that soft, husky voice.

And she was there, standing over him, dressed in a hospital gown, black hair framing a wry smile. She had combed it forward to cover her forehead; beneath her bangs was a hideous purple-green bruise, and the skin around her eyes was red and raw. For a moment he thought he was dead, or mad, or dreaming. "It's all right. Tacky. I'm okay. I'm here."

He stared up at her numbly. "You're dead," he said dully. "I was too late. I heard the shot, I had him by then but it was too late, I felt the gun recoil in his hand."

"Did you feel it jerk?" she asked him.

"Jerk?"

"A couple of inches, no more. Just as he fired. Just enough. I got some nasty powder burns, but the bullet went into the mattress a foot from my head."

"The Turtle," Tach said hoarsely.

She nodded. "He pushed aside the gun just as Bannister squeezed the trigger. And you made the son of a bitch throw away the revolver before he could get off a second shot."

"You got them," Des said. "A couple of men escaped in the confusion, but the Turtle delivered three of them, including Bannister. Plus a suitcase packed with twenty pounds of pure heroin. And it turns out that warehouse is owned by the mafia."

"The mafia?" Tachyon said.

"The mob," Des explained. "Criminals, Doctor Tachyon."

"One of the men captured in the warehouse has already turned state's evidence," Angelface said. "He'll testify to everything—the bribes, the drug operation, the murders at the Funhouse."

"Maybe we'll even get some decent police in Jokertown," Des added.

The feelings that rushed through Tachyon went far beyond relief. He wanted to thank them, wanted to cry for them, but neither the tears nor the words would come. He was weak and happy. "I didn't fail," he managed at last.

"No," Angelface said. She looked at Des. "Would you wait outside?" When they were alone, she sat on the edge of the bed. "I want to show you something. Something I wish I'd shown you a long time ago." She held it up in front of him. It was a gold locket. "Open it."

It was hard to do with only one hand, but he managed. Inside was a small round photograph of an elderly woman in bed. Her limbs were skeletal and withered, sticks draped in mottled flesh, and her face was horribly twisted. "What's wrong with her?" Tach asked, afraid of the answer. Another joker, he thought, another victim of his failures.

Angelface looked down at the twisted old woman, sighed, and closed the locket with a snap. "When she was four, in Little Italy, she was run over while playing in the street. A horse stepped on her face, and the wagon wheel crushed her spine. That was in, oh, 1886. She was completely paralyzed, but she lived. If you could call it living. That little girl spent the next sixty years in a bed, being fed, washed, and read to, with no company except the holy sisters. Sometimes all she wanted was to die. She dreamed about what it would be like to be beautiful, to be loved and desired, to be able to dance, to be able to *feel* things. Oh, how she wanted to *feel* things." She smiled. "I should have said thank you long ago, Tacky, but it's hard for me to show that picture to anyone. But I am grateful, and now I owe you doubly. You'll never pay for a drink at the Funhouse."

He stared at her. "I don't want a drink," he said. "No more. That's done." And it was, he knew; if she could live with her pain, what excuse could he possibly have to waste his life and talents? "Angelface," he said suddenly, "I can make you something better than heroin. I was . . . I *am* a biochemist, there are drugs on Takis, I can synthesize them, painkillers, nerve blocks. If you'll let me run some tests on you, maybe I can tailor something to your metabolism. I'll need a lab, of course. Setting things up will be expensive, but the drug could be made for pennies."

"I'll have some money," she said. "I'm selling the Funhouse to Des. But what you're talking about is illegal."

"To hell with their stupid laws," Tach blazed. "I won't tell if you won't." Then words came tumbling out one after the other, a torrent: plans, dreams, hopes, all of the things he'd lost or drowned in cognac and Sterno, and Angelface was looking at him, astonished, smiling, and when the drugs they had given him finally began to wear off, and his arm began to throb again, Doctor Tachyon remembered the old disciplines and sent the pain away, and somehow it seemed as though part of his guilt and his grief went with it, and he was whole again, and alive.

The headline said TURTLE, TACHYON SMASH HEROIN RING. Tom was gluing the article into the scrapbook when Joey returned with the beers. "They left out the Great and Powerful part," Joey observed, setting down a bottle by Tom's elbow.

"At least I got first billing," Tom said. He wiped thick white paste off his fingers with a napkin, and shoved the scrapbook aside. Underneath were some crude drawings he'd made of the shell. "Now," he said, "where the fuck are we going to put the record player, huh?"

Acknowledgements

"The Rock in the Park" © 2010 Peter S. Beagle. First publication: *Mirror Kingdom: The Best of Peter Beagle* (Subterranean Press).
"Cryptic Coloration" © 2007 Elizabeth Bear. First publication: *Jim Baen's Universe*, June 2007.
"The Horrid Glory of Its Wings" © 2010 Elizabeth Bear. First publication: *Tor.com*, 8 December 2009.
"The Land of Heart's Desire" © 2010 Holly Black. First publication: *The Poison Eaters and Other Stories* (Big Mouth House).
"Blood Yesterday, Blood Tomorrow" © 2011 Richard Bowes. First publication: *Blood and Other Cravings*, ed. Ellen Datlow (Tor).
"A Huntsman Passing By" © 1999 Richard Bowes. First publication: *The Magazine of Fantasy & Science Fiction*, June 1999.
"Caisson" © 2015 Karl Bunker. First publication: *Asimov's Science Fiction Magazine*, August 2015.
"The Tallest Doll in New York City" © 2014 Maria Dahvana Headley. First publication: *Tor.com*, 14 February 2014.
"Painted Birds and Shivered Bones" © 2013 Kat Howard. First publication: *Subterranean*, Spring 2013.
"The City Born Great" © 2016 N. K. Jemisin. First publication: *Tor.com*, 28 September 2016.
"Le Peau Verte" © 2005 Caitlín R. Kiernan. First publication: *To Charles Fort, With Love* (Subterranean Press).
"Shell Games" © 1987 George R. R. Martin. First publication: *Wild Cards*, ed. George R. R. Martin (Bantam Spectra).
"Red as Snow" © 2013 Seanan McGuire. First publication: *Hex in the City*, ed. Kerrie L. Hughes (Fiction River/WMG Publishing).

"Priced to Sell" © 2011 Temeraire LLC. First publication: *Naked City: Tales of Urban Fantasy*, ed. Ellen Datlow (St. Martin's Griffin).

"Salsa Nocturna" © 2010 Daniel José Older. First publication: *Strange Horizons*, 20 December 2010.

"Weston Walks" © 2011 Kit Reed. First publication: *Naked City: Tales of Urban Fantasy*, ed. Ellen Datlow (St. Martin's Griffin).

"Grand Central Park" © 2002 Delia Sherman. First publication: *The Green Man: Tales from the Mythic Forest*, eds. Ellen Datlow & Terri Windling (Viking).

"How the Pooka Came to New York City" © 2011 Delia Sherman. First publication: *Naked City: Tales of Urban Fantasy*, ed. Ellen Datlow (St. Martin's Griffin).

"Pork Pie Hat" © 1994 Peter Straub. First publication: *Pork Pie Hat* (Orion).

About the Authors

Peter S. Beagle was born in Manhattan and raised in the Bronx, but has lived in California for most of his life. He is the author of a number of works considered to be classics of modern fantasy, including *The Last Unicorn* and *A Fine and Private Place*. The animated film version of *The Last Unicorn* has become a cult classic. Beagle has also written short fiction—his 2005 novelette "Two Hearts" won both the Hugo and Nebula awards—nonfiction, screenplays, poetry, and song lyrics.

Elizabeth Bear was born on the same day as Frodo and Bilbo Baggins, but in a different year. She is the Hugo, Sturgeon, Locus, and Campbell Award–winning author of twenty-seven novels (the most recent is *The Stone in the Skull*, the first of a new fantasy trilogy) and over a hundred short stories. She returns to science fiction with her novel *Ancestral Night* in 2018. Bear has never lived in New York, but grew up in Connecticut, which she notes is basically New York's lawn. She now lives in Massachusetts with her husband, writer Scott Lynch.

Holly Black is the *New York Times*–bestselling author of contemporary fantasy books intended for kids and teens, but also loved by adults. Some of her titles include The Spiderwick Chronicles (with Tony DiTerlizzi), The Modern Faerie Tale series, the Curse Workers series, *Doll Bones*, and *The Coldest Girl in Coldtown*. Her most recent novel is *The Silver Mask*, fourth in the Magisterium series co-authored with Cassandra Clare. A new series by Black will launch early in 2018 with *The Cruel Prince*. She is the recipient of both an Andre Norton Award and a Newbery Honor. She lives in New England with her husband and son in a house with a secret door.

Richard Bowes moved from Boston to Manhattan in 1965 and has lived there ever since. He has published six novels, four story collections, and over seventy short stories. He has won two World Fantasy Awards, and Lambda, Million Writer, and International Horror Guild Awards. His novel *Dust Devil on a Quiet Street* was on the World Fantasy and Lambda short lists. His novelette "Sleep Walking Now and Then" was on the Nebula short list. Recent appearances include: *Tor.com*, *F&SF*, *Lightspeed*, *Interfictions*, *Uncanny*, and the anthologies *XIII*, *The Doll Collection*, *Black Feathers: Dark Avian Tales*, and *Best Gay Stories 2016*.

Karl Bunker's short stories have appeared in *Asimov's*, *Fantasy & Science Fiction*, *Analog*, *Interzone*, *Cosmos*, *The Year's Best Science Fiction*, and elsewhere. In the past Bunker has been a software developer, jeweler, musical instrument maker, sculptor, and mechanical technician. He currently lives in a small town north of Boston, Massachusetts, with his wife, sundry pets, and an assortment of wildlife.

Maria Dahvana Headley is the *New York Times*–bestselling author of the young adult novels *Magonia* and *Aerie*, the dark fantasy/alt-history novel *Queen of Kings*, the internationally bestselling memoir *The Year of Yes*, and *The End of the Sentence*, a novella co-written with Kat Howard. With Neil Gaiman, she is the *New York Times*–bestselling co-editor of the monster anthology *Unnatural Creatures*. Although she grew up in rural Idaho, she now lives in Brooklyn.

Kat Howard lives and writes in New Hampshire. Her short fiction has been nominated for the World Fantasy Award, performed on NPR, and anthologized in "year's best" and "best of" volumes. In the past, she's been a competitive fencer, a lawyer, and a college professor. Her debut novel, *Roses and Rot*, was released by Saga Press in 2016. Another novel, *An Unkindness of Magicians*—a fantasy thriller featuring New York City's magicians—was published in fall 2017. Her short fiction collection, *A Cathedral of Myth and Bone*, will be released in 2018.

N(ora). K. Jemisin lives and writes in Brooklyn. She won the Locus Award for her first novel, *The Hundred Thousand Kingdoms*, and her short fiction and novels have been nominated multiple times for Hugo, World Fantasy, Nebula, and RT Reviewers Choice awards, and shortlisted for the Crawford and the James Tiptree, Jr., awards. In 2016, she became the first black person to win the Best Novel Hugo for *The Fifth Season*, which was also a *New York Times* Notable Book of 2015. Her latest novel, *The Stone Sky*, is the final title in The Broken Earth trilogy. She currently writes a *New York Times* book review column covering the latest in science fiction and fantasy.

World Fantasy Award–winning author **Caitlín R. Kiernan** is the author of numerous comic books and thirteen novels, including *Silk*, *Threshold*, *Low Red Moon*, *Murder of Angels*, *Daughter of Hounds*, *The Red Tree*, and *The Drowning Girl*. She has authored more than 200 works of short fiction, much of which has been collected in fifteen volumes. Kiernan's most recent long work is *Agents of Dreamland*. Born in Dublin, Ireland, she was raised and trained as a vertebrate paleontologist in the southeastern United States. She currently lives in Providence, Rhode Island.

In the last seven years, *New York Times*–bestselling author **Seanan McGuire** (and her science-fiction thriller-writer pseudonym Mira Grant) has published more than two-dozen novels and over seventy-five short stories. The most recent novel is the eleventh book in her Hugo-nominated October Daye series, *The Brightest Fell*. Winner of the 2010 Campbell Award for Best New Writer, McGuire is a native Californian who now lives in Washington State. Her 2017 standalone urban fantasy/ghost story novella *Dusk or Dark or Dawn or Day* (Tor.com Publishing) has been called "a spooky, atmospheric love letter to New York."

George R. R. Martin is best known for his international bestselling A Song of Ice and Fire fantasy series, which has been adapted into the HBO dramatic series *Game of Thrones*. Martin serves as *Game of Thrones*' co-executive producer—for which he has received two Emmys—and has scripted four episodes of the series. *Time* named him one of the "2011 Time 100," a list of the "most influential people in the world." The winner of many other awards—including six Hugos and two Nebulas—he was given the World Fantasy Award for Life Achievement in 2012. Martin was born and raised in Bayonne, New Jersey, and now resides with his wife, Parris, in Santa Fe, New Mexico.

Naomi Novik's first novel, *His Majesty's Dragon*, was published in 2006 along with the next two novels of the Temeraire series: *Throne* *of Jade* and *Black Powder War*. She won the John W. Campbell Award for Best New Writer, the Compton Crook Award for Best First Novel, and the Locus Award for Best First Novel. The fourth volume of Temeraire, *Empire of Ivory*, was a *New York Times* bestseller, and was followed by bestsellers *Victory of Eagles*, *Tongues of Serpents*, *Crucible of Gold*, and *Blood of Tyrants*. The ninth and final volume of the series, *League of Dragons*, was published in 2016. Her novel *Uprooted* (2015) was nominated for a Hugo Award; all of Temeraire was nominated for the Hugo for Best Series in 2017. Novik lives in New York City with her husband and eight computers

Daniel José Older is the Brooklyn-based writer, editor, composer, and *New York Times*–bestselling author of *Salsa Nocturna*, the Bone Street Rumba urban fantasy series, and the Young Adult novel *Shadowshaper*, a *New York Times* Notable Book of 2015, which won the International Latino Book Award and was shortlisted for the *Kirkus* Prize in Young Readers' Literature, the Andre Norton Award, the Locus, the Mythopoeic Award, and named one of *Esquire*'s "80 Books Every Person Should Read." His most recent novel is *Shadowhouse Fall*, sequel to *Shadowshaper*.

Born into a Navy family, **Kit Reed** moved so often as a kid that she never settled down in one place. Author of sixteen novels, the most recent of which is *Mormama*, which unfolds in a deteriorating mansion on a once-distinguished street in Jacksonville, Florida. Other recent books include the collection *The Story Until Now*. A Guggenheim fellow, she is the first American recipient of an international literary grant from the Abraham Woursell Foundation. A longtime member of the board of the Authors League Fund, she serves as Resident Writer at Wesleyan University and lives in Middletown, Connecticut.

Delia Sherman was born in Tokyo and brought up in Manhattan. The author of numerous short stories, her adult novels include *Through a Brazen Mirror* and *The Porcelain Dove* (which won the Mythopoeic Fantasy Award), and, with Ellen Kushner, *The Fall of the Kings*. Her novels for younger readers are *Changeling*, *The Magic Mirror of the Mermaid Queen*, *The Freedom Maze*, and *The Evil Wizard Smallbone*. Sherman lives in New York City with her wife and sometime collaborator, Ellen

Kushner, loves to travel, and writes in cafés wherever in the world she finds herself.

Author, screenwriter, and musician **John Shirley** spent some of the eighties in New York City where, with his band, Obsession, he signed a record deal, made a record, and played at CBGB, the Pyramid, and other NYC venues. The city in the 1980s is the scene and inspiration for his terrifying cult classic novel *Cellars*. He is the author of more than forty novels and many of his numerous shorter works have been gathered in nine collections. He lived in California for many years and now resides in Washington State near Portland, Oregon.

Peter Straub is the *New York Times*–bestselling author of nineteen novels. His shorter fiction has been gathered in five collections. Straub is the editor of numerous anthologies, including the two-volume *The American Fantastic Tale* from the Library of America. He was born in Wisconsin, eventually got an MA from Columbia, lived in Dublin and London, and in the early eighties moved with his family into a brownstone on the Upper West Side where they lived until recently. He and his wife, Susan, now live in Brooklyn.

About the Editor

Paula Guran has never lived in New York City, but she loves to visit there. She's the senior editor of Prime Books and has edited more than forty anthologies as well as more than eighty novels and collections. She is the mother of four, mother-in-law of two, and grandmother of three (so far) fabulous grandchildren. Guran resides in Akron, Ohio (not to confused with the village of 2,868 in Erie County, New York), in a house three years shy of being 100 years old.